The Heart
By
Iris Bolling

Siri Enterprises
Publishing Division
Richmond, Virginia

This is a work of fiction. Names, characters, places and incidents are either the product of the author's imagination or are used fictitiously, and any resemblance to actual persons, living or dead, business establishments, events, locales is entirely coincidental.

The Heart
Copyright©2011 by Iris Bolling

ISBN-13: 978-0-9801066-7-1
ISBN-10: 0-9801066-7-2
Library of Congress Control Number: 2011918500

Cover and page design by: Judith Wansley

The Heart Series
By Iris Bolling

Once You've Touched The Heart
The Heart of Him
Look Into My Heart
A Heart Divided
A Lost Heart
The Heart

www.irisbolling.net
www.sirient.com

Acknowledgements

Thank you my heavenly father.

Chris and Champaine, thank you for your love, support and patience.
Judith Wansley, thank you for sharing your talents, your kindness and your unyielding dedication and belief in the dream.

Roz Terry, LaFonde Harris, and Gemma Mejias: the roots to my tree, thanks for always answering the telephone.

Kathy Six, Erica George, and Cathy Atchison, thank you for your time, knowledge and encouragement.

To the beautiful people, Monica Jackson, Sakeitha Horton, Justin Wansley, Jason Wansley and Stephen Howell, may God's blessings always be with you.

To Beverly Jenkins and Gwyneth Bolton, thank you for sharing your knowledge and experience.

To my mom, Evelyn Lucas, my sister Helen McCant and brother Albert "Turkey" Doles, family is the strength that binds us forever and always.

A special thank you to Loretta Walls, you encourage me to improve with every stroke of my pen.

To all of my readers, the final installment is here. You embraced the Harrison's family and friends and I thank you. My prayer is that The Heart Series touched your life and continue to bring you enjoyment for years to come.

Dedication

This book is dedicated to,
Raymond Franklin Washington, Jr.
The man who taught me how to love.

Prologue

Jeffrey Daniel Harrison stood at the podium, as a sea of people looked on. The Convention Center in downtown Richmond was lined with red, white and blue banners, balloons, posters, hats and any other paraphernalia available to mankind. The atmosphere in the room was more than electrifying; it was explosive. He looked to his left and saw his wife Tracy beaming with love and pride in her eyes. The intensity of the unspoken message that passed between them was more than he could handle. He stepped away from his podium, placed his arm around Tracy's expanded waistline, then proceeded to give her the most passionate kiss ever witnessed by a national television audience. The crowd cheered louder, as they basked in the joy of knowing they had just elected another African American for President of the United States, which essentially meant that the country was progressing into becoming exactly what the Declaration of Independence states: *We hold these truths to be self-evident that all men are created equal.* American's hearts were warmed by the knowledge that the couple standing before them truly loved each other and The White House on Pennsylvania Avenue would once again be filled with children—an American family they could all look up to.

As the cameras scanned over the crowd, the commentator spoke in awe of the array of people and the hope that America had become, truly one nation under God. Every ethnic group imaginable stood side by side cheering at the prospect of having a better future under the leadership of Jeffrey Daniel Harrison, President of the United States.

A hush came over the crowd as they waited to hear the words from the man who they believed had jumped the first hurdle to becoming the new leader of the free world. Every eye was looking toward the stage where the Harrison family and friends smiled brightly. The attendees waited patiently, anticipating the words of encouragement and hope they had become accustomed to receiving from the young man facing them.

Jeffrey Daniel Harrison, better known to all as JD, returned to the podium, smiled and looked at the eager faces in the crowed. "Marrying my wife was the smartest thing I have ever done." He bowed his head and chuckled, "Her love has made me rich beyond my imagination in so many ways. The most prominent is being able to stand before you today and accept the faith you have placed in me, to be the next President of the United States of America." The crowd cheered wildly, peaking to a frenzy, as JD scanned the room smiling.

A Secret Service agent whispered into his earpiece. "We have another President with rock star status, we need to tighten up." At the command the agents on the stage moved closer to the family, as more agents entered into the room at floor level and spread throughout the crowd of thousands. JD continued with his speech as the agents moved about unnoticed, but vigilant. Midway through the speech, JD reached down to pick up his two-year-old daughter,

Gabrielle who was tugging at his pants. She captured his cheeks between her small hands and kissed her daddy. As the crowd clapped, Gabrielle joined in smiling. JD smiled at his daughter and turned back to his speech. She then laid her head on his shoulder, put her thumb in her mouth and listened as her daddy talked.

Brian Thompson, the President-Elect's personal bodyguard, scanned the room from his position directly behind JD. His trained eyes took in each level of the room searching for anything he considered a threat to the family on stage. After scanning the top levels of seats, his eyes drifted to the rafters, where some of the television cameramen took shots of the crowd below. A stream of light caught his eye as he scanned over the cameras. It was only a split second that it took his eyes to go back to light, another second for recognition, then one more second for his body to react before shots rang out, with center stage as their target. The loud sound of the automatic weapons continued to flow through the air like shock waves. Awe and then screams filled the room.

Secret Service sprang into action, covering the children and Tracy as ordered by the President-Elect. JD covered Gabrielle as Brian immediately hit him from behind propelling him forward. He hit the floor with Gabrielle beneath him and that's when he heard a heart-wrenching scream that he was certain came from Tracy. With Brian and agents' bodies surrounding him, his movement was limited and his line of sight was blocked. Reaching out he grabbed her hand, "Tracy!" he yelled out, to no avail. When the firing stopped, the room was half-empty, the crowd was still buzzing and agents were surrounding the stage with weapons drawn. JD looked down at Gabrielle, who was now crying. "It's alright Gabby, Daddy has you. It's alright." He held her tightly as he scrambled to stand. Tracy was pulling her hand from his frantically reaching for something.

Following her line of vision, he saw the blood and his heart literally stopped.

The frenzy that followed was all a blur as JD scrambled to get to the body on the floor next to Tracy. His mind snapped as he realized his worst nightmare had occurred. How would he live his life knowing he was responsible for the events happening at that moment? How many lives would come to an end on that night, trying to accomplish a dream

Chapter 1
Six months earlier

A l "Turk" Day was living proof that any person with a heart had the propensity for violence. Even a mild-mannered skinny kid from the North Side of Richmond, Virginia could become a cold-blooded murderer if the person he loves is threatened. Al wasn't one of the cool kids in elementary or middle school. How could he be with a name like Albert? To top things off he was a genius at the age of ten. Anything he read he could repeat verbatim. He could run numbers better and faster than any bookie in Las Vegas or on the street. Adding to his uncool status, he lived with his grandmother, his older sisters, Valarie and Joan, and was the baby of the family, at least in this house. Cool, he was not. Hell, he didn't even have a mother, not a real one anyway. The woman that gave birth to them only appeared once a year around the holidays or when she needed something. He had a simple life with his grandmother, his sisters and books. He loved books.

At thirteen that simple life was turned upside down when his grandmother suddenly passed away. Almost immediately after his grandmother's funeral, Al and his sisters were moved to Norfolk, Virginia to live with his mother, Lena, and their stepfather, Billy Washington. Life changed quickly. At his grandmother's house they came home from school to a house filled with love, a firm hand and dinner. At Lena's, that's what he called his mother, there was no firm hand for they rarely saw her. Thanks to Valarie, who had learned to cook from their grandmother, there was food to eat. As for love, well that came to Al in the form of a pint size five-year-old little sister he had met once when his mother came home for Thanksgiving. That was the year he earned his nickname, Turk.

On that particular Thanksgiving, Lena had come home with her then three-year-old daughter, Tracy. Her husband, she said, was spending the holiday with his family. The family still didn't believe Lena was married, but hey who cared. He was around nine and they were all at his Grandmother John's house. Grandma John, yes her name was John Russell, had cooked the turkey for dinner and left it on the kitchen table. Tracy, whom he called Sugie, was sitting on the steps playing with her doll when he came in from playing.

"Sugie, did grandma cook?"

She nodded her head and pointed to the kitchen and said, "Table."

Hungry from playing hard outside, he walked through the swing doors into the kitchen and started eating the only thing that was on the table—the turkey.

Grandma John walked in the kitchen and Al smiled up at her with a turkey wing in his hand. "The turkey is good, Grandma."

His grandmother looked at that turkey then at him. "Boy!" she yelled. "You ate my turkey."

From the tone of his grandmother's voice he knew he was in trouble. Before he could explain, she grabbed him off the stool and commenced to whipping his behind. Sugie came running into the kitchen and just stood in the doorway with a scared look on her face. After whipping his behind, his grandmother stood him in the doorway. "Stay there," she said as she fussed and tried to salvage what was left of the turkey for Thanksgiving dinner. Lena came running through the swing doors and stopped dead in her tracks.

She looked at the children standing in the doorway. "Where's the rest of the turkey?"

Sugie looked up at her and pointed to her brother's stomach. "Turkey."

Lena looked at the turkey, then looked at him and fell out laughing. Ever since then, his baby sister called him Turkey.

The first day at Lena's house was awkward until Tracy came in from kindergarten. She walked in the door holding her father's hand and looked around the room at the people. When her eyes landed on him sitting on the sofa, she giggled and ran to him with her arms open wide.

He picked her up and sat her on the sofa next to him. She smiled and pointed at his stomach. "Turk?"

He smiled back. "Hi, Sugie."

Without saying another word, she crawled up in his lap, put her thumb in her mouth and went to sleep. His baby sister made him feel loved, wanted, and needed. Now he was a big brother, it was his job to protect her. She also gave him a way to be cool. Tracy changed his name, but he knew the name Turkey would give him more grief. So the first day of freshman year at high school, when the teacher asked what name he wanted to be called, he replied, "Al." That was the same day he met his friend Tucker.

Because of his test scores, Al was placed in all advanced classes at the new school. When he walked into his first class it was a culture shock. His old school was predominately Black. The AP Algebra class consisted of fourteen Caucasian males and females, two Black girls and one Black male. Naturally Al migrated to the back of the room with the brother.

"Al Day." He introduced himself with a slight nod of his head.

"Donovan Tucker. What's up, man?"

Al looked around the class, leaned over and asked, "Where are the brothers and sisters?"

Tucker smirked. "Very few have been in my class since the first day of middle school."

"What's up with that?" Al questioned.

"These are advanced classes. You don't see brothers and only one or two sisters in here."

"Why?"

"It's not cool to be smart."

Al leaned back in his seat and huffed. "I'm cool."

"Yeah? Well welcome to the smart-ass cool class." The two laughed.

"Is there a problem back there, Mr. Tucker?" The teacher asked in an accusing tone.

"No sir. No problem," Tucker replied.

"Well," he hesitated, "Maybe your new friend will not mind sharing with the class what type of equation is written on the board." He asked in an arrogant tone.

Tucker whispered, "He's trying to piss you off by putting you on the spot."

Al looked at the board. "It's a quadratic equation." He turned back to Tucker. "Why would he want to do that?

"To get you kicked out of his class. He doesn't believe the brothers are smart enough to be in his class."

"Good guess." The teacher stated. "Perhaps you would be kind enough to solve the equation for us."

Al looked at Tucker as he stood. "Watch the cool kid at work." He walked up to the board frowning. Turning to the teacher he asked, "Factoring or Square Root Method?"

The teacher's eyes narrowed. "Square Root," he replied with a smirk.

Al took the chalk from the teacher, "Thank you." After a moment, Al read the equation to the class, then proceeded to give a step by step break down as he solved it. When he finished, he put chalk on the board tray and returned to his seat. The teacher examined the equation on the board and turned to Al. "I'm impressed, Mr.?"

"Day, Al Day."

"Mr. Day. Forgive me for questioning your abilities."

Al leaned back in his seat. "I'm cool," he grinned. One of the sisters that were sitting up front turned to him and smiled. Al winked and she turned back around. He held his fist out in the aisle. Tucker gave him a pound and they both turned back to the teacher grinning. As it turned out Al and Tucker were in every class together.

Refocusing on the events taking place around him, Al wondered for at least the hundredth time today, how in the hell did fate put him in this place and time? Watching the last minute activities taking place over the rolling lawn of the Brooks' Estate where his sister Tracy now called home, the events leading to this moment played in his mind like an old black and white movie. The multitude of people that gathered for the announcement seemed to fade as his life replayed in slow motion. The announcement the world was holding baited breath to hear as evidenced by the many television camera crews, political commentators, and reporters that were present.

Nothing in Al's life indicated he should be in this place. Most in law enforcement would have placed odds that he would be dead before reaching his twentieth birthday. But Al had beaten the odds in more ways than one. He'd led a life of intrigue since the age of fourteen. Fifteen years as the leader of one of the most successful street organizations to date, four years in prison, and the last five years organizing communities to help combat gang violence.

No, he should not be a VIP at the announcement of a candidate being declared the Democratic Nominee for President of the United States. Only a hand full of people knew Al was the reason the man who was about to be introduced would have the opportunity to change all their lives. Al would never admit or take credit for it. However, on this warm June evening, he was as proud as a father watching his baby emerge into the world.

Al closed his eyes and hung his head. His shoulder length locs covered his face shielding his thoughts. His stance, legs braced apart, arms folded across his chest, was relaxed to him, but to others it may have seemed intimidating. That's what his past life dictated, that others fear him. His past was the reason he really was the last person on earth that should be standing there. He shook his head at the thought. His brother-in-law, JD Harrison, now ex-Governor of Virginia, refused to treat him like an unwanted relative. No, JD was a special man in Al's book. But then, only a special man would be good enough for his baby sister.

A smile creased the face of his caramel brown skin. It took him a moment to accept the reality that the two were destined to be together. After all, this was his baby sister, the one that he put his life on the line to protect. The one he killed for and would kill again for if it were deemed necessary. Al's and JD's lives were irrevocably intertwined on that day over twenty-years ago before either of them knew of each other. It all began the summer he turned fourteen.

At fourteen, Al was doing what young boys did, shooting hoops and watching girls. During his freshman year of high school, he had grown by leaps and bounds. Not just in size, but in popularity and coolness. Basketball or better yet, dreams of the NBA had become his and Tucker's focus. But, Tucker's mother was determined to have him go to college on an academic scholarship, so Al was determined to do the same. However, they had to keep their skills on point just in case the NBA thing came through.

The basketball court wasn't fancy; in fact grass was growing between the cement cracks. There were no rope hoops for the ball to swish through and no seats from which the spectators could watch. All that was there was cement, more cement and linked fence surrounding the full court.

Al and Tucker ruled the court, outdoor and in. At school, Al at six feet directed the game as the point guard and Tucker, at six two, stood back and took shots at will. On the cement, positions weren't defined. It was street ball. In Norfolk, Virginia, there was no Midnight league where the teenage boys were organized and played exhibition games. But whenever an organization came through with a tournament, you better believe, teams were lining up to recruit Al and Tucker. Some would offer them money to play for their team. The highest bidder was usually granted with their special talents. But, even in their youth, Al and Tucker had their own set of rules they lived by. The two were selective in who was allowed to purchase their services and they never—never played against each other. And no one challenged their decisions. Their connections to Ms. Sunshine, the owner of the 'anything-you-may-be-looking-for' house in the neighborhood, legal or not, ensured their protection on the street.

On that dreadful day, Al and Tucker had just finished a game and were standing on the sidelines having an intense conversation. The two girls standing outside the fence were their main focus. Al's rap had worked, now he was attempting to persuade her friend to accompany Tucker for a little one-on-one. Al's glance wandered over the girl's shoulder where his stepfather stumbled into his line of vision. It was a good thing the gate leading to the house he lived in was open. It seemed his stepfather was fully loaded and would not have been able to open the gate. He never liked to see his stepfather drunk. Usually when he was that drunk it meant his mother and Bill would be fighting before the night was out. Deal with a drunk or Tameka, who was smiling up at him, ready and willing. No brainer, he returned his attention to the girls. This was a hell of a lot better than having to go home. Home quickly became a distant thought.

When Al finally made his way home that night, it was to the flashing lights of emergency vehicles in front of his house. Something kicked in the pit of his stomach with each step he took. Walking towards the house, nothing could have prepared him for what he was told. Officer Wilber T. Munford stopped him at the walkway to his house and told him his sister Joan was being taken to the hospital. The story told to him was that someone had tried to rape her, but she fought back and it looked like she lost the battle. Al tried to break away from the man, but he couldn't. Tucker stood by his side as they watched Joan being rolled away with his mother Lena next to the gurney trying to get her daughter to talk. But it was all to no avail. Later that night, his mother came home alone. Billie was nowhere to be found and no one had any answers to his questions. No one could tell him who came into his house and killed his sister.

The days and nights that followed that gave him some answers. He didn't want to believe it, because his stepfather was a good man when he wasn't drinking. And Al knew that Lena was hard on the man. But when Billie was drunk, Lena and everyone else in the house stayed away from him. For days Al wondered why they ever came to live with Lena. All of them would have been better off staying on their own when their grandmother died. But a nice little check from Social Services and a good amount in food stamps convinced Lena the children should be with her.

The months that followed Joan's death, were hell on Al's mental state. He believed if he had just gone home, Joan would still be alive. From that day on, he became his little sister Tracy's protector. He was not going to let what happened to Joan affect his little sister. Every day he had her at his side. It didn't matter that she was only eight years old and he was fourteen. Where he went, she went. Where he stayed, she stayed. His mother actually enjoyed not having to come home and deal with the little brat, as she called her. She had her freedom again and could hang out in the clubs or wherever. But Al didn't care. After Social Service and Child Protective Services completed their investigation, the welfare checks continued coming and that was all Lena was concerned with. As for him, Tracy's safety was his number one concern. He wasn't going to lose another sister.

A few months later, on a September afternoon, the day before Tracy's birthday, Al and Tucker had stopped by the corner store after school. It was one of those rare occasions when Lena actually had Tracy with her. He didn't feel the need to rush to get home when he stopped by the corner store to pick up a candy necklace for Tracy's birthday. He had all of two dollars on him, but that was enough to buy the gift for Tracy.

Al and Tucker made plans as they walked the few blocks to his house. Whenever they needed a few extra dollars, they would help Ms. Sunshine with her accounting books and she gave them a few dollars. She had been trying to get the two to work for her full time, but the boys refused. They were trying to stay clean for possible basketball scholarships. Neither could afford to have a record. Later that night they planned to talk to Ms. Sunshine about working part-time, just on her books, nothing illegal. As they turned the corner, they could hear the yelling coming from Al's house. The two looked at each other then took off running. Al burst through the front door just as Billie grabbed Tracy by the arm and flung her back into the bedroom. Lena jumped on Billie's back swinging with her fist and screaming. Tracy was crying as Billie yelled and turned on Lena with rage in his eyes. Al knew somebody in his house was about to die. It wasn't going to be his mother and it damn sure wasn't going to be Tracy.

Al grabbed Billie's arms. "Get Tracy," He yelled at Tucker as he tried to pull Billie's hands from around his mother's neck. Instead of following Al's demand, Tucker walked to the kitchen. On the table was the butcher's knife Lena always used. Turk moved just as Tucker stuck the knife in Billie's back. It was hard to believe, but Billie didn't as much as blink as he released Lena's throat and turned on Tucker. The backhand hit sent Tucker flying. He slammed into the wall and fell to the floor. Billie walked over to Tucker with the knife still lodged into his back and began to repeatedly kick him. Seeing his friend in danger, Al grabbed the cast iron skillet pan off the stove and swung on Billie knocking him to the floor. He didn't stop with one swing; Al continued to bang Billie's head with the pan until Tucker pulled him off. Lena took the pan from his hand.

Suddenly, everything was eerily silent. The only sound was that of the television show Good Times playing in the background. Al stood over Billie, not sure if he was dead or alive, his adrenaline speeding through his body, and his shirt covered in blood. He looked at Lena, then at Tucker. There were blank expressions on their faces. Someone had to do something and it was clear neither of them had a clue.

Al pulled his bloodied shirt over his head. He walked into the bedroom, where Tracy was sitting in the corner on the floor with her head on her knees whimpering. Dressed in a little blue jumper with pink flowers all over it, with a little pink shirt underneath and pink barrettes at the end of her two ponytails, she looked up at him and hiccupped.

"Turkey, Daddy hurt my arm," she cried.

With each hiccup, her two ponytails jiggled. With the traumatic scene she was still the cutest little girl he'd ever seen. Now, she was his responsibility. He held his arms out, "It's all right Sugie. I will never let anyone hurt you again— never." His frightened little sister walked right into his arms and held on to her big brother.

Al placed her in Tucker arms. "I trust you with my sister. Don't let anything happen to her. Take her to Ms. Sunshine's house. Tell her what happened and that I need her special friend at my house."

Once Tucker was out of the house Al turned to Lena. She standing there, rooted to the spot with the skillet in her hand. He calmly walked over and tried to pry it away, but her grip was strong. "Lena," he called out to her and for a moment she didn't respond. He pulled the bloody skillet from her hand, took it over to the sink, washed it, then put it back on the stove. He then went into the bedroom and came back with a spread from the bed. He bent over Billie's still body and covered it. Reality set in for Lena when he stood. She turned on him swinging her fist, screaming. "You killed him. You killed Billie. You stupid son-of-a-bitch." She slapped him across the face. "Who in the hell is supposed to take care of me now? Who?"

At first Al was stunned. Didn't he just save her life? He wasn't hearing are you all right son, are you hurt? Or at the very least thank you for getting that crazy man off me. No this woman—his mother was cursing him out because he killed the man that had terrorized their lives for four years. Yeah it was nice when he first came around, but after Tracy's car accident, Billie changed and so did their lives.

The shock wore off as Lena swung to strike him again. The vision of his sister Joan on the gurney hit him in the gut. He caught her hand mid-swing then pulled her to him with a strength he didn't know he had. "You?" he said calmly—too calmly. "You want to know who is going to take care of you! What about your daughter Joan? Who took care of her? What about your daughter, Valarie? You practically sold my sister to the first man that came along offering marriage. How much did you get? Let me see if I got it right, $5,000.00. That's right. Hell, if you had protected Joan, she would have brought in twice that, after all she was the spitting image of you."

"Don't you talk to me like that. I'm your mother. Let me go!" Lena tried to pull away, but Al was too strong for her and held her wrist tight as he spoke his mind.

"You don't know what the word means. If you were a mother, you wouldn't have allowed that man near your daughters. You knew what he was doing every time he got drunk and you weren't here. You knew, and you still let him come back into this house. A mother would have protected her children—especially her daughters."

"Don't you judge me! You don't know the hell I've been through."

"I don't, but it's going to be nothing compared to the hell I'll bring on you if anything happens to Tracy."

"You won't know. Your ass is going to jail. I'm going to make sure of it!"

Al released her hands, then pushed her hair over her shoulders. In the smoothest, chilling voice, Al spoke. *"Lena, you are a beautiful woman. My boys always say they could hang out and just look at you all day."* Then he stepped so close to her, they were nose to nose. *"Say one word to anybody and no man will ever want to look at you again."* He could see the fear and surprise in her eyes. In a way the look hurt him, for she of all people should know he would never hurt her or any woman. But he would beat the hell out of a man that tried to harm his women and that included her. Al stepped away. He saw her rub her arms as if she had a chill.

"What are you going to do now?" she snarled. *"You can't run. The police will track you down."*

He didn't respond at first. Al walked away from her to think. *"I'm going to handle my business and you..."* he hesitated, *"are going to stay out of it. Anybody ask you about your husband, you will just say he walked out one day and you haven't heard from him since. You got that?"*

"I heard you," she snapped. *"How am I supposed to live now? That little check I get from Social Services is*

barely enough to put clothes on our backs. At least the money Billie was making was getting us by. But that was barely enough to get my hair and nails done."

Al just stared at his mother. He knew she'd had a hard life growing up, but what made her so self-centered? Then it really hit him. He only thought he knew this woman, but really didn't know her at all. They were standing over her dead husband's body talking about getting her hair and nails done. No, he didn't know this woman and the longer he stood there, the less he liked her. And to think, the whole time he lived with his grandmother he always prayed that his mother would come and get them. It just goes to prove we all have to be careful what we wish for. Every woman is not mother material just because they have a womb. But he had to wonder, why it took her four children to reach that conclusion?

Unfortunately for them, she was the only relative they had. They didn't have a choice in coming to live with her. And look where it got them. Valarie was the only fortunate one. She was old enough to know when to get the hell out of dodge. She got married as soon as she turned eighteen and never looked back. Joan, her problem was she was just as pretty as his mother. Once, his mother tried to get one of her friends to take Joan in, just to eliminate the competition for the male attention. How could a mother be jealous of her own daughter?

Tracy was going to be just as pretty as Lena and Al knew it. There was no way he could take Tracy where he was going. Ms. Sunshine's house was not the place for a little girl. So again, he was left with no choice. Tracy was better off staying with Lena. At fourteen, he felt he had the weight of the world on his shoulders. If he went to jail for killing Billie, there was no telling what would happen to Tracy. Therefore, he had to put the fear of God in Lena. He had to let her think that he would kill her if anything happened to Tracy.

The only thing Lena valued was money. Therefore, he had to work that angle to his advantage. "I'll give you $500 a week to keep Tracy."

Lena took a step back as she thought about his offer. Where are you going to get that kind of money?

"It doesn't matter," the young boy, said to his mother. "You keep your mouth shut and take care of Tracy. You keep her safe and I'll give you $500.00 a week."

Lena glared at Al with a look of disbelief. "$1,000."

"$500 for now and more when you prove you can be a mother." Lena nodded. Al sighed as he walked back over to her. "I have one question. Billie wasn't like this when we first came. What in the hell did you do to make him drink?"

"No woman has the power to make a man do anything unless he gives it to them."

Al made up his mind then and there, that no woman would ever have that power over him.

The applause of the people brought Al's attention back to the present. Pearl Lassiter, JD's press secretary, stood at the podium. "Ladies and Gentlemen, the Honorable Governor of Virginia, His Excellency, Jeffrey Daniel Harrison."

The crowd of a few hundred applauded as JD walked on the stage with his wife Tracy by his side. He winked at Pearl as she whispered, "It's the last time I can use it." Smiling as JD and Tracy took the stage, she knew he never liked the term 'His Excellency' so she had to tease him one last time.

Al smiled, as JD and Tracy took center stage. He was right. Tracy Washington-Harrison turned out to be more beautiful than Lena and Joan. For her beauty was more than skin deep, it was to the soul. How he wished he could find a woman that was as beautiful and as sweet as his Sugie.

As if it were ordained, his eyes drifted to the woman standing on stage behind his sister. Now—she is sex on spiked heels. He loved that commanding walk and sassy sway of her hips that carried her from one point to the next. Al stood there watching her as her eyes scanned around the room, looking for any sign of a threat to his sister. A lump formed in his throat, as it had many times before. How could someone so dangerous appear to be so vulnerable every time he looked into her eyes? Slowly he reached inside his suit jacket, pulled out a pair of black shades and put them on. The shades allowed him unlimited access to the woman. He could look at her as long as he wanted without detection. But the shades also served as a mental shield from the affect the woman had on him.

"When are you going to stop staring at that woman and do something about that itch?"

Al didn't have to look to his side to know who had the nerve to call him out on his undercover surveillance of Morgan Ryan Williams, better known as Ryan. "I thought you were in Washington visiting Julianna, the woman you have an itch for and are doing nothing about?"

"That was cold." Tucker pulled out his shades then put them on, taking his stance next to his friend. Folding his arms across his chest, he smiled. "I'm back."

Morgan Ryan Williams was child number five to Franklin and Mary Williams. Her crime in life, according to her father, Detective Franklin Williams of the Richmond Police Department, was being born a female. That was the crust of the wedge between father and only daughter.

She was only eight years old when her mother passed away from cancer. That event left her as the only female in a house filled with alpha males. As a little girl, the only examples she had were over-achieving males. So she emulated what she saw day in and day out. All four of her older brothers were police officers or detectives. Learning how to be a lady was out of the question. However, learning to play ball, any kind of ball, was a definite, as well as how to fight and shoot guns. The girl knew how to break down a weapon, clean and store it better than her brothers. In fact, it was one of the things she would do regularly to get her father's attention. It didn't work. She stopped trying. Once she grew up, she began to rebel against everything her father stood for on general purpose. He didn't treat her like a boy the way her brothers did. No, he simply ignored her existence. It was as if his family line ended with his last son. That's probably why, for a brief period of her life, she ventured on the other side of the law.

It was during that time that she worked for Al "Turk" Day's organization. She never met the man back then, for she took orders directly from his right hand man, Donovan Tucker. They were in the midst of taking the organization completely legal when they hired her as the muscle to help them accomplish the task. Yes, she was that good and Tucker recognized her skills and her ability to reason out situations without violence. Their goal was to take the organization legit with as little loss of life, on either side, as possible.

During that time Ryan was assigned to a case involving Cynthia Thornton. That's when Ryan met Samuel Lassiter, who was working for Thompson Security Agency, which handled personal security to now Governor Harrison. Lassiter liked the way she handled herself and recommended her for the position she held now- personal security to Tracy Washington-Harrison, wife of JD and sister to the man she was staring down at the moment, Al Day.

As soon as she walked onto the stage behind Tracy, she scanned the area for any possible threats. Like always, her eyes found and settled on Al. Her shades protected her from detection, as she watched the brother who literally took her breath away.

Al Day towered at six foot-one, boasting a solid one hundred ninety-five pounds of pure unadulterated man.

Today, he was dressed in an Armani suit, royal blue, crisp white shirt, with a red, white and blue stripe tie. What set the ensemble off was his crowning glory of locs that fell to his shoulders. How she would love to run her fingers through them, just once. Ryan watched as he reached into his pocket and pulled out his shades. She held her smile, for she knew he was doing the exact same thing she was doing—checking her out undercover. She felt the familiar tingle the moment his eyes were on her.

"I love this cat and mouse game you two play," her partner, Magna Rivera stated as she scanned the lawn.

As much as she liked her partner, Ryan was at a point where she simply wanted to get Magna in a room and knock her hell out. The only thing stopping her was the fact that Magna was a martial arts specialist who would probably kick her butt then ask whose next. "Keep your eyes on the children, not me."

"We are in the safest place in America today."

"If it was that safe we wouldn't be here."

"Touchy—touchy, aren't we. That's what five years of celibacy will get you."

Ryan turned, lowered her shades and glared at the woman standing next to her. "Do I look amused to you?"

"You look horny to me and I wish you would man up and do something about it."

Ryan pushed the shades back up then returned to scanning the lawn. "I wish you would mind your business and leave mine the hell alone."

Magna sucked her teeth, "You are my friend, which makes you my business."

"I'm good watching from afar."

"You're chicken, that's what you are. Keep sitting back—watching. Some other woman is going step in and take your man." She hunched her shoulders. "Hell, I may give the brother a try myself. From what I understand he doesn't discriminate. A little Spanish fly might do him some good."

Ryan turned to her partner with eyes blazing. Magna threw her hands up. "Hey, I was just joking. Stop shooting lasers at me through those shades."

Tracy turned to them with a look that meant she could hear the conversation. Ryan straightened up resuming her position. If she thought for one minute she could tame Al Day, she would go for it. But two things stopped her. One was her father. He would never accept Al as the man in her life, simply because he has a record. All the other things the man had accomplished would never be considered. The second reason—Al. In her estimation he did not come across as a man that could be tamed unless he wanted to be. And he clearly didn't want to be. So for now, she would continue her life of celibacy and covertly watching the man who had captured her heart years before she'd even met him.

"Ladies and gentleman," JD spoke, "It is with a heavy heart mixed with joy and excitement that I stand before you today." He reached his hand out to his side. Tracy took a step to her right and joined their hands together as she smiled up at him. That smile did exactly what it had done for the last twelve years—took his breath away. He shook his head, "For those of you, who do not know, I love my wife, Tracy." The crowd applauded as Tracy waved to them. "I make no decisions, small or large without her counsel and blessing. "With that in mind, we stand here, together, before our friends and supporters to announce that your hard work has paid off. As of tomorrow, I will officially be named the Democratic Nominee for President of the United States of America."

The statement was barely out of his mouth before the crowd erupted in cheers, applause, cat whistles and music. People were literally dancing on the lawn. JD held up his hand to silence the crowd, but they weren't ready to stop the celebration. He stepped back and allowed the crowd to have the moment. Pearl stepped up and whispered, "Primetime news cycle is due to start within the hour, and this announcement needs to be completed before then." JD raised his hands again and waited as the crowd began to settle down. "Now," he hesitated, "This journey is not going to be easy. The road is a long, arduous one that will take us months to complete. But we knew that when this journey began twelve years ago here, in Richmond, Virginia. I believe on the first Tuesday in November, we will complete our mission by receiving the keys to the front door of 1600 Pennsylvania Ave, Washington, D. C." The crowd erupted again. "Are you ready to take this journey with me?" JD asked over the roar of the crowd. "If you're ready, just say— Yes, I'm ready."

The crowd yelled, "Yes, I'm ready!"

"If you're ready for a better economy, a stronger educational system, stability in our inner cities and peace in our foreign lands, just say, I'm ready."

The crowd yelled, "I'm ready!"

Once the crowd quieted down, JD turned to his campaign manager and brother-in-law, James Brooks and said into the microphone. "James," he said as he shook his head, "I think a call should be placed to Washington to put Congress on notice that the people have spoken. We're ready and we're coming!"

That was the sound bite that flooded the national news cycle. The governor's mansion in Austin, Texas, was filled with the family of the Republican nominee, Governor Jeremiah McClintock III, better known as Jerry, as they watched the announcement. "Well, the wait is over. He's clinched the nomination. It should be a hell of a race." Jerry proclaimed as he swallowed the last of the scotch from his glass. Surrounded by his father, US State Senator Jeremiah McClintock, Jr. who went by Jeremiah, and his grandfather ex-governor of Texas, Jeremiah McClintock, Sr., who everyone simply referred to as Mac, the room took on a solemn tone. "Cheer up, everybody," Jerry said with his southern drawl, "Hell, I haven't lost the damn race yet."

"You won't lose to that colored boy." Mac stated as he shook his walking cane at the television. "You have my word on that."

"Grandfather, you know I don't like that kind of talk in my office. We represent everyone in the state of Texas. Now, we are going to win this race. But it's going to be won fair and square. There will be no behind the scenes schemes. Do I make myself clear?" He looked decisively at his grandfather.

"Boy, I was winning elections before you were born. Ain't nobody younger than the hats going to tell me what to do. Do I make myself clear?"

"Father," Senator McClintock chimed in as the peacemaker. "This is Jerry's race to win as he sees fit."

"Or lose," Jerry's wife, Eleanor, slurred as she downed another glass of scotch.

"If I lose it will be due to the discovery of your fondness for scotch," Jerry reprimanded his wife.

"Here, I thought it would be due to your fondness of all things dark," she sharply replied.

Senator McClintock stood. He walked over and took the drink from Eleanor's hand. "You both have a point. I think it would be wise for both of you to let the dark side go until the campaign is over." He looked pointedly at his son and his daughter-in-law. "Can we all agree that it is going to be difficult enough beating JD Harrison without the added drama?" Everyone nodded their heads in agreement.

"Good. Do we all agree this country will be better off with Jerry as President? Eleanor hesitated, then nodded her head. "Good. Then let's all do our part to see that it happens."

Jerry and Eleanor, turned away lost in their own thoughts, As Mac whispered to Jeremiah. "Put our people on notice. I want Harrison eliminated."

Jeremiah looked from his father to his son. This was one time he wasn't sure which way to lean. His son was a good man thanks to his mother. His wife, may her soul rest in peace, made sure that their son believed in right and wrong, good would prevail over evil and that the world would be better once America was united. His father, on the other hand, believed strongly, the old way of segregation and bigotry was the only way to preserve the true American way of life. In fact, Mac had spent his entire life ensuring that people knew and stayed in their place, by any means necessary. The Senator believed in his son's abilities. However, the country was ready for a change. Hell, they were demanding it and JD Harrison was the man they clearly favored to bring the change about. Like it or not, Jerry was going to need all the help he could get to win. Be it behind the scenes or in front of the camera. There was no way he could beat Harrison in a clean campaign. His belief that his son would be good for this country was the deciding factor. The Senator turned back to his father. "I'm with you father."

Chapter 2

The campaign trail took over their lives. JD and Tracy hit the road for days and sometimes weeks at a time. However, it was their policy that one of them would be home with the children as much as possible. The couple now had four of the twelve children they'd discussed having during the first year of their marriage. The final decision came from Tracy when she declared she would have five children and if JD conceived and carried number six, then they could talk about seven through twelve. Needless to say, the couple settled on five children.

During her visits home, Tracy would always do things with the children. Their favorite place was the park, not far from their home. She sat on the park bench with Al as they watched the children playing. "This is the life I've been waiting for. Spending time with you and your children is like being in heaven." It was good to see that none of the negative effects from Tracy's childhood had filtered down to her children. They were happy, healthy and surrounded by love. Unlike their mother, they were wanted and from what Tracy had told him, JD wanted more. Al had to laugh at the expression on Tracy's face whenever she talked about having more children.

"Wait until you have more than just Monique and let's see if you are singing the same tune."

Shaking his head, Al smiled. "I don't know if more children are in the cards for me. I'll just wait for you to have more."

Tracy laughed, "You sound as bad as Jeffrey. He wants more children, too. I'll give him one more, but he is going to have to wait."

The glow in her eyes told Al a completely different story. She was happy. If anyone deserved happiness, it was Tracy. Her childhood was not like the one he was enjoying with her children today running around in the park. No, Tracy spent most of her life in a library reading books, just to stay off the streets and away from their mother.

Their mother, Lena, Al shook his head as he thought of her. It was because of her that at thirty-eight he was still holding to a promise he made to himself at fourteen. He would never, under any circumstances, give his heart to a woman. Lena Washington was a bitch on wheels. Oh, that's right, he thought as he watched Tracy run after Gabrielle, her youngest. Her name is now Lena Roth. She is the wife of Senator John Roth, who was declared Tracy's biological father a few years back. Now, that was a surprise that she couldn't have planned, or could she? Hell, the way his mother operated, one never knows. For a while he had wondered if Billie knew that Tracy was not his daughter. He thought of Billie often, wondering if there could have been another way for his life to end. But then, Al learned a long time ago not to question his path in life. All he could do was embrace it.

"Al," Tucker whispered in his ear. "We have a situation."

Al looked over his shoulder to see Tucker's hand on his weapon. As an ex-felon, a weapon in Al's possession could cost him five more years of his life. Fortunately, none of his men from his street days had records. He took a plea and did the time to make sure of it. "Get the children." Tucker said as he walked swiftly towards Tracy. From the moment years ago when Al put Tracy in Tucker's arms, he took the responsibility of protecting Tracy to heart. To this day, Tucker had never wavered on that trust.

Al moved quickly as the peaceful scene quickly turned tensed. Tracy's security team moved into action. Ryan and Magna had proven to be an impenetrable team for the last five years. Back then the dirty police chief attacked JD and Tracy's home, almost fatally injuring their boss, Brian Thompson. Since that time no one got within twenty feet of Tracy or the children without the threat of serious bodily harm. Today, it appeared someone wanted to test their resolve.

Al took ten-year-old Jon-Christopher--JC, and his seven-year-old sister Jasmine, or Jazzy, by the hand and moved quickly towards one of the black SUVs parked at the curb. Tucker grabbed six-year-old Brianna, who was playing in the sand box away from the others. Magna placed Tracy and four-years-old, Gabrielle safely inside another black SUV parked at the curb. Afterwards, Magna and Tucker circled the vehicles with weapons drawn and alert while they waited on backup. Once Al placed JC and Jazzy in the vehicle, Al turned to assist with the assailants, but found no need.

Confronting the two men that dared to penetrate the security barrier was Ryan. Dressed in a white tee, black skin-tight jeans, and four-inch knee high boots, she was a force to be reckoned with. Apparently, the two men on the attack doubted her abilities.

"Another step forward could be hazardous to your life." She calmly stated, with her arms folded across her chest, her stance steady and her eyes lethal.

"You and what army little lady," one man had the nerve to laugh.

"Who said I was a lady?" Ryan bent, stuck one leg out striking the man at the ankles. Before he hit the ground, she had two weapons pulled. One pointing at the fool on the ground with the spiked heel of her boot at his throat, and the other pointed at the man that hadn't had a chance to react. Within a matter of seconds the situation was under control. By the time she had disabled them, the cavalry had arrived. Brian Thompson, Ryan's brother, Donnell and members of the Secret Services were on site. Just like that, the attack plot was derailed, as the park area flooded with agents.

"Having fun Ryan?" Brian called out as he and Donnell cuffed the attackers.

"Not yet," she replied. She walked over and kicked the one on the ground between his legs. "That's for making me break my nail. I've been trying to grow them for months," she yelled.

"Damn! That woman turns me on." Al said as Tucker joined him.

"That's the first time you've really seen her in action?"

Al nodded, "She handles herself well."

"She definitely handles her business," Tucker nodded.

Ryan walked toward the vehicles, "Everyone inside the vehicles, we need to move." She walked by Al as he watched her. "That means you too, Mr. Day. You will have to be debriefed."

"Are you going to be the one debriefing me?" Al asked with a crooked smile.

Ryan turned to him. She tilted her head a little to the side and replied. "I don't believe you could handle my debriefing, Mr. Day. I suggest we keep things on a professional level. We'll have one of the men handle you." She slipped into the driver seat and started the engine.

Tucker cleared his throat to cover his laugh. "Man, that was the first time I've ever seen you flirt and she shut you down." He walked by shaking his head. "Inhumane I tell you—inhumane." He laughed and walked away.

"She doesn't know she is supposed to be intimidated by you," Brian smirked as he walked by. "I forgot to send her that memo."

"That's cute, Thompson." Al said then slid inside the back seat of the vehicle with JC and Jazzy. They watched as Donnell and the other agents pulled off with the two assailants and Brian climbed into the vehicle with Magna, Tracy and the girls.

Senses still alert, Ryan put her shades back on as Al secured the children in their seatbelts. "Was those bad men, Uncle Al?" Jazzy asked.

"Yes Jazzy, they were."

"Didn't they know Ms. Ryan and Ms. Magna were going to be with us?" JC questioned as he shook his head. "They should have sent more than two people. Wouldn't you think, Uncle Al?"

Al looked up into the rear view mirror at Ryan, who was just as startled by JC's remarks. Ryan held his stare through the mirror, both thinking the same thing.

"Yes, I would think so, JC," Al replied, never taking his eyes from Ryan.

Ryan touched her earpiece activating the communication device. "Stay alert people. I don't think this was the main event." Between the driver's door and her seat she passed a weapon to Al. Not thinking twice, he reached out concealing the weapon from the children's view then secured it in the back of his pants.

"Jazzy, lay down on the seat. JC, cover your sister."

"I don't want to lay down, Uncle Al." Jazzy whined.

Ryan turned in her seat and gave Jazzy a stare that would weaken most grown men. The child immediately spread out on the seat. JC covered her.

"I see you have a way with children," Al smirked as he pulled out his phone. "Tucker where are you?"

"Right behind you," Tucker replied from his SUV.

"Something doesn't feel right."

"I'm fully loaded back here."

"Good." Al stepped out of the vehicle and scanned the area. He walked around and took the passenger seat. "The open park was on our left and a row of houses on the right. If a car pulled out in front of us from the corner ahead and another from the corner behind, the only area for escape would be the open park. We're sitting ducks here. We need to move."

Ryan looked around accessing the situation. He was right. They could be blocked from the front and behind. She spoke into her earpiece, "Boss, lead us home."

"Is Day with you?" Brian asked.

"Yes."

"Is he carrying?"

"He is now."

"Good. Something doesn't feel right."

"We have the same sentiment back here," She replied.

"We'll take the secondary route. We might have to fight our way home."

Al raised his phone, "Tuck, my brother, take the lead. Clear the way if you have too."

Tucker took the lead, Magna and Brian followed with Ryan and Al taking the rear. The concern for all involved wasn't driving through town. It was once they reached the outskirts of the city, precisely the single lane off of New Market Road that led to the Brooks' Estates.

As they approached Charles City Road, Al did what he always did. He made the plan his own. What would he do? After a few moments, he pulled out his cell. "Tucker, have Melissa Sue meet us at Varina High School football field."

Ryan looked over at Al with a startled expression. "I didn't know Melisa Sue was still around."

"We use her every now and then. Tell Thompson to follow Tucker."

She raised an eyebrow. "You don't know the boss real well do you?"

"What's the problem?"

"He doesn't take orders."

"Dealing with Thompson's ego is not on the top of my agenda at the moment. Just call him."

Not liking the way the order came out, Ryan turned away. "Apparently you don't know me real well either." She touched the device in her ear. "Boss, we have a change in plans. Lay back and follow Tucker."

"Why?"

"We're going to take them in a different way."

"There's only one road going in. There is no other way."

"Boss, trust me on this one."

The line was silent for a moment. "You better know what you're doing, Ryan."

The entourage made a quick right, then a left and pulled into the parking lot of the football field.

"Why the change Ryan?" Brian asked as he stepped out the vehicle with Magna in tow.

"We have another form of transportation." Ryan replied.

"Where?" Brian asked concerned with his protectee' safety.

"Right behind you."

Brian turned to see a chopper approach. He could fell the breeze from the propellers as it landed. He watched as Al approached the pilot. The pilot threw her arms around Al's neck and planted a kiss on his lips. They spoke for a moment then Al walked back to them.

"She can carry Tracy, the children and one other person. The rest of us will have to take the road."

"I'm taking the road." Ryan and Magna said simultaneously.

Brian stared at them. Hell, he wanted to take the road, too.

"You have a family now, Boss," Magna stated. "Too much to lose. We'll handle them."

Brian hesitated, then conceded. This was his place now. "Let's get the children."

These security situations were now a normal part of Tracy's life. There was and would always be an element of danger for them. She knew the calmer she was, the better the children would react. The team surrounded Tracy and the children the moment they stepped from the vehicle. She spoke to Al. "Don't get caught with that gun. I need you out here for this very reason."

"I'm good, Sis. My friend Melissa Sue is going to take you and the children home," he replied.

"Everything is set." Brian said trying to comfort Tracy. "We'll have you home in five minutes."

"Where are you going?" She asked Al.

They reached the chopper and had the children in before he answered. He smiled, "We're going to get the bad guys." Tracy frowned while JC gave his Uncle Turk a pound.

"Do what you do." JC smiled at his uncle.

Al laughed. "See you in a bit, little man."

The chopper took off as Ryan, Magna, Tucker and Al watched. "How do you want to roll in?" Tucker asked.

"They are only expecting two cars. I'll take the lead." He pointed at Magna and Ryan, "You two take the middle. Tucker you're loaded, you hang back. You'll know when to hit."

"I think we should take the lead." Ryan protested. "We're legit, you're not."

"We protect our women," Al replied as he began walking away.

"Oh Lord," Magna sighed as she turned away, "Wrong thing to say."

Tucker and Magna leaned against one of the SUVs and waited for the argument that was sure to pursue.

"We are not some little women that need the big strong man to protect us." Ryan explained in a rather hostile manner. "In fact, we could easily take you down."

Al walked towards the other SUV. "You have a problem with men being protectors." Al questioned over his shoulder as he continued walking. "It's in our nature to want to protect the weaker species."

"What in the hell makes you think I'm weaker than you?" Ryan asked walking behind him toward the vehicles.

Al stopped suddenly and turned to her. She walked right into the stone wall of his chest. He reached out, catching her around the waist before she fell backwards. He would have laughed at the irony if he had the time, but he didn't. "Because you are," he said as he pulled her to him.

Ryan's body slid down his until her feet touched the ground. The sensation of being held by him stunned her momentarily. The moment her mind cleared, she pushed away. "You caught me off guard." She said composing herself. "I can still take you out."

It was a second or two before Al said anything. He liked the way she felt in his arms way too much, and that bothered him. "We're wasting time here. He calmly replied. "Get in the car, let's move."

"I'm going, but it's not because you ordered me to."

"It wasn't an order, it was a request."

Magna and Tucker looked at each other. "I give it six months before they will be doing the wild thing." Magna snickered.

Tucker laughed as he walked towards his vehicle. "I have a grand that says it will be six weeks—tops."

"I don't have a grand, but I'll take that bet. My girl is not going out like that." Magna climbed into the driver's side of the vehicle as Ryan entered on the other side. "Do me a favor?"

"What's that," Ryan asked still bothered by the feel of Al's body next to hers.

"There's two weeks left in June. Four weeks in July." She nodded her head satisfied with the calculation. "Hold out on Day until August and I'll give you $500.00."

Ryan turned and frowned at Magna then declared. "I don't plan on giving him any—ever."

"Good," Magna laughed as she pulled off. This was the first time she had seen a man affect her partner this way. She liked seeing Ryan rattled. "Just as long as ever doesn't end until August, we're good."

As Al predicted the attack took place about a mile before the entrance into the estates. Ryan had just received the call indicating Tracy and the children were safely inside the house, when she saw the back window of the SUV Al was driving shattered. "They're using silencers pull it over!"

Magna slammed on the brakes and swung the vehicle to an angle. "What direction did it come from?" Magna called out.

"Every direction," Ryan replied as they both hit the floor of the vehicle. Crawling to the back, they looked at each other, counted to three, then kicked the back door open and hit the ground crawling under the vehicle.

Al's vehicle was under heavy fire. He was on the floor trying to determine where the shots were coming from. It was hard to figure because of the silencers they were using. One thing was certain. There were more than two shooters on each side.

He crawled to the back of the SUV, kicked the door open and hit the ground. Looking back he spotted Magna and Ryan under the other SUV. He motioned to them he was rolling left, into the wooded area and they were to go right.

"Tracy is going to have our ass if anything happens to him." Magna hissed.

"Why are men so damn controlling?" Ryan exhaled.

"That's a conversation for another day," Magna stated as she checked her ammunition.

Ryan did the same. "Once he rolls, we're following.

"Got you covered," Magna replied.

As soon as Al made his move, the women rolled right and came up shooting over his head. They both slid into the ditch, feet first as if they were tagging home plate to beat the throw. Under cover of the woods, they made their way to where Al should have landed. They split up to search for him. Magna was the first to come across a body. She smiled, "One down," she said into the earpiece.

"I have two over here," Ryan replied as she crept through the woods alert.

"I have another. That's four," Magna relayed.

Ryan did not have a chance to reply. A body fell on her from the tree above causing her to hit the ground hard and her weapon to drop. She reached behind her back, pulled out another weapon and placed it in the gut of the man on top of her.

"You pull that trigger and your man goes down."

She looked up to see the attacker's laser pointed right at the back of Al's head. "Where's the boy?"

"What boy," Ryan stalled hoping Al would sense the danger.

"Don't play with me. Where is Harrison's son?"

"Safe and secure at home," she sneered.

There was a momentary look of disbelief in the man's eyes. It disappeared. The look in his eyes now almost made Ryan wish it would return. He angrily knocked the second weapon from her hand. That was the split second she needed to react. Bringing her knee up full force she connected with his jewels causing him to pause for a moment. The man apparently had a high tolerance for pain. The kick would usually give her a good minute to counter act, but this man had it together in half that time. And he was not happy. He raised the butt of his gun to hit her but she never felt the impact.

Al cursed when he ducked after seeing the laser reflection on the tree bark in front of him. From the ground, he looked behind him to find the target. The sight of a man on top of Ryan with a gun made him curse. He was normally a quiet, laid back kind of man. Soft spoken, some would say, but certainly capable of protecting himself and those that he loved. There were only a few things that caused him to lose his cool. This stubborn woman seemed to be one of them. Another, he determined was seeing her in danger.

Al exhaled, then doubled back behind the man, the whole time muttering to himself, *The woman apparently doesn't know her left from her right.* Without thinking twice, Al reached down, yanked the man from Ryan and slammed him against the tree trunk. The man kicked his feet from under him and Al landed on his back. He quickly jumped back to his feet swinging the butt of his gun against the man's jawbone, knocking him out cold.

Al turned to Ryan, who was now on her feet with her weapon drawn. He took one deep breath to calm himself before he spoke. He had learned early in life that anger works against good judgment. With his organization, he always handled his people with patience and tolerance. When they made a mistake, he did not take them out and shoot them. He would sit down and explain what they did incorrectly, then show them the correct way.

He exhaled again and spoke softly. "The signal I gave was to go left. You rolled to the right, which put you in a dangerous situation. Let's try to avoid that in the future. ."

Ryan stood there for a moment, not sure how to respond to the man. He was speaking to her as if she were a new recruit that did not know her way around a fight. Normally she would be offended, but he said it in such a sincere manner that it threw her off—for a minute. That's when the first blast sounded.

Al smiled. "Sounds like Tucker's having fun without us." They followed the sound.

"The good guys are here," Magna said through the earpiece.

Ryan relaxed then turned to Al. "Give me the gun." He handed her the weapon as they began walking back out to the road. "I didn't need your help back there. I had that situation under control."

Al followed behind her shaking his head trying to weaken the effect of her hips swaying in front of him. "You're welcome," he said as he reached the conclusion it was time for Ryan 'the warrior princess' to become his.

Tucker had gathered, five attackers, while Magna had another four on the ground. "There's another one about twenty feet in." Al stated.

"This was a professional team. That doesn't give me a warm fuzzy feeling" Ryan added. The thought put an uneasy feeling in Al's gut.

Tucker was the only person that could read Al. What showed on his friends face concerned him. "You ladies have this covered?" he asked.

"We're good," Magna replied as she secured one of the assailants."

Tucker looked at Al, "Let's roll out."

Al nodded as he pulled off the band that held his locs back. "You're going to be okay?" He said as he walked by Ryan.

"I'm fine," Ryan replied agitated that he asked the question.

Al turned to her and smiled. "That you are Morgan Ryan Williams—that you are."

The impact of his full blown smile on her was indescribable. This was the first time in her life that a man had affected her in this way. *What in the hell was she going to do about it,* she wondered as Al and Tucker pulled off.

Magna looked at Ryan watching the fleeting vehicle. "August is all I'm asking for—hold out until August."

Chapter 3

A few days after the incident, Al was sitting at his home in the influential area of Richmond called Chamberlayne Farms. The homes ran from a modest three hundred thousand to a cool million or more. He loved the area because some portions of it were considered secluded, although it was located in the city. Al liked the city life. He liked having neighbors nearby, hearing the traffic in the distance, seeing children playing together. Gated communities like the one Tracy and Tucker lived were nice to visit, but he didn't want to live there. The city was just fine to him.

To the outside world the home resembled a modest four bedroom two story rancher, surrounded by a beautifully manicured landscape and circular drive way. But, once you stepped inside, you knew it was a luxury home. The foyer provided a spectacular view into the great room and beyond through the floor to ceiling windows surrounding a fireplace. A sixty-inch flat screen was anchored above presenting a welcoming area to relax. To the left was a library with books on shelves as tall as the windows in the great room. To the right was what appeared to be the living room with a dining room on the far side. Walking towards the great room a portion of the kitchen came into view. A marble island separated the kitchen and the great room. The furniture was placed in a circular pattern, with a huge round table in the center. A spiral staircase led to the second level, which housed two bedroom suites, with walk in closets and bathrooms fit for a queen. The hallway to the right was the master suite that spread the entire length of the right side of the house. The double doors opened to a sitting area with tray ceilings, a fireplace, comfortable seating and another library with books from floor to ceiling. Turning left was the archway that led to three steps. The platform had a king size sleigh bed anchored with a rich leather headboard. Once inside the room, to the right was a walk in closet. One wall of the closet had shelves filled with shoes. The walk, straight ahead had shirts arranged by color at the top and suits at the bottom. The wall to the right had shelves filled with tee shirts, sweaters, sweats and hats. In the center was a chest with drawers on each side. On top was an assortment of watches, rings, bracelets, and chains. Next to the closet was the bathroom or spa would be a better description. The bathroom was the size of a small house. The walk-through shower literally encircled the spa tube on one side of the room. One vanity sink was at the entrance from the closet, the other was across the room from the bedroom entrance. The commode was enclosed in its own room.

Walking back into the bedroom, there was another door, but it was not apparent to the naked eye. It was only accessible by reading the iris of your eye. A picture of a couple in an embrace was the single item on the wall. Looking closely at the picture you will see the man is wearing a ring. The right eye standing in front of the picture, looking into that ring will activate the opening. Once activated, the wall literally slides open. Five seconds after the sensor reads a body walking through, the doors close and lights activate. Inside the sound proof room, was the most sophisticated surveillance system in existence. After the incident with Tracy, The CIA would be impressed and would have to be trained to use it. On the monitors mounted throughout the room, the exterior of JD, Tucker, and Al's homes were displayed. There were two entrances to the room, one from the bedroom and the other from the utility room connected to the kitchen. Only two people had access, Al and Tucker.

It was 5:45 in the morning. Al was sitting in his enclosed patio that overlooked the pool in a pair of shorts, tee shirt and flip flops. This was his favorite part of his home. It was where he relaxed, and where he met regularly with his brother-in-law. Brian and Samuel entered the wrought iron security fence that led to his back yard. The men's presences indicated that JD was about to make an appearance. The two nodded then took their surveillance positions. Wearing sweats, a tee shirt, hat and sneakers, JD walked in and took a seat across from him. Al handed him a cup of tea. JD took a sip and frowned. "Man, you have to do better than that." He held the cup out to Al.

Al reached over to the stand next to him, pulled out a bottle of Hennessey and added it to the tea. JD took another sip. Laying his head back he sighed, "Much better." He savored the moment. "I prefer to have this straight but diplomacy dictates that I not indulge at this time."

"I feel for you my brother." Al smiled just as the sun began to rise. He knew why JD was there. Tracy wasn't happy about the recent events and that had a direct impact on JD's frame of mind. "You have to make her feel secure." Al stated, "What happened the other day has her on edge. It's not so much about her, as it is about the children. Those men were well organized, fully armed equipped and highly trained. That equals money and power." Al sat forward. "They were missionaries and they were after your family."

JD sat up. "I only trust certain people with my family. Secret Service is good, but I've been in the position before of trusting officials and they were the very people that went after my family. My personal detail travels with me and they are stretched to their limit. I will walk away from this campaign before I put my family in jeopardy. I need your help to continue."

"You know I will protect Tracy and the children with my life. But JD, the people that we encountered were professionals. They were organized and well financed. You will need a lot more than me to protect your family." Al grinned, "You may not want to hear my suggestions, but it's guaranteed to keep your family safe."

"I'm listening," JD exclaimed, "Who...." He stopped and began shaking his head. "Don't."

Al smirked, "He's the best whether you like his methods or not."

JD stood and looked out at Samuel. "The last time we were together he damn near blew up a town."

"It was an island," Al replied. "And from what I understand it needed to be blown up."

JD put his hands in the pocket of his sweats and looked down at the ground as if waiting for the answer to jump up at him. Knowing the combination of Al, Hurricane and Absolute would keep his family protected did not make the decision easy. If anything were to go wrong, and with Absolute around the odds increased the possibility, he would have hell to pay.

"Al, I love Tracy. She is the fiber that keeps my blood pumping." After a moment, he looked out at the sunrise. A smile creased his lips, "That's what Tracy is to me—my sunrise every morning." He sighed. "I believe I can move this country forward, but I can't do it without knowing Tracy and my children are safe." He turned to Al. "What do I do here? I want my family safe but have a responsibility to protect this country. The best way to do that is to keep Absolute busy in other countries."

Al laughed understanding JD's hesitation. He stood and walked over to stand next to his brother-in-law, looking out over the yard. "Here's what I see. This attack is the first of many to come. Since this attempt failed, we have to be prepared for other. We will need his skills to determine where the threat is coming from. And let's be honest, as extreme as his antics are, they work."

JD shook his head, "Tracy is not going to like this."

"I'll handle Tracy."

JD nodded. "I'll get him on board." He was silent for a moment. Having Al around had been a godsend to JD. The circumstances in which they first met were less than desirable. During his stint as District Attorney, JD was the prosecutor responsible for bringing Al Day down. It was during that time that Al placed Tracy's protection in JD's hands. At the time neither of them knew he would fall in love and marry Tracy. Despite how they first met, JD knew Al was a good man and cared deeply about people, especially those he loved. In addition to that, Al was one of the most intelligent people he had ever met. That was saying a lot, when you consider those who surrounded JD. With all of that aside, Al was a good listener and always gave good advice where Tracy was concerned.

"Tracy doesn't like campaigning. If I could get this job any other way she would have no issues with it at all. She thinks this is the moment she has feared for ten years. I don't know how to get her to realize I'm not going anywhere. She is going to have me until death we do part plus some. There isn't a woman on this planet that could take me from Tracy. She loves me and all my faults. Believe me, I have plenty. In spite of them she has given me four beautiful children and not one day of regret. Seeing her worried, concerns me. Tell me what to do."

Al chuckled softly. "You're asking me for relationship advice." He laughed, "You must be desperate."

JD smiled. "Not on the relationship, just on how to convince Tracy I'm not going anywhere."

"Tracy is insecure when it comes to love. Your years together have helped, but it hasn't diminished. The only time she is secure is when she is pregnant."

"She said I can't have any more children right now."

"She put you on lockdown?" Al teased.

"In a way. She said I can have another child once we move into the White House."

Al laughed, "That's months away, my brother."

JD shook his head, "She can't hold out. Tracy will be all over me in less than a week."

"That's too much information, my man. You're talking about my little sister."

"She's my wife."

"Are we going to have this argument again?"

JD grinned. "Do you remember when I came to the prison to tell you about Tracy?"

"I was ready to kick your ass that night."

"That would have been an ass kicking I would have to take. There was no way I was not going to have Tracy. I didn't care what you did."

"It took balls for you to tell me that back then. That's why I didn't object. I knew you had to be in love with her."

JD sat back in his chair and crossed one knee over the other, placed his forefinger and thumb against his chin and stared at Al in thought. "You've been behind the scene pulling strings for a long time. Did you set us up?"

Al smiled then sat back down. "Not intentionally." Al sat in the same comfortable position as JD. "I didn't know you were Tracy's roommate's brother until the spring break she spent at your condo. That was all fate. I had nothing to do with it." Al smiled, "One of my men saw you and Tracy on the balcony at a club. He took pictures of you kissing her.

He wanted to take you out." Al laughed. "Lucky for you, by then my focus had changed." Al took on a faraway look. "When Munford killed your father, something snapped in me. Seeing Munford take him out like that," he shook his head, "for no reason, changed me. That was when we reorganized our business. I figured if cops were killing cops, we didn't stand a chance. Taking a life needlessly just did not make sense to me." Al shrugged. He looked over JD's shoulder as Tucker joined Brian and Samuel in the yard. "One could say Munford made me. My focus became getting my people off the streets and into legit businesses that would keep them out of the line of fire."

"When your man Charlie came to me with the story of Munford, I began to understand why the man had it in for me." JD stated, "What I never understood was why he was after you. What did you have that he wanted and couldn't take?"

Al smiled, "Ms. Sunshine."

"Who's Ms. Sunshine?"

Al laid his head back and smiled at the memory. "Ms. Sunshine was a Madame that lived two doors down from us when we were kids." He sat up, "Man that was a beautiful woman and could handle her business. Munford was one of her main clients, but she couldn't stand the man. She had to deal with him to keep the police away. When I was just about thirteen, Ms. Sunshine caught me looking up the dress of one of her girls." He laughed, "She told me don't be a little pervert. If you want something from a woman, be a man and step to her. From that point on, she taught me how to make love to a woman. I can truly say I was taught by a professional. She took a liking to me, found out I was smart and began teaching me about her business. It was her hope that I would work for her, but at the time I was into basketball and school. The day Tracy's father died changed all of that. I began working in the business, handling the books and from time to time, the muscle. When she died, Munford thought he was going to take over the business. Hell, he was running everything else on the streets. But on her deathbed, she made me swear not to let Munford near her business or her girls. I made the promise and I meant to keep it. A few months later Munford approached me about taking over the house. I turned him down cold. That's when the battle began."

"Why did he want Ms. Sunshine's business if he was controlling everything else on the street?"

Al laughed again, "Between the weed and the girls, Ms. Sunshine was pulling in over a million a year with no effort. Munford may have been pulling in that kind of money, but he was greedy for power. He wanted to control the police force and the streets. I interfered with that on the streets and you interfered with it in court. Munford merged our lives."

JD chuckled, "He unknowingly fused us into a bond that will never be broken." JD sat up and clasped his hands. "What about Gavin?"

Al smiled. "Roberts was a rookie back then. His only problem was trying to impress the brass. He didn't find out until later that Munford was dirty. He didn't know about your father, JD. Gavin was being politically blackmailed. Munford knew Gavin wanted a political career and he used that knowledge against him."

"I appreciate you sharing that." JD sat forward, "Al, I want you at the table."

Al shook his head. "As much as we want to believe, once a man pays his debt to society all is forgiven and he starts on a clean slate, it's a myth. The far right Republicans will use that to incite the general public. They will have half of the country believing you will have thugs running the White House. I've been in the background of your life for over twenty years. This is where I work the best."

JD nodded his head, accepting Al's decision. "Do you still have those pictures?"

"Those, and some woman giving you hell afterwards. It's not often you see a real player caught in the game." He laughed.

"I wasn't caught, man." JD had to laugh. "Oh hell, I was, but not by Vanessa. Tracy caught me that night and she still got me."

Al stood and tapped him on the knee. "Yeah man, you are good and got!"

"Like Ryan got you?" JD smirked.

The statement made froze Al in his seat. Then he nodded. "Ryan has my interest, but not my heart. There is a difference."

JD laughed. "Yeah, I said the same thing."

Not truly ignoring JD, Al looked to the men in the yard. "Breakfast?" he called out. "You're soft. I'm not."

"Soft!"

"Yeah," Al looked over his shoulder as the men followed him into the kitchen. "Soft. You let a pair of light brown eyes control you."

"Just like you're letting a pair of dark brown eyes have you so wound up you can't even look at another woman. Like it or not, Ryan's got you the same way Tracy got me. We are good and got, my brother. The men laughed. "Al." He turned to JD. "If I haven't said it before, I appreciate all you've done for Tracy and me."

"I know."

JD patted him on his back as he followed him into the kitchen. "Prepare yourself, Absolute is hell on wheels."

Al's face lit up. "I'm looking forward to working with him."

JD shook his head. "That's what you say now—just wait."

Mac was sitting in his home office looking over some papers when the Senator walked in. "You summoned me, father?" he said taking a seat in front of the desk.

"Have you seen the polls? The boy is double digits ahead of Jerry. I've made a phone call. We're flying to Miami tomorrow."

The Senator was not comfortable with the arrangements his father had made and shared with him earlier. "Do you think this is wise?"

The one thing Mac hated about his son was his lack of balls. He was raised to take out whatever competitor he had with all the force he could. His son, as much as he loved him, was raised with a conscience. He got that from his mother. "No. The writing is on the wall. You don't let the enemy get stronger. Once his party base solidifies around him it's a wash, son."

"I agree with your thinking. I just don't agree with your methods. Your solution should be the last option, not the first. I'm merely suggesting we try another approach to get him to drop out of the race. If that doesn't work, then we do things your way."

"Your plan failed. It's time to move forward." Mac held his son's eyes until he looked away. "We'll meet with my people tomorrow. Set things in motion."

Jeremiah looked up at his father, somewhat surprised he knew about the failed attack. However, he knew not to show the weakness of surprise. You must be confident in all things you do, his father once told him. "When at first you don't succeed, try again." Jeremiah stood. "I'll meet with your people tomorrow. If this backfires, I will distance myself from you quicker than a politician with a sex tape.

Chapter 4
Miami, Florida

Alejandra Mateo stood at the window of his home office overlooking the veranda where his household staff was busy setting up for the meeting with an American Senator. The calm of the clear blue Atlantic Ocean just beyond his veranda was a definite contrast to the turmoil raging inside him. Dealing with politicians was what he had to do at this level of his organization and as the Americans always say, politics is a dirty business. It always left a bad taste in his mouth after dealing with an elected officer. In Mexico, he controlled the politicians and the police. Hell, he even controlled a few in just about every major city in America. That was precisely the reason he despised them. The politicians, that is. Most of them had a price tag. Money, women, and drugs—all politicians crave one or the other. But most of all, they craved power. Power—the word alone generated immense pride inside of him, as he patiently listened to the request placed before him. Again, the American Senator is in search of what he has—the power to control a country.

"Our contact indicates the senator is offering a few million for the completion of this contract," Miguel Santiago stated as he swallowed his tequila. "However, I brought this directly to you. Under the circumstances, I thought you might require more than just monetary compensation."

Mateo, standing just at five-eleven, with a solid body weight of one hundred ninety-five, dark, almost coal black hair, dark black eyes and as always, impeccably dressed in an Italian tailored suit and loafers turned to the man he considered his lieutenant and friend. "You were right to bring this directly to my attention, amigo." He spoke casually at times mixing Spanish, his native language and English his second. "How many know of this meeting?"

"Only Raul Cortez from the Houston operations," Miguel replied. "He has previously handled a few situations for the Senator's father. This request, however, in his words was fire. Raul wanted no parts of it. In fact, he marked it for your eyes only." Taking a seat in front of Mateo's mahogany desk, Miguel asked, "Any thoughts on the matter?"

Mateo sat in his leather chair with a marked grin. "Men at this level seek only one thing, power." His dark eyes leveled on Miguel, "But to acquire such you have to have the heart to seek it, take it once found and then control it once you've conquered. What we have to determine is does the American Senator have the heart to take what he desires. More importantly, what will the benefit of honoring his request be for the organization?"

"They're offering a few million," Miguel smiled.

Mateo rendered a laughable look at his friend. "The organization could pay off the Americans debt to China and not miss a meal." He stood, resuming his stance at the window. "I don't trust the Americans from Texas. No, the Senator would have to offer significantly more than money."

There was a soft knock at the door of his office. Before he could respond, a burst of energy by the name of Ariella came through. Standing, holding the handles to both doors, dressed in a flowing white sundress and white sandals, with her raven black waist length hair flowing behind her, Ari, as he called her, beamed a smile so bright, he knew all was right with the world.

In addition to the meeting, they came to Miami to visit with her family. A family that tried to turn her against him, but for some reason God had blessed him with her love.

"Ale, you would never believe what I've just learned."

"Apparently not how to wait until you are invited into a closed room," Miguel replied testily.

The smile faded, along with the gleam in her eyes as Ari looked to the imposing figure sitting in her husband's office. She turned back to Ale. "Forgive the interruption. I wasn't aware you were in a meeting." She turned to leave.

"Ari, you are never an interruption, my love." He held his hand out to her. As she crossed the room to him, Mateo turned to Miguel. "Ensure all is in place for the meeting," he said to his friend in a tone clearly indicating he did not appreciate the comment made to his wife.

Miguel stood, rising to his full six foot figure as he winced at the tone Mateo had taken with him in front of her. Adjusting his suit jacket, he bestowed a menacing glance at Ariella. "It's always interesting to see you, Mrs. Mateo."

Forcing a smile for her husband's friend, Ari replied, "It's nice seeing you again Miguel and I do apologize for the interruption."

Miguel nodded, not sure how to take the woman that seemed to have caused his friend to lose focus. He looked at Mateo, "I'll see to the arrangements." He closed the doors behind him.

Ariella stared at the door with her hands on her hips. "I have no idea why that man dislikes me so."

Taking her hand, Mateo pulled her into his embrace. Looking down into her now smiling eyes, he smiled back. "He fears you have taken my concentration away from the business."

Wrapping her arms around her husband's neck, she was simply radiant with her contagious smile. "Well, he's really going to be pissed when he hears my news."

Kissing her neck, right below her earlobe he asked, "What news is that?"

Ariella placed her hands on his face cupping it and bringing his eyes to meet hers. She softly kissed his lips, then pulled back to see his reaction. "You, my handsome husband, are going to be a father."

The look of pure male satisfaction is all that Ariella saw. She laughed joyously as he ravished her with kisses.

Miguel watched the exchange through the windows from the end of the veranda. His boss, the head of the largest, most influential crime cartel in the world was acting like a teenage boy getting his first piece of a woman. The sight disgusted him.

An hour later, Mateo and Miguel sat at the table on the veranda, covered with a variety of Mexican dishes, fruits and drinks. Across from them sat the ex-governor of Texas, "Mac" McClintock and his son, Senator Jeremiah McClintock Jr. With the pleasantries out of the way, Mateo was more than ready to hear what the men wanted. They were powerful men in the United States, what could they want from his organization?

"Have one of those gals bring me another tequila," Mac demanded in his condescending southern voice. The pool off of the veranda was surrounded with women. This seemed to be the way to attract Americans when it came to business, but as for Mateo, he would prefer to do without them. Either way, there was no reason for the ex-governor to speak to the women in that tone. Mateo placed a hand on Miguel's arms, stopping his advancement to honor the old man's request. "Before we become inebriated let's move the conversation to the business at hand."

Miguel retook his seat as Mac replied, "I do my best negotiations when I'm," he paused then tried to mimic Mateo's accent, "inebriated," he drawled.

Showing no reaction to the old man's attempt to rattle him, Mateo spoke. "I prefer to handle business when everyone's mind is clear and focused. It tends to limit future misunderstandings."

"I believe Mr. Mateo has a valid point father," Senator McClintock spoke with the polished southern drawl similar to his fathers, but more respectful in its delivery. "To the business at hand," the Senator began but was interrupted by Mac.

"Are you telling me how to negotiate, boy?" Mac snapped.

"Not at all father," the Senator replied smoothly. "Mr. Mateo has been hospitable to a fault and he is after all a very busy man. And as you say—time is money." The Senator looked pointedly at his father.

Apparently satisfied with the response, Mac turned to Mateo. "We will pay you two million dollars to kill a colored boy. Five million if it's done at the right time."

Mateo learned early in life to mask his reactions around people. Miguel had not completely acquired the skill. "What color is the boy?' He asked with a clearly agitated voice.

"It's not one of you Mexicans if that's what you're asking." Mac waved him off.

"Allow me to clarify," the Senator interjected, trying to keep the talks from turning into murder.

"Please do," Mateo replied with a raised brow.

"The coolness of Mateo's response shook the Senator to his core. He'd much rather deal with men like Miguel. You knew his thoughts and feelings, for he never spared a reaction to the conversation at hand. Alejandra Mateo was different. Other than the coolness in his eyes that had been there from the beginning of the meeting, you had no idea what he was thinking. And that could be dangerous.

The Senator sat forward. "My son is the governor of Texas. It is our wish to see him become President of the United States. But there is an obstacle."

"The colored boy?" Miguel asked.

"Yes!" Mac shouted. "That colored boy is trying to take what is my grandson's birth right," he slammed his fist on the table.

"Father," the Senator cautioned with a look. Giving his attention back to Mateo, he explained. "As you can see, we are very passionate about this obstacle."

Mateo remained calmly seated with his legs crossed and his eyes leveled on the Senator. Without as much as raising his voice he clearly reprimanded the ex-governor. "Passionate or not," he coldly stated, "You will pay the one point two million to replace this table I had imported here for my wife from Italy if the foundation is damaged." He could see the respect for the reprimand on the old man in the Senator's eyes. "What is the man's name?" Mateo continued.

"Before we tell you that boy, we need to know you're going to take the job." Mac stated holding Mateo's stare.

Mateo looked out to the ocean as a cynical smile touched his lips. He slowly uncrossed his legs then placed his arms on the table and clasped his hands together to keep from strangling the old man. "Governor McClintock," his mother always told him to show respect to his elders, "I'm a patient man." He turned his cold dark glare to Mac. "I pride myself on being accepting of others. However, if you refer to anyone else in this meeting as a boy....." he let the word hang. "I will chop your body up into pieces so small the sharks in the ocean would have to search for hours to find a complete meal." He held the old man's eyes to make sure he was completely understood. Then he turned to the Senator. "An obstacle deters progress. It does not stop it unless you allow it to. For example, your father's southern nature is an obstacle that I will not allow to impede the progress of this meeting. The obstacle in this scenario can be walked around, over or through. Or, I could simply choose to ignore it. Your obstacle at the moment is the lack of the name of the man you want eliminated. Mateo sat back in his seat and crossed his legs. "So, what shall it be? Are you going to provide the name of the individual or will you allow this obstacle to bring this meeting to a close?"

The Senator held Mateo's glare, as minutes ticked away. He slightly turned his head towards his father who gave a slight nod of his head. Senator Jeremiah McClintock turned back to Mateo, and then sat back in his seat. "The obstacle we want removed is Jeffrey Daniel Harrison, the Governor of Virginia."

On the same day, a meeting was called at JD's home to discuss the security detail. The participants of the meeting were as different as they were committed to one goal. The goal simple—get JD elected as President of the United States. To ensure his cooperation in reaching that goal, each knew his number one requirement was the safety of his family. This meeting was set to determine just how far they were willing to go to guarantee their safety.

As always, Al stopped in to see Tracy before the meeting was set to begin. The kitchen was the heart of the Harrisons' home. Instinctively that's where Al headed. Outside the entrance from the foyer Ryan stood next to the door. She straightened as he approached.

"I need you to wait here, Mr. Day." She stated as she put her hand out.

Al took in her black jeans, white tee shirt and of course her boots. The woman affected him just by standing there. "Good morning, Ms. Williams. I'm here to see Tracy. Since you're here, I assume she's in the kitchen."

"She is." Ryan nodded, shaking off how good he looked. "But she's busy."

"I'm pretty handy in the kitchen. Maybe I could give her a hand." He took a step forward.

She placed her hand on his chest to stop his progression. The touch sent sensations throughout her body. She jerked her hand back. "She's not alone. Her husband is with her," she stated while taking a step back.

Al gave her a knowing smile, "I see." He turned, "I'll wait for them in the office."

Not able to let the opportunity go Ryan stopped him. "You know," she began, "Mr. H asked you to the table. That's an honor not many would turn down, but you did. Why?"

Al turned back to her with a curious look. "How do you know he asked me to the table?"

"I hear things."

"That's good to know the next time I'm here." He turned to walk away.

"You didn't answer my question. Why did you turn him down?"

"I don't see how that should be your concern," Al continued to walk.

"I never took you for a coward." That stopped him dead in his tracks. He turned back with a frown. "The man asked you to the table because he needs you there. I can only assume you are too afraid to venture into the world of politics."

He walked back towards her. "Ms. Williams, I believe you have over stepped your boundaries. Your job, as I understand it is to protect Tracy. Not to interfere in family business."

"Sometimes it's one and the same." Ryan held her stance. "You ever wonder why he asked you? Of all the connected people he has around him, why did he ask you?"

Al stood there as he placed his hands in his pockets wondering where she was going with this. "I'm sure you have a theory."

"I do," she walked up to him. "You remind him of why he started down this path in the first place. You're his proof that this world can be better. The people at the table with him, they don't understand the depth of his passion the way you should. Or could it be you have forgotten where you started. How you got to this point in your life."

Looking down into her eyes, Al's first thought was how beautiful, yet vulnerable they were. Those deep dark brown eyes could easily make a man forget the outside world. But that was something he couldn't allow to happen. Yes, he wanted her with a passion that was almost overwhelming. But that was just until he had his taste of her and then he could and would let her go. "Ms. Williams, I pride myself on my patience level, but you are testing it." He stepped away from her. "I'm going to walk away now and pretend this conversation never took place."

"I never thought the great Al Day would be afraid of the Carolyn Roberts' in this world."

Al stopped and walked back until he was standing over her only a breath away. "In five minutes you've called me a coward twice. Yet, I'm willing to forgive you. However, please don't for a minute take that as a sign of weakness on my part. Any person can speak their mind, but it takes a wise man to know when to hold his tongue." He was so close to her his lips touched her cheek as he spoke. "I'm walking away."

Ryan watched as he walked away. "Damn." She mumbled to herself. Just listening to him while he stood that close to her made her wet. She definitely had to keep away from him. He could easily affect her mental stability.

J D, Brian Thompson, Calvin Johnson and Douglas Hylton went to high school together. JD never took a step without their input then and he refused to do so now. They was his core—his boys that had supported him in every endeavor from girls to jobs. Their advice had been invaluable. James Brooks had become just as valuable. As his campaign manager and brother-in-law, James' wisdom and support had resulted in a prestigious political career. He was number five at JD's round table. Now there was his other brother-in-law, Al. Over the years, he found Al to be a complete oxymoron.

The so-called thug he put away nine years ago was the quietest, most mild mannered person, other than Tracy, that JD had ever met. Al loved children, especially his daughter, Monique and his nieces and nephew. He had and will do whatever it takes to protect those that he loved. That elite group of advisors now included Al. JD trusted his advice and had learned to never question or ask the reason why, when it came to Al. For one, he probably would not tell you and two, he always had an intelligent reason for whatever he did.

All were in attendance for this meeting. And though JD admired and welcomed their advice, he did not always agree. This was one of those times.

"I don't understand the problem." Samuel Lassiter grinned. JD looked at the person that was now his main body man. He had come to respect and accept the fact that Samuel was physically able to break him in half if he wanted to. It didn't make him less of a man because Samuel could restrain him at any time. It just made him wise to recognize and respect the fact. At least that's what Tracy told him. "You all know how my brother works."

"That's the problem," James stated. "Everywhere he goes, something blows up."

"That's a problem?" Samuel asked as he laughed at his own joke. The others in the room turned to him as if he had lost his mind.

"Only if you are a political candidate that unleashed him on the city," James replied.

"You make him sound like a monster," Magna stated. "If I remember correctly didn't he save your son?" She asked Brian.

Brian, who had not added to the conversation, nodded his head. "He did."

"Look, all I know is he was there when Sammy and I needed him. I'm with Sammy." Ryan added, "I don't see the problem."

"Let's cut to the chase." Brian stood, "James, if Ashley's life was in danger, what would you want, someone that shot whoever dared to put their hands on her or someone that's going to ask questions?"

James looked at Brian, "If I remember correctly, it was you that stopped me from killing David Holt."

"That was your brother's doing. I would have let you kill him then helped you hide the body."

JD turned to Douglas. "What's your take Douglas?"

Douglas looked around at the people in the room. There is no reason he should be there advising the presumed next president of the United States, but that's the man JD was. He had his core friends and no one will ever convince him to turn from them. "I trust Al's judgment. If he said he needs Lassiter here to protect your family, there should be no discussion—get the man here."

"Ask and it shall be granted." Everyone turned to the doorway leading to the patio, where, Joshua "Absolute" Lassiter stood in his signature designer suit, Italian loafers and sunshades. "At this point boys and girls, the conversation is mute. I'm here to serve at the will of the President of the United States." He walked, correction, the man did not walk—he swaggered over to where JD stood near the fireplace. "SQ2, this is for you." He gave JD two letters then turned to the people in the room. "Big brother, what's up?"

Samuel gave him a brotherly hug. "Your niece misses you. Drop in before Cynthia kills me."

"You sure it's not your wife that misses me?" Joshua grinned. "Thompson, how's little man?"

"He's good man," Brian smiled as he shook the hand of the man who had saved his son.

"Douglas," he shook his hand. "James." He spoke, "Not liking this-huh? I understand. But on the serious tip, you need me." He walked over to where Magna stood. "Hello. I don't believe I've had the pleasure." He extended his hand. "Joshua Lassiter."

Magna returned the smile, "Magna Rivera. No, you haven't."

Joshua displayed a seductive lopsided grin. "I like a confident woman. You wouldn't happen to be free tonight?"

Magna laughed as he turned his attention to Ryan. "Hello, gorgeous."

Ryan smirked, "Hello, pain."

"He looked down her body, then back up. "You still want me—don't you?"

JD tuned out the conversations going on in the room as he read the letters with the Presidential seal affixed to it. The first letter gave Joshua a get out of jail free card for any actions taken to protect JD and his family during the campaign. The other letter somewhat explained the first and a bit of advice. JD read the letters then handed them to James.

The first letter James read quickly and knew it needed to be placed in the safe. The second letter had him nodding his head in understanding.

JD,

  Congratulations on your accomplishments thus far. When we spoke a few years ago, I knew you would be my successor. As President it is my duty to protect the United States of America by any means necessary. There will be times when you will have to make life or death decisions to honor that pledge. This is one of those times for me. You are the future of this country. As President it is my duty to protect you. Our Christian belief states Thou Shall not kill, therefore the thought is an issue for you. I'm happy to know that, for the decision to take a life should never be easy. When that commandment must be broken, I want no doubts that the task is swift and complete. Absolute leaves no doubts. Learn to trust his instincts and his abilities, you will not go wrong. It may come in an unconventional package, but he is a true patriot of this country. Use him to protect your family so that you can protect this country.

  Decision made, JD turned to Joshua. "Do you play Bid Whist?"

  Joshua turned as if he had been insulted. "As well as I can love a woman."

  "Good, this should be easy." JD joked, "Shall we begin the initiation?"

  The people in the room smiled, then stood to follow JD into the game room. James had placed both letters on the table in front of him. Suddenly one of the letters burst into flames. Everyone turned to the small fire that quickly dissipated. "What the hell?" Douglas, who was just walking by the table, knocked the paper to the floor and stomped it out.

  "Oh, my bad," Joshua said to the stunned group. He turned to JD. "I forget to tell you the letter will self-destruct fifteen minutes after your DNA touches it."

"The paper is standard equipment used during covert missions when a secure message is sent," Samuel explained as he frowned at his younger brother." As an ex-Navy Seal, Samuel knew and used highly classified equipment that this security team would not be privy to. That included Brian, who was ex-FBI.

"My bad don't work here Joshua," James exclaimed a tad bit aggravated. "You have vital information to share you damn well better share it before the "my bad" occurs—understood."

The serious look on everyone's face amused Joshua. "This is going to be fun."

JD patted Joshua on the shoulder, trying to smooth over the reprimand from James. "Joshua, SQ2?" he questioned.

"The principal of the Square Root of 2 also known as root 2," Al responded as he walked by.

"That's your code name, The Squeal." He walked away, "Hey who's the brain?"

JD laughed. The name eased the tension.

The group entered the game room. There were two in the house. The one upstairs, for the children, contained every electronic gaming device known to man. This one was JD's man cave. It had the traditional pool table, card tables, and a fifty-two-inch flat screen for the games at one end then a door leading to a full size basketball court at the other end.

Al, who had sat back and observed the legendary "Absolute" preform, nodded his head. "This is going to be interesting." But Al knew the jokester on the outside, was the best covert operative in the world. If someone out there is planning to derail JD's campaign, Joshua will find and eliminate the threat. If that meant they had to put up with his antics, so be it. Let him have his fun, as long as that fun did not include Ryan.

The initiation, as it was called, consisted of round robin bid whist. Partnered off was, JD and Calvin, Brian and

James at one table in the far corner of the room. On the other side, seated at the table were Al and Tucker against Samuel and Joshua. Magna and Ryan were seated at the bar ready to handle the losers for either game. Douglas, kept the glasses on the table filled with whatever poison was ordered. As the game progressed, decisions were made on security while on the road and at home. "A large security detail is not needed." Brian stated as he played his hand. "A small contingent of experts can be just as effective as an army."

"I agree, but do we have the right combination of experts?" James questioned as he frowned at the card Brian played. "Are you watching the table?" he asked.

"What?" Brian questioned, wondering why James was frowning.

"You just cut his King of Hearts," Calvin, stated as he tried hard not to laugh.

"It's on the table now," JD stated as he collected the book. "Let's evaluate who we have," he suggested as he placed the ace of spades on the table.

"Donnell is the best techie in the area. He can handle the control room." Brian stated. "Magna is no slouch when it comes to surveillance equipment. She can be his back up."

"Magna may be needed in the field. I'll begin a search for a few computer techs." James stated as he realized JD was running the board with spades.

"Get the names to me and I'll run a background check on them before we let them into the room." Brian said as he watched JD pull in another book.

"You and Samuel will be the only security on the road?" JD asked Brian as he played the small joker.

"Secret Service will increase the field staff," Brian stated. "I have a call into a few friends at the Bureau to add to the personal security team. I like to recruit experienced agents, but it will cost."

"Cost is not an issue." James said as JD raked in the last book. "Experience and skill it is. Speaking of which, are you ever going to get better at this game?"

The conversation at the other table was—different. "We have access to unlimited armor," Joshua stated.

"Define unlimited and armor," Tucker said as he pulled in another book.

"Weapons you've never heard of and technology to detect your blood type in a matter of minutes if I needed it. Unlimited simply means whatever, whenever I need to get the job done." Joshua said as he watched Tucker fold another book, "Sometimes before I even know I need it."

"Are you paying attention to the table?" Samuel asked not too subtly.

"No," Joshua replied and then turned to Al who had remained silent throughout the game. "Do you ever talk?" he asked Al.

Al smiled, "There are talkers and there are thinkers. I listen, think things through then speak." Al laid his cards on the table and sat back. "I believe you just reneged."

Joshua looked at the table then at the cards in his hand. "When?"

"Book three, card number two. You cut the ace of cubs with a three of diamonds."

Samuel and Tucker sat back and watched.

"Are you sure?" Joshua questioned. "Maybe you want to think about your answer before you take the next step."

Others in the room thought tension was building, but Al and Joshua knew this was a test of testosterones. "Don't have to think about it. I'm calling you on it. Book three."

"I don't cheat."

"No, you act without thinking about the consequences at the time." He smoothly replied. "In this instance that's something we cannot afford." Al nodded, "I know you reneged and I know you did it purposely. Pull the book. If I'm right, you will take direction."

"I'm a natural leader, I don't take directions."

"To be a great leader, you first have to be a good follower. You will take directions. Pull the book."

Joshua glared at the man. He had to chop his balls a little. If he didn't it wouldn't be fun. "If you're wrong?"

The end of Al's lips curved, "Pull the book."

Joshua grinned, "It's going to be fun working with you." He nodded to Tucker never taking his glare from Al. "Pull the book."

Samuel smiled when the cards were flipped over. Sure enough Joshua had reneged. "This is going to be interesting."

The tension at the table quickly changed to laugher. "Your game," Joshua conceded.

Douglas brought over a drink and placed it in front of Joshua. "Your security deposit is half a million."

"Why so much," Joshua protested.

"Because this is my home," JD said from across the room. "You destroy it and you will pay for it."

"Double that deposit," James laughed, "My house is next door."

"Hey, can a brother get some love from somebody around here?" Joshua pouted as he looked over at Ryan.

"Looking in the wrong direction, my brother," Ryan laughed.

Joshua turned back to the table, "She wants me."

Al turned to look at Ryan. It wasn't often he saw her smile. The fact that she was smiling at another man rattled him. He didn't like it.

Chapter 5

The security house on the twenty-seven acres of gated area where both James and Ashley Brooks and JD and Tracy Harrison lived was located in the center of the entrance. The Estates had two seven foot double gate wrought-iron fencing entrances about ten yards apart. The driveway on the left led to the home of James and Ashley Brooks, and the driveway on the right led to the home of JD and Tracy Harrison. The two-story structure looked more like a beautiful brick home than a security building. The building consisted of five executive offices and a conference room on the top floor. The first level held the weapons storage room, a computer room with state-of the art equipment, flat screen monitors that covered every inch of the compound, a huge kitchen and two bedrooms, each containing double beds, for the night crew. The basement was a panic room that was divided into two secure living areas. Each area had an entrance tunnel, one from the Brooks home and the other from the Harrison home. The area was built to secure the families for months if needed from any type of attack, foreign or domestic. It consisted of six bedrooms, two full baths and two half baths, a kitchen, great room and a security room.

The initiation of Joshua into the crew ended and all, involved with the personal security of the family, were now in the conference room of the security house. Brian stood at the front of the room as film footage of the area where the attack took place was being viewed. Al, Tucker, Joshua, Samuel, Magna and Ryan listened as Brian discussed security issues associated with the area.

"The land on both sides leading up to the Estates is owned by Davenport Industries, a development company that plans to build in the next year or two. The owner, Zackary Davenport built the estate and granted permission for the road to be placed. He has now granted permission to use the area for security purposes as needed until construction on the new planned development begins." He hit the pause button to stop the video at the turn onto Brooks Road leading to the property. "We need to secure this five mile radius." He used the area on the screen. "Man power is limited. How do we cover this area 24/7?"

"Sensors," Al stated. "Place sensors on both sides of the road about a quarter of a mile apart."

"Stagger them," Joshua suggested. "Starting at the turn, put a sensor at the beginning on the right, then a fourth of the mile on the left then so on up the road. Place the eye where it can rotate around the area."

"Any movement will not only send a signal to your computer system it will also send you a visual of what's happening in the area." Al turned to Joshua, "Adding sound could be useful."

"Metal detector would pick up any weapons within a ten mile radius."

"Yea, but that includes any vehicles going down the main highway, he stated. "Depending on the sensitivity, some of them may pick up anything from the airport."

The group in the room watched as the conversation went back and forth between the two. Most had no idea what they were talking about. "That may be true however, if the invaders are well-financed," Joshua shrugged, "they could have access to choppers."

"Excuse me, geek one and techie two," Brian interrupted the private conversation, "Do either of you want to explain what in the hell you are talking about?"

Al and Joshua looked at Brian then each other, then back to Brian. "You're making up names for us?" Joshua laughed. "That's cute." He turned to Brian. "The sensors we are talking about are not available on the open market. They can detect any movements in a wide area, effectively eliminating the need for actual man power."

Samuel sat forward, "You and I know how to get pass those sensors."

"If you can detect them, you can by pass them." Al stated, "These are undetectable by any devices we have in the U.S. Now, if the enemy is able to detect the sensors, then we have a larger issue."

"Foreign enemies," Brian replied. The men nodded their head in agreement. Brian sighed. "Have we gotten any information from the men that were captured? Do we know who we are up against?"

"Donnell is still on them and has not reported anything new," Ryan stated. "So far, no one is talking."

"We need to determine if the threat is foreign or domestic." Brian looked at Joshua. "That's on you. We need to know like yesterday, what we are up against. Acquire the sensors and I don't want to know how. Just do it and have them installed before the day is out. Al, Samuel and I will be leaving in the morning for a Midwest stomp with JD and Tracy. The children will remain here with their grandmother. Ryan and Magna will remain with you until Tracy and JD go in separate directions. At that time you two will be on the road with Tracy. Let's play nice and get JD through this election without any loss of life, theirs or ours. Any questions, concerns—good. Let's roll."

As the group dispersed, Samuel and Joshua stood outside the door talking. Magna and Ryan walked towards the staircase. "Look at those two," Magna said as she touched Ryan on the shoulder.

Ryan glanced over her shoulder as she continued walking. "Yeah, and?"

"Hold up," Magna stopped Ryan at the top of the steps. "Don't they look like Tyson Bedford and Tyresse Gibson?"

"The model?" Ryan question.

"Well, one is an actor in the Transformer movies— but yeah."

Ryan shrugged her shoulder, "Okay," then turned to walk down the stairs.

Magna stared after her from the top of the steps. "You know how to determine if a woman is totally gone for a man?"

Ryan stopped on the lower step and looked up at Magna as she came down. "Not really. But I'm sure you are going to tell me anyway."

They both continued walking down the steps together. "Yes. Any time you can see two fine brothers like that and it don't faze you, you are gone."

When they reached the bottom of the steps Al, Tucker and Brian were talking just outside the door. Ryan's attention strayed to them. "Open Webster's dictionary. I bet a picture of those two brothers is next to the phrase tall dark and handsome." Magna laughed, but there was no response from Ryan. Looking out the door, she saw Ryan's attention was on Al. Magna rolled her eyes, "You are so gone. Give me until August. That's all I ask—August." She brushed by Ryan.

"What?" Ryan asked as Magna opened the door.

As they walked by Brian turned to Ryan. "Tracy is at the house. She wants to see you before you leave tonight."

"Will do Boss." Al watched as she walked away.

"Al. Al the duck just walked out of the pound."

"Yeah," Al replied, then turned back to Brian. "What?"

Tucker and Brian shook their heads and laughed. "You are so gone."

To the outside world, Tracy Washington-Harrison had the life. She had four wonderful children, a beautiful home and a husband that loved her beyond reason. Now she was about to travel all over the world meeting dignitaries, country leaders, all while being treated like royalty. What the general public did not know was that she would give it all up in a heartbeat just to have a normal life with her family. Proof of just how abnormal her life was, was walking through the door. Not every wife had a bodyguard.

"Hey Tracy, the boss said you needed to see me." Ryan said as she began helping Tracy put the girls' to bed.

"Hi Ms. Ryan," Gabby waved.

"Hey Peanut butter and jelly," Ryan smiled as the girls giggled. She pulled off Gabby's slippers as Tracy pulled off Brianna's.

"Brian said you'll be staying here with the children until we hit Iowa."

Ryan knew Tracy very well. She had been her body woman for years. Tracy taught her more about family and friendship than her father ever did. The ladies, as Ryan called Tracy's group of friends, were like sisters to her. So when one of them was in trouble or worried, it was easy for Ryan to pick up on feelings. "I'll be here with the little rug rats." She covered Gabby and kissed her as Tracy did the same with Brianna. She watched as Tracy walked over and kissed Gabby then stood at the door watching them as she turned out the light and closed the door.

"Walk with me to Jazzy's room." She put her hand through Ryan's arm as they walked. "I need you to do me a favor."

Ryan raised an eyebrow, as she looked sideways at Tracy. "What do you need?"

"Well, I understand Turk will be working with you on security while I'm away."

"Yes," Ryan hesitantly replied.

"I think it would be a perfect opportunity for you to really get to know him." They reached Jazzy's room and found her standing in the mirror posing with a hairbrush. "Jazzy, bed right now!"

Jazzy put her hands on her hip. "I told you I'm waiting for Daddy to tuck me in."

"Daddy is in a meeting and it will be late before he's done. He'll come afterwards. In the meantime young lady, as I said before, it's lights out."

"But I want to wait for Daddy," the child whined.

Tracy took her daughter's hand and walked her over to the bed. "Not tonight. Daddy will come in when he is finish. Bed."

Jazzy huffed as her mother tucked her in. "I'm going to tell Daddy you wouldn't let me wait for him," she huffed and turned away from her mother.

Tracy tucked the child in and kissed the back of her head. "Good night, Jazzy." Tracy turned the light out and closed the door.

"What are you going to do with her?" Ryan asked.

"Let her father handle her. He's the one that spoiled her rotten. Now back to you." They continued on to JC's room. "I think it is time for you and Turk to stop teasing each other. Life is too short not to spend as much time as you can with the man you are in love with."

Ryan jerked away. "I am not in love with anyone. I don't mean any disrespect but you don't know what you are talking about."

Tracy stood there in her black trousers, red shell top, pearl earrings and necklace looking like a Black Jackie Kennedy Onassis. Arms folded across her chest and hair up in a roll, she smirked at Ryan. "Yeah—Right." She walked over and put her arm back through Ryan's arm and walked to JC's room. "You save that for someone that doesn't know." She turned the light on her sleeping son. The spread was on the floor. She picked it up and placed it over him, kissed his head and walked back out the door. "You like Al. I know it, Ashley knows it, Cynthia knows it, Roz knows it, and hell even Carolyn knows it. So, on a serious note, what's holding you back?"

They walked into the upstairs family room. Tracy sat on the chaise lounge facing the window, while Ryan took the chair. Both kicked off their shoes and pulled their feet up under them as they had done many nights before. "Okay, Talk to me."

"Your brother has enough women."

"He doesn't have that one in his life that makes it meaningful. I think it's time you let him know you are that woman."

Ryan laughed.

"You two having fun without me?" Ashley asked as she ascended the stairs.

"Hey Ash. We're talking about Turk."

"Oh good," Ashley sat in the loveseat next to Ryan. "We're finally letting that horse out of the barn."

"Whatever you two are thinking—you're wrong."

Ashley looked at Tracy. "I'm thinking Ryan is hot for Al. What do you think?"

"I'm pretty sure you're right. I also think Turk is hot for Ryan. Let me qualify that. I know he is hot for Ryan."

"Professor Woods," Tracy and Ashley laughed together. "So, what are we going to do?" Ashley pulled her feet under her after kicking off her shoes. "I'm so tired of waiting for the two of them to do the right thing."

"Well Brian said Turk and Ryan will be working security together while we are gone. I was thinking this would be a perfect time for Ryan to put some moves on him."

"You mean like using her womanly wiles?"

"Yes. That's exactly what I was thinking."

"You two do realize I'm sitting right here," Ryan sighed, "And I don't have womanly wiles."

"All women have wiles," Mrs. Gordon, Tracy housekeeper said as she walked into the room. "Some women just need help bringing it out." She glared at Ryan. "Men like to see the feminine side of their woman every once and a while. Now, a man like Mr. Al is special. He's one of those rare men that can see inside a person and know what's in their heart. And Ms. Ryan that rough exterior of yours is a smoke screen that intrigues him." She grinned, "You need him as much as he needs you."

"I don't need a man. I can take care of myself quite well."

"Try as you might, but there are one or two things that need a man's touch every now and then." She laughed. "You know what I mean? Ask Ms. Cynthia one day about her brotherman and how she threw it away the moment she met Mr. Samuel. She'll tell you, there are certain things that only a man can handle."

"Ha, no she didn't go there," Ashley laughed.

"I think she did," Tracy joined her.

"I get mine, Mrs. Gordon," Ryan laughed.

"Really? When was the last time you got yours and was it good?"

"Mrs. Gordon," Ryan blushed. "You can't ask questions like that!"

"Don't avoid the question, child. When was the last time?"

Ryan looked at Tracy, then Ashley. Both of them were waiting for her response. Ryan stood, "I'm not answering that question."

"Just what I thought," Mrs. Gordon snickered. "Girl, you better stop playing shy and go get that man. You ain't going to give nobody else none because that man has gotten under your skin." She waved Ryan off. "Do you ladies want something to drink before I retire for the night?"

"I'll take a glass of wine," Ashley replied.

"I'm good Mrs. Gordon, thank you," Tracy replied.

Mrs. Gordon looked at Ryan, "Do you want a beer?"

"I want to know why you're calling me out like this?"

"Child, you are walking around here pining after Mr. Al, when all you have to do is strip out of those jeans, throw on a dress with those spiked boots and add a little lipstick. Mr. Al will bang your brains out." Mrs. Gordon turned and walked off, fussing. "Lord these young ones don't know nothing about getting a man."

Tracy gave Ryan a sympathetic look. "I'm sorry Ryan, but I do agree with her. I want to see Turk happy and I think you could do that for him."

"She's right about something else," Ashley crossed her legs and smirked. "A little makeover wouldn't hurt."

Ryan stood, "I am not a girly girl and you two know that. If a man can't accept me the way that I am, the hell with him." She stormed out of the room.

"That didn't go the way we planned," Ashley looked at her friend.

Tracy smiled, "I disagree. You know, Professor Woods once said, the result of the seeds you sow is not always immediately visible. The garden has to be cultivated and nurtured."

"So you sowed the seed with Ryan. Now you're going to sow a seed or two with Al." Ashley laughed, "Okay, while you do that, I'll put Cynthia and Roz on notice that their services will be needed soon. I suggest you find and hide all of Ryan's guns. She is not going to like us playing matchmaker."

Tracy smiled, "Well someone had to start that train, neither of them was making a move."

"You remember that when she pulls out her guns."

Al "Turk" Day sat in his sister's family room laughing at JD's renditions of one of Jazzy's antics. "I swear to you Al, Jazzy is going to be the death of me. I spanked her little behind when she threw the dirt in JC's eyes. Then she had the nerve to look at me and say it was mommy's fault because she wouldn't make JC play with her."

"What did JC do?"

JD took a sip of his drink and smiled. "You know JC takes after Tracy. He told me, as her older brother it was his job to teach her right from wrong. Since he didn't do his job he should get a spanking, too."

"I have to have a long talk with him. I hope you're ready." Shaking his head Al laughed. "You are going to catch just as much hell with Jazzy as I caught with Monique."

"Hell, I certainly hope not," JD laughed as he sat his glass down. "Monique was hell on wheels before you came home."

Turk turned to JD, locs swinging as he shook his head, "She is still hell on wheels, just in a different way now." He turned back to the window. "I thought four years at Howard would have slowed her down. But it seems like it fueled her even more. Tell me how she can hit the dean's list every semester and stay in the streets like she do?"

Learning comes easy for her, just like it did for you and Tracy. Not many people can say they were accepted into

Georgetown Law on the first try, without connections. You should be proud of her."

"Yeah, I know." Turk shrugged his shoulders but did not say anymore.

JD picked up the bottle of scotch and poured the smooth brown liquid into Al's glass. "What's bothering you, Al?"

Turk took the glass but didn't reply. JD looked over his shoulder to the Secret Service agent standing at the door. He had become so used to having a protection detail around him. But there were times, like now when he needed privacy. Nodding his head at the agent he waited until he walked outside the door.

After swallowing the scotch, Turk looked knowingly at JD. "How many people you know do that?"

"Do what?"

"Get into Georgetown without a hookup."

"I don't know the numbers, but I'm sure Calvin would be able to tell you."

Turk laughed. "Hell, Calvin could tell you the names and years of graduation. "Seriously, what do you think the odds are that a girl from the projects, who attended Howard, would get into Georgetown without a recommendation from you or any of your connections? I understand how intelligent Monique is and I know she will handle her own at Georgetown. But let's be real, her reputation is not pristine and her attitude leaves a lot to be desired."

JD knew the look Turk had on his face indicated pieces to a puzzle did not fit for him and he wanted answers. "What do you think happened or should I say who do you think happened?"

Turk sat the glass on the table and clasped his hands together. "Someone gave her the necessary reference to get in. I want to know who. I don't have access to the people that can answer that question, but you do."

JD put his hand up, "Say no more. I'll get the information. But don't be surprised if she did this on her own. After all, she is your daughter."

There was a knock at the office door. "Is it okay to come in?" Tracy asked from the doorway.

JD's eyes brightened. "Of course you can." Tracy walked behind the desk and kissed her husband, then took her place in his lap. "Ashley went home already?"

"Yes. She knows this is our last night home for a while and thought we could use a little private time."

Al stood, "That's my cue."

"No, Turk, don't leave. I wanted to ask a favor."

"Sugie, you know whatever it is the answer is yes."

Her eyes brightened and her smile spread. "Thanks Turk. I will feel so much better if you stay here with the children while we are away. With everything that happened, it would give me piece of mind knowing you are right here in the house with them."

"You want me to stay here at the house?" Turk asked as he noticed the questioning look on JD's face.

"Babe, mom is going to be here with the children and so will Ryan and Magna."

"I know, but I would feel so much better about the children's safety and Momma Harrison's safety too if I knew Turk was here at the house. You can stay in the west wing. That will give you all the privacy you will need. And it'll just be until we come off this road trip."

Turk was not in the habit of saying no to his sister even when he had the feeling she was up to something. However, his baby sister had an unusual flaw—she couldn't lie worth a damn. "Okay, Sugie. I'll bring a few things over tomorrow."

Tracy jumped out of JD's lap and ran over to Turk and kissed him on the cheek. "Thank you, Turk. Love you." She turned to walk out of the room. "Sit back down, Turk.

I'll let you two get back to what you were talking about." She ran out of the room.

JD began laughing as Turk sat back down. "You know that was a bunch of crap, right?"

Turk laughed, "Yeah, she's up to something. But have you learned to say no to her yet?"

JD shook his head, "No, is that normal?"

Turk laughed, "I haven't either and of course it's not normal. You two are perfect for each other. You were never meant to have a normal life. You are destined for great things, my brother. That's why God gave you an extraordinary woman. Embrace your destiny."

Chapter 6

Al was walking into his house just as his cell phone vibrated. Checking the number he saw it was his daughter, Monique. "Hey, baby girl. Where are you?"

"Hi Daddy, I'm still in DC. I was calling to let you know I found a little place here."

Al snickered, he knows his child. A little place is not in Monique's vocabulary. "Where?"

"NW. It's really a nice area and it has a great view of DC."

"How far is it from the university?"

"Walking distance Daddy, and it has a wonderful walk-in closet. You wouldn't believe how hard it is to find a place with a decent closet in DC."

"How much?"

"Not too much. It has granite counter tops, original hardwood floors throughout, with Berber carpet in the master suite. And Daddy, you wouldn't believe the size of the master bath!

"How much?"

"You already asked me that Daddy. Did I tell you it has a doorman and twenty-four hour security?"

"Yes. But I couldn't help but notice you haven't answered my question."

"The price shouldn't be your biggest concern. I've found a place that I am comfortable in and it meets your security standards. But most of all, it has all the comforts of home. Isn't that what you want for your baby girl?"

"Avoidance will not get you the condo. How much is your comfort going to cost me?"

"Daddy, it's only one point two."

Al laughed. "I'm sure you mean has only one and a half bathrooms?"

"No Daddy. It's one point two million dollars and it's a good investment for you. Besides, you won't have to worry about my safety anymore."

"I will always worry about you, Monique. Have the paperwork faxed to my office number tomorrow."

"Thank you, Daddy. I really want you to come and see. You're going to love it. And Daddy, this place is fabulous enough for me to live here."

Al shook his head at his daughter's antics. She could have simply told him she needed the money to buy a condo and he would have had the funds transferred to her account. For whatever reason, Monique felt she had to justify things with him. It wasn't necessary. He would give her the world on a platter if he could—no questions asked. For the first few years after his release from prison, they went through some rough times.

When he came home Monique was on the wild side, hanging with the wrong people. The first thing he did was get custody of her and moved her in with him. It was hell there for a moment. Telling a teenage girl who was used to hanging out all hours of the night, that she had a curfew and chores did not go over well. By the time she reached her senior year of high school they understood each other very well. He was her father and she was the child. What he said was law. If she wanted it different all she had to do was get a legal job, an apartment she could afford and she could do whatever she wanted. To prove his point, he gave her a job. Her job was to go to school. If she skipped a class, her paycheck was deducted. If she did a mediocre job and brought home mediocre grades her paycheck was adjusted accordingly. He charged her rent for her room and gave her a portion of utilities to pay for the house. If she did not pay the electric bill, he had the electricity in her room disconnected. She had to pay for her own cell phone and Internet service. After several disconnections, she learned how to manage her money and time. During her senior year of high school she wanted a Mercedes. He told her she had champagne taste on a beer budget. She needed to look at what she could afford. She asked why, you can afford it— you're loaded. He said yes I am, but you're broke. He ended up buying her a small Mercedes more because of her grades then her antics. Just like this condo. He was certain there were other condos in the area that were less expensive. But his daughter had champagne taste in everything—except men. She still wanted to hang out with the boys on the corner. He was the last person to judge them, for that was how he made his living for years. However, the street game was different, more dangerous than before. The last thing he wanted was to lose her to the street. Al was determined to keep her from the street life the way he did with Tracy, whether Monique liked it or not. It seemed those moments of chaos between father and daughter was worth it.

Monique was now a graduate from Howard University and was accepted to Georgetown Law School. As a father, he could not be prouder of her. Whatever he could do to make her journey easier he would do. If she wanted the condo, he would make sure she had it. However, there was something puzzling him and until he had the answer, his baby girl was still on his watch list.

Walking upstairs to his bedroom, he pulled out his cell phone to call Tucker when it rung.

"Hola amigo."

Recognizing the voice, Al frowned. "Dos minutos." He walked into the bedroom, looked at the picture and watched as the wall separated. He stepped inside and waited for the wall to close. Taking a seat at the desk in the secure office, he pressed a button on his console. A few seconds later the monitor filled with the face of an old friend.

"We have three minutes. It's good to see you my brown brother."

"You as well, my black brother."

"I understand congratulations are in order." Al sat back and smiled. "You got married on me, my man. I wish you the best."

"I have the best and that's not an exaggeration my friend." Mateo smiled. "What about you? Have you found that special lady yet?"

"I don't think there's one around that can handle me. But then again, I'm not looking."

"Ah, my man, there is nothing like having the woman you love to come home to. I tell you what I know." The heavy Spanish accented voice replied.

"Listen to you. You're getting soft man?" Al chuckled.

"Some say yes. I say I'm just getting wiser."

Al nodded, "You need wisdom in your line of work."

"Ahhh, that is true. But so do you playing both sides."

"Just one—totally legit."

"I still can't believe it, Turk, working for the government. That brother-in-law of yours is indeed a miracle worker."

"He's a good man."

"Then you should protect him at all costs."

Al sat back in his chair and frowned. "Is there a cost?"

"A great one I'm afraid."

"Cartel?"

"We refused, however tempting."

"Foreign or domestic?"

"Domestic my brother—practically in his back yard."

"Appreciate the call."

"If he is indeed a good man, watch his back and yours, my brother." The call ended.

"Babe," JD called out as he entered their bedroom suite. There was no answer. Walking through the room he pulled his shirttail from his pants and began unbuttoning the shirt. After reviewing foreign and domestic policies with Calvin there was only one thing on his mind—his wife. Her visit to his office left a few questions. What was she up to? He couldn't think of one reason why Al needed to stay at their place while they were away. His mother always stayed with the children whenever they had to travel. That's why the mother-in-law suite was added to the house. His sweet innocent little wife was up to something. He just had to decipher what?

JD stopped when he reached the bathroom doorway. The vision in the tub did exactly what it always did—stopped him dead in his tracks. His wife was in the Jacuzzi tub with her hair pinned up, her body submerged in bubbles. The sensuous vanilla scent was like a mating call to his nostrils. Whenever he went away, he would take a pair of her panties with him to help him sleep at night. Did that make him a freak? Hell, he didn't care one way or another, as long as he had the essence of his wife near him. Seeing her in the tub brought back memories of the first time they made love. He had multiple memories of his wife, but two stuck with him just about every day, the first time they made love and their first conversation about the propensity of violence. At the time he wondered why a person so young had such a sad take on life. After learning about the ups and downs of her life, he definitely understood her stance. Watching her now and thinking of the first time they made love was making him hard as steel. Making love to her eleven years later was still as sweet as it was the first time. Stripping out of his clothes, a smile instantly appeared on his face.

The sound of the door closing caught her attention. Tracy opened her eyes to see her husband walking towards her. The look in his eyes told her all she needed to know. That was the look of pure sexual intent. The man was so good looking, in or out of his clothes. Her nipples hardened just at the sight of him. His body clearly displayed how physically fit he was. The six pack was still intact from his football days and those thighs—they looked so strong and powerful she closed her eyes and moaned. Riding them had always been her joy. "Are you joining me or are you going to just tease me with your sexy body?"

JD climbed in the tub behind her. "Was that supposed to be a trick question?"

"You want to get the thingy off of me?" Tracy giggled.

"That thingy wants to get inside your thingy. We still have eight more children to produce." He kissed the side of her temple.

"You get one more from me, mister. Remember, number six is on you."

JD took the sponge from her hand, dipped it into the water, than squeezed it between her breasts. "I may need your help with that one."

"You're about to become the leader of the free world. Surely you can handle carrying a baby full term then take a few hours to squeeze it out of your body."

"Baby, the leader of the free world can do a lot of things, but if it's a male, I'm not sure he can do that. Besides, you do it so well. Look at our children. They are beautiful and well behaved."

"Ha." Tracy laughed. "Is Jasmine still a part of this family?"

"Jazzy isn't bad, she's just spirited."

"I don't know how it happened, but Jazzy is a little Lena Washington."

"Lord help me if that's true." JD sighed. "I guess I should pull out the shotgun and have it cleaned. Jazzy, Briana and Gabby are going to have boys knocking on this door before you know it. We should have been a little more specific when we asked God for children. We should have told him we wanted all boys. I knew girls were going to have your eyes and that smile that caught me."

Tracy laid her head back against his chest and smiled. "I wouldn't give them up for anything in the world."

He wrapped his arms around her and kissed the top of her head. "I would kill anyone that tries to take you or them away."

"See, there's that propensity for violence I told you about."

"I remember that conversation at the old condo," he smiled. "It was the first night you stayed at my place." She could feel him growing against her backside. "You called me on a few things that night. You said if someone I love was in danger that the propensity for violence would rear its ugly head and you were right." He rubbed the sponge down her stomach. "If someone harmed you or the children I would kill them."

"No you wouldn't. It's not in you."

JD kissed the side of her temple, thinking yes he would. But he didn't say that to her. "Yes baby, you're right. I'd have Al do it and I'll watch in case he missed."

Tracy laughed, "Turk doesn't miss. If he wants you eliminated, you might as well start planning your funeral. That's why I want him here with the children while we're away."

"Is that the only reason?" JD felt her body tense.

Tracy turned in the tub, sitting at the other end facing him. She lowered her eyes, hoping he wouldn't detect the little white fib she was about to tell. "What do you mean is that the only reason?"

JD smirked, "You know exactly what I mean. Al can very well handle the security on the children without staying at the house." He pulled her leg down to him, effectively pulling her into his lap. He placed a finger under her chin tipping her head up so her eyes met his. "Are you playing matchmaker?"

"No." She stammered. "With whom?"

"Al and Ryan," JD replied as he held her head up.

"Why would you think that? I'm not sure they even like each other." JD gave her that look that said you can do better than that. Tracy smiled, "Okay, maybe a little." She hurried on before he could speak. "I'm so tired of watching those two watch each other. I want Turk to have what we have, Jeffrey. And I believe Ryan is the woman that does it for him. I want him happy." She pouted.

"Babe, did it ever occur to you that Al might have a reason why he hasn't stepped to Ryan yet?"

"What reason could there be? I mean, he's free and so is she."

"Al is single, but he only recently became free." JD pulled Tracy closer and wrapped her legs around his waist. "It could be that Al wanted to clear up his past obligations before bringing someone he really cares about into his life. I know I would." He ran the sponge down her back as she eased a little closer to him.

Her voice dropped an octave as he used his other hand to massage the lower part of her back. "So you think he really likes her, too?" she kissed his neck and draped her arms over his shoulders.

JD dropped the sponge, gathered her at the waist and pulled her barely a breath away from his manhood that was now throbbing to slide into home plate. "I do," he spoke barely above a whisper.

Tracy sat firmly on his powerful thighs as she tilted her body to him. "You're not upset with me for interfering?"

JD lifted her by the waist and entered her with one powerful thrust. His head rested right above her breast, and her chin rested on the top of his head as they both exhaled from the intense impact. "Ahhh, babe," he sighed, "No, I'm not upset." His heart began to race.

Tracy ran her hands down his back, "I'm glad," she breathed, as JD lift her until only the tip of him was embedded in her, then he eased her back down. They both sighed. "Oh, God, I want him to feel that."

JD began to chuckle between her breast. "No, babe." He sighed, "I don't want Al or any other man to feel that." He lifted her and pulled her back down again, "or that," he did it again, "or that."

Tracy tightened her legs around him, no longer listening to his words, only feeling the impact of his touch. She leaned back to allow more access and JD complied. He took her nipple between his lips and sucked then gave the other the same treatment. The water pulsating around them intensified the sensations flowing through them. "Jeffrey," Tracy urgently whispered.

"I know babe—I feel you. God, you feel so good." Her nails scraped the skin on his back just as he increased their movement. Both bodies, merged as one, cascading into the depth of their love, until the explosion left them both breathless.

JD sat up and pulled her to him, tucking her head under his chin, her ear right above his heart, listening to the racing rhythm caused by their lovemaking. Moments passed before either of them could speak. He held her gently as he spoke. "Tracy, Al is a man. He will approach Ryan when he believes the time is right. I'm not sure he will appreciate you interfering in his life."

Tracy drew circles around his nipples. "Are you telling me to back off?"

"No. I'm telling you to tread lightly. I would hate to have to kill Al."

There was a light knock at the door. "JD."

It was Brian's voice on the other side of the door. "Yeah." JD answered.

"We have a situation."

JD exhaled as he held Tracy a little tighter. "We have a situation, babe."

Neither of them moved. They weren't ready to break the connection.

"JD?" Brian called again.

"Get away from my door, Brian," JD yelled.

Brian laughed. "I get pulled from my wife, so do you. Let's go."

Monique knocked on the door of the hotel suite in the Grand Hyatt in Washington, DC. The man answered the door with a smile as he wrapped his arms around her waist and pulled her inside. "Howdy do, my little chocolate drop?" He closed the door.

"Surprised you are here while your father is away."

"I'm full of surprises, darling. How did the apartment hunting go?"

Grabbing the lapel of his blazer, she pushed him backwards onto the bed. Then she straddled him. "I found the perfect place," she said as she ripped his shirt apart. She ran a sharp nail down his chest. "It's secure, private and discreet."

He grabbed her hands and held them from him. "And the interview?"

"Hired. I'm sure the idea of JD Harrison's niece working for him thrilled your father."

He smiled, "How much do you need for the apartment?"

She pulled her hands from him and ran them up his chest. "I don't want anything from you. I like being an independent woman."

He reached up and pulled her down by her neck until their lips met.

A few hours later, while the man slept, Monique went into the bathroom, closed the door and sent a simple text –In.

Chapter 7

Early Monday morning, Al arrived thinking this would be a normal first day on a new job. Well, officially, he never really had a real job. Everything up to this point in his life had been about adventures. First there was the adventure of being a brothel house manager. Ms. Sunshine taught him that business, regardless of its nature should be run as such. You go to work on time, work hard then play harder. During the adventure of the leader of a street organization, he learned that if you help others achieve their goals, you would gain a lifetime of loyalty. Alejandra Mateo was proof of that. They were enemies on the street when Mateo attempted to take him out. The failure was the best thing to ever happen to Mateo. Instead of Al retaliating, he took Mateo under his wing and taught him how to strategize. Those lessons led him to the leadership role he now has and gained Al as a friend for life. His last adventure as a mediator between the government and street gangs taught Al that there are different levels of gangs, the government being the largest and most powerful. However, none of those positions had prepared him for the adventures this day had in store for him.

It began at 5:30 am. That was the normal wakeup time for him. Most of the things he needed to do within a day were finished by the time most people were going into the office. Entering through the back door that led directly to the kitchen he found Mrs. Gordon was there to greet him.

"Good Morning, Mr. Al. How are you this fine morning?" she said while setting a hot cup of tea on the island for him.

Al kissed her on the cheek. "I'm fine. How are you?"

"Same aches and pains as before."

"Here," he took her by the shoulders. "You take a seat. I'll cook breakfast this morning." Al pushed the cup of tea she'd prepared for him in front of her. "Give me that apron."

"Now, Mr. Al, you going to cause me to lose my job."

Al laughed as he took the apron and put it on. "Tracy will never let you go anywhere and neither would JD." After washing his hands, he walked over to the large refrigerator and pulled out eggs, milk, butter, strawberries and blueberries, then placed them on the island. "Besides, if they did let you go, I would hire you on the spot." He walked over to the cabinet and pulled out flour, baking powder, and confectioners' sugar. Opening the cabinet under the island, he pulled out a large bowl and the mixer. "Are waffles and fruit okay with you today?"

Mrs. Gordon sipped her tea. "Sounds good to me. What are you doing here so early? You know Mr. JD and Ms. Tracy are leaving today."

"That's why I'm here. I'll be staying in the east wing while they are away."

"I thought Mrs. Martha was staying with the children."

"She is. I'll be around to help with security." He continued preparing the batter.

"Are they expecting trouble? You know I know my way around a gun as well as I know my way around a kitchen."

Al smiled up at the woman. "I know you do. But we won't tell Tracy that."

"What are we keeping from my wife?" JD asked as he came down the backstairs wearing sweat pants and a black t-shirt. He kissed Mrs. Gordon on the cheek. "Good morning, Mrs. Gordon. Al."

"Morning, son."

"Hey, man."

JD walked over to the coffee pot. "What are we keeping from Tracy?"

"Mrs. Gordon's gun," Al replied as he put the batter into the waffle maker.

JD took a sip of his coffee and sat at the island next to Mrs. Gordon. "No, we don't want to mention that." He looked up at Al. "I don't think that's enough batter."

Al laughed. "I'll make more for the kids when they wake up."

Mrs. Gordon laughed, "He's not talking about the children, at least not the small ones."

"I know Brian will be walking through the door any minute. It's enough here for him, too." He walked back over to the refrigerator and pulled out some bacon. Taking a pan from the baker's rack above, he sat the pan on the stove and placed the bacon in. "What time are you pulling out?"

"We're scheduled to leave at ten. I'm sure Brian has the car scheduled for around 9:30."

"We made a small change in those plans. Melissa Sue will be taking you to the airport in the helicopter. We think it's safer."

"Did you clear that with James?"

"I'm sure Brian will handle it."

"Speak of the devil," Mrs. Gordon said smiling at the man walking through the door.

"You're doing homemade waffles, man?" Brian asked as he took a seat next to JD.

"And good morning to you too," Mrs. Gordon laughed.

"Caitlyn didn't cook this morning?" JD asked laughing at Brian.

"Yeah man, she did." He poured a cup a coffee. "It just wasn't food."

"TMI man," Al said as he placed a plate of waffles, fruit and bacon in front of Mrs. Gordon and JD.

"Don't be jealous." Brian smirked.

Al sat a plate in front of him. "Man, we don't need to hear about your love life this early in the morning."

"Don't knock it until you try it."

"I'm good like I am."

"That's what we all said right before we fell." JD said as he gave Brian a pound and continued eating. "Any other changes made after the meeting?"

Brian and Al exchanged a look. "Nothing you need to know." They decided not to mention the tip Al received until they had more information. "Joshua will report in this morning. Donnell has a report on the men from the attack he wants to brief us on before we leave."

"What time is that meeting?

"This morning at seven."

JD looked at his watch. "I should be able to make that." Al and Brian exchanged another look. JD caught it, "What?"

Al sat his plate on the island and took a seat. "You don't need to be in on the security meeting."

"Why not?"

"It's our job to worry about your protection," Brian replied with a fork full of food going to his mouth. "It's your job to worry about getting elected."

"We're talking about the protection of my family. It is my job to worry."

"True," Al stated, "And that's exactly why you have us here, to handle that worry for you. Between, Mrs. Gordon, your mother, Ryan, Magna, Joshua and myself, your family is well covered."

Brian shrugged his shoulders, "You have Samuel and me on the road with you. As soon as Donnell finishes the investigation on the men from the attack, he'll join us on the road. Let us worry about the security, that's why we are here."

JD looked up as Tracy walked into the room. "Hey babe," he said as they shared a kiss.

"Don't stop talking because I came—continue. I heard most of it anyway." She walked over to Al, "Hey, Turk," she hugged him. "You made waffles?"

He kissed her cheek, nodding. "Yours are right there." He pointed to the counter.

Tracy took the covered dish and sat next to Al. Taking the top off, she had waffles with two blueberries for the eyes, a strawberry cut in half for the nose, several strawberries for the smile and whipped cream around the edges. Everyone looked at their plate, then hers, then up at Al. "What? You want a happy face, JD?"

They all laughed as Mrs. Gordon stood. She patted Al on the shoulder, "Thank you for breakfast, son."

"Mrs. Gordon, Turk will be staying at the house while we are away. Is that okay with you?"

Mrs. Gordon laughed and shook her head, "This is your house, baby. Anyone can stay here that you want. Besides, anyone that knows their way around a kitchen like Mr. Al is welcome here anytime."

Al smiled, "Thank you, Mrs. Gordon. When I grow up, I'm going to marry you."

"Son, you couldn't handle me."

They all fell out laughing just as Ryan walked through the back door. "Good morning."

Everyone spoke as Al took her in from head to toe. Her hair was tapered back with a part on the side similar to the way Nia Long wore her hair. She wore a short black jacket, white top underneath, black jeans and of course her signature black spike boots. *She filled out those jeans quite well,* he thought.

"Good morning Ryan," Mrs. Gordon responded. "You ready for some breakfast? Al made waffles."

"So I see," Ryan said as she looked around the kitchen at everyone eating. "You know I don't really do breakfast, Just coffee is fine."

"Breakfast is the most important meal of the day. You shouldn't skip it," Al stated as he drank his tea.

Why he had to look so damn good in the mornings, Ryan thought as she took him in. Today his locs were hanging lose, his tan linen shirt with the sleeves rolled up and open at the 'top, tan dress pants that stretched across his thighs and Italian loafers. Yes he looked good, but it was those eyes—those light brown eyes that seemed to look straight through her that got to her the most. She hated the effect the man had on her and wished she could stop it from happening. As always, she used the only defense she had. "I don't need another father, thank you very much. I have one at home."

Brian moaned, JD grunted, while Mrs. Gordon looked up, surprised at the young woman's response.

"I don't think he meant anything by it, Ryan. He was just concerned about your health. Isn't that right, Turk?" Tracy turned to her brother.

Al held Ryan's stare and watched as she raised an eyebrow daring him to respond. He took his napkin and wiped his mouth as he stood. "It wasn't a criticism." He put the napkin in the seat. "You're welcome to mine if you like." He looked at Tracy. "I'll catch you guys before you leave."

He turned to Brian. "We're meeting at seven in the conference room."

Brian nodded, "Yeah."

"I'll see you there. Mrs. Gordon," he kissed her on the cheek, "Thanks for breakfast. I'll see you later." He walked by Ryan and out the door. Just like that the atmosphere of the room changed.

All eyes turned to her. "What?" she asked.

"Don't ever disrespect a guest in my home again." JD walked out of the room.

Brian just looked at her and shook his head. "See if you can get that chip off your shoulder before you come to the meeting." He walked out the back door.

Tracy smiled, "I know. That didn't come out the way you meant it. And I think you know Al wasn't criticizing you." She scraped her plate and put it in the dishwasher. "I'll see you upstairs." She walked out of the room.

Mrs. Gordon reached for the plate Al was eating from and scraped the food. Ryan sat down at the island in a huff. "Go ahead. Give it to me."

Mrs. Gordon chuckled. "I'm not going to say a word, child. But you know," she put a cup of coffee in front of Ryan, "I've learned you can catch more bees with honey than you can with venom."

"I'm not trying to catch any bees."

"Then you're the fool. Cause honey, Al Day is a 100% honeybee. I believe you have been stung."

The seven am meeting began with Brian giving a rundown on duties while he was away. The entire security staff was in attendance, Brian, Samuel, Joshua, Ryan, Magna, Donnell and Al. The first line of business was to place Al in command and the meeting over to him.

"We received a tip indicating there is a possible contract out on JD. The caller indicated it was a domestic threat. However, until it is confirmed, we are going to proceed as if that determination hasn't been made. All leads are to be investigated and followed up on." He looked towards Donnell, "What did you get from the assailants?"

"Not much. None of them are talking. But we did find money transfers from the same corporation in each of their bank accounts in Switzerland."

"A dummy corporation?" Al inquired.

Donnell nodded, "We believe so. As of this morning, we still have not been able to get any names connected with the corporation."

"Give me the name of the corporation." Al replied. "I'll see if my resources can get what we need."

"What was the amount received?"

"Most had transfers totaling $50,000, but one had a single transfer of $100,000.00."

"That was probably your friend, Ryan," Magna stated. "He seemed to be the leader of the group."

Al nodded, "Since he specifically asked about JC, I think Magna should double up on the children with Ryan."

"I've been protecting the children on my own just fine," Ryan stated.

"You have. However, with a viable threat out there, I think the added coverage would be best." He turned to Joshua, "Do you have anything for us this morning?"

Joshua smiled, "I'm glad you asked." He put a file on the table with a variety of pictures. "I checked satellite from the day of the attack. It showed how they got into the area and set up. The sensors were placed based on that information and a few other spots."

"Did you put any surprises in the wooded area?" Samuel asked.

"You know me too well."

Samuel and Brian laughed.

"With the sensors in place, I believe the grounds are well protected." Brian stated, "My only concern is with the children."

"I don't believe the children are the true target," Al stated. "I think it was a test of security to see how close they could get. They saw our strength and weaknesses. We've made the necessary adjustments. We'll be better prepared if they come at us again."

"Are you calling me the weak link?" Ryan sneered.

Al did not respond immediately. He mustered up all the patience he had acquired over the years of dealing with people before he replied. The people at the table looked from Ryan to Al as they waited for his reply. He swallowed hard once, then looked directly at her. "No. I actually believe you showed them you are one of our strengths. "With what we have ahead of us for the next six months, I don't have time to stroke your ego or build your confidence. I'm going to say this once. I realize JD has had issues with you in the past. That is the past. JD and Tracy value your service to them. You are very good at your job. No one is questioning your abilities to handle the job. But, the attitude, as adorable as it may be, will remain outside these doors. When we gathered at this table it is about the security of my family and nothing more."

Although Al's voice was smooth and calm, the tension in the air had gotten a little thick. The group looked from Ryan to Al waiting for the next move. It was as if they were playing a game of chess.

"I can help you with that tension—you know," Joshua smiled. Ryan looked at Joshua with daggers in her eyes. "I have six sisters, that look don't scare me. It just turns me on."

She couldn't help herself; a smile touched her face as she shook her head at the fool.

Al liked her smile, but it was again point towards Joshua. "Any further concerns? Good," Al said before anyone could reply. "Let's get the family on the road.

As the group dispersed, Brian approached Al. "Do me a favor."

"What's that?"

"Don't kill her before I return. She's one of my best."

Al smiled, "We'll handle things. You keep JD and Tracy safe."

They shook hands and Brian walked out. He hit Samuel on the shoulder, "Let's make moves, man."

"I'll be right with you," Samuel replied as he turned back to Ryan. "What's going on with you?"

Ryan shook her head, "I'm good."

"Are you sure? Seems to me you're a little on edge."

"I'm always on edge."

"Today is a little more than normal. Remember, Day is on our side. Don't shoot him."

Ryan smiled, "I'm good."

Donnell waited until Ryan was alone, then he pulled her to the side. "Morgan, you are playing with fire. You know you cannot bring Al Day home to Dad."

"What are you talking about?"

"Morgan, I know you better than anyone in that room. You are fighting your feelings for that man. I strongly suggest you continue to do that. If you don't you will be cutting any chance of you and Dad having any kind of relationship."

"Don't talk to me about losing something I never had. You're my brother and I love you but stay out of my business." She walked away, stopped then walked back, kissed him on the cheek then walked away again.

Al and Joshua stood in the hallway as Ryan and Magna walked down the stairs. The conversation stopped for a moment as Joshua nodded to the ladies. "I wonder if she brings all that sassiness to bed with her."

Ignoring the comment, Al continued with the conversation. "I don't like unknown factors. We're checking with our sources for any chatter on a hit. I need you to check yours."

"Done. I have one or two leads I'll be following. We also have someone on the inside checking around." He reached inside his suit pocket and gave Al a small monitor about the size of a cell phone. "This is for you. If there is any movement around the sensor it will vibrate. If it's human a picture will appear giving the location. If you hit this button the screen will give you a wider view. This button will give you sound. Now this button with the protect cap, well now that button will make things disappear."

Al looked at him, then at the device. "Did you set bombs in the woods?"

"No. No. Man I wouldn't do that. No. No." he answered frantically. "Would I do something like that?" He laughed as he started to walk away shaking his head. He stopped at the top of the steps then turned and walked purposely back to Al. "You may want to, you know," he tilted his head to the side, "be careful with that button. Lasers, you know, don't just zap any more. They kind of make you disappear." He patted Al on the shoulder. "I'm out."

Al watched as Joshua walked away. Looking at the man and thought, he's just joking. But then Al looked down at the device and knew Joshua was serious. He took the device and hooked it to his pants. "I like that man."

The foyer at JD and Tracy's house was packed for the sendoff. JD's supporters were a group of who's who of the political world. His father in law, ex-Senator John Roth was one of his political advisors. He was there with his wife, Lena, who also happened to be Al and Tracy's mother. JD's brother-in-law and campaign manager James Brooks was there with his wife, Ashley. Their four children were there, including James Jr, who was now sixteen, the twins, Jaden and Jayda, and their five-year-old son Anthony. James parents, Avery and Gwendolyn Brooks were there. Avery was also a political advisor to JD. Calvin Johnson, JD's legal advisor, his wife Jackie and twelve-year-old son Calvin Jr. were there. Brian's wife Caitlyn, their sixteen year-old son Elliott and his two-year-old baby sister Cheyenne were present. Samuel was there with his wife Cynthia and their five year-old daughter Samantha.

With the adults busy with unimportant details for their trip, the children gathered in the game room downstairs to make their own plans. JC, Calvin, James, Elliott and Jaden were in a corner strategizing. "Hey, my mom is cool, but she's not going to let us do it." Jaden explained. "Grandma will."

"I don't know." Calvin shook his head. "I still remember that whipping your grandma gave us for taking her stones to build our fortress."

"But those were her good stones that Grandpa James put there." Jaden defended. "This time we are not using anything but our own stuff. My dad showed me how to do them himself. If it was something bad, he wouldn't have showed me."

"Dad also told you not to do them without an adult present." James Jr. stated as he tied little Anthony's shoe.

"You and Elliott will be there."

"We are not adults."

Jaden huffed. "You always try to stop me from having fun."

"I'm trying to protect you. That's what older brothers do."

Elliott turned. "What do you think, JC?" the boys all looked to JC waiting for his decision.

JC shrugged his shoulders. "If we do them right, I don't think it would hurt anything. Since we're all out of school now, I'll ask grandma if all of you can sleep over. That will give us more time to plan."

"Okay," Elliott agreed. "Are we going to tell the girls?" The boys all turned to the corner where the girls stood.

Jada looked over her shoulder to see the boys. "He's looking at me again."

"Who?" Jazzy asked as she began to turn.

"Don't look," Jada demanded.

"If I don't look how am I supposed to know who you are talking about?"

"If you look he will know we are talking about him."

"I'll look," Samantha sighed. "They're just boys." She stood with her two ponytails swinging with the movement. "Hey," she yelled. "Stop looking at Jada." She returned to her seat with Briana and Gabby.

"You are so childish," Jazzy snapped at Samantha, as Jada put her hands over her face embarrassed.

"We are children. And I'm going to tell Mommy if you keep looking at those boys." Brianna told them, while playing on her computer.

"You can tell Mommy, I don't care." Jazz rolled her eyes at her sister.

"You'll care if I tell Daddy," Gabby looked up nodding her head.

"You better not tell Daddy." Jazzy pushed her little sister.

Samantha stood and pushed Jazzy, "Don't you push my friend."

The boys walked over. "What's wrong, Gabby?" JC asked seeing crocodile tears about to fall from her eyes.

"Jazzy pushed her," Samantha told.

"She should mind her own business," Jazzy yelled back.

"You should stop looking at boys," Samantha shouted back.

"Okay." JC said trying to calm everyone down. "Jazzy, you shouldn't push Gabby, she's smaller than you. " He turned to Gabby and hugged her. "She was just upset Gabby she didn't mean it."

"I didn't even push her that hard," Jazzy huffed as she turned away.

"It's not about how hard you pushed her." James Jr. said. "You hurt her feelings."

"That shouldn't come from you," Elliott added, "You're her big sister. You should protect her from others. Not be the one pushing her."

"Jazzy didn't mean to hurt her feelings. She's sorry." Jada said as she turned to Jazzy. "Aren't you, Jazzy?"

Sometimes Jazzy wished she was her father's only child. Sometimes she just wished they would all disappear, especially JC. He always got to do things with Daddy just because he was a boy. And now Gabby was always in Daddy's arms lying on his shoulder. That's where she was supposed to be, not Gabby and not Mommy either. But they were her family and so she had to be nice to her brother and sisters. "I'm sorry, Gabby."

The little girl ran to her sister and hugged her.

"What's all the fuss about?"

Smiles spread like wildflowers on the children faces. "Hey, Grandma," JC called out as Jada, Jaden, Grabby, Brianna ran to Martha's open arms.

"How are my babies?"

"Hey, Grandma Harrison," James Jr. said as he kissed her cheek along with the other children. "Can we spend the week over here with you?"

"If your mom says it's okay of course you can."

"Can all of us stay?" Elliott asked.

Martha looked around at the faces of her grandchildren and their little friends and thought it's wonderful being a grandmother. "Of course you may. Check with your parents and let me know who's staying."

The children ran by Lena and Gwendolyn as they went in search of their parents. Martha turned to the other grandmothers as they watched the children running off.

"Where are all those kids going to sleep?" Lena asked.

"There is a combination of twelve bedrooms and four guest houses each with two bedrooms, not to mention the two pool houses with bedrooms on this compound. No one is going to be sleeping on the floor, including you two. Which guest house do you want?" Martha raised an eyebrow daring either of them to say no.

Lena stood with her hands on her hips, brushing her hair away from her face, "I don't do the grandmother thing."

"Well you are doing it this week." Martha declared. "Bedroom upstairs or the guest house?"

"Guest house," Lena frowned.

Martha turned to Gwen, who was laughing at the look on Lena's face, "I'll be staying in my suite at James' house."

"Ryan," Martha called over the women's shoulder. "We are going to need your help. The children will be staying here while JD and Tracy are away."

"Yes ma'am I know." Ryan nodded her head.

"No." Lena stopped Ryan. "You don't understand. She said all," Lena spread her hands out "the children will be sleeping over her. That means Tracy's, Ashley's; Cynthia's, Caitlyn's and Jackie's children will be staying under this roof for a week."

"Oh hell," Ryan yelled as she turned and walked off.

Martha smiled. "I think this is going to be fun."

Lena frowned as Martha walked off, "You would."

"Come on Lena. Where's your sense of adventure?" Gwen laughed as she pulled her along.

Ryan walked through the group of people in the foyer. She noticed the children talking to their parents. Walking up to Al she stopped. "I need to speak with you."

JD raised an eyebrow as he watched Al's reaction. The man had the patience of JOB. After the way Ryan spoke to Al this morning, it's a wonder he could stand to be in the same room with her. But, as calm as a summer breeze, Al excused himself, placed his hand on the small of her back and stepped away. "Is there a problem?" Al stood with his hands in his pockets giving her his undivided attention.

Damn, those eyes are dangerous when they are directed at one target. She put her sunshades on. "We have an issue," was all she managed to say. Al held her glare as he waited for the issue to be revealed. "Mrs. Harrison has agreed to let all the children stay here."

"They are all usually on the compound every day away. That shouldn't be an issue."

You don't understand. All ten of them," she pointed for emphasis, "under one roof."

Nodding with a slight smile, Al replied, "I understand the concept." He shrugged his shoulders. They're just children. How much trouble can they be?"

The statement brought Ryan out of her temporary fantasy of his lips and frowned. "Have you ever been around a lot of small children at one time?"

"No, but it can't be that bad."

Ryan put her hand on her hips. "Can't be that bad? Are you serious?" She walked away mumbling. "You're going to wish you were still dealing with the gangs in the streets before this week is out."

"We can handle them."

She looked over her shoulder. "You are going to eat those words."

Chapter 8

Magna was working the first shift at the gate while Ryan completed the walk around the compound. She was still laughing at the expression on Al's face when he found out not only were the children staying on the grounds, but so was his mother. The look was only a moment long, but she caught it and it was priceless. Being around Tracy for the last few years she knew a little about their story. Lena and Tracy did not have a good relationship in the past, but it seemed they were a little more than civil to each other now. But Al apparently still had issues with Mrs. Roth.

Ryan walked in the back door leading to the kitchen of the house thinking at least Tracy understood the value having a mother, even a bad one. She looked up, "What are you still doing in the kitchen? It's after nine."

Mrs. Gordon laughed, "We have ten children in the house ranging from 4 to 16. Somebody is always needed in the kitchen. It might as well be me." She looked up at Ryan with that concerned motherly glance. "Are you doing better tonight?"

"I'm good." She knew what the woman was asking. She shrugged her shoulder, "He gets to me, alright." She hesitated. "I don't know how to handle what he makes me feel."

"Don't fight the feelings."

That sounded so simple, but it was not. Ryan thought as she stood to walk up the steps, but stopped. She turned back to Mrs. Gordon with her hands wedged into her back pockets and pleading eyes. "I don't know how."

"You can start with a smile. I'm sure Mr. Al will take it from there."

"Just a smile, huh."

"That's all—a smile."

She nodded. "I'm going up to check on the children before turning in at the bunk house." Ryan walked up the back stairs.

"Have a good night, just in case I don't see you when you come down."

"You too, Mrs. Gordon."

Mrs. Gordon watched as the woman walked up the stairs wondering how long it was going to take Al to tame the beast.

Ryan heard a voice as she turned the corner to the children's playroom. But it wasn't a child's voice; it was Al's. Strangely, the children were nowhere to be seen, as she approached the room. Walking into the room the children were still nowhere in sight. "Where are they?" She walked further in looking around. Noticing the French doors leading to the balcony were open, she walked quickly across the room. The children were not allowed on the balcony without adult supervision. Realizing Al was on the balcony, she began slowing her pace. Al's voice was the only thing she could hear and it was mesmerizing her.

As she got closer to the opening, Mrs. Harrison and Gwendolyn Brooks came into view. They were both sitting in lounge chairs with their feet up and drinks in their hands.

As she moved closer to the doorway, she could see all the children sitting on the deck looking to the front. They seemed to be spellbound. As she reached the opening she saw the children were as mesmerized by Al's voice as she was as he told them a story.

The top two buttons were open to his white linen shirt and his sleeves were rolled up to his elbow. Sitting on one knee were Gabby and Samantha with Brianna on the other. Sitting at his feet were JC, Jaden, and Jada. Elliott and James Jr. sat behind them all engrossed in his story.

It appeared Al had his own version of The Wizard of Oz, called The Knights of Oz. Locs hanging around his shoulders, moving along with the motions of his body, as he glanced up at her and smiled. The smile was so seductive, at least to her; she had no choice but to smile back. For a moment she stood in the doorway thinking Mrs. Gordon was right. It wasn't that hard to smile at Al.

"What happened to the Knights after they saved the little girl?" JC asked his uncle.

"Well the knights were given the most precious gift of all. The honor of protecting the little princess forever."

"What happened to the princess?" Brianna asked with her thumb still partially in her mouth. "Is she still scared?"

Al twisted the old id bracelet his then little sister had given him years ago. He kept the bracelet with him wherever he went to remind him there was a God somewhere out there, for he had created his little sister. It reminded him why he did the things in his past and proved that there was good in this world. "The princess," he said as he looked up at Ryan, "is still afraid sometimes. But just like all princesses, if they really think about it, they know, they will never have a reason to be afraid. The Knights of Oz will always be there whenever they need them."

The stare from him sent goose bumps up Ryan's arm. She rubbed the area thinking, any man that could make her feel jittery just from a look could definitely be trouble. But then again, any man that enjoyed being around children couldn't be all bad.

A movement near the fireplace at the end of the room caught her attention. It was Al's mother. She started to speak, but Mrs. Roth put her finger to her lips asking her not to.

What is that about? Ryan thought, but adhered to the woman's request as she turned back to the children.

Al returned his attention to the children. "You know what happened next? The Princess of Oz married the King of the region. They are about to embark on a journey to protect families all over the world."

"Will the bad people try to attack them again?" Jada asked.

"Probably," Al replied.

Gabby pulled down on one of Al's locs. "The Knights of Oz is not going to let them. Ain't that right, Uncle Turk?"

Al looked down at the expectant face of his niece and smiled, "That's right."

"I want to be a Knight," JC said with his head resting in his hands as he sat Indian style on the balcony

Al looked down at JC. The boy had captured a piece of his heart the first day they met when he just walked to him with his arms open ready to be picked up. The child had no restraints when it came to people. He reminded him so much of Tracy at that age. "You will be so much more JC, you and your friends. You will be a great leader, just like your father."

The always attention-seeking Jazzy, stood with hands on hips. "What about me, Uncle Turk?"

"You," Al laughed, "Are going to have all the knights dropping at your feet, just like your Grandmother Lena." Ryan peeked in the room to glance at Mrs. Roth. The woman simply held her head down as a small smile touched her lips. *Hmm*, Ryan thought. She never expected to see humility on Lena Roth.

Jazzy turned to Martha. "Grandma, did you have knights?"

Martha laughed, "I had one good one. I didn't need anymore."

"Well, I'm going to have all the knights."

"And I'm going to have your behind. That's what grandmothers do."

The adults laughed, as Al looked up to see Ryan walking onto the deck. She bent over and whispered something into Martha's ear. That was his cue to leave. It was difficult to be in the same room with the woman and not be affected by her. Rather than having another dose of her bitterness towards him, he sat Gabby and Brianna down.

"Are you leaving, Uncle Turk?" JC asked.

"No, but I think Ms. Ryan is here to get the little ones ready for bed."

"Do we have to?" Brianna cried.

Al smiled, then bent down to kiss her cheek, "Yes chubby cheeks, you do."

Gwen turned to Martha, "You take this group. I'll take the next."

"Sounds good," Martha stood, "Okay, Brianna, Samantha, Gabby and Anthony," Martha called out. Let's get ready for bed. The rest of you can hang out in the game room a little longer."

"Can Uncle Turkey tuck us in tonight, Grandma?" Gabby asked.

"No. Uncle Turk has to talk to Ms. Ryan. But you can see him tomorrow." The small children followed their grandmother pouting, as the older children ran into the game room.

Ryan stood on the balcony giving Al the evening report as Lena watched them from her seat near the fireplace. Gwen walked over and sat next to her. "Have you two talked yet?"

Lena continued to watch the two on the balcony. "There's really nothing to talk about. The past cannot be changed."

"True. But acceptance and progress can. Believe me, I know—I've lived it."

"Look at those two," Lena instructed her friend. "What do you see?"

Gwen sat back for a moment and watched. She smiled, "I see two people attracted to each other and trying not to show it."

Lena nodded, "That's what I see, too." She sat back and smiled. "It's kind of nice to see. Maybe he's ready to let a woman in."

"Maybe."

Ryan walked from the balcony, through the room and out the door. Al stood just inside the French doors watching her exit. He turned to see Lena and Gwen watching him. He looked from one to the other. "Mrs. Brooks, Lena."

"Al," Lena and Gwen replied.

"That was a wonderful story, Al. You are surprisingly good with children." Gwen complimented.

"I had a lot of practice with my little sister. Good night, ladies."

"Good night, Al."

An hour later, Ryan was at the computer when Al walked into the situation security house. "The children weren't a problem after all," Al said as he leaned against the door jam.

Ryan turned and looked up at him. "Don't call it a victory yet, you still have six more days to go."

He tilted his head and gave her the crooked smile. "I can't believe you're afraid of a few children."

"Those sweet little children can turn into devils at a moment's notice."

"Tomorrow is going to be a breeze, just like today." Al said over his shoulder as he walked away.

"We'll see," Ryan turned back to the computer.

Day two began and ended with a bang. The small children, Samantha, Brianna, Gabby and Tony decided they were going to help Grandma Martha with the wash. They meant well, they really did. It just turned out all wrong. At the bathroom sink between Gabby and Brianna's bedrooms was where the innocent brainstorming began.

Samantha and Brianna were complaining about the small children being put to bed early while the big kids got to stay up late. "Grandma Martha said we wore her out last night when she put us to bed." Brianna explained. "She said we had to go to bed early so she could get some rest."

"Well," Samantha said as she washed her face, "maybe we can help her with her work and then she won't be so tired."

"But we are little children. What can we do?" Brianna sat down on the stool and propped her elbow on her knee and her chin on her hand.

Brianna sounded so sad and Samantha wanted to make her friend feel better. She sat down on the stool next to her and sighed. "You know, I help my mommy all the time. We wash clothes, dust the furniture and I even help her cook sometimes. Most of the time my daddy cooks. But sometimes my mommy cooks hot dogs and I help her."

"But Grandma Martha don't cook at our house. Mrs. Gordon does." Brianna pouted.

Samantha frowned more. Her friend was still feeling sad. A moment later she turned to her friend, excited.

"Your Grandma Martha said she was going to have to wash a heap of clothes. We could help her wash clothes."

"Do you know how?" A curious Brianna perked up.

That encouraged Samantha more. "I sure do. All you need is some washing powder and a lot of water."

Brianna sat up. "I know where there's a lot of water."

"You do?"

"Yep and we can ask Mrs. Gordon for the washing powder." Brianna stood. "If we wash the clothes for Grandma, she won't be tired and we can stay up late tonight."

"Okay," Samantha smiled, "Let's go do it before your grandmother wakes up and we can surprise her."

"Okay." The two little girls ran into the bedroom and began dressing.

Gabby appeared in the doorway with her thumb in her mouth. "Where you going Brianna?"

"We're going to help Grandma Martha."

"Can I go?"

"Sure you can. Go get dressed."

The excitement was spreading. "Can Tony come too?" Gabby asked.

"Yes he can come," Samantha replied, "But don't tell the big kids. They will just try to stop us."

"Okay." Gabby ran in her room to get Tony.

Ten minutes later the children walked into the kitchen. "Good morning, Mrs. Gordon. Where does mommy wash the clothes?" Brianna asked barely reaching the counter top.

Mrs. Gordon looked over the island to see four children standing there with their arms filled with clothes. None of the girl's hair was done, and they were dressed haphazardly. "Good morning, my angels. Aren't you being helpful little bees early this morning? The laundry is right by the bathroom at the back door." Mrs. Gordon replied smiling brightly at the children as they marched by. "Isn't that sweet, they're trying to be helpful." She smiled and continued preparing breakfast.

After reaching the laundry room, Brianna climbed up the step stool to reach the detergent. "It's heavy. How are we going to carry it?"

Eager to help, Tony put his bundle of clothes on the floor. "I can go get my wagon to carry the 'tergent to the water."

"That's a good idea. You go get your wagon and we'll wait here for you. Hurry up so we can surprise grandma before she wakes up."

"Okay," Tony smiled and ran out the door.

"I'm going with Tony," Gabby dropped her armload of clothes and ran out behind him.

The two children began the journey down the road leading to Tony's house. Neither considered the distance or how long it would actually take to get there.

Ryan was sitting in the security rooms watching the monitors drinking her second cup of coffee for the morning, when she noticed the two children walking up the road. "What are they up too?"

"Who?" Magna asked from the doorway.

Ryan turned her way, "Good Morning. Take over the monitors while I see what those two rug rats are up to."

Ryan walked out the door and down the road until she was a few feet away from them. The two were holding hands, swinging as they walked along. Gabby's hair was all over her head and Tony's clothes were hanging off of him. "Where are you two going?"

The children turned and smiled up at Ryan. "We're going to get my wagon so we can surprise Grandma Martha."

Ryan returned the children's smile. She walked over, pulled Gabby's hair together and put it in a single braid. "Your mother would have a fit if she knew you were outside with your hair like this." She finished the braid. "Now, that's better." She then turned to Tony and fixed his clothes properly. "Now, how about if I give you a ride there." The children bobbed their heads up and down. Ryan took them by the hand and walked them to her truck.

Al watched the scene from the office window upstairs. "She's good with kids," he said, then went back to what he was doing.

Ryan and the children walked in the back door of Ashley's house. "Good Morning Clair."

"Good morning, Ms. Ryan. What brings you by so early in the morning?" The Brooks' housekeeper asked.

"This little one would like to get his wagon. Is that okay?"

"Of course it is." Clair pushed a button. The doors to the garage slid open. Tony ran in and came out with his wagon in tow.

"Thank you, Clair," Ryan said as she loaded the wagon in the back of her truck and pulled off. She dropped the two at the back door of Tracy's house. She watched as the children walked inside with the wagon, before she pulled off.

Now armed with the laundry detergent in the wagon, and clothes in their arms, they were off to the water.

It was a little before eight in the morning when Lena awakened to water running. She sat up and looked out the bay window of the guesthouse and noticed the fountain that sat in the center of the lawn was on. The fountain was not always running, but whenever there was a function on the lawn, it was turned on. Thinking nothing of the fountain, she returned to her pillow and closed her eyes. They didn't stay that way for long as visions of Al and the Ryan girl came back to her. It would be nice to see him settled down and happy. Lord knows he deserved it. She wasn't the best mother in the world, but she did the best she knew how. Her other children seemed to have accepted who she was and had forgiven her, but there was still a polite rift between her and Al. The telephone chimed. Lena picked up her cell phone and saw her husband's handsome face. "Good morning, darling. How was the trip?"

"It was a great gathering." Senator John Roth replied. "There were at least five thousand people there to hear JD speak. The place rocked, as the kids would say."

Lena smiled. It was her husband's dream to get JD elected. She hoped it all worked out. "How was Tracy?"

"Lena, that girl is a natural. She has your charm and my brains."

"Not to mention my good looks," Lena joked.

"She had the crowd eating out of her little hand."

"You sound like a proud daddy."

"I am, sweetheart. I know it was difficult for her to accept me as her father, but I think we are doing all right. I have a nine o'clock meeting I need to prepare for. But I had to hear your voice first. I missed you last night."

"You didn't miss me. You missed that pole in our bedroom."

"That too," John laughed. "Love you."

"Love you back." Lena closed the phone, stood and stretched. The fountain came into view. "Now that's different," she said. She shrugged her shoulder, began striping out of her nightclothes and walked into the shower. Fifteen minutes later, Lena was standing at the kitchen window fresh from her shower pouring a cup of coffee. Something about the fountain caught her attention. "Now that's over doing it a bit." She laughed at the sight. She poured the coffee into a cup and walked out of the door thinking she would get an early start with the children.

Lena walked into the kitchen from the patio door, for that was closer than the back door. As she walked in she watched Brianna, Gabby, Samantha and Tony walk by. "Good morning, little soldiers."

"Hi, Grand'Mere," Brianna and Gabby smiled.

"Hi, Ms. Roth," Samantha smiled. A wave was al Tony managed.

Lena stood there watching the children. "They're on a mission," Mrs. Gordon said.

"Looks like it." Lena turned, walked over to the island and took a seat. "How are you this morning, Mrs. Gordon?"

"I'm better than alright, but not quite good."

"I can understand that. I thought I'd give the real grandmas a little help with the kids this morning."

"Those are the only ones up. I haven't heard a peep out of the others yet."

"They were up kind of late playing on that Wii game." Lena said as the four children marched back through the kitchen with clothes in their hands. "What are they doing?" She asked as they walked out back.

Mrs. Gordon smiled. "They think they are helping by putting the dirty clothes in the laundry room."

"Aw. That's nice."

At the security house, Al was making sure his signature was everywhere the x was on the mortgage papers for Monique's new condo. Tucker assured him it was in a nice area of DC and a good investment. Once Monique finished Georgetown, he could sell it for twice the amount he paid for it, or possibly rent it out. All in all, it was a good investment. When he reached the last page, he heard Ryan scream. Then he heard footsteps running out of the guardhouse. Al quickly made his way downstairs to see what the commotion was all about. Ryan and Magna had left their post, but had not sounded the alarm. Al walked over to the monitors to see what was going on. One monitor showed Ryan running full stride across the lawn, Magna with her long raven black hair, not far behind her. Another monitor showed four children walking in the same direction with something in their hands. The third screen showed the water fountain streaming beautifully upwards and cascading down the sides. The fountain itself was filled with bubbles. "Bubbles?" Al said aloud. The next thing he saw sent him into shock mode. Each of the children empty the load of clothes from their arms into the fountain turned and was marching back towards the house. "Oh, hell!" he ran out the door.

Lena watched as the four children marched back by them and walked up the stairs again. Then she looked up to see Ryan and Magna running across the lawn at full speed. Not a minute later, Al was running behind them with his locs flying around him. "What in the hell is going on?" She stood and walked out the back door. She walked around the patio until the fountain came into view.

Mrs. Gordon came to stand behind Lena with her gun in her hand. "What is it she called out?"

Just then the children walked out with another bundle of clothes. "'Scuse me, Mrs. Gordon," Brianna said.

Mrs. Gordon stepped aside, her attention still on Lena. The children marched around the other side of the patio, right up to the fountain and dumped the clothes in.

"Stop," Ryan yelled as Magna was handing her wet clothes from the fountain. She knew JD and Tracy did not curse around their children, but this situation called for something strong. "What in the hell are you doing?"

"Awe, Mrs. Ryan you said a bad word. Daddy is going to spank you." Brianna said pointing a finger at her.

Lena began laughing hysterically.

"Hi, Uncle Turkey. Are you going to help us wash clothes for Grandma Martha?" Gabby asked as she ran into her uncle's arms.

Al lifted the child for he couldn't think of anything else to do and because he couldn't think of anything else to do, he smiled.

Ryan turned to the other children with her hands on her hips. "Brianna, you are the oldest. Explain."

"We're washing the clothes so Grandma Martha won't have to."

"Then we can stay up late, cause she won't be tired," Samantha finished.

"Does this look like a washing machine to you?" Ryan yelled.

"The washing 'chine was too small," Tony explained.

"Yeah," Brianna agreed, it would take too long in the washing machine."

By this time, Lena was bent over laughing. Al had sat Gabby back on the ground as Mrs. Gordon, put her gun in her apron pocket and walked over to the fountain. "Ain't no need trying to understand their logic. It'll just make you crazy. Take the children in the house and let's get the clothes inside."

Ryan stood there with her mouth wide open. She turned and looked at Al who was only smiling, but she could tell he wanted to laugh. "Don't you dare!"

Al threw his hands up in the air, "What," he laughed?

Ryan grabbed the children by their hands and stormed by a laughing Lena who was now on the ground rolling.

Thirty minutes later, the other children came down stairs had their breakfast and were heading outside to play. James Jr had the basketball in his hands as, Elliot, JC, Jaden and Calvin, followed him out the door. A minute later, JC came back into the house. "Hey who put the bubbles in the fountain?"

Lena and Mrs. Gordon fell out laughing, Ryan looked at the boy as if she was ready to kill and Al just smiled. "We thought it would look nice with bubbles."

"Cool," JC shrugged. "Next time we need some with color. You know, like the rainbow." He turned and walked out the door.

Ryan frowned at Lena, who just could not get herself together. Al gave Lena a pleading look and she took a few deep breaths, just as Ashley and Cynthia walked through the door. "What happened to the fountain?" Lena let go again as Ryan slammed her coffee cup on the island and stormed out the door. Al walked out and brought her back in.

"Okay, let's all take a breath." He sat Ryan down in the chair facing Lena. "There's enough responsibility to pass around. For example, let's examine the adult's responsibility in what took place." Al looked at Lena and Mrs. Gordon. "You two sat here and watched the children march back and forth with clothes in their arms and said nothing." He looked at Martha and Gwendolyn, "You two weren't even up with the children as you should have been. And you," he turned to Ryan, "you not only helped them get the wagon, you made sure they looked good doing it." He folded his arms across his chest. "You all are just as responsible for what happened this morning as the children."

Everyone in the room looked from one to the other until finally, Ryan began laughing. "I can't believe they washed the clothes in the damn fountain."

Finally, her smile was directed at him. He liked it. He liked it a lot. Within minutes the adults were all laughing with the exception of Ashley and Cynthia. The two just looked at each other. "I guess you had to be there," Ashley said as she shrugged her shoulders.

That was round one. Round two happened a little after two in the afternoon. Jada and Jazzy were watching America's Next Top model when they decided it would be more fun in real life. "My mom has a lot of pretty dresses in her closet and she don't even wear them." She twisted and turned for emphasis. "And my daddy buys her a lot of pretty jewelry, like diamonds and stuff and she won't wear them either."

"My daddy buys my mommy jewelry, too." Jada replied, "But they keep them in a safe."

"My mommy lets me wear hers all the time. Want to see how pretty I look in them?"

"Your mommy won't be mad?"

"No, we play dress up all the time." Jazzy stood up, "Come on, I'll show you."

Magna was the first to see the silent alarm flash across the screen. She adjusted the monitors to the room indicated on the monitor. In the room she could see, Jazzy and Jada near the door. "Hey Al, the outer door of the safe in Tracy's closet was just opened. Any chance JD or Tracy gave Jazzy the combination to the safe?"

Al stood behind Magna as they watched the screen. "I don't think so?"

"So how do you suppose Jazzy opened that door?"

Al stood there and watched as Jazzy manipulated the numbers until the safe door popped open. "I'll be damned. She popped that safe."

Magna stood, "The little safecracker." She looked over her shoulder at Al who appeared amazed. "I can't believe you are marveling at a little girl's skill at safecracking."

"She's what, eight years old." Al bragged. "There are maybe ten people in the world that can do that in less than five minutes.

"Oh, no. No!" Magna screamed.

"What?" Al looked at the monitor. "Oh, hell." He took off running. Magna wasn't far behind.

Ms. Gordon was wrapping things up in the kitchen when the patio doors flew open, followed by Al and Magna running up the back staircase. At the top of the steps, Martha, Lena and Gwen were relaxing with drinks and sandwiches in Tracy's office as Al and Magna flew by them running towards the master bedroom. Martha sighed, "What now?"

Lena laughed as she stood and quickly followed them.

Gwen shook her head and looked at Martha, "Shall we wait here, or follow?"

Martha walked down the hall to the game room. JC, James Jr. Elliott and Calvin were on the Xbox playing a football game. "Well they're accounted for. The small children were taking a nap. That only left Jazzy and Jada."

Gwen stood, "Lord only knows what those two busy bodies have gotten into." The two grandmothers walked down to the double doors that were wide open. They walked through the sitting area, then the bedroom and into Tracy's closet. They walked by the everyday clothes, the gowns, shoe racks and coatroom until they reached the last turn. From there they could see Al at a door working on a number pad and Magna standing over him with a hand held monitor in her hand. "What's going on?" Gwen whispered to Lena.

"I'm not sure," Lena replied as she leaned casually against the outer doorframe.

"Why are you trying to break into the safe?" Martha asked.

Al ignored the question as he continued maneuvering the numbers. Magna walked back to them and showed them the monitor.

On the monitor, the drawers inside the safe were hanging open as Jazzy and Jada were sitting on the floor covered in bracelets, necklaces and earrings. Lena began to laugh.

"Oh my lord," Gwen chuckled. "Oh, I like that one."

"Which one?" Lena asked.

"The rubies and diamonds Jada has around her neck."

"That is nice, but look at the sapphire ring Jazzy has on. Oh, I could work that."

"Al," Martha called out as the two women continued gawking at the monitor. "Are they getting any air in there?"

Everyone looked up at her, then to Al's back. "Not for long." He continued to work.

"Shouldn't we call somebody? Does anyone have the combination to the safe?" Gwen asked.

"Yes," Magna replied, "Tracy and JD. Either of you want to call them and ask for it. Grandmothers that were supposed to be watching the children?" She smirked, "I didn't think so."

The grandmothers just looked at each other. "Well how did they get in there in the first place?" Gwen asked.

"She cracked the safe." Magna replied then walked back to where Al worked on the door.

Martha and Gwen looked at each other, "Who did?"

"Jazzy."

"Awe, that girl is after my heart," Lena placed her hand on her heart and just shook her head.

"How are we going to get them out of there?" A concerned Martha questioned.

"Al will get them out. This is child's play to him," Lena boasted.

Just as the sentence was complete, the doors opened. Al stood and sighed.

"Hi, Uncle Al," Jazzy looked up at him smiling. "What took you so long?"

The child looked so much like Tracy with those big brown doe eyes all he could do was smile. "How did you know I was coming?" he asked as he reached down to begin placing the jewelry back in the compartments.

"Only you and JC could open the door."

"I was scared when the door closed," Jada smiled. "But Jazzy said we could get out just like we got in." She held a diamond bracelet up to him. "Isn't this one pretty?"

"Yes," he replied as he took the bracelet and placed it in a drawer.

"Both of you come here." Martha called in that grandmother means business tone.

She began taking the items off of them and handing them to Gwen to put back in the drawer. "Your mother is going to have a fit when she finds out about this."

Jazzy proceeded with caution around Martha. "Grandma we play with mommy's jewelry all the time."

"Your mother does not allow you to play with this jewelry and you know it. And I know she didn't teach you how to open a safe. Now did she?"

Jazzy turned and looked at her Uncle Al, then back at her grandmother. "No." the child replied and hung her head.

Martha gave Al that you are in trouble look as she took her two granddaughters' hands and stormed out of the closet with Gwen following.

Magna and Al had replaced all the items and were walking out of the safe when Lena smiled at Al. "I'm proud of you son, passing on the family skills and all." Then she laughed, "But you are in trouble. Those are real mommas and you are going to catch hell for this." She shook her head and walked off.

Magna looked at him with empathy. "I'm sorry, Al."

"What? I'm not scared of them."

Fifteen minutes later, Al was sitting in the kitchen at the island. Lena was standing behind him, while Gwen stood next to him with her hands on her hips and Martha in front of him laying him out.

"As enjoyable as this scene is, let's be real. There is enough blame for the events of the day to go around. Pointing fingers at Al is not going to change anything that has happened." Ryan said from the doorway. She walked over and sat at the far end of the island. "Besides Mrs. Harrison, you were the one that said all the children could stay. And you two," she pointed at Lena and Gwen, "said you would help watch the children. Al is here for security. So when JD and Tracy hear about all of this, they are not going to be looking at Al. Oh no, they will be gunning for you. So I suggest we all settle down, laugh a little and enjoy the rest of the afternoon."

"You have a point," Martha acknowledged. "I'm still upset with you." She said to Al. "Teaching a child how to crack a safe is wrong—it's just wrong."

"Look at it this way, if you ever get locked out again, we don't have to call a locksmith. That's a special talent," Lena offered. "Come on ladies, let's go have a drink."

"I could use one," Gwen said as she turned to walk up the stairs.

"I second that," Martha followed.

Lena walked towards the stairs and looked back at Al. She liked the way Ryan came to his defense. She winked at him then followed the ladies.

Ryan bit into the apple she took from the bowl, as Al turned to her. She smiled and pointed a finger. "Let's examine the adults' role in all of this."

The laughter that filled the room sparked something deep inside of her. Examining it would cause her to get angry because it touched her heart. Instead she decided to enjoy the moment.

Round three took the cake. It was well after nine. The July sun had just set with the stars shining brightly in the sky. It looked to be the beginning of a peaceful night as the grandmothers sat in the game room playing Gin Rummy. The grandmothers had laid down the law on the children. They could not make a move without asking them first. The adults were now in charge.

"Grandma," JC called from the doorway. "Is it okay if we go outside just for a little while?"

"It's dark out," Martha replied without looking up.

"We just want to sit out back for a little while," Jaden replied.

"They're boys and they haven't given us any trouble today," Gwen smiled. "Let them go out for a little while."

Lena grunted and shook her head. "Sounds like famous last words to me."

Martha looked at her grandson. "Stay away from the fountain and the pool."

"Okay, Grandma," JC kissed her on the cheek and ran from the room.

Martha smiled, "Little devil, looks just like his granddaddy."

Ryan and Magna were sitting at the monitors with their feet up taking a breather. It had been over six hours and no issues out of the children. They were not completely at ease, but a lot more settled than a few hours ago.

"This day reminds me of why I don't have kids," Magna laid her head back against the chair.

"I don't know. I think it would be fun to have a boat load of kids," Ryan replied.

Magna's head shot up, "The way those kids acted today, no way."

"Come on. You've been around these kids as much as I have. You know they don't act like this when JD and Tracy are home."

"Really, none of them are bad separately. All of them together is an entirely different story."

"But, I have to agree. It has been a trying day." Ryan laid her head back. "I could use a little down time."

"Hey ladies," Al called as he entered the room. "All quiet on the home front?"

"For now," Magna sighed.

He looked at Ryan, "You did good today. With the kids, I mean."

She was almost tempted to smile at the sincerity of his voice. "Is that an admission that I was right to be concerned?"

He shrugged his shoulder, "No. We made it through the day and they are all still alive," he joked—maybe a little too soon.

Suddenly, sounds of gunfire filled the air. Ryan and Magna pulled their weapons and ran out the door as Al hit the button securing the grounds and all entrances into the house. "What direction, Boss?" Magna asked as she activated her Bluetooth.

"Back of the house!" Al yelled while examining the scenes from the monitors that had all come to life. He could see the women in the game room looking around startled at the sound. The next monitor showed the small kids looking out of the window. The girls were in the bedroom looking out the back. "Where are the boys?" he wondered as he looked at each monitor. He scanned around the pool house, stopped, then went back. The boys were behind the pool house kneeling on the ground. Suddenly, all them ran back towards the structure just as the sound erupted again, this time the sky lit up with an array of fireworks.

Magna and Ryan looked up at the sky from their position on the ground and cursed. "What the hell?"

Ryan stood, holstered her weapon and angrily marched towards the pool house. "I'm going to kill them with my bare hands."

Al watched as Magna stood, but then the small computer on his belt vibrated. "Ryan take cover. We have an intruder on the grounds. Magna, go to your left, circle around the fountain, and stay low."

Al grabbed a gun from the rack and ran around the house to the right with the handheld. "Ryan, can you reach the boys?"

She was on the other side of the pool house, when another round of firecrackers went off.

"Wow. Look at that one," she heard Jaden say.

"Yeah," she stayed close to the house until she reached the back then looked around the corner. The boys were standing in the shadows looking up at the sky. She watched as their heads traveled up following the spark as it went backwards and landed on the roof of the pool house. "Oh, hell."

Al watched the figure on the monitor as he came through the woods to the grass area. He ran faster to get to the pool house. The monitor picked up a second figure he believed to be Magna approaching from the other side. "Ryan do you have the boys?" he yelled. He waited, and waited, no reply. He cut through the flower garden to reach the right side of the pool house. That's when he saw the fire. Al ran past the commotion of Ryan and the boys with his gun raised high ready to fire, just as he recognized the figure. "Shit! Stand down, Magna, its Joshua."

Al and Magna ran back and turned their attention to the fire on the roof of the pool house. "Go get a bucket and some water from the fountain," Al yelled at the boys.

"Grandma told us not to go near the fountain," JC explained.

Joshua walked by all of them, pulled out what looked like a laser gun from his inner pocket, sprayed a liquid on the roof and the flame evaporated in a snap. He then pulled out a pin, which was actually a flashlight to examine the roof. "It's out." He turned to the group. "No one told me we were doing fireworks tonight." He said with his hands held out. "I had some serious stuff we could have used."

The boys ran to Joshua, "Like the ones you had before? Do you have them with you?" Elliot asked.

"Better man—better."

"Whoa, let's light them up," James Jr. grinned.

Al grabbed James and Elliott by the back of their shirts. Magna snagged Jaden. Ryan grabbed JC and Calvin. As she walked by Al she snarled, "They're just children. We can handle them." She rolled her eyes and continued dragging the boys along.

"What?" Joshua yelled as the boys were marched towards the house, "No more fireworks?"

By ten o'clock that night every child was with their own mother, with the exception of Tracy's. They were each in their own room forbidden to leave until Al allowed it.

Ryan walked around the perimeter just for her own peace of mind. Al decided to join her.

"You knew all this would happen. Didn't you?"

She laughed. "I've been around these kids all of their lives. I know them as if they were my own and love them just as much." They continued to walk. "They are good kids, but when their parents aren't around they will try you. Four, you can handle. Double that and you are asking for trouble."

"I should have taken you a little more seriously. Will you forgive my stupidity?"

She stopped and looked up at him. Her body immediately reacted to those smoldering eyes and that crooked smile. This time she didn't fight it. She punched him on the arm. "This time, but don't let it happen again." She smiled.

The air crackled as they held each other's stare.

"You are a beautiful woman. Do you know that?"

The blush on Ryan's face could be seen even in the dark. "No. But thank you for saying it."

Al took a step to close the distance between them. He tilted his head toward her lips. The anticipation of kissing her was so strong he licked his lips as he watched her mouth tilt up to him.

"Hey. What are you two up to?" Joshua grinned. The daggers sent his way by both parties as they turned to him would have killed a normal man. But not Joshua, he just smiled at them. "I'm not interrupting anything—am I?"

Ryan sighed, "I'll be in the bunkhouse," and walked off.

Al stood watching her with his hands in his pockets then turned to Joshua. "I could kill you right now."

Joshua threw his hands in the air and laughed. "What?" He shrugged his shoulders. "I had to let you know I'll be out of the country for a minute."

"Why?" A frustrated Al asked.

"I'll find out when I get there." He hit Al on the shoulder. "You need to get laid. You seem a little grouchy—tense. You need to loosen up." Joshua laughed and walked away.

If Al could carry a gun he would have shot him.

Chapter 9

Joshua stood on the roof top balcony of Prince LaVere' Ashro's of Emure palace. He had received a message that the Prince had requested to see him. Joshua had a number of feelers out regarding the possible assassination attempt on JD. But so far, nothing had panned out. Normally, nothing would deter him from his mission. But LaVere' was a friend and he'd indicated the situation was urgent. "Shall I check my rooftop for explosives," LaVere' greeted Joshua as he extended his hand.

It was good to see LaVere. The last time they saw each other his brother Samuel was marrying the woman LaVere had selected as his wife. "Not this time." Joshua shook his hand. "How are things with you?"

"Quite well, thanks to you. I can never repay the debt of you saving my sister's life. However, I do hope the information I'm about to give will be beneficial." LaVere pointed to the chairs around the table on the rooftop. "Please have a seat." They both sat as a servant placed a bottle of wine and two glasses on the table. Once the servant walked away, LaVere pulled out a hand held computer. "I think it would be beneficial for you to find this man."

Joshua looked at a video clip of what appeared to be a Mexican man meeting with a Middle Easterner. The clip showed the two talking then an envelope being passed between them.

"Why would this interest me?"

LaVere pulled out a manila envelope. "This is the envelope obtained from this gentleman when my brother's men apprehended him on another matter. The man is a well-paid assassin. My brother, who is now King, knew of my connection to this family and thought I should be made aware of the discovery."

Joshua opened the envelope to discover a picture of JD Harrison and his travel itinerary.

After interrogating the assassin, Joshua was a little on edge. A few facts troubled him. The realization that the contract was real and the target was a man he liked and respected. Some of the men he had worked for in the past he really didn't give a damn about, it were the Country that he vowed to protect. With JD, it was different. He liked the man and everything that he stood for. Did he understand that once JD became President, he would have to curtail the way he operated—yes. He could deal with that. JD didn't have it in him to take a life. Well there was that one time when Joshua had to talk him down from killing the man that killed his father. But other than that, JD was a good man and Joshua would count it as an honor to serve him. Someone was trying to take that from him. The disturbing fact was the itinerary the assassin had was a duplicate of the one Joshua had. That meant that someone from JD's camp supplied that itinerary. The last issue was the most dangerous. With assassins, there was always a contingency plan.

Joshua sat on the private jet provided by LaVere, stretched his legs across to the other seat and crossed them at the ankle as he pulled out his phone. "Hey big brother, where are you?"

"Iowa."

Joshua laughed, "That sounds like fun." He became serious, "The threat is real. The first wave has been eliminated, however, other layers exist."

"That's not good. Where are you off to next?"

"The trail leads to Mexico."

"Hostile territory to travel alone."

"It's the only way I travel."

"You need to be vigilant, big brother." He hesitated for a moment. "The man's itinerary was found on the assassin."

Samuel took in the information. "We have an insider."

Joshua disconnected the call, then hit another button.

"Al, are you finished playing with children?"

"Funny. You did not help matters much."

"You should be happy that call came in from LaVere' or I would have never been at the house that night. Kids playing with firecrackers, you should be ashamed of yourself."

Al sat back at his desk and laughed, "Imagine my surprise to discover you provided those fireworks."

"Man, they talked." He laughed. "They gave me up."

Al smiled. "All right, on a serious note. What did the Prince have?"

"More than we want to deal with. I need you to arrange a meeting with your contact."

Al could hear the change in Joshua's voice. "Dangerous territory."

"So I've been told."

"I consider him a friend."

"As a friend you should tell him I'm coming. He can open the front door or I can knock it down. You know what I prefer."

"Where are you?"

"On my way."

"I'll arrange a hook up." Al disconnected the call, then dialed Tucker.

Twenty minutes later Ryan was at the monitors laughing at Magna, who was telling her about her date the night before. "Did you hurt the boy is all I want to know?"

"Wore his little soul out," Magna laughed. "I taught him about playing at the grown up table."

"Hell, I'm not mad at you. At least you got your cookies wet even if it was with 2% and not whole milk."

"I'm sure he has some friends that could wet those cookies for you."

"Thanks for the offer, but I'll pass."

Magna smiled, then looked away. "I see you and the man are doing better. No bickering for a few days."

She shrugged her shoulders, "He's not so bad."

"Seems like a pretty decent person to me. Last week certainly showed me another side of him."

"With the children?" Ryan grinned while shaking her head. "No, I've seen that side of him before. He loves kids." She looked sideways at Magna. "What surprised me was actually hearing them talking to the kids together. Tracy is going to be happy to see the progress those two have made. I think he feels pretty good about it, too."

"And, what about you? How do you feel about him now?"

Ryan blushed a little as she nodded her head. "He's really a good brother."

Magna smiled. "Finally let someone in," she shoved her shoulder. "About time." She turned back to the monitor. "Whoa, I don't think I've ever seen legs that long."

Ryan looked at the monitor, smiled, then pushed the button. "That's her style. Melissa Sue. What in the hell are you doing here?" she asked as the woman walked through the door.

"The man calls, I come no questions asked."

Magna tiptoed next to her, "How tall are you?"

"With or without the shoes?" Melissa Sue turned with the grace of a gazelle.

Magna looked down at the four inch stilettoes and frowned, "Never mind."

"Melissa Sue." Al called out as he walked off the elevator.

"Good to see you again, Boss." She walked over kissed him on the lips. "Which way?"

Al held his hand out towards the elevator as Ryan and Magna looked on. "Well," Magna said as the elevator doors closed. "What do you make of that?" Ryan watched as they stepped off the elevator upstairs, walked down the hallway into the office and closed the door. "Are you going to just stand there and watch until they come out?"

Ryan turned to Magna about ready to spit fire. "I'm going to walk the grounds." She stormed out of the building. Magna turned to the monitor with mixed feelings. Ryan was just letting Al in. Seeing him kiss another woman was not good. "Looks like my grand is still safe."

This was her own fault. She let this happen. How many times had she watched as her brothers tossed one woman after another aside? She knew how the game was played, but she let him get inside. Ryan mumbled to herself as she began walking the acres of land surrounding the Harrison's home, kicking herself all the way for letting Al Day get under her skin.

For the third time Tracy watched as Ryan walked by the window. "Something has upset her," she said to her mother who was visiting.

Lena looked out the kitchen window and watched as Ryan stormed by. "She's not walking, honey. She's taking that I'm pissed stroll." She smirked.

"I wonder what has her so upset."

"It's not a what, it's who. That stroll has Al written all over it."

"Turk?" Tracy looked at Lena surprised. "Did something happen between them while I was gone?'

Lena put her magazine down and stared off into space for a minute. "In my opinion it did. I think Al is falling for Ryan."

"You do?" Tracy turned eagerly to her. "I think so too. What should we do about it?"

"Stay out of it," Lena opened the magazine and continued reading.

That wasn't what Tracy wanted to hear. "I want to see Turk happy." She sighed.

"I do, too," Lena replied, "but I want to stay alive."

"Turk wouldn't hurt you or me." Tracy walked out the door to catch up with Ryan.

"That child really doesn't know her brother."

"Hey Ryan, wait up." Tracy spoke as she ran to catch up with her. "Are you ready for the party this weekend? I'm pretty excited about it." No response as she continued to walk. "It's not public knowledge yet, but the polls have Jeffrey double digits ahead of the opponents."

Surprised by the news Ryan stopped walking. "Really? That's a good solid lead with four months to go." She looked at Tracy with melancholy eyes. "This is really going to happen, isn't it?"

"We're pretty sure of it."

"My God, Tracy, you may actually become The First Lady. I mean, I know we've been talking about it and thought it would happen. But, Tracy, now it's becoming a reality."

"Well, we still have to win the election."

Ryan smiled, "I've been with you for seven years. Your family is my family and I love you guys. I'm going to miss you." She hugged Tracy.

Tracy pulled away. "Where are you going?" She looked shocked.

"Not me, you and JD—The White House. Once you win, Secret Service will really take over."

"Oh, that. You'll still be here," Tracy waved her off and continued their walk. "Now about the party, what are you going to wear?"

Ryan smiled at the woman that was like a sister to her. It never failed. Whenever she was feeling down, Tracy always made her smile. She began walking with her again. "What I normally wear to one of your parties, black pants, white collar blouse and black blazer."

Tracy laughed, "I should have known. I think we need an intervention. How would you like to go shopping?"

Ryan paused, "I don't do girly things like shopping."

Tracy continued walking. "I can tell."

Al walked Melissa Sue out to her car. On the way back in he stopped by the command room. "Where's Ryan?"

Magna looked over her shoulder then turned back to the monitor. "She stormed out when you went behind closed doors with Melissa Sue."

"Stormed out—why?"

Magna knew she was about to step over her boundaries, but Ryan was like a sister to her and she really did want her to be happy. "Al, I don't know you well. But any fool can see that Ryan has a thing for you."

The statement caused Al to take a moment. "And?" he said with a raised eyebrow.

Magna stood and faced him, "Do me a favor—hell do all of us a favor. Take Ryan somewhere and screw her brains out." She walked out of the room, then came back. "Um," she held a finger up pointing at him. "I would personally appreciate it if you wait until next week." She winked and then she walked out.

Al went to the monitors to try to locate Ryan. He saw the look in her eyes when Melissa Sue had kissed him. It was a running joke between the two of them. Back when Al was on the street, he managed to get Melissa Sue out of a sting operation, by pulling her in a corner and kissing her until the cop following her ran by. Ever since then, whenever they met she would kiss him. There was nothing to the kiss. Al sat at the desk as he watched Tracy and Ryan walking. The two of them together made him smile. They were not just employer, employee. They were friends. The knowledge warmed him. Ryan clearly loved the children as much as he did. Hell, she even got along with Lena.

Thoughts of Ryan were clouding his judgment. How could he open his heart to a woman when he knew how destructive it could be? Billie loved Lena. That love drove him to alcohol. Alcohol led to the death of his sister and the obliteration of his family. That was what forced him to turn to the street life. Lives changed all because a man loved a woman.

"Man, you still staring at that woman?" Tucker joked as he sat next to Al. "You and I both know you are in love with that woman."

Al thoughtfully looked at his friend. After hesitating a moment, he revealed his thoughts. "Billie loved Lena too. Look what it got us."

"Al, Ryan is not Lena and you damn sure are not Billie."

"The result is the same."

"Al."

"Not up for discussion. What brings you by?"

Tucker knew when Al shut down there was no getting through to him. He'd wait and try again later. "Monique."

"Did she get moved in okay?"

"Let's just say she is having fun decorating," Tucker laughed.

"With my money," Al laughed.

"You really need to put some type of limit on her."

"Have you ever been able to control Monique?" Al smirked at the look on Tucker's face. "That's what I thought." He hit Tucker on the leg. "Okay what are you trying hard not to tell me? What has she done?"

Tucker hesitated before he spoke. "She's seeing someone."

"Just one?" Al knew Tucker loved Monique and would protect her even from him. He was pretty sure that's what Tucker was doing now. "It can't be that bad."

Tucker smirked, "Yes it can."

"Did she go to the other side?"

"You mean women?" Al nodded. "Hell no," Tucker laughed. "There isn't a woman alive that can do anything for Monique. That girl loves...men." He stopped himself from saying what he was thinking.

Al laughed, "Nice catch. You remembered you were talking to her father."

"Well, you have a tendency to go a little crazy when it comes to Monique."

"And so do you. So, tell me what you know."

"Monique told you she has an internship. What she didn't tell you was that it's with Senator Jeremiah McClintock."

"A Republican?"

Tucker nodded, "Not just any Republican, he's the father of the man running against JD."

"Don't tell me she's sleeping with him."

"Okay I won't tell you that. I'll just tell you she's sleeping with the Governor himself."

Al jumped out of the chair. "She's sleeping with Jerry McClintock!" He looked at Tucker as if he had lost his mind. "The man running against JD?"

Tucker took a seat and stretched his legs out crossing them at the ankle. This was not going to be a pleasant conversation. "I do believe they are one and the same."

"Has she lost her damn mind! Does she have any idea what kind of damage this could cause the campaign?"

Tucker spoke in a voice meant to bring his friend down a level or two. It was rare to see Al lose it. The last time was when he had to tell him about the attack on Tracy. That night he was sure Al was going to break out of prison and kill every member of the Eagles gang. "Al."

"Al my ass! You can't save her this time, Tucker." Al stormed out of the office heading for his truck.

"Al, wait!" Tucker called out.

Tracy and Ryan were walking up to the building when she saw Al and then Tucker running after him. The anger on Turk's face was as clear as Tucker's need to stop him from getting into his vehicle. "Turk?" Tracy increased her speed. "What's wrong?"

"Nothing, Sugie," he replied as he opened the door to his vehicle. "I'll be back."

Tracy saw the concerned look on Tucker's face and knew instantly Monique was involved. "You're leaving me?"

Al stopped and turned to her. "Sugie, I have something I need to handle."

"I'll go with you," Concern filled Ryan's offer as she walked to the other side of the vehicle.

"No!" he snapped, narrowing those now angry grey eyes at her. "This is about family."

Angrily, Ryan threw her hands up in the air. "Excuse the hell out of me. Oh, I forgot you don't need anyone to have your back." She stormed off.

Al who was standing with the door open, slammed it then leaned against it. He didn't mean to snap at her like that.

"Al." Tucker interceded. "We don't know all the facts. I suggest we talk to her and see what's up."

"Talk to her." Al swung on him. "I'm going to beat the living crap out of her."

"Al you've never put your hands on her and you are not going to start now."

"Look," Tracy walked over to Al, "I don't know what's going on, but why don't you come up to the house. Have a glass of wine with me and we can talk." She leaned into him, "Please, Turk."

Al wanted to hit something, but kicked the tire instead. "Wow, now that was a manly thing to do. Did you break your toe?" Ryan smirked sarcastically from a few feet away. The look Al sent Ryan would have told a rational person to step back. But, Ryan was known to be a little less than rational at times.

Tracy reached over, put her arm into Ryan's and pulled her along. With Turk on one arm and Ryan on another, Tracy began walking. "I think we all can use a little cooling off."

Tucker and Magna looked at each other but didn't say anything. Both were thinking before the day was over Tracy may need protection from Al and Ryan. They turned and followed the trio to the house.

Once inside, Tracy prepared a glass of wine for everyone as they sat around the family room. "Okay, Turk, what's going on?"

Al sat down in the chair near the window. He took a long sip from his glass, trying to calm down. The walk to the house helped enough for him to at least be a little more rational. "Monique."

"What about Monique?"

"Monique has accepted an internship with a Senator in DC," Tucker began.

"Well, that's wonderful—isn't it?" Tracy looked around curiously.

"It would be if it wasn't in Senator Jeremiah McClintock's office," Al snarled.

Tracy sat up, "Governor McClintock's father?"

Al sat forward, sat the glass on the table and nodded, "The one and only."

"Whew." Tracy thought for a moment. "Maybe it's the only position she could get. Jobs are hard to come by in this economy, even for college graduates."

"Do you really believe that, Sugie?" He angrily replied. "You know Monique's history as well as anyone. This is another of her defiant moves. But for the life of me, I didn't see this one coming."

"Is it really that bad that she works in his office?"

Al stood and began pacing, "If it was any other Senator, I would say no, but this is the opposition."

"Turk, you know Monique is not really into politics." Tracy explained. "She probably thought this was a good opportunity, that's all."

"By sleeping with the man's son? She needs to find a better way!" Everyone was silent as they absorbed that bit of information.

"What did you expect?" Ryan asked a tad bit annoyed. "Monique has been doing things like this for years to try and get your attention."

All eyes turned to her. "What?" Al replied tensely.

"You heard what I said," Ryan shot back.

Tucker, Tracy and Magna all looked at each other, surprised at the tone of the conversation.

Al's eyes narrowed, as the eyes that were normally light brown turned a darker grey than before. "I heard you. I just don't recall anyone asking your opinion."

"Oh." Ryan put her hand to her chest. "I stepped out of bounds—again. I forgot I was supposed to speak only when the great Al "Turk" Day gave his permission." She said sweetly, then her tone changed. "Forgive me, all mighty one."

"What is your problem?" Al's voice rose a little more than he intended.

"I don't have a problem. You, on the other hand do. Walking around here wondering why Monique acts the way that she does, when all she wants is a little attention from her father."

"What in the hell are you talking about?" Al turned on her. "My daughter doesn't want for anything. I make sure of that."

"Really?" Ryan sat her glass down on the table and stood. "Who went to check out the condo you purchased for her? You? No, it was Tucker. Who arranged to meet with her and the realtor? You? No. That was Tucker, too." Tucker saw Al's jaw clench tight. That was a dangerous sign. He stood. "What about last year when Monique had a little trouble with the Dean, who went to check on her? You? Oh, no, that was Tucker, too. For a while I wondered whose daughter she was, yours or his. You know what they call fathers like you—deadbeat."

Al stormed towards her in three ominous steps. "What did you call me?"

"Oh, now you have a hearing problem again. I didn't stammer," she stood up to him. "You give her all the material things a girl could want. But all she really wants is your love and acceptance. So she gets into things that she thinks will get your attention. When one doesn't work, she tries another and another. And she thinks eventually you will give her just a little piece of your heart that you seem to give to others so freely." Standing toe to toe with him she could see the anger in his eyes, the jaws tightening and his eyes turning dark. Did any of that stop her—no. She kept going.

"You want to know why she jumps on every man that comes around, because it's what she sees you do. She imitates what she see!"

Al's voice was soft and as his eyes were lethal as he looked down at her. "I'm a little confused." He was standing so close to her; she could see the steam coming out of his nose. "Are you talking about Monique, or Morgan?" The tone of Al's voice caused a reaction from Tucker. He'd heard that tone before and knew the end result would not be good. "Daddy casted you aside, wasn't giving you enough attention at home. So you decided you had to prove you were just as much of a man as your brothers. Is that why you came to play with the street boys? There were no complaints about my lack of attention to my daughter while I provided a safe haven for you, was it!" He stepped closer, "Tell me, did you and your brothers compare notes on the women all of you pulled? Do you need a man to show you that you are indeed a woman?" She took a step back. "When you figure out who the hell you are, then you can tell me how to be a man." He saw the hurt reflected back in her eyes, but it needed to be said. "Are those tears I see forming in your eyes? What, you can't take the criticism—too damn bad!"

"Turk," Tracy jumped between the two to stop the discussion from escalating any further. Tucker reached in and pulled her back. She turned and frowned up at him and was a little taken back to see him grinning.

Ryan stepped back to Al with hands on her hips and speaking slowly punctuating each word she said, "I can take anything that you throw." She stepped closer and held her chin up higher, "When it comes to parents neither of us had a hell of a lot to brag about. I refused to be like my father. But you—you are more like your mother than you think."

The air in the room ceased to exist as everyone present held their breath. Tracy wasn't sure what to do. What happened next surprised the hell out of her and everyone else in the room.

Al looked down at the fire-eyed dragon woman standing in front of him. He wanted to knock the hell out of her, but he had never hit a woman. Not sure what his intent was, his hand wrapped around her throat and he jerked her to him. The next thing he knew, his lips were descending to hers. The first touch was rough, determined, meant to take command and control that sassy mouth of hers. Then suddenly a startling sense of oneness came over him. Her taste was as sweet as the strawberries fresh from the vine. Her tongue was strong, but easily surrendered to his will. It would be so easy to give in and let go, as the kiss turned sensuously scorching. That thought caused him to pull away. Staring down into her dark brown eyes he saw the same thing he was feeling—turmoil. What in the hell just happened? He dropped his hand and walked out of the room.

Ryan stood there, with her hands still on her hips in a haze. What in the hell just happened? She thought as she reached up and touched her lips that were still shivering.

No one moved or said a word. The expressions on their faces spoke volumes. Ryan looked around the room at the others. She didn't know if she should laugh or cry. But the old emotion of anger took over. "What? You never saw a man kiss a woman before?"

Magna's eyebrow rose as her lips curved into a smirk. "Not one that wanted to choke you at the same time."

"Well," a giggle escaped Tracy's lips. "If that don't beat all."

Tucker turned to leave. "I think I'm going to catch up with Al before he kills someone." He smirked at Ryan. "I'll see you ladies later."

"Chicken," Tracy teased. As he walked away she swore she heard him making a quacking sound. She turned to Ryan and caringly asked, "Are you okay?"

Ryan shot her a look that indicated she was treading on dangerous grounds. "Hell yes, I'm okay. Why wouldn't I be?" she yelled.

Magna, who knew that Ryan's bark was worse than her bite, in this case, laughed. "One reason could be the way that man just shut you up." She snapped her fingers. "Like that. Now what are you going to do?" Magna asked. "The door is open. Are you going to slither away like you've been doing or are you ready to accept why you get so angry at the man?"

The look on Ryan's face would have warned any sensible man or woman off—but not Magna. "You want your ass kicked today—don't you?" Ryan asked still reeling from the aftermath of the kiss.

"Look at you." Magna teased, "You can't even threaten me with any real force you are so seared by that man's kiss. Hell, now I know how to keep you in line. All I have to do is call Al over." She laughed.

Steam was now replacing the warmth from the kiss as Ryan stood there trying to come up with a remark that would shut Magna up. But nothing came forth. She turned in her signature spiked heel boots and stormed out of the room yelling, "I carry a gun and I will shoot you."

Magna stood, pushing her hair behind her ears. "Well, my job is done for the day. I must say, Tracy there is never a dull moment in your house—never."

Tracy stood in the room now alone wondering what in the world just happened. One minute they were talking about Monique and the next minute her brother was kissing her security guard. A smile touched her face. "I wonder what's going to happen next."

Chapter 10

Al stayed in his room at the house that night. Words from Ryan still vibrated through him. Was he a bad father to Monique? Has he allowed Tucker to take on the role he should be doing? He threw the comforter aside and stood. Walking over to the window he glazed out over the back lawn area. There was nothing he loved more than his child. Her mother, Kayla Perry, was street through and through, but damn if she wasn't hot. That girl would send him into over drive every time she walked by. Kayla was hard to resist. They burnt some sheets up back in the day. But Kayla's problem was she wanted that street life. But for Al, it was just a means to get what he needed. This was not going to be a way of life for him. So they had to part ways. He was surprised to find a few months later he was going to be a father. Kayla was a lot of things, but she wasn't a fool. She knew that having Al's child meant she would be financially secure and well protected. No one was going to do anything to Al's child or her mother. Unfortunately, Kayla wasn't ready to be a mother. The street was still calling her, but she wasn't giving up the hold on Al by giving him custody of Monique. Al played the father role until he learned Kayla had taught Monique the only thing he was good for was money in your pocket. That's how Monique treated him, like he was the bank. To some extend she still did, but unlike before, they had established one vital fact, her father loved her. She knew her father would kill anyone that hurt her and if not her father, definitely her Uncle Tucker.

Al opened the doors to the balcony and stepped outside. It was three a.m. in the morning and he hadn't closed his eyes. He sat in the lounge chair with nothing on but his shorts. Tucker crossed his mind. The man understood the difficulty he had with Monique and her mother. He would step in whenever things got a little out of hand. Tucker could always get Monique and Al under control before things escalated to a point of no return. For a while Tucker was the glue that kept them together. He hated to admit it, but it was possible Ryan had a point. Tucker was more of a father to Monique than he was. Maybe it was time to make some changes in his life. He walked into the room, picked up his cell and sent Tucker a message to meet him in an hour. He threw a few items into an overnight bag, took a shower then made his way to Tracy's room. He knocked lightly on the door. He wasn't surprised to find her awake.

He sat the bag beside the door before he walked inside. Tracy was sitting in the veranda of her bedroom reading. The skyline of downtown Richmond loomed in the background.

"Couldn't sleep?" he asked as he walked over and kissed her cheek.

"I can never sleep when Jeffrey is away." She closed her book and moved her legs over so he could sit. "Did you get any sleep before you decided to go see Monique?"

Al smiled, she could always read him. With his elbows rested on his thighs, he pushed the locs back from his face and sighed. "I need to talk to her. I need to make sure she knows I'm her father. That I'm proud of her and I love her. It's my job to make her feel secure, if she doesn't then I've failed. It could be she's doing these things because she is insecure." He turned to his sister. "If any of what Ryan said is true, I haven't done a good job with Monique."

Tracy sighed. "I think I may be a little responsible for that as well."

Al frowned. "Why?"

"Turk, you spent your life looking out for me. You have been my personal guardian angel. In the past you have forsaken others, including Monique to make sure I was safe. But you never neglected the child in any way. Ryan wasn't totally wrong, but she wasn't one hundred percent right either. Some of her feelings came into the conversation. You just happen to be on the receiving end of her anger because you hurt her feeling when you let that woman kiss you." His locs fell when he dropped his head. She pushed his locs back over his shoulders. "Ryan's in love with you and doesn't know how to handle those feelings." She smiled, "I suspect the same thing is happening with you."

Al shook his head, "I don't think I can do the love thing, Sugie. I mean, Billie loved Lena and you know how that turned out."

"That's their story and everyone can do the love thing. It can't be controlled. I tried for the very same reasons you are trying now. Our mother was not the best, hell, she was probably the worst, but she had four remarkable children."

"And we're good looking, too." He smiled.

"A little arrogant are we?" she smiled.

He stood, "I have to go. I'm asking Tucker to hang out here until I get back."

"Okay. You will be back in time for the party on Saturday—right?"

"Yes," He kissed her cheek. "I'll be back."

"Turk." He stopped and turned back to her. "What are you going to do about Ryan?"

"You mean besides wring her neck?" he shrugged his shoulders, "I'll have to deal with that when I get back."

Tracy nodded her head, "Be careful on the road."

"I'll call," he said as he closed the door. He picked up the bag and wondered what he was going to do about Ryan.

This could not be happening, Monique thought as she opened her eyes and looked at the clock. It was showing 6:15 a.m. The last time she looked at the device that she was beginning to despise it read 4:05 am. That was the time she finished her first field report and sent it through the secure email to her boss. Because she was a new recruit on her first assignment, it was imperative that contact was made at the designated times. If she went as much as fifteen minutes past that time, someone would be busting through her door. After the aggressive training program, Monique was intent on being not just successful, but also an elite operative for the Central Intelligence Agency, like her trainer.

When she was first approached, during her junior year at Howard, she thought the people that pulled her from class had lost their minds. But then they explained their reason for coming to her. Her analytical mind when it came to formulas was impressive and her ability to decipher codes was a skill that was desperately needed in the agency. But her ability to read or hear something once and repeat it verbatim made her a candidate they couldn't afford not to secure. Talking with Joshua Lassiter convinced her, this was the direction in which she wanted to go. However, it wasn't easy convincing the brass to bring her on board. With all her skills and abilities, they feared her family connections. The decision was made after a one-on-one interview with the

Director. He was so impressed with her understanding of the threat to America, foreign and domestic, that he not only approved the appointment, he assigned her to Joshua for training. His words were simple, "If you're going to do this, I need to ensure that you stay alive. I value my life."

She laughed, but understood his concerns. If her father ever found out what she was doing, he would probably have Uncle Tucker kill everyone that had had a hand in recruiting her.

There it was again. It sounded like a scuffle going on outside her door. But she lived in a secure building. Fights should not be happening in the hallway. She groaned as she crawled angrily out of bed. Not bothering to put a robe on over the boy shorts and tee shirt, she walked to the door and yanked it open ready to do battle.

"Who in the hell is this?" Her father stood in the hallway of her building with his hands around a man's throat holding him up against the wall with his feet dangling.

That woke her up. "Daddy? What are you doing?" She ran over and tried to pull him off the man.

"I want to know why this man is peeping under your door."

"I don't know, Daddy." She replied with her hands on her hips frowning. "But he is my neighbor, so let him go."

Al looked at the man whose face was red as a beet. "Why were you looking under my daughter's door?"

The man attempted to answer, but Al's grip was so tight he could barely breathe. "Daddy, the man can't answer you. His voice box is in his throat. Your hand is constricting the box."

The anger in Al's face was displayed purposely to the man. "Don't let me catch you near my daughter's door again." He released the man and he fell to the floor.

Monique bent down next to the man. She didn't know his name, but she had seen him in the building before. "Are you okay?"

The man crawled a few feet down the hallway. "I swear," he whispered while holding his throat, "I was just reaching for your paper. I swear that's all it was."

"Well get your own damn paper," Al stated as he turned and walked into the condo.

"I'm so sorry," Monique said to the man who was clearly too afraid to move. Walking back into the condo, Monique gave her father an angry glare as she walked back to her bedroom to get her robe. She wondered what he was doing outside of her door at six o'clock in the morning. Not looking where she was walking she hit her toe on the leg of the chair near her bedroom door as she was returning to the great room. "Ouch, damn it," she cried out.

"You should be careful walking in the dark."

"Really—you think!" Monique replied hopping around on one leg with the other foot in her hand.

He had to smile. It was good to see her. "Hey, baby girl. Having a rough morning?"

Monique put her foot down and frowned at him. "It's not morning. Most people are still asleep."

"You apparently have been on the internet." He looked around.

Monique smiled as she watched him surveying the place. "Do you like it? I'm still getting used to the furniture." She frowned, thinking about her toe.

Al nodded his head in approval, "Looks nice."

Eagerly, she took his hand. "Let me show you around." She wrapped her arms through his and pulled him along. "This of course is the great room. Look at this view." She pulled him over to the bay of windows that covered an entire wall. From the window you can see the White House and all its surrounding buildings.

"Nice view."

Then she took him through the rest of the house. When they returned to the kitchen she pulled out a box that had an assortment of teas. "Select your poison," she said as she turned on the stove and placed the teakettle on the eye. "What are you doing here and why are you harassing my neighbors?"

Al sat at the breakfast bar and stared at his daughter. She had her mother's coco brown skin tone, her silky wavy hair that Monique kept braided, but everything else was all him. Her light brown eyes, five-six sleek frame, and that room-brightening smile. He clearly understood why men wanted to be in her presence, but as a father, he just couldn't accept any man being good enough for her. She placed the cup in front of him and waited. "Your neighbor should stop being cheap and buy his own paper." He sighed, "I need to ask you something."

She turned to the kettle as it began to signal the water was about to boil. "Okay," she looked up at him as she poured the water into his cup. Noticing his hesitation, Monique put the kettle down and gave him her undivided attention. "What is it, Daddy?"

"Am I a deadbeat dad?"

Of all the things Monique expected to hear, that was not it. The question caught her off guard. She picked up the teakettle poured her water into the cup, then sat the kettle back on the stove. "No, daddy. You are not and never could be a deadbeat dad. You were not always there when I wanted you to be, but you were always there when I needed you—just like God."

Al laughed. "Baby, I'm not God."

"To me you are—always have been." She pushed her cup across the counter then walked around and sat next to him. "Where is this coming from?"

After sipping his tea, he blew a long steady breath out. "Someone said I've allowed Tucker to be your father figure. That at times I haven't been there for you."

She nodded her head, "That's a good assessment." She shrugged. "There were times I felt the only way I could get you to pay any attention to me was if I acted out. Really push you to your limits."

"Is that why you are sleeping with McClintock?"

"Whoa." She held up her hand. "That's crossing the line. You are my father, but who I decide to sleep with is my business. We have been through this already."

Al inhaled to keep his temper under control. This was not the first time they'd had a round or two about her sexual habits. "This one is different. This can have rippling effects if it were ever discovered." He calmly replied. "If this is one of your rebellious antics, to get my attention, you have it."

Monique sat her cup down and looked at her father. "I grew up, Daddy." She stood and walked into the bedroom.

Al followed her and leaned against the door jam. "Then explain to me why you are working for his father?"

Pulling her clothes from the walk-in closet to get dressed for work, Monique walked back into the room and laid her suit across the bed. "It's an internship, Daddy. I need the experience and you said I had to contribute to my living expenses, so the little pay I get help."

"Why McClintock? You know he is running against your uncle for the presidency. How do you think this will play in the media?"

"The economy is bad, and a sister needs a job. No one else offered a paid internship." She continued walking around.

He grabbed her arm as she went to walk by him again. "Monique, stop. Listen to me. I love you. You know that, don't you?"

Looking up at him, she smiled, "Of course I do."

"And you are sure you are not sleeping with the enemy to get my attention?"

She sat the shoes down she had just pulled from the closet then turned to her father. "Daddy, I'm going to say something and I want you to remember that you started this conversation."

Al folded his arms across his chest. "Hit me."

"All right you asked for it." She laughed at him. "Daddy, I am sleeping with Jerry because he is a damn good lay."

"Awe, man." Al threw his hands up in the air. "Did you have to go there?" Al turned from his daughter and walked out of the room.

Monique had to laugh. This happened every time he initiated these conversations with her about sex. "Look, Daddy," she followed him back to the kitchen. "I realize you showed me love the only way you knew how. By making sure I was provided for." She placed her hand on his thigh, "We are not the Cleavers from Leave It to Beaver family or the Walton's. We are the Day's. Remember, Lena Washington is my grandmother. If nothing else she taught me to be comfortable with my sexuality, because you didn't know how."

"Modeling your life after Lena isn't the best thing in the world, you know."

"No not all of it. But, Daddy, she was a female and was there to answer questions you couldn't. I'm glad she was there. At least I didn't have to grow up without someone to talk to about love, sex and men. Mommy always equated men with money. Lena, taught me they were very different things."

"Lena said that?"

"Yes. Her exact words, "Love without finance is a nuisance."

"Now, that sounds like Lena." He laughed.

"Yeah, but she also said real love is priceless. It's a good thing I had Aunt Tracy and Uncle JD around, too. While Lena gave me the practical, they gave me the ultimate. They showed me that real love is out there. You just have to recognize it when you see it. So I apply a little of Lena's theory and Tracy's and established my own."

Al leaned back in the chair and stretched out his legs. "Which is?"

She smiled and spoke softly. "Be patient. Wait for love and be wise enough to recognize it when it appears." When he smiled she put up a hand. "However, while I wait for that love to come around, I'm going to enjoy my life with no interference from my father." She kissed him on the cheek. "Now, I have to get ready for work. You, on the other hand look like you've been up all night. Why don't you crash in the guest room and I'll see if I can get free for lunch. You can take me to The Capitol Club restaurant," she smirked as she walked back to her room.

"Make the reservation." He grabbed his bag from near the door and noticed the security system. It was one of the most sophisticated systems on the market. He wondered how much that cost him.

Monique came out of the bathroom while brushing her teeth. She studied her father as he walked towards the guest room. "It was Ms. Ryan, wasn't it?" Al didn't reply he just kept walking. Pointing her toothbrush at him, she called out. "You don't have to say anything. I know you've been after that." She walked back into her bathroom and was surprised to see her father standing in the doorway.

"You do have the right to share your body with whomever you choose. As your father you need to know if I see you in danger, I will eliminate that danger, regardless of who it may be." Al turned and walked out of the room.

Monique looked around the bathroom and then her bedroom. "How in the hell did he get in here?"

Joshua tried to sleep on the plane, but something about the information he received continued to bother him. He reached for his suit jacket to retrieve the itinerary that was taken from the assassin. The fact that it was the current schedule of events produced that morning ate at him. He pulled out his cell again and dialed a number. Brian picked up on the second ring. "Thompson."

"Question. Who has access to the daily schedule?"

"What color is it?"

"Pink."

"Pink is senior staff. Why?"

"Send me yesterday's list of everyone that was with you."

"Why?"

"No answers at the moment. Send me the list."

"It's on the way to you now."

Joshua disconnected the call, then reached into another pocket of his jacket and pulled out a hand held computer. He turned it on, then connected to a friend through video conferencing. "Good morning. I need a favor."

"You muscle types always need something from us geeks." Ned Gerhardt was the typical dark curly-hair, eyeglass-wearing computer specialist, with one exception. He was the best in the world. In the IT underground world he was known as AZ meaning, he knew everything from A to Z. The honor was not in vain. When it came to weaponry technology, he was always on the cutting edge. "What is it this time?"

"I'm sending you a document. I need to know its origin."

"Continent, state, city, house, computer?"

"That and whose fingers prints are on the keyboard."

"Never a dull moment with you, Absolute." Ned nodded. "Document received. Give me twenty-four hours."

"You have twelve."

"You don't ask for much do you?" Ned smirked. "Hey, you tried the new suit out yet?"

"Have it on now."

"Have you tested it?" He anxiously asked.

"Hell no."

"What are you waiting for? I need to know if that material works."

"No one has taken a shot at me lately."

"You must be losing your touch. You've gone a day without being shot at."

"Give me twenty-four hours. I'm sure that will change. Any word from my trainee?"

"Routine report was received on time. A message came in. Her place is off limits for the moment."

"Did she indicate why?"

"Father's in town."

"Keep a close eye on her. Anything goes awry you contact me."

"On it." The connection ended.

Placing the computer back into the jacket, Joshua ran his hand over the material. The comfort and the weight of the full body armored suit were amazing. He was sure the suit worked, but he wasn't ready to put it to the test by allowing someone to shoot him. If no one attempted to kill him in the next twenty-four hours, he'd ask Samuel. With that settled Joshua stretched out in the seat and slept.

The command center was quiet when Ryan walked in. She took her position at the monitors and found all was quiet at the house. Tucker walked into the room. He handed her a cup of coffee and took a seat next to her. The two sat in silence for a moment allowing the hot liquid to prepare them for the conversation that was about to take place.

"I don't want to talk about it," Ryan advised, then took another drink.

"Cool. You can sit there and listen. Al and I are a lot alike when it comes to women. We have those we play around with and those that we admired from afar. But there is only one that we let get under our skin. There's always one that we can't control no matter how much we try. Julianna is that one for me. You—Morgan Ryan Williams are that one for Al. It's time for both of you to stop circling the wagon. I've given you the day off."

Ryan's head whipped around to him. "Why? Al's not here. There shouldn't be any issues."

"I'm giving you the day off because you have some prep work before your next assignment."

"Which is?"

Tucker stood and began to walk away. He wanted some distance between him and the woman that could probably break him in half. "Your mission, and there is no choice, you will complete this mission, is to get laid. Preferably by Al."

"I can't do that!"

"Can't or won't?"

Ryan shook her head and sighed. He was asking her to face her biggest fear. "I can't, Tucker."

"That's what I thought."

"You don't understand," Ryan walked over to stand in front of him. She put her hands on her hips. "Look," she dropped her head. "I don't um...I've never, you know," she looked up at him and exhaled as he looked expectantly at her. "I've never seduced a man before. I wouldn't even know where to start."

Tucker smiled inwardly. The tough Ryan had to admit to a weakness. One of the reasons he took her on when he worked the streets was because of the vulnerability he saw in her. Any other organization would have turned her out, simply because she was a cop's daughter. He couldn't let that happen. She was nineteen, trying to find her way. He pushed her face back up to him with a finger under her chin. "I know." He said like a protective big brother. "I've set everything up. Your first appointment is at eight."

"Appointment with whom?" She asked as he walked away.

"You'll see."

Chapter 11

Precisely at eight a.m., Magna met Tracy and Ashley at
the door of the command center. "Be easy on my girl,"
she said as she escorted them to the office. "You have
visitors," she said to Ryan.

Ryan turned to see the ladies smiling brightly at her.
"Good morning. Are you two my eight o'clock
appointment?"

"We are," Tracy replied smiling brightly, dressed in
a pair of jeans, cardigan top and dress sandals.

"Grab your purse." Ashley grinned, "We don't want
to be late."

Magna laughed at the expression on Ryan's face.

"I feel like this is the first visit from Marley in the
movie Scrooge." Ryan smirked as she stood. "I don't have a
purse. Where are we going anyway?"

"We're going to find Morgan," Ashley replied as she
walked over and pulled Ryan along. "Come on, let's go. I
love shopping."

Magna shook her head as the women climbed into
Ashley's SUV. "This is going to be interesting."

Fifteen minutes later, Ashley was pulling into the mile long driveway that led to Cynthia Lassiter's home. It was more like a hideaway secluded behind miles of trees on the front, and by the James River on the back. The doors to the mini ranch style mansion opened and Cynthia stepped out to greet them. The vehicle had barely stopped when she pulled the back door open and practically pulled Ryan out. "I have been waiting to get at you for years. I can't wait to get started."

"You seem just a little bit too anxious for this," Ryan said as they all walked inside.

"You're afraid of me?" Cynthia teased.

Ryan looked the five-four, hazel-eyed, petite woman up and down. Then replied, "I remember what you did to Carolyn Roberts the last time you were called to make her over. You're damn right I'm scared."

They all laughed as they walked into the kitchen. "Hey ladies," Roz Marable reached out giving each of them a hug.

"Hey Roz," Tracy and Ashley returned the hug.

"Is anyone else in on this?" Ryan asked as she hugged Roz.

"Girl," Cynthia laughed, "We called in a village to transform the train wreck you call Ryan into the sophisticated Morgan. And we're doing it because we love Al."

"Cynthia," Tracy scolded.

"So, all of this is for Al's sake?" Ryan asked raising an eyebrow.

"No," Tracy replied. "This is for you, too. God Ryan, we all owe you so much. You have protected my children and me for years. This is our way of giving back."

"Hey, I'm first in that line. You came to my aide when I didn't even know I needed you around." Cynthia said while eating a piece of fruit off the breakfast bar. "Giving you a little makeover is the least I could do."

"Is that food for all of us or just you?" Ashley asked as she sat at the bar.

"These are new items Marco and I added to the breakfast menu at the restaurant," Roz smiled. "We need to get feedback, and what better way than a girls spa day."

"Spa day?" Ryan questioned as she walked over to the sink to wash her hands.

"Oh, we didn't tell you," Ashley said as she wiped her hands dry. "This is your day."

"Actually two days," Tracy added as she washed her hands, and then took a plate. "Today is skin care, hair and makeup. Tomorrow is shopping at Ashley's."

"Yeah, then Saturday is reveal day," Roz grinned.

"You know," Ryan said as she bit into a quiche tart, "you all sound like one of those programs on TV. This is good." She pointed to the mini tart, "What is it?"

"That's a variation to our spinach quiche dish. Do you like it?" Roz smiled.

"It's like a small taste of heaven." Ryan reached for another.

'That's a great name for it," Roz pulled out her cell phone and made a note to herself.

Cynthia took the plate from Ryan and smacked her hand. "You have to be fitted tomorrow. No more for you." She then put the other tart in her mouth.

"Oh, but you can eat the hell out of them," Ryan replied.

"I already have a husband. A damn fine one at that," she smirked.

Ashley ate one, "Hmm, this is good." She took another and looked at Ryan, "I have a husband, too."

Tracy laughed. "You two should be ashamed of yourself. What time are we starting?" she asked Cynthia.

"They are downstairs waiting for us."

"Who's downstairs?" Ryan asked.

Cynthia smiled. "Well," she took Ryan's hand and pulled her along. "When I got the call to arms, I figured I would need some real professional help with you."

"Thanks," Ryan sarcastically replied as she followed Cynthia down the stairs and the other women followed.

When they reached the next level, they walked by the indoor pool, basketball court, game room and the home theater. Cynthia opened the door to the last room. It was a spa. "I called Blake's manager, Shannon P and she sent an entire crew of professionals from LA just for you."

The room was filled with five massage tables, three male and two female massage therapists. A stand containing a variety of oils and a man dressed in a linen shirt and matching pants with what Ryan would call flip-flops greeted them. "Good morning ladies. I am Raphael. My team is ready when you are."

The voice and the build of the man surprised them all. He glanced at Cynthia. "Which of these magnificent specimens is the guest of honor?" he asked.

"That would be me," Ryan replied as she extended her hand.

The ladies glanced at each other and smiled. "Ah, I can see you are unique. You have a style of your own." He placed her hand on his arm. "I'm going to handle you personally. We're not going to change a thing. We are simply going to enhance what you already have."

"He sounds like Kyle Barker from Living Single. Remember that show?" Tracy smiled.

"Please tell me he is not gay." Ashley grinned.

"Not in your wildest dreams," Raphael said over his shoulder, as he handed a robe to Ryan. "There is nothing that I love more than a female body." He nodded to his team. "Please prepare the other ladies."

Ryan turned to the women. "All of you are joining in?"

"There is no way in hell we would let you go through such a dramatic experience alone," Cynthia declared as one of the males approached her with a robe. "The two females are for Roz and Tracy," she pointed accordingly. "They are shy about their bodies."

Roz and Tracy looked at each other. "Who said that?" Roz asked.

Cynthia opened the door to the changing room. "Has any man other than JD every touched your body, Tracy?" Tracy shook her head no. Cynthia turned to Roz, "Roz?"

"JD's never touched my body, but I get your point."

"See I was just looking out for you two."

Ashley smiled at the man that approached her. "Good looking out, Cynthia."

An hour later, all of the ladies were sitting in lounge chairs out on the patio. Not one of them was able to move. Their bodies were limp and feeling good. If anything had jumped off Ryan would not have been able to protect anyone. "I think I just died and went to heaven," she said aloud to no one in particular.

"That was heaven," Ashley replied. "After running around the house with three kids, my body needed this."

Raphael appeared on the patio with two assistants. One had a tray of crystal flutes, while the other had treats from the kitchen. "Here's a little nourishment for your bodies ladies." He took the tray of drinks from the assistant. "Four glasses of champagne and one apple cider."

Everyone turned to Roz with a look of anticipation. "No, it's not me," she laughed as she pointed to Cynthia.

"Cynthia, you're working on the tribe called Lassiter?" Ashley smiled as she took her glass. Raphael and his team returned inside the house once everyone was served.

"Yes, number two is on the way," she took the apple cider.

"Congratulations." Tracy laughed. "Does Samuel know yet?"

"No. I'll tell him when he returns tomorrow."

"Have you started preparing Samantha?" Roz asked, "You know that child is spoiled. She is not going to like sharing her mommy and daddy with a little brother or sister."

"My baby is not spoiled."

"Yes she is," every person on the patio, replied.

They all laughed. "Well, she will figure it all out just like Jazzy had to," Tracy smiled.

"I never ran into that problem with the twins." Ashley stated. "They loved Tony from the start."

"Oh, I think Jazzy loves her brothers and sisters," Tracy said.

"She certainly has enough to love," Roz laughed.

"Ashley has four children just like I do. It's not like I have a house running over."

"Yes you do," Roz teased.

"I think we should send the extras over to her house," Ashley teased.

"Send them on. I would love to have a house filled with children." Roz replied.

Tracy and Ashley looked solemnly at each other. "I'm sorry, Roz," Tracy said. They all knew that Marco and Roz had been trying to have children unsuccessfully for the last five years. "I didn't think before I spoke."

Roz waved them off. "Nothing to be sorry for. Marco and I have decided to take in a foster child."

"That is wonderful Roz!" Tracy beamed.

"When are you going to start the process?" Ashley asked.

"We filled out the paperwork and are just waiting for approval."

"You'll get it with flying colors," Cynthia waved the conversation off. "Samuel and I returned our reference letter last week."

"I didn't get one," Ashley stated.

"Neither did I." Tracy added as she sat up and looked at Roz.

"What's up with that, Roz?" Ashley asked.

Cynthia looked over at Roz with an 'I told you so' look. Roz exhaled. "I didn't want to put down JD or James as reference. I didn't want the agency to think I was name dropping. You know what I mean?"

Ashley and Tracy looked at each other then back to Roz. "No." they both replied.

"It's a state agency we're going through. What type of response do you think they would have with the ex-Governor's or his campaign manager's name as a reference?

"A positive one," Ashley replied a little testily.

"I wanted us to be approved on our own merit. Not because we are friends with JD."

The tension on the patio grew a little thick as silence built. Suddenly a noise came from Ryan's direction. "Is she snoring?" Cynthia frowned.

They listened. "I believe she is," Ashley began to laugh.

"By all means let her sleep." Tracy smiled, "She's going to need it when Turk returns."

"I hope he's getting some rest," Ashley sat back in her chair. "Once they get started, it will be days before they come up for air."

"Weeks," Cynthia added. "She has at least a five year backup."

Roz laughed. "Tracy I hope you have a replacement in mind for her. The way Al's been watching her, we may not see her for months."

They all started laughing. Ryan suddenly sat up and looked around. "What?" she groggily asked. The ladies looked at her and laughed harder.

Saturday morning, Ryan was at Ashley's house at nine o'clock a.m. as instructed. She had to admit, she'd had the best sleep of her life last night. Raphael had magic hands, she was sure of it. And it definitely did not hurt that the man reminded her of Al. Thinking about him still hurt. She was wrong to say the things she did to him. Anger was her fall back emotion. Whenever someone got a little too close, she would lash out and push them back. The problem for her was the man was already ingrained in her soul. Her fear was no longer keeping him away; it was now how to get him closer. The ladies, that made her feel like one of them, were all successful in getting that one special man in their lives. If she had to suffer through shopping malls filled to capacity with hormone-raging teenagers, she would do it, just to have a chance with Al.

"Hello, you must be Ryan."

With an eyebrow raised, Ryan looked at the woman and knew she was familiar she just couldn't put her finger on it. "I am," she said slowly.

The woman laughed. "I'm Ashley's sister-in-law, Nicole Brooks. I've heard so much about you." She stepped to the side, "Come on in. We've been waiting for you."

"Okay," Ryan said as she walked in.

"Ryan," Ashley called out from the stairs. "I see the hair is still working," she said as she walked around the woman. "You must have brushed it into a wrap and put on a silk scarf." She stopped in front of Ryan with hands on hips, nodding her head. "Looking good."

"She's a little taller than what I thought," Nicki said thoughtfully.

"It's the heels." Ashley explained. "Come Ryan, everyone's downstairs."

Ryan hesitated, "I thought we were going shopping."

Ashley and Nicki looked at each other. "You mean like go to the mall or something?" Nicki asked.

"Yeah," Ryan replied.

A huge grin appeared on Ashley's face as she took Ryan by the arm. "That running from store to store is for the screaming teenagers. I can't deal."

"It's not my thing either." Nicki added. "I like when the stores come to me," she said as they walked down the stairs into Ashley's ballroom.

Ashley pushed the doors open. The ballroom did not look anything like the last time Ryan had been there. This room was filled from corner to corner with racks and racks of clothes, shoes, handbags, lingerie; you name it and it was in that room.

Lena walked from behind one of the makeshift dressing room curtains in a skimpy two-piece teddy set. The woman's body was toned for a sixty-year-old.

"I see why John had to retire." Gwen said, "He had to keep up with you."

"I do look good, don't I," Lena pranced in front of the mirror.

"Mother, I think you need to put on some clothes."

"Girl at my age, you don't hide something like this."

"Ladies, need I remind you that this shopping spree is for Ryan," Ashley said as she pushed Ryan forward.

"That's right," Nicki added. "I brought these people in from New York to get a sister hooked up. So she gets first rights to any and everything." She turned to Ryan. "I suggest you decide on a gown first, then the lingerie, jewelry, and shoes." She turned back to the women in the room. "Once Ryan has her choices down, then and only then can the rest of you shop until you drop."

"Ryan the rules of this game are simple," Ashley stated, "Each person has picked out a gown for you to try on and we will each vote on our favorite. As you can see there is a camera and a cameraman, say hello to Jay."

"Hello," a rich deep voice sounded from above.

"Whoa, he sounds delicious," Lena laughed.

"He will video stream each outfit to the men in the other room. They will vote on which gown they believe will knock Al to his knees."

The women in the room all nodded their heads confirming the process. "Oh, here's the best part. Everything that you select, including the jewelry is on the house."

Ryan looked at the racks of clothes. "This is just for tonight, right?"

"Well," Tracy stood, "We thought you might as well get a few other things for the future."

"Yeah," Lena added. "For example, this little number would wreck Al's mind on Sunday morning before going to church."

"Ain't nobody going to church if she's wearing that," Martha laughed.

"I know that's right," Roz joined in.

"Alright," Nicki chimed in, "Let's get started. "She grabbed Ryan's hand. "Allow me to introduce, Shanti, Carrie and Danielle. They are personal shoppers from different boutiques in New York. Your wish is their command."

Ryan felt a little overwhelmed, as she looked around at all the items. Black pants or jeans, white dress shirts or tees, and her selection of boots were her wardrobe. She had no idea where to start with gowns or dresses or lingerie. Ashley sensed her hesitation. "I always start with the basic black dress," she whispered as she pulled a dress from the rack and gave it to one of the girls. "She'll start with that."

An hour later Ryan had finished shopping and was worn out. It was four hours later before the other women were finished. Ryan was surprised when Ashley loaded up her truck with all the purchases made by the other women. "My apartment can't hold all this stuff."

Ashley waved her comment away. "Don't worry about it. Al's closet is larger than my ballroom."

Everyone had returned to the estate, with the exception of Joshua. From what he was told Joshua was tracking down a viable lead on the contract. Having Brian back in place was a welcome relief for Al. After spending a few days with Monique he was still not clear on how to approach things with Ryan. The sensation from the kiss they shared still lingered on his lips. They only reason he stayed in DC as long as he did was to try and get the feeling of longing out of his system. But that wasn't working.

At home sitting on his patio thinking about her wasn't helping matters much either. The fear of letting this woman take a piece of his heart consumed him. Now, he realized the fear of not letting her in was stronger. His cell phone rang. He recognized the number and stood. Walking through the kitchen he stopped, looked at a picture of Tracy's family, and walked inside as the doors slid open. He waited until the doors closed, then answered the call.

"Yeah."

"I'm sending you some still shots." Joshua said into the phone. "We need to know if you recognize any of them." The monitors were displaying an array of snap shots of men flashing across the screen. "We've traced through three layers of contacts, however, I still don't think we're at the top."

"I'm looking through them as you speak. Nothing so far," Al replied as he continued to look at the monitor. "Did my package arrive?"

"Whew, man I like the way you send a message. You know she wants me—right?"

Al smiled, "Melissa Sue will hurt you, man. I'm just warning you." Al stopped at one of the pictures and frowned. He enlarged the picture of the man to ensure he was right. "Where are you?"

"Still in Mexico."

"Shit," Al hissed as the hard copy of the picture printed out,

"We have a problem?"

"I'm not sure. Tread lightly."

"I always do." Joshua replied as he disconnected the call.

Al sat back wondering if Mateo was playing him or was there dissension in the Cartel as he stared into the face of Miguel Santiago. Mateo indicated he did not accept the contract. If that was the case, why was Miguel in this photo? Either way, Joshua was in dangerous territory. Al called Tucker. "I think we may have an issue with the Cartel."

"Ms. Day," Anna called from the hallway door of Senator McClintock's office. Monique stood with her head down reading a letter from a constituent and walked towards the woman. She looked up from the letter. "Yes?"

"The Senator left the notes on the Crenshaw Bill on his desk. Get them and meet us in the chamber."

"Will do." Monique walked back into the closet they called an office to put the letter down. She hurried to the Senator's office and almost ran into a woman walking out. "Oh my goodness, I'm sorry. I didn't see you there."

"Not a problem." The woman rushed off.

Monique continued looking back at the woman. Something about her was familiar. She dismissed it and walked into the office. There were several piles of paper on his desk. She was scanning through them looking for the bill, when she saw a document with JD Harrison at the top. She pulled it out and quickly realized it was his daily itinerary. She looked at the date. It was today's date. Then, something else caught her eye. It was marked, "Not for public distribution." Careful to place it exactly as she found it, Monique continued looking for the bill. Once she found it, she ran it over to the Chamber.

The security system in the mansion was a little more sophisticated than Joshua had anticipated, but not enough to keep him out. The office he invaded was nice, a little too conservative for his taste, but nice. Hell, he didn't plan on spending a lot of time there, he thought as he took a seat. According to his estimation, someone should be coming through the door right about now.

The double doors swung open. The blast hit him dead center in his chest.

Joshua looked down. "Damn, it works." The momentary surprise to the man that fired the weapon was enough time for Joshua to react. He quickly disarmed the man, knocking him to the floor unconscious then retrieved the weapon, broke it down into pieces and dropped them to the floor. "Ouch," he finally felt the impact of the bullet that was now lodged in the suit jacket.

Mateo stood in the doorway watching the action. "Raul's wife is going to be very upset with you for injuring her husband."

With a scowl on his face Joshua turned to Mateo. "Well she should teach him how to be hospitable when visitors drop in."

Mateo walked over to his desk and took a seat. "Most visitors use the front door."

"I'm not your average visitor." He reached inside his jacket and pulled out a small envelope, then placed it on the desk.

Keeping his eye on the dangerous stranger, Mateo reached for the envelope, opened it and placed the contents on the desk. He smiled. "So, you are Absolute." He pulled out his wallet and retrieved the connecting card. Placing it on the desk he matched the severed Ace of Spades to ensure the pieces fit together. Satisfied, he looked up at Joshua. "Tell me," he said coolly as he replaced his card back inside his wallet and the other inside the envelope. "Is someone digging my grave or Al's?"

Joshua pulled out his handheld computer. "Depends." He turned the monitor to Mateo. "Do you know this man?" Joshua saw the flicker of recognition before Mateo could conceal it.

Keeping his cool on the outside, Mateo was reeling internally. But until he had more facts he would not believe Miguel had defied him. "What proof do you have that this man is now my enemy?"

Joshua displayed another picture showing Miguel and another man. "My sources say this man was hired to assassinate JD Harrison." He then pointed to Miguel, "They also say this is the man that gave the order." Joshua closed the computer. "This man works for you. That makes me believe you gave the order. Did you?"

"No."

"Do you know who did?"

Mateo returned the envelope to Joshua. "Give Al my gratitude for sharing the information. We'll take it from here."

Joshua took the envelope and replaced it in his pocket. "My job is simple—eliminate threats to the United States of America. I'm very good at it. Either you give me this man or I'll consider you a part of the threat."

"I will handle my family. The other man is a German national. He goes by the name Rabbit."

Satisfied for the time being, Joshua nodded. "That will do for now. But if I can't locate him, I will be back."

Mateo smiled, "You're a cocky son of a bitch."

"Thank you." Joshua smiled.

"Question," Mateo said as Joshua turned to leave. "My man shot you dead center. Any other man would be dead."

"And your question would be?"

"Why in the hell aren't you dead?"

"I'm not your average man."

Mateo laughed and turned to walk back to his desk. "I can see..." the reply trailed off as he looked around the office and found himself alone.

Joshua made it to the woods outside Mateo's compound out of pure determination, but there was no way he was going to make it back to the chopper and Melissa Sue. He pushed a button on his jacket to indicate he was in trouble just before his knees buckled. The sound of guns pointing at him clicked just as he lost consciousness.

TNT Event Planners had outdone themselves. The basement to Tracy's home looked as if it was a ballroom in a luxury hotel. It was exactly what she wanted. No, she was not entertaining a prince, senators or congressmen. This black tie affair was strictly for those men and women who had spent the last ten years of their lives protecting them. JD and Tracy wanted to take this night to thank each of them for being such an important part of their lives. Since this seemed to be the last time she would really have any down time, Tracy decided to invite the employees who made up the executive branch of her company, Next Level. JD invited his campaign staff to show his appreciation for their long hours and dedication.

"Let's go people," Cynthia shouted as she entered the main level of the house.

JD and Tracy were at the entrance for they intended to greet every person that walked through the door. "We're right here, Cynthia. There is no reason to yell." JD stated.

"I need to be heard and know that my commands are being followed," she said as a few waiters lingered in the foyer of the house. "Downstairs people—downstairs." She clapped her hands.

Tracy took JD's hand and whispered. "Be nice. She's pregnant and everything that does not go her way gets on her nerves."

"Well, I didn't impregnate her and I'll be damned if I'm going to be yelled at all night."

Tracy put his hand around her waist. "Did I tell you how good you look in that tuxedo, Mr. Harrison?"

JD smiled down at his wife, "Not half as good as you do. You are wearing the hell out of that gown." He twirled her around, and then pulled her back into his arms.

"You like?"

He kissed her temple, "I do."

"Would you two cut that out please?" Cynthia frowned as she reached to open the double doors.

"Okay, prego." JD smiled.

Cynthia turned to Tracy and frowned. "Traitor."

The couple stood at the door and greeted everyone for at least thirty minutes. They followed Cynthia's instructions and waited to be introduced before entering the room filled with their special guests. "These are friends and family." JD complained to Tracy as they stood behind the closed doors. "Why do we need to be introduced?"

"Jeffrey, there is a reason we hire Cynthia to handle these things. Now stop complaining and just follow."

"She's getting on your nerves too, isn't she?"

"Immensely," Tracy smiled.

"As soon as we are seated, I'm going to have a few words with Samuel. I know he can get her under control."

Tracy reached up and kissed him, "Thank you, baby. Thank you."

JD smiled at his wife just as the doors were opened. The people in the room applauded as the couple walked to the table in the front of the room. Once there, Cynthia handed JD a microphone. "Good evening everyone. Since this was shoved in my hand, I take it I'm supposed to say a few words. But I have a better idea. There's food, drinks, and a room filled with beautiful people. Cynthia," JD called out. "I believe it is time to party—music please."

Before the words were out of his mouth Candy by Cameo boomed through the speakers. Everyone jumped to their feet and made their way to the dance floor. Anyone that really knew this couple knew how much both of them loved to dance. The fact that they were in black formal wear did not affect the intensity of party time for them. Next up, the DJ mixed smoothly into the Electric Slide, and the Cupid Shuffle. To take it down a notch before people began to drop, the DJ followed up with Before I Let Go, then Joy and Pain by Frankie Beverly and Maze.

Within a matter of minutes the party was in full swing. After a few dances, Tracy and JD left the floor and began to mingle. Tracy met up with Ashley and Cynthia near the entrance. "Everything is really great, Cynthia." Tracy huffed as she tried to cool down from dancing. "Thank you for pulling this together."

"It's what I do," Cynthia replied. "But in all honesty, it really is nice to see everyone together, even Gavin and Carolyn."

Tracy and Ashley looked at each other, surprised at Cynthia's comment. "You're happy to see Carolyn?" Ashley had to ask.

"Don't be silly. I still don't like that heifer. But it's kind of nice to see Gavin happy."

"Okay, that's better," Ashley smiled as Roz walked over. "You've finished in the kitchen?"

"Actually, we turned everything over to the trainees." Roz replied as she looked around the room. "We'll evaluate their performance tomorrow." She continued looking around the room.

"We're looking at a location in Northern Virginia." Cynthia added. "The manager of that location will be selected based on tonight's function."

"That is wonderful Cynthia." Tracy beamed. "TNT is growing."

"Yes it is. However, we are going to need your support once you move into the White House. We expect a lot of business from you."

Tracy's smile seemed surreal. "I guess now is as good of time as any to tell you this." All eyes turned to her.

"What?" Ashley asked.

"Jeffrey received a call from Stanley Davenport. According to the polls he is double digits ahead of his opponents."

"Oh my goodness," Roz declared. "It is really going to happen."

Cynthia put her hands on her hips and smiled up at Tracy, "Damn right it's going to happen."

"Oh Tracy," tears formed in Ashley's eyes. "You're going to be the first lady of the United States."

"We still have months to go. And according to Jeffrey it will not be easy."

"Nonsense," Cynthia smacked Tracy's hand. "You might as well get ready. Come next January we will be partying at the White House."

"You don't party at the White House," Roz responded, as she began looking around the room again. "You have functions."

"Same difference," Cynthia snidely replied. "And who in the hell are you looking for?"

"Ryan. Have you guys seen her?"

All of them began looking around, "As a matter of fact I haven't." Cynthia replied. "Hell after all the work we put into that girl over the last two days, her ass better show up."

"You know, you are going to have to clean up your vocabulary when we move to DC." Roz said as she continued looking for Ryan.

"Why? The people in DC curse like sailors."

"WOW!" Tracy exclaimed. "She just walked in the door."

Al had his back to the door while talking with Lena and Senator Roth, when Lena suddenly changed the subject. "You know, I usually stay out of your business son. But..."

"That means she is about to get into your business," Senator Roth chuckled as he took a drink.

"Thanks for the support, Bottles and James," Lena smirked.

"No. Lena knows better," Al replied as he stared at his mother. They were doing better at the talking thing, but his days of needing a mother were long gone.

"Alright, I won't say anything. But your woman just walked in the door and was immediately surrounded by a number of rather good looking young brothers. How old are you now, Al?"

Al turned to the door to see Ryan surrounded by several men. Exactly who they were never came into focus as his eyes were on the dress that was clinging to her body. He was used to seeing her in skintight jeans and knew she was curvy. But the dress she was wearing tonight revealed just how well endowed she was. The sleeveless, Chinese collared black gown fit over her body like a glove. There was an opening from the bottom of her breasts, until it reached the top of her hips; it showed the curve of her small waist. The Commodores line from the song, Brick House, 36-24-36, what a winning hand, was the only way to describe the woman.

"Son, I don't mean to get into your business either," Senator Roth chuckled, "But if you have any plans on getting that you better make a move."

Al turned to look at the Senator, somewhat conflicted. Then he turned back to see Ryan walking onto the dance floor with a man.

For an hour Al literally stood in a corner and watched Ryan dance with one man after another in that dress. Every time she did a dip or swing, he could feel himself groan in pain as his manhood strained against its zipper.

"I've been watching you watching her and frankly I can't take it anymore," JD stood behind Al and pushed him on the shoulder. "The time is now, Al. Go get your woman."

Al reached back, practically throwing his drink into JD's hand. "It's time." He stormed across the room onto the dance floor, grabbed Ryan by the hand and practically dragged her off the floor, and through the French doors leading to the backyard. A few people stopped and stared at the commotion, as Brian yelled out, "It's about damn time." The crowd clapped and continued dancing.

Chapter 12

Literally pulling her behind him, he could hear her protesting. "This is not prehistoric times. You don't drag me around like a damn caveman."

Ignoring her protests he continued his determined pace to find a secluded area, as his mind came to terms with his actions. The mild mannered Al had just lost all his cool points in front of a roomful of people. Why did the mere sight of her invoke an increase in his heart rate? Why now, after years of securing his heart from all women with the exception of Tracy, did this woman make him want to throw caution to the wind? Just a few steps away and his respiratory system was wreaking havoc on his body. He could feel the sweat beads forming on his forehead as the gazebo in Tracy's backyard came into view. In the past he had watched this woman in her jeans and spiked heels, with her gun strapped to her waist, day after day. But nothing had prepared him for the vision that stepped into that room tonight.

Pulling her up the steps, he released her hand. She pushed him away. Chest heaving, eyes narrowing, he walked in a circle in an attempt to ease his temper. Why in the hell was he so mad at her? Jealousy. He frowned at the word that came to mind. Al Day doesn't get jealous. He could have any woman he wanted at any time. He stood there and just stared at her, with her hands on her hips ready to beat the crap out of him.

There was barely a step between them and damn if he didn't like her boldness. Staring into her dark seductive eyes, Al tilted his head slightly to the side and gave her a half smile. "I don't intimidate you at all, do I?"

"Should I be?" She asked shifting the balance of her stance to one hip and folding her arms.

"Some believe me to be an unrepentantly powerful man."

"Yeah, well Al you may be a powerful man, but it kills you every time you have to step on a bug. You can save the unrepentant," she put up quotation marks with her hands, "for somebody that's going to buy it. I see something different."

Al prevented the smile that was itching to appear on his face. Damn if she wasn't the sassiest woman he had ever met. Then it hit him. She reminded him of a young Lena. Keeping his thoughts from his face, he took a step back. He wasn't sure he wanted to lose his heart to a woman like his mother. "Don't fool yourself Morgan, I will kill if threatened."

"What are you going to do? Shoot me because I make you feel?" Ryan bent over, pulled up the front of her gown and pulled her revolver from the strap around her thigh. "Here, use my weapon." She shoved the gun towards him, as she stared him in the eyes.

Al laughed, jerked her hand and pulled her closer to him. With their lips a breath apart he whispered as a single brow rose, "Don't tempt me." He watched the play of emotions on her face as her chin raised and she met his eyes.

"Don't call me Morgan," she breathlessly responded.

He ran a finger down her cheekbone, not surprised by the silky feel of her skin. "I like the name Morgan." He mumbled against her lips as he slowly took the weapon from her hand. "Morgan is a very sensuous name." He gently kissed her lips. "Almost as sensuous as the woman it belongs to." He ran his tongue across her bottom lip then took it between his and suckled until he heard her moan. He smiled against her lips, "You like that." It was a statement more than a question. "Good, I like it too. But I want more." They held each other's eyes as the tension surrounding them steadily built. He watched her eyes narrow and felt her body shiver. She was hesitating. "Before you decide, know I play for keeps. There is no turning back." He pulled her body flush with his. "Can you give me more, Morgan?"

Ryan wasn't sure in what direction to go. Her heart and body were clearly betraying her mind. The steel of her weapon in his hand flush against her back was as hard as his manhood, which was positioned at the very core of her. She wasn't sure which turned her on the most. The way they stood, at that moment, had been her mind's nightly companion for years now. And she expected it to remain that way. However, there was something in his light brown eyes that screamed sincerity, loyalty, and the wildest sexual experience of her life. How in the hell could she walk away from that? She wrapped her arms around his neck, then took his lip between hers and returned the sensual assault he had graced her with moments earlier. "I got more," she murmured then released his lips. "But I don't share and I don't play nice with others."

Momentarily engrossed in the feel of her lips assaulting his, Al simply moaned his response before taking full control of the kiss. His tongue liked the cranberry taste of her lips, but now he longed for the mango flavor of her tongue. Slowly, he began stroking his tongue with hers, taking his time, tasting every bud, every crevice, every juncture of her mouth. He left no corner of her mouth untouched with his oral assault. Without breaking contact, he placed the weapon in the small of his back and gathered her more snuggly around her waist. Then his hands followed the same leisurely assault of her body as his tongue continued to tango with hers.

The July heat was nothing compared to the temperature rising in the gazebo. It was becoming dangerously hot, and there wasn't a damn thing either of them could or wanted to do to reduce the heat. When her fingers entwined with his locs, his senses soared and nothing or no one could pull him away from that moment. His male grunts and moans of pleasure broke the silence of the quiet night as he pulled the bottom of her gown up to her waist, feeling the silkiness of her thighs against his fingers. The heat soared as his hands captured the globes of her soft naked behind. That blew his mind. There was not a string or barrier between her sex and him, except his own clothes. He lifted her by the waist, braced her body against the pole and held her in place while he released his belt, unzipped his pants and allowed them to fall to the ground. Her legs tightened around his waist as he entered her with one powerful thrust. The air they were breathing became one as they both sucked in at the touch, the feel of the moment. Life ceased to exist as their lips stopped moving, their eyes wide open, staring, amazed at each other. Holding her stare he lifted her by the waist from his sex until only the tip of him remained. He thrust into her again. "Ah." They both closed their eyes as the feeling of sheer ecstasy built.

This was five years of longing, wanting, wondering, and fearing. Both fought a good fight, but now they'd surrendered. And there was absolutely nothing either of them could do but ride with the tide. This was not going to be a sweet first love excursion. This was a joy ride of the highest magnitude and they were both ready as Al slammed into her again, savoring the feel of her surrounding him. Each thrust was more powerful than the last. The more Ryan pulled on his locs, the harder and deeper he went. When she bit into his neck, sucking on the vein that throbbed with each thrust, his control vanished and all he wanted—needed was to hear her scream his name. He plunged deeper, holding her as if his very life depended on her pleasure. "Free me, Morgan. Take all of me," he whispered in her ear.

Her body shivered at his words. The pure power of him inflamed the desire she had carefully suppressed for five years. There was no defense against the yearning building within her. No mechanism to stop the inferno that was now raging with each thrust. All she could do was throw caution to the wind and ride. She squeezed her inner muscles to feel the steel of the man. God, he was so hard, so smooth and so damn hot. She wanted every inch of him deeper inside of her. She crossed her legs behind him and threw her head back, arching her body. Holding on to his arms, her body leaned across the banister. Al couldn't hold back a second longer. He pulled her waist to him with a force so strong he heard the banister crack as they both screamed out their release that was five years in the making. His juices flowed, mixing with hers as they were both suspended in time.

He pulled her body up to him and held her tight. Her breasts to his chest, heaving until the sensations eased within them. He slowly lifted her from him and placed her on her feet. They both moaned at the loss of the connection. Holding her with one arm around her waist, he lowered her dress and brushed it down neatly. "Where are your panties?" he asked.

"I didn't wear any."

Those light brown eyes were as dark as grey coal as he stared at her.

Her boldness was making him hard as a rock—again. He reached down and picked up his pants and the gun that had fallen to the ground.

"Where are your panties?" she asked with a raised eyebrow.

"I don't like being confined," he replied as he zipped his pants.

"I don't either."

"You're a woman."

She smiled. "Yes, I know."

He stood and stared at her with his crooked smile. "Damn," he said as he took her hand and practically dragged her down the steps, across the yard into the pool house, kicking off his shoes as they entered. Closing the door behind him, he pulled the dress over her head and threw it across the room. His suit, shirt and tie soon followed.

"You've got to stop with the caveman action." She pulled off her sandals and threw them across the room as he pulled her into the walkthrough shower. Al hit the cold water button and six powerful showerheads rained down on them.

Pushing her back against the shower wall, he allowed the cold water to hit his back, hoping it would diminish some of the heat emanating from his body. But in his mind, he knew it was hopeless. He held her hands above her head and stared into her eyes. "I want you, Morgan, to be my woman."

The intensity of his stare, seeing his eyes change from dark to light brown again caused Ryan to inhale. He must have sensed her fear of the moment for he pulled slightly away and stared at her. He cupped his large hands, with the long fingers around her face, making her a hostage to his eyes.

That's when she saw it—the vulnerability. He was just as afraid as she was. The irony astounded her, but it aroused her as well. He rubbed his thumb across her lips as if to ensure they would stay in place. She took his thumb into her mouth, as she held his glaze. She could feel his manhood growing against her thigh. His eyes narrowed at the touch and it was in that moment, Ryan knew this man would love her like no other dared. No one could or would ever, pull her away. "I'm yours," she whispered.

The kiss that followed began as sweet as a gentle rain that could barely be heard on the inside but it soon grew into a raging storm. Al's lips and hands were everywhere, leaving burning sensations with each touch. He knelt at her feet, and his hands slowly ascended up her calves, then her thighs. He reached under her, squeezing the round meat of her buttocks. Each squeeze caused her inner lips to release more moisture as freely as if it were a waterfall. Slowly, he kissed her inner thigh. Before she could grasp the action, his mouth gulped her feminine center and was drinking as if he were a man dying of thirst. The sensations shot throughout her body demanding more, deeper, powerful strokes of his tongue. Her hands reached for his head, holding it in place at the same time praying the onslaught would not stop. Her prayer was answered a split second later when his tongue hit a spot that caused her body to jerk repeatedly, losing all control.

Al's smile was one of pure male satisfaction when he emerged from between her legs. The look on Ryan's face was one of unbelievable pleasure. He pulled her fingers from his hair and raised them above her head. "Tell me what you want, Morgan," he whispered as he captured one of her nipples between his lips.

"You."

"Where?" he switched to the other.

Still reeling from the wondrous feeling his mouth had given her; she still hadn't regained control of her body. She licked her lips, then slowly opened her eyes. "Everywhere."

The heated look tore through Al, sending his blood to a boiling point. As if guided by radar, he entered her slowly. His body knew exactly where it needed to be. Hesitant, he closed his eyes and allowed his forehead to rest against hers. He knew, this was going to be his last first time with any woman. "There's no turning back," he barely mumbled before filling her completely. The second time around was more amazing than the first. It could be because he was taking it slow, savoring the feel of every glorious inch of her inner body.

They both moaned, "Ahhh...", then paused to savor the moment.

He waited, but once she tightened her thighs around his waist to pull him deeper, he lost all sense of decorum. Pulling out to the tip, he surged back into her. The warmth of her inner muscles heated his manhood like a cashmere blanket, and it was just as smooth. Each withdrawal and reemergence warmed his blood and stole a piece of his heart. Her inner muscles squeezed and pulled until he had no choice but to burst, just like the tea kettle cap would release its steam. His head shot up as he howled just like a wolf that had just captured his prey.

After they showered, he took a fluffy towel from the rack and began to dry her off. His touch was just as arousing as his tongue. He gathered her into his arms as they cuddled together on the bed in the bedroom of the pool house. He wasn't prepared for the protective instinct that engulfed him when her head touched his chest. From this moment on, he would live his life to protect, love and cherish this woman that gave him the feeling of finally being home.

Ryan had never been so content, she thought as she wrapped her arms around Al. This man, some called ruthless, her family called a thug, made her feel secure, loved, and for the first time in her life, happy to be a woman. From this moment on, she would protect him and his heart

with her life. She closed her eyes, sighed and fell peacefully
asleep.

An hour later, a movement or a sound, awakened
Ryan. She slowly reached over and pulled her weapon from
the nightstand where Al had placed it. She swung around
quickly with the weapon drawn and ready to fire.

Al quickly reached out and lowered her arms, taking
the weapon and securing it. "Turn your head man," he said
to Tucker as he stepped inside the room. Tucker did as he
was told as Al placed the weapon back on the table then
covered her with the bedspread. "What's up?"

Tucker turned back around. A grin as wide as the
state of Texas was on his face. "So," he said as he took a seat
across from them then crossed one foot over a knee, "you
two finally scratched that itch. It's about time. You two were
driving me and everyone around you crazy."

Ryan looked over her shoulder at Al. "If you had
allowed me to shoot him, we wouldn't have to listen to this."

Al kissed the back of her neck. "I take it you have a
purpose for this visit." He said to Tucker.

Sitting forward, Tucker's smiled faded. "Intel just
came in. We have a situation in Mexico."

Al sat up. "Don't coat it."

"Someone took exception to our visitor."

"Would you give us a minute?" Ryan hesitated, then
wrapped in the bedspread she walked out of the room to the
shower.

As she walked away Al found his pants then walked
to the gazebo. A moment ago he was in heaven, now his life
was going to hell. "Captured?"

"Yes." Tucker nodded. "Our messenger is safe."

"Contact the council. Advise them we will meet
within the hour."

Tucker smiled. Whenever the council met, it led to one of Al's undercover missions. He always enjoyed them. The last one was on a dirty police chief. The sight of the man literally pissing in his pants had them laughing for weeks. "You know, we are getting too old for this stuff."

Al smiled, looking over his shoulder as he walked back to the pool house. "Never." Seeing Ryan in the dress disappointed him. He wasn't ready to let the night end. "Will you come home with me?"

The question surprised Ryan. She wasn't sure what to expect, but she certainly didn't expect him to say that. "I thought you had business with Tucker."

"I do." He walked over to her, "But I'm not nearly finished with you." He started to kiss her, but stopped. "Are you finished with me?"

"Not nearly."

Al smiled, "Then I say let's take this show to a more comfortable location." He kissed her, leaving no doubt that they had more to do tonight.

Thirty minutes later Ryan was standing on the inside of Al's kitchen. She had been there before whenever Tracy and the children visited, but this was her first time at Al's invitation. Well it really wasn't an invitation, it was more on the line of, you're going with me and don't ask any questions. Ryan was in no way complaining, for she enjoyed the tools he used to convince her.

"Are you ready to step into my world?" He reached out his hand.

Looking at his outstretched hand she wondered if she was truly ready for this man. She wasn't sure. But one thing was for certain she decided as she closed her hand around his. After the way he made love to her, she never wanted to be outside of his world. "I'm ready."

Al smiled as he turned and looked at a picture.

To her surprise the wall in the hallway of his kitchen parted. Stepping inside she was amazed at the equipment.

The room looked like the command center at the estate and more. As she stepped inside, the wall closed as if the opening never existed. She hesitated before taking another step.

Walking over to the console, Al took a seat and watched as she took it all in. He pushed several buttons and the monitors mounted on the walls above came to life. Ryan took a few steps in to see what was on the monitors. She immediately recognized the exterior of Tracy's home on one monitor. Walking over and standing next to him, she pointed to the second monitor.

"Monique's condo in DC."

Nodding her head in understanding she moved on to the next, "Where's that one?"

"Julianna St. Clair, in Spokane, Washington."

She looked down at him, "The woman that Jonas Gary kidnapped." Al nodded. "Why are you doing surveillance on her?"

"She is special to Tucker. Whoever is special to him has our protection as well as all that are special to me." He held her gaze.

Slowly pulling her eyes from his trance she looked at the last monitor. "Whose place is that?"

Al frowned at her, "You don't recognize that place?"

Taking a closer look she gasped, "Is that my apartment?"

"The one you never stay in, yes." Al replied.

Placing her hands on her hips in defiance she replied, "That's because I'm always working. I don't spend a lot of time there." He pushed another button and the monitor that previously showed her apartment, split into four smaller pictures. "That's my father's house," she declared, "And my brothers' homes. Why do you have them or me under surveillance?" she asked a little disturbed.

He took her hand, pulling her down into his lap. "Because you—are special to me," he said as he looked into her eyes. "The people that are special to you are now special to me as well."

"Is that so?" she asked staring at his lips.

The pupils of his eyes turned darker as he held her stare, "That's so."

Looking up into his eyes she couldn't turn away. "Suppose we don't want or need your protection," she seductively asked the question.

Her voice soothed him, especially here, inside his home. "Needed or not you have it."

Normally she would have a good comeback for him, but she couldn't think when she was this close to him. She stood to try to clear her mind, not sure how she felt about being watched constantly.

Al could read the thoughts going through her mind. She was fighting those old demons of proving she was just as much a man as any of her brothers to her father and didn't need anyone to watch over her. Taking her hand, he walked to the far side of the room where a conference table and chairs sat next to several office machines. He placed his hand on a pad near the wall. The walls separated.

"How many damn walls do you have around here that open?"

Laughing, Al guided her into another room. The only thing in the room was a king size bed. Al walked towards the bed as he stripped out of his clothes. "Join me," he said as he leaned back against the leather covered headboard.

The sight of his naked body turned her on. She reached down, pulling the gown over her head and stood there with her hands on her hips with nothing but her weapon strapped to her thigh.

His erection began to jump at the sight of her. Damn if she wasn't the sexiest gun toting woman he had ever seen. The only thing missing to complete the vision was a cowboy hat. "There appears to be a new Sheriff in town," he smiled, "Are you going to take me down?"

The smile that radiated from him was contagious. She couldn't stop herself from smiling back until she saw his body react to watching her. Suddenly the smile disappeared as heat rushed through her body. She wet her lips with her tongue as she stepped over to him.

Al closed his eyes as he waited for the moment she would straddle him. His eyes shot open as he felt her lips close around him. The next few moments were a blur as surges of pleasure forged through his body while she did exactly what he asked. She took him down.

It was thirty minutes later when the doors to the command center opened. Tucker looked at his watch. It was two in the morning. "Nice of you to join us."

Al took his seat at the console. On the monitor above were two other men, representing territories 1 through 4 of the United States. While working for the government, Al had divided the Gang Reduction Initiative into regions. The regions were referred to as T1—Northwest, T2—Southwest, T3—Northeast and T4—Southeast. Each region had a commandant. Their job was to know every gang, its leaders, its product and its control area. They did their jobs well. To protect them and their families, their names were never used. They were referred to as T1, T2, T3, or T4. This was the first time he'd needed them since leaving the organization and they were more than willing to assist with whatever information he needed.

Tucker pulled up a group of pictures on another monitor. "This is where he is being held. These satellite pictures were taken about an hour ago."

"Who has him?" Al asked as he reviewed the terrain of the area.

"That's the problem." Tucker responded curiously. "Is it possible that the Cartel infrastructure is in disaccord?"

Looking up from the pictures, Al shook his head, "It wasn't mentioned. Why?"

Tucker nodded to T2, whose territory covered the Southwest. "Recent activity shows Miguel Santiago has been quietly recruiting. He seems to be creating an elite force within the Cartel. In fact, Santiago is indicating that the request for elite soldiers is coming directly from Alejandra Mateo. However, our source indicates Mateo is not aware of the activity."

"Is Santiago descending from the Cartel?"

T2 put a picture up on his monitor. "There seemed to be a discord between Mateo and Santiago centering on this woman. Her name was Ariella Vasquez. She is now Ariella Vasquez-Mateo."

"Mateo's wife." Al smiled. "She's beautiful."

"Quite," T4 replied. "Her family owns Vasquez Imports, specializing in Cuban cigars-drugs."

"Ahhh, Mateo is strengthening his stronghold in Cuba." Al summarized.

"All are not happy with the move."

"Santiago being at the top of the list," Tucker questioned.

"I'm afraid so," T4 replied.

"Here's where things get a little complicated." T2 chimed in. "None of the commands to the recruits come directly from Santiago, therefore, no one can prove to Mateo that his right hand man is making a move to dethrone him."

"The person that has our friend reports to Santiago, not Mateo." Al stated as he looked up at Tucker then back to the men on the monitors. "Thank you for the intel, gentlemen. Until next time." He waited until the monitors were clear, sat back in his seat and chuckled. "Do you remember how we eliminated the two fractions in the 34th street gang?"

Tucker nodded his head, "I do. But this is another country and the Cartel, uncharted territory." Al gave him that look. The one that tells him everything he needed to know. "I'll make the arrangements. When are we leaving?"

Al grinned, "Give me a few more hours."

Tucker stood, shook his head and laughed as he walked towards the exit by the kitchen. He waved his hand in front of the monitor. "I sure hope you two are using protection."

Al froze at the opposite side of the room just as he was about to wave his hand in front of the monitor at the exit to the bedroom. He turned with a deer in the headlights look. Tucker laughed harder as he walked out of the exit. Unlike other men, Al did not walk around with condoms in his wallet, frankly because he did not have unplanned sex. Whenever he was intimate with a woman, he had planned every encounter. He placed his hand on the pad and the exit appeared. Standing on the other side in his bedroom, he marveled at the sight of Ryan spread out in his bed. Bringing her home with him was the best decision he had ever made, she belonged there. He kicked off his slippers and stripped out of his clothes. Lying next to her warm body was playing havoc on his senses but he was determined to let her sleep.

Not sure if it was the heat from his body, or the intensity of his stare, but something reached the recesses of her consciousness and told her to open her eyes. The sight that rewarded her made her smile. Al had his back to the headboard, bare chest; locs loose, arms folded staring at her with a crooked smile. "Good Morning,"

He leaned over and kissed her lightly on the lips. "Are you always this breathtakingly beautiful in the morning?" Her skin became flushed at his compliment. He tilted his head to the side. "Hasn't anyone ever told you how beautiful you are?"

Not sure why, but she suddenly became aware of her nakedness and pulled the sheet, that felt like pure silk, up to cover her breast. "Look," she hesitated as she scanned the room. "You don't have to do this." She sat up, not sure how to leave.

"Do what?" Al asked, as he watched her trying to determine what she should do next.

"You know the whole, you're beautiful thing. I'm comfortable with who I am." She pushed her hair down, thinking it must look a mess. "I'll get dressed and leave," she looked around the room for her gown.

Reaching out, Al pulled her and the sheet to him. They were face to face, her clinging to the sheet and him clinging to both. He held her chin up with his free hand to get her to look into his eyes. She tried to look away, but he refused to let her. "In 1588 Shakespeare wrote, 'Beauty is bought by judgment of the eye, not utter' d by base sale of chapmen's tongues.' Benjamin Franklin in 1741 wrote: 'Beauty, like supreme dominion, is but supported by opinion.' David Hume's Essays, written in 1742 state, "Beauty in things exists merely in the mind which contemplates them'. Then Margaret Wolfe Hungerford broke it down in 1878 when she wrote, "Beauty is in the eye of the beholder". My words to you are simple. Your beauty is as rare as a pure heart and as admired as a Nubian Queen. For your beauty is more than skin deep. It lies within your soul."

When he began talking Ryan held his eyes, because she had no choice. His voice was as sensual as it was commanding. She had been privy to both and she had to admit, the sensual voice was lethal. As he continued he held her eyes captive, for she felt he was revealing his soul to her. Then the words began to touch her in a place she'd never allowed anyone in—her heart. When he said *my words* her gaze fell to his lips. She felt a shiver travel down her spine. "Damn, that's good." She murmured.

He dropped his hand from her face. The sheet slid to her waist. "I didn't wait all my life to allow any woman in,

Morgan." He kissed her lips softly. "I waited for you. What makes you think I would let you walk out of here?"

"Let?" she raised an eyebrow.

"Lips as sweet as wine, words as sharp as knives."

"I think that was a criticism, but you said it so sweetly, I'm not sure."

"Morgan you can physically leave anytime you like, but your soul will always be here with me." He'd lain back against the headboard and folded his arms across his chest. "I'll wait until you come to terms with that."

Her eyes narrowed as she stared at him. Ryan knew he was right. The truth was, in five years she had not been able to shake this man and she really didn't know him. Now, she knew he loved children, his family and friends to the point that he cared about what they cared about. Loyalty should be his middle name, and protective should be his surname. Yet, he had the gentlest way about him. If he weren't so handsome, you would never notice he was in a room.

Watching her come to her own conclusion wasn't easy for Al. He was used to saying this is the way things are going to be and that was that. But with this woman, he had to let her reach her own conclusion. When her eyes began to soften, he knew she had accepted the situation.

"I'm mouthy, blunt and opinionated." She pouted, "I don't like men treating me like I'm helpless because I'm not. I don't like being told what I can and cannot do." A tear slid down her cheek. "I get evil when I'm on my monthly period, and I get cramps real bad." She wiped the tear away. "And I lash out at times." She looked up into his eyes.

"I like mouthy, opinionated, man hating evil women. I can apply heat and rub your back when your monthly period comes around. Then, there's the lashing out thing. I have a cure for that too." He pulled her to him. "I'll simply kiss you to shut you up." He proceeded to demonstrate.

When he finished, he pulled her to his chest. Ryan lay in his arms so content; she never wanted to leave.

Al lazily rubbed her back as he spoke. "I have to leave for a while. Will you be here when I return?"

"I'll think about it," she replied. He felt her smile against his chest. Then the smile changed and tension filled her body. "I need to see my father. I should be the one to tell him about us."

"Do you want me to go with you?"

"No—," she quickly replied. "I would like you both to still be alive at the end of the day."

Chapter 13

Who in the hell set his chest on fire? That was the first question on his mind as Joshua regained consciousness. The second was, what in the hell was sticking him in his back? The cobwebs were clearing from his mind. The damn suit. Yes, it had saved his life, but it hurt like hell when the bullet compressed the material. Ned definitely had to make adjustments to the material. Moving his left side was a bit of a challenge, but he managed to sit up. His chest was bare, with the exception of a white gauze bandage wrapped around him. The only clothing he had on were his pants and he was sure that was because he was naked beneath.

Looking around, the room was about a 12x12 box with one door and one window, both had bars and in the center a hole at the top. The floor was little more than dirty wood and the bed was more straw than mattress. The object he sat on, disguised as a bed, was the only furniture in the room. Of the four walls, two were covered with dried blood. He laughed inwardly. They needed to do a hell of a lot more than that to intimidate him.

Joshua glanced up from the bed and stretched as if he were bored instead of captured by an unknown enemy. Due to his height, it wasn't a problem seeing out the window. Outside the door there were four men talking. He smiled as he watched a man approach the guards with a heated temper. "Someone is not too happy," he murmured. The men spoke in Spanish, which he was well versed in. They were informed Miguel was on his way to interrogate the prisoner. He didn't think it was wise to hang around for that visit. With his clothes gone, so were his gadgets. He was going to have to escape the old fashioned way. "Okay, I can handle four." He turned to look out the window. "How many more will come?" Outside was nothing but a field. In the distance he could see, a larger house and a few men standing around. "Hmm, less than ten." He felt his chest to test its sensitivity. It was a little tender to the touch, but what's a little pain when you are fighting for your life.

Joshua turned his back to the window and did a mental measuring of the distance to the door. He grinned. "This should be fun." He took one giant step then karate kicked the door with both feet, knocking it down. He hit the floor at the same time bullets were fired. The wood door knocked the four men to the ground with guns still firing off.

Joshua grabbed two of the semiautomatic weapons and ran down the hall. In one of the rooms he spotted the other pieces to his suit. Looking around to gauge the response to the gunfire, he had a minute. He slipped his shoes on and grabbed his jacket. Hell, the shoes alone cost a grand. He wasn't leaving them unless he had to. Running to the far side of the building, he opened fire on several men that ran towards him. When they fell he saw what appeared to be a herd of men running to the area with guns drawn. "Oh hell!" He looked around. Going backwards was not an option. He was sure the fencing would send a surge of electricity if he touched it. Going forward meant taking on an army and under normal circumstances, he would try it, but he had no back up and no one coming. Up was his only option. He put his jacket on and strapped both guns to his shoulder. He climbed the side of the building until he reached the roof. "That's better." He laid flat on the roof and began taking out the multitude of men running towards him. The rifle he was using jammed. "That's not good," he threw that one to the ground. "What ever happened to the good old Smith and Wesson made in the USA?" He pulled the other gun up as he looked below. He was clearly outnumbered. For a moment he considered surrendering.

Just then an explosion from behind him rocked the area, sending debris everywhere. He ducked to cover his head. "What the hell?" He looked up to see the army that was marching towards him a moment ago was obliterated.

Joshua had raised his weapon to fire, then froze. "Damn those are some long legs."

Looking over his shoulder, Melissa Sue was strutting towards him with her weapon pointing in the air, resting on her hips with the smoke from the blast surrounding her like she was in an action movie. Beside her was Tucker, with a gun holster around his chest and a semi in his hand ready to fire. Behind them in the center walked Al Day, with nothing.

Melissa Sue and Tucker stopped as Al walked through them. He stood looking up at Joshua with a crooked grin. "Couldn't wait?" he asked with a raised brow.

"Who in the hell are you supposed to be walking in here like someone from the Wild Wild West?" Joshua asked as he slid down the building brushing the dirt off of him.

"I'm the Sheriff." Al grinned then pointed to his side. "These here are my deputies."

"You walked up in here without a gun?"

"No. We flew in." Al turned to walk back to the chopper. "I'm a felon. You know I can't carry a gun." He looked over Joshua's shoulder. "We are about to have company gentlemen." He turned back to Joshua.

"Chopper's in the field. The plane is waiting for us in Brownsville. Are you riding with us?"

He followed them through the fence that now had a hole large enough for a few men to fit through. "I didn't need to be recused you know." Joshua felt the need to explain.

Melissa Sue and Tucker just looked at each other. "Sure, that's why you were shooting your way out." She smirked.

As they climbed into the chopper Tucker took the front with Melissa Sue. Al sat in back across from Joshua He tilted his head as if he was contemplating something. "You ever blow up fifty million dollars in cocaine?"

"Not recently." Joshua laughed. "Why?"

"I need to send a message to a friend." Al reached behind his seat and pulled out a handheld missile launcher.

Joshua's eyes lit up. "Man," he said in awe, "Where did you get that? I thought felons were not supposed to carry guns."

"It's not a gun." Al replied. "It's a missile launcher. Nothing in the code said anything about missiles."

Unable to help himself, Joshua laughed at the comment, while testing out the weapon. "Where are we stopping?"

"We're doing a fly by." Al replied. He then told him about the Intel received from his people on Miguel Santiago. He also explained Mateo's part in disclosing the assassination plot in the beginning.

"So you want to get him to question why he has lost 50 million dollars of his product in retaliation from the Americans." Joshua summarized. "All of this is based on Miguel telling him the truth."

"No." Al replied. "Someone else will tell him."

"How do you know one of the men Miguel recruited will turn?" Joshua asked.

Al shrugged his shoulder, "I'm the one that taught Mateo how to interrogate. He'll get the message. I left one or two of Miguel's men alive just for that purpose." Al looked out of the chopper window then tapped on the window separating the front from the back. "Take us down." Melissa Sue complied. He motioned to Joshua to look out of the window. "X marks the spot. Take it out."

Joshua raised the launcher, balanced it on his shoulder and took the shot. As soon as the missile was released, Melissa Sue turned the chopper in the opposite direction and headed back to Brownsville, Texas.

It had been two days since Al had disappeared. Two days since he sent her world into a tailspin and he hadn't as much as called. And it pissed her off that her body was tingling at just the thought of him. It didn't seem there was a damn thing she could do about it. They were scheduled to fly out the next day for a weeklong campaign stomp through the west, so this was her off day.

As always, Ryan would stop by her father's house before leaving on a trip, just out of respect. She usually allowed him an hour to complain about her lifestyle, and then she would say her good byes and leave. Today was going to be especially hard, for she was walking in the door pissed and she needed to tell him about Al. "Father?" she called out as she walked into the kitchen of the split level home.

She walked towards the family room and there he stood—Franklin Williams. He was an imposing figure, standing six feet, with not much fat around his waist. It was clear why her mother fell for him. Even at the age of sixty-five he was still an attractive man. She often wondered why he never married again after her mother's death, but never felt close enough to the man to ask. "Hello, father. How have you been doing?"

Placing the cup of coffee, his one and only vice, on the stand near the door, he folded his arms across his chest and stared at his only daughter. "It wasn't enough embarrassment for you to work for criminals. Now you're sleeping with them too."

It wasn't a question; it was a statement. "I'm going to kill Donnell." She huffed. "I'm leaving with the Harrisons on a campaign trip and will be gone for a few days. I thought you should know."

"You don't have anything to say for yourself, young lady?"

"I stopped trying to explain myself to you when I turned eighteen and you put me out of your house." She looked around the kitchen. The only good memories she had here were when her mother was still alive and they would make cookies in the kitchen. After her mother passed away, her father became withdrawn and worked twenty-four hours a day, leaving her to fend for herself at eight. Her brothers were older and always involved in sports or something in school. She, on the other hand, never had the opportunity to do the things girls would do, like join the choir, become a cheerleader, ballet, nothing. Just like now, she was always the black sheep of the family and she never really knew why. "I don't know why I continue to try with you." She turned back to him.

"Did you think working for a gang would endear you to me?" he asked. "And now you are giving yourself to a man that has killed people, sold drugs to children and brought weapons into this city."

"I think you have that backwards father. You worked for Munford—the man that took a vow to protect the citizens of Richmond. He's the one that controlled the drugs, weapons and gangs in this city. The man you are condemning fought against Munford and what he was doing.

He turned himself in and paid his debt to society. Then he came out and made a difference to thousands of children across the country." She put her hands on her hips and smirked. "But don't worry father, I'm sure he will desert me just like you did."

"I've never deserted you," he took an angry step forward. "I've always provided a roof over your head and food in your mouth." He pointed a finger in her direction. "If your mother could see you now, she would be so disappointed."

That hurt. The only thing Ryan kept dear in her heart was the love she knew her mother had for her. To think her mother would be disappointed in her cut deep. But she would never let her father know that. "Take care of yourself Father. I won't be back." She turned to walk out the door and saw Donnell standing there.

He had no idea why his father was like this with Ryan. There was never a time his father was not one hundred percent supportive of him and his brothers. But when it came to Ryan, he just could never seem to support her in anything. Hell, it was Ryan that put him in the position to be working for the next President of the United States. It was Ryan who helped save Cynthia Thornton's life and it was Ryan that helped to rid the city of a bad police chief. There is no way he could believe his mother wouldn't be proud of her. He held her by her arms. "Don't leave like this Ryan. Let me talk to him."

"Help yourself. I'm out." She left Donnell standing there staring angrily at their father.

Once inside her vehicle she allowed the tears to flow. Usually their confrontations were simple. This one cut a little deep. *Hell*, she thought as she wiped a tear from her cheek, *I'm twenty-nine years old. If things haven't changed with him by now they never will.* It was time to give up. That was the last time she would go back to the house.

By the time Ryan pulled into her apartment complex, she was over it. She had learned as a little girl how to shield herself from her father's tirades about her behavior. Walking into her apartment she reached to disable the alarm system and found it was already disarmed. She immediately reached for her weapon.

"You know, you need something stronger than tea in the house." Monique said as she walked from the kitchen. "I couldn't even find a bottle of wine or anything in this place. Do you eat here?"

Ryan looked around confused as she put her weapon away. "What in the hell are you doing here and how did you get into my house?"

Monique plopped down into a chair by the kitchen. "That's part of what I need to talk to you about."

"Start talking before I commence to whipping your ass."

Monique smiled, "That's not going to be as easy as it was before, Ms. Ryan." Still not comfortable, Ryan took a quick walk around the one bedroom apartment, just to ease her mind. "No one else is here. It's just me. I need to talk to someone. Normally that would be Daddy, but I can't find him or Uncle Tucker. I thought Daddy would be here, but I was wrong."

Ryan sat in the chair across from the woman, placed her hands on her knees anxious to hear what she had to say. "Talk."

Monique exhaled. "While I was at Howard I was recruited by the CIA. I joined them about a year ago. Joshua Lassiter is my handler."

Ryan sat back in the chair. "Whoa. Does your father know this?"

"No." Monique shook her head. "And if this situation hadn't arisen, I wouldn't be here looking for him now to get advice."

"What situation?" Then Ryan held up her hand. "Hold on. I'm not sure I want to know." She stood and walked into her kitchen.

Monique followed her, determined to pass the information to a responsible party. She watched Ryan turn the stove on where the teakettle sat, then open a box filled with assorted teas. "You are as bad as Daddy with the teas" she sighed. "Look, you are the only person I can trust to pass this information on with Joshua and Daddy out of reach."

"Don't you have a commander or someone to pass information to?" Ryan asked as she waited for the hot water.

"Yes, and I will pass it on to them. But this concerns Uncle JD."

Ryan stared at the young woman. She knew Monique well from all the hell she put JD and Tracy through when she was a teenager. But since her father had come home, she'd slowed down considerably. They were just dealing with normal father-daughter things. To Ryan it seemed Monique was concerned about whatever was going on. Ryan prepared two cups of tea and they sat at the table. "Okay what's going on?"

"I've been placed in Senator McClintock's office to report on any activity with unfriendly entities. There were some sightings with the Senator and his father that were questionable. My assignment was to clear him or discover what they may be up to. Simple enough, I thought until yesterday." She sighed as she sipped her tea.

"What happened yesterday?"

Placing her cup on the table, Monique explained what she found. "Senator McClintock's secretary, Anna Murray, sent me into his office to pick up a folder for her. On his desk was a copy of Uncle JD's itinerary. The document was on pink paper which from what I understand is senior staff colors."

"Who did it come from?"

"I don't know. There was no cover sheet or name on the document I saw."

"Is it possible you may have missed something?"

Monique looked incredulously at the woman across the table. "Ms. Ryan, I have a photographic memory. Do you know what that means?"

Ryan shook her head. "Should I be impressed?"

"Yes, you should. It's the reason I was recruited in the first place. Everything that I hear, see or read is stored in my brain. Believe me, there was nothing else on the document. It's not the first time I've come across his name in the office. But this was not a document that should have been in the opposition's hands."

"Isn't his schedule public knowledge?" Ryan asked. "I mean McClintock's son is the Republican nominee running against JD. I would think the opposition would have his schedule. Maybe his intent is to pass it on to his son."

"I could go with that if it were his scheduled events and not his private itinerary."

Ryan frowned as the implication of what Monique was saying began to set in. She pulled out her cell and called Brian. "Boss, who has access to Mr. H's itinerary?"

"The security team and traveling staff. Why?"

"I'll call you back." She disconnected the call.

"Everyone on the staff has access to the itinerary. What was the date on the document you saw?"

"Tomorrow," Monique replied as she sat forward. "Someone in Uncle JD's staff is passing information to McClintock."

"The question is who."

Monique stood, "That's what you need to find out. In the meantime, since you were here and Daddy wasn't, there is no need to tell him about my new career path."

"Oh no, you are not putting me in that position." Ryan stood. "You are going to tell your father what you are into or I will."

"Ms. Ryan, let's be reasonable here. Daddy is not ready to hear his daughter is working for the CIA. He is just dealing with the fact that I'm sleeping with Jerry McClintock. That's enough of a shock for his system right now."

"You're really sleeping with the Governor—your father knows—and the man is still alive?"

"Yes, yes, and yes." Monique almost laughed at the expression of disbelief on Ryan's face.

An hour later everyone was called into the office. Which usually meant something had happened or was about to happen. Ryan walked into the command center to find the downstairs empty. Walking up the steps she could hear voices coming from the conference room. To her surprise Al, Joshua, Samuel, Tucker, Melissa Sue and Brian, were sitting around the table while Magna leaned against the doorjamb listening to the account of events.

As soon as Al's eyes reached hers, she saw him rise from his seat. It seemed as if everything around them ceased to exist. Not sure what to do or how to get her stomach to stop fluttering, she just stood there and held his glare. "Hello Morgan," he said as his lips descended upon hers.

"Oh, it's like that now?" Joshua teased.

The kiss was so tender and thorough the voices in the background did not register. The memory of just how mad she was at him for not contacting her since they made love vanished for a moment. She suspected he knew that, as she pulled away. "Two days."

He gave her that crooked smile, "It was business."

Magna glanced over to Tucker and nodded, "I owe you." Tucker laughed.

"If you two don't mind," Brian interjected, "We are in the middle of a meeting here."

Al looked into Ryan's eyes, "Forgive me?"

"No." She walked by him and took a seat at the table.

Al retook his seat directly across from her.

"It seems the case may have international implications." Brian stated. He clicked the remote in his hand. "According to intel received, this is the man of interest." A picture of a man appeared on the monitor.

The idea of Ryan being mad at him was eating at Al. He took a piece of paper folded it up to make a paper football. He sat it on one of its points, took his finger and plucked it over to Ryan.

The paper flying across the table caught everyone's attention with the exception of Brian, whose back was to them. Ryan was stunned and slapped the paper with her palm on the table. For a minute she looked up at him surprised. Her eyes narrowed as she unfolded the paper. Inside the note was simple. *Circle one. Do you like me? Yes – No – Maybe.* As hard as she tried not to, she had to smile. She picked up her pen, circled an answer folded the paper back, then plucked it back over to him.

Al caught the paper football just as Brian turned to them. He didn't move a muscle as Brian continued to talk. "The information indicates this may be our assassin. Those of us that will be on the road need to be vigilant." He turned back to the monitor as the proposed itinerary was displayed.

Slowly Al unfolded the paper and read the response. *Maybe.* He tilted his head and looked at her sideways. He wrote another note. *Dinner—you—me—candlelight—and music. Yes—Maybe. Circle one.* He repeated the action.

This time Ryan was ready for the note when it landed in front of her. Unfolding the paper, she read the note, circled her answer and refolded the note. She waited until Brian's back was turned again then plucked it to Al. Joshua reached out and snatched the paper football down just before it reached the intended receiver. He took the note and placed it in his suit pocket. Al and Ryan both turned to him with angry eyes. Neither of them caught what Brian said at the end of the meeting.

Afterwards, Ryan made a beeline to Joshua. Al watched the two in the corner as the talk turned intense. Finally Joshua walked away. As he passed Al he just shook his head, pulling the note out of his pocket and gave it to Al. "She threatened my life. Can you believe that? Ya'll are no fun."

Al's eyebrow rose as he watched the man walk out the door. He turned to see Ryan now conversing with Brian.

Brian looked over Ryan's shoulder as Al walked towards them. "How long are you going to keep him waiting?"

"Two days," Ryan replied.

Brian had to laugh as he saw Al approaching, "Good luck with that."

"Morgan, it's time to go," Al stated.

"This is business," Ryan replied

Al looked at Brian, "This is her off day—right?"

"Sure is." Brian replied with a little laughter in his eyes. Ryan gave Brian a deadly look.

Al took her hand, which she immediately tried to pull away. "You can't just come in here and carry me out whenever you feel like it."

Al sighed, "Is it going to always be a battle with you?"

Hands on hips, Ryan frowned at him, "It's been two days." She put her fingers up in the air. "Two days since I've heard from you."

He kissed her fingers than calmly replied. "You will be gone for eight. Do you want to be mad at me for the next twenty four hours or do you want to make up for lost time?"

He got on her nerves with those sexy eyes, crooked smile and those damn locs. She huffed as she walked away, "Your place or mine?"

Al smiled as he watched her walk towards the door. "Damn if that girl don't turn me on."

Brian laughed as Al followed Ryan out the door.

Al waited at the door of his house as Ryan parked her car. It had been two days since he last touched her and the memory had played havoc with his mind. But his instincts told him something more was needed. Al closed the door behind her and locked it. He took her hand in his. "I apologize from the bottom of my heart for being so thoughtless. At no time do I ever want you to think I took what I wanted then disappeared. The situation called for my immediate, undivided attention. A man's life was at stake. I humbly ask for your forgiveness."

She was tired of trying to figure out why this man's words touched her so deeply. Emotions were something she did not like dealing with, but he always forced the issue. "I forgive you." Her voice sounded so weak, feminine. "But don't let it happen again." She added with more force.

Seeing the wariness in her eyes, he smiled. "Looks like you could use a little loving. Come with me."

Thinking he was going to the bedroom, she was relishing in thoughts of the last time she was there. But when he reached the hallway, he turned towards another room. He opened the door; there was a sunroom overlooking the gardens with a huge Jacuzzi in the center. "There's swimwear in the closet. Make yourself comfortable and I'll return in a moment."

Ryan dropped her bag from her shoulder and opened the closet. She smiled. There was a small store of swimwear inside. Everything from one piece suits, to bikinis, to robes and cover ups in every color. For a moment she wondered how many women had worn the sets. A closer examination showed the tags were still on them. Then she thought about how good the water would feel against her body and all thoughts of other women vanished.

Upon his return, Al was pleased to find Ryan in the water relaxed with her head back and her eyes closed. He placed the tray with fruit and cheese, a bottle of champagne and two glasses on the base of the tub, lowered the shield to control the sunlight, then pushed another button that lit the candles surrounding the tub and turned on the music.

"Will Downing. Nice."

He climbed into the tub behind her, gave her a glass of champagne. "I'm glad you like it." He began to massage her temples. "Tell me about your day."

She sighed, "It was hell. How was yours?"

He smiled as he fed her a strawberry. "I was in hell."

"Hmm, that is delicious. Where did you get strawberries that big from?"

"I have them shipped in." He fed her another. "Why was your day so hellish?"

Ryan hesitated. "It just was."

"Who made you cry?"

"I don't cry," she declared as she tried to turn around.

Al placed his hand around her waist to hold her in place. He set his glass down, pushed her head back against his chest and began to massage her temple. "Tell me what your father said to make you cry." He felt the moment her body tensed.

"I don't like the idea of you spying on me."

He kissed the top of her head. "I didn't spy on you. I could still see the traces of tears on your face." Her body relaxed. "I know you well enough to determine who affects you and who doesn't. The only person that could cause you to shed a tear is your father."

She exhaled, then downed her drink. "I really don't want to talk right now. She rubbed his thighs. "I would think after two days there was something more intimate we could be doing. Don't you?"

Al placed his hand on top of hers to stop the motion. The sensation of her touch was causing him to lose his concentration. "There is nothing more intimate than two people that care about each other sharing their joys and pains." He kissed her temple. "I'll show you how it's done. Someone is trying to kill my sister's husband—a man whom I've come to care a great deal about. Nine times out of ten when that person takes that shot my sister will be in the vicinity and may get hurt if not worse. My purpose in life, for over twenty years has been her safety and well-being." He pinched his fingers together. "I think they are this close to accomplishing all their dreams and truly being happy, but someone is trying to stop them. My fear is I will not be there to stop it from happening."

"I'll be there." She tried to reassure him.

"Hmm. That should make me feel better." He picked up his glass and downed the contents. "It only doubles my fear." He placed the glass back on the table and wrapped his arms around her waist. "Now that I've dropped that shield and let you in, I'm just as afraid of losing you as I am of losing Tracy."

"Why?"

"Well, because, Morgan Ryan Williams, somewhere along the last five years, I fell in love with you. And I want to spend the rest of my life making up for the five years we wasted."

Ryan exhaled as a tear ran down her cheek. That was the sweetest thing anyone had ever said to her. "I don't know if I can love anyone. No one has ever loved me before."

Al smiled against her temple. "I don't believe that. They may not have shown it but your brothers' love you and so does your father."

For a moment, the only sound that could be heard was the motion of the water from the jet motor in the tub. "He said my mother would be disappointed in me." Al felt the tears falling onto his arms. He tightened his hold around her and listened as she talked. "My mother was the only person that showed me any kind of emotion. Until I met Tracy, no one had hugged me after my mother died."

"Tell me about your mother."

"I don't remember much," she shook her head. "But I know she used to make the best blackberry cobbler."

Al smiled. "Did you help her pick the berries?"

She nodded her head like a little girl. "Yes, I did. And they were the biggest and the best."

"How many did you eat before they made it to the kitchen?"

Ryan laughed and laughed at Al's question. "My mom and I had to go back several times to make sure she had enough." She wiped a tear from her face. "One time I ate so many I was sick for days. My mom started calling me her blackberry baby."

He listened as she continued to talk. The thought crossed his mind that this was the first time she'd had someone to talk to about her mother. He loved the sound of her voice like this, it was whimsical. She sounded like a carefree little girl as she talked. Her talking freely this way touched his heart. He had no idea how this woman got so deep under his skin. But he was certain of one thing. He would never allow her father to hurt her again.

Chapter 14

There was someone on the inside passing information to the McClintock camp and they needed to find out who. The problem for Brian was two-fold. He hated not trusting people he had known all his life. Getting the same information from two different sources indicated some element of truth to the claim. He refused to believe it was any of the core people. But finding the culprit was going to be more difficult once the Secret Service stepped in. There would be more people that would have access to the daily itinerary. This meant he had to work quickly. Brian picked up the telephone; it was time for an emergency meeting.

An hour later, Douglas, Calvin, James and Brian sat at a table in the command center. None of them could believe what they'd just heard. "You believe someone within our organization is giving information to the republicans?" Calvin asked, not believing the accusation.

"It's worse than that." Brian added. "The assassin captured by LaVere's men was carrying the itinerary that was distributed to the touring staff that day. A week later another itinerary was found. Whoever is passing the information on, it's not just reaching the McClintock's. It's getting into the hands of whoever put the contract out on JD."

Douglas sat forward. "Is it possible they are one in the same?"

Everyone at the table looked from one to the other. Calvin sat forward, shocked by the suggestion. "You think McClintock would go as far as to hire someone to take JD out of the election? I can't believe that." Calvin turned to Brian. "You know Jerry McClintock better than any of us. Do you believe he is capable of murder? No not just murder, but the assassination of a political candidate?"

"Jerry," Brian shook his head, "No. His grandfather-- definitely."

James sat forward. "I think you better get my father in on this discussion."

Everyone turned to James. "Why?" Calvin asked.

James stood and walked over to the computer and turned it on. He continued talking as he waited for the system to populate the monitor on the wall. "Back during the sixties when Mac McClintock was governor of Texas, some civil rights activists went missing. My father and a group of other men went to Texas in search for them. Two of the members of the team were hung. The group swore Mac was involved in those hangings." The monitor filled with an article on the incident. "Another incident took place when Jeremiah Jr, ran for Governor of Texas. That incident was investigated by the Feds."

"Do you remember who handled the investigation?" Brian asked.

"I do. Samuel Lassiter."

"You mean to tell me the McClintock's have been winning elections by eliminating the opposition?" Calvin asked.

"I can't say for certain. I can only give you the facts, as I know them. However, I think it's imperative for us to talk with my father and Samuel."

"We have to find whoever is leaking this information before it's too late." Brian declared.

"Where do we start?" Douglas asked.

"As hard as it is to believe." Brian stated, "We have to start with our own people."

"Not really," James stated. "We start with those that were on the last tour. They are the only ones that would have access to the two days in question."

"We then need to know what computers have been assigned to whom. The document was emailed from one of our computers. We need to know which one."

Looking forward to a little down time, Joshua walked right into the suite in Samuel and Cynthia's house that was home for now. But first he needed to talk to Ned. "The damn suit doesn't work."

"You're still alive," Ned smirked. "Therefore, technically it worked to some extent.

"Granted. However, I can't be rendered helpless for hours after impact."

"Okay, so it needs a little tweaking. We'll look into strengthening the material."

"You do that. In the meantime, I need you to run a facial recognition on the man I'm sending over now." Joshua sent the scanned picture over his computer to Ned. "I need to know where he's been in the last forty-eight hours and his exact location now."

"Give me an hour."

The call was disconnected. Stripping out of his clothes, Joshua was ready for a nice long shower. The man in the picture was assassin number two. They needed to know precisely where he was. But for now, a nice shower was all he needed to rejuvenate his body.

Unfortunately, that shower was interrupted by a knock on the door.

"Uncle Joshua," he heard his niece Samantha call out to him. "Are you in there?"

"Yes Pumpkin. I'll be out in a minute."

"Okay."

When Joshua emerged from the bathroom he found Samantha sitting in the middle of his bed playing with his cell phone. He picked the child up and sat her on his lap. "What are you up to Pumpkin," he asked as he took the phone from her. He noticed the light blinking indicating there was a secure message waiting for him.

The child smiled up at him with her mother's hazel eyes and her father's smile. "Daddy said you are going to stay with us."

"I am," he said as he tickled the child and she fell back in a fit of laughter, legs kicking and arms flinging. He finally let her up.

She laughed. "Mommy said you're going to blow up the swing set. Can I help?"

Joshua laughed as he sat the child on her feet. "I'm not going to blow up the swing set." He walked towards the dressing room to dress, but the child followed him. He took her by the hand and carried her back into the bedroom. "Stay," he said pointing at the child.

He walked back as he heard her ask. "Why can't we blow up the swing set?"

Dressed in trousers and buttoning his shirt, Joshua frowned as he walked back into the room. He sat on the side of the bed putting on his shoes. "It's not time for the swing set to die."

"Why?"

"Well," Joshua thought. "Is the swing set bad?"

Samantha shook her head. "No."

He ruffled her hair. "Uncle Joshua only blows up bad things."

"Oh." She replied, as Joshua continued dressing. Thinking real hard she looked up at him again. "Can we blow up Jazzy? Mommy said she is bad."

That question caused him to look down at the child. She was standing there all smiles and bright eyes expecting an answer from him. That's when he realized she had no idea what she was asking. "You have to stop repeating what your Mommy and Daddy say."

"Why?" Samuel asked from the doorway.

"Daddy," Samantha ran and jumped into her father's arms.

"Hello, Angel. You're do what Mommy told you and keeping Uncle Joshua company?"

Joshua shook his head laughing. "I should have known Cynthia sent her in here."

"Daddy, Uncle Joshua said he only blows up bad things. The swing set wasn't bad so he can't blow it up. But Jazzy was. Can we blow her up? Please Daddy?"

Samuel looked from his daughter to Joshua. "What have you been telling my daughter?"

"Me?" Joshua questioned. "It was your Angel that wants to blow up her friend."

"Can we, Daddy?"

Samuel put his daughter down. "Go ask your mother."

"Okay," the child happily ran from the room.

Samuel turned back to his brother. "You can't talk about blowing up things around children."

"Your wife started it."

"Cynthia wasn't the one that blew up the garage."

"That was ten—twenty years ago."

"And you are still blowing things up."

"Hey, what can I say? I'm good at it." He picked up his phone to check the messages. "Is there a point to this visit?"

"Glad you asked. Brian called. There may have a connection between the assassin and the itinerary."

Joshua grabbed his jacket and started walking towards him. "Who?"

"The McClintock's."

Joshua stopped dead in his tracks. He hit the button on his cell phone and reread the message from Monique. "My sources have the same connection."

Samuel grinned, but it disappeared quickly when Cynthia appeared at the door.

"Which one of you Neanderthals, told my daughter she could blow up Jazzy?"

It was bright and early Tuesday morning when Monique sat at her desk in her closet-size office when Joshua and his brother Samuel showed up. Her office was the first one on the left when they walked in. She almost had a heart attack at the sight of seeing Joshua there.

"Excuse me." He said to her. "Could you tell me where I can find Senator Jeremiah McClintock's office?"

She pointed, "Right through there."

"Thank you," he replied.

Monique stood in the doorway watching the two as Anna greeted them. "May I help you gentlemen?"

"Yes. We need to speak with Senator McClintock." Joshua stated. "Is he available?"

"Do you have an appointment?"

Joshua pulled out his ID badge. "This is our calling card."

A strange look came to Anna's face. "One moment gentlemen."

"Who is that?" Brandi, another intern whose office was across from Monique's, asked.

Monique shook her head, "I don't know."

"I could do both of them."

Monique stared at the Malibu Barbie look alike as if she had lost her mind. "They are brothers."

"And what, I'm not supposed to be down with the brothers. Hmm, you better get a clue, girl."

"Alright now," Monique smiled. Once Anna escorted the men into the Senator's office and closed the doors, Monique and Brandi ran to her desk. "Ok Anna, who are they?"

"Ladies, this is a professional office and you are to conduct yourself as such."

"Cut the crap, Anna—gives?" Brandi huffed.

Anna looked around to ensure no one was listening. "I'm not sure. But one of them flashed an FBI badge."

The two women looked at each other. "FBI?"

Anna nodded. "That's all I'm going to say on the matter. Now, go back to your desks and get to work."

Monique and Brandi returned to their individual offices as instructed.

Inside the Senator's office things were going a little less cordially. "Gentlemen, my secretary indicated you are from the FBI. I'm always willing to help the bureau. Have a seat. What can I do for you?"

Joshua took a seat, while Samuel remained standing. "Senator McClintock," Joshua extended his hand. "I'm Special Agent Lassiter." He pointed to Samuel. "He's ex-Special Agent Lassiter. We have a few questions regarding a possible assassination plot against Governor Jeffrey Harrison. You wouldn't happen to know anything about that—would you?"

"Gentlemen, what possible reason would I have to harm Governor Harrison?"

"He is running against your son for the Presidency." Samuel stated.

"According to the recent polls, Harrison is leading your son with double digits."

"Then it would be my son that would have reason, not I. However, I can't believe my son would have anything to do with this so-called plot." He sat forward in his chair. "Is the fact that my son is running against Harrison your only reason for assuming he is a part of this?"

Joshua got the distinctive felling that the Senator was fishing. "Not really," he replied before Samuel could. "It's a political campaign. The Bureau's first instinct is to check out the opposition. So, here we are." He stood, "Frankly Senator, I believe this is a waste of our time. There is no way a family as well connected and established as yours would take such a risk. However, my brother here works for Harrison. When this issue came to his attention, your son was the first name he contemplated. If I hadn't at least looked into this situation he would have told our mother and that's a whole other can of worms you don't want to open."

The Senator laughed and stood. "I understand Agent Lassiter." He extended his hand. "I do hope this plot is nothing more than a political ploy from the Harrison camp."

"No one in the Harrison camp plays political games Senator." Samuel declared. "We're leading. We don't have to."

"For now Mr. Lassiter—for now."

"Senator," Joshua shook the man's hand. "I hope you understand we will have to speak with your son."

"And your father," Samuel added with a scowl.

"I encourage you to speak with either. I'm sure it will put your mind to rest. In fact, I'll give them a call to let them know you will be stopping by."

Joshua gave his brother an, *I told you so look.* "I would appreciate that Senator."

Samuel stared intently at the Senator before following Joshua out the door. When they walked down the hallway Joshua spoke. "He was searching to see how much we know."

"He's definitely involved," Samuel stated as they strutted out of the door.

Senator McClintock called his father. "I just had an interesting visit from the FBI. It seems they received a tip about an assassination plot against Harrison. I'm flying in tonight. We'll talk then."

Chapter 15

Al decided he wanted to make Ryan a permanent part of his life. However, before he could do that it was his duty to speak with her father. Knocking on the door of the Williams' home, he wondered how the reception would be. It wasn't long before he found out.

"Mr. Williams. My name is Al Day. I was wondering if I could have a moment of your time."

Frank Williams could not believe the audacity of this criminal standing on his front porch. "What could you possibly have to say to me?"

The attitude towards him was clear. "It would be much easier to answer the question if you would be kind enough to step outside."

"Easier so you can have one of your thugs to gun me down."

"I have no reason to do that Mr. Williams. I would like to talk about your daughter."

"Who is it, Dad," his oldest son Devin asked as he walked to the door. "Al," Devin stepped out the screen door and extended his hand. "How're you doing man?"

"I'm good, Detective. How about yourself?"

"I can't complain. What are you doing here?"

Al looked through the screen door at Mr. Williams. "I was hoping your father would give me a minute of his time."

Devin looked from Al to his father, whose face clearly showed displeasure at the thought of talking to Al. "You two have met?"

"I don't socialize with criminals," his father replied. "I lock them up."

"Dad?" Devin questioned.

"Mr. Williams, I was a criminal. I paid my debt to society and have made amends for my past. I'm standing here today as a man that cares deeply for your daughter. I'm here to ask you for her hand in marriage."

"What?" Devin exclaimed, surprised at the statement. "You and Ryan?"

Al just held Mr. Williams' surprised glare. "Mr. Williams?"

"My daughter stopped asking my permission to do things years ago. She definitely doesn't need it now." He angrily replied.

"She may not need it sir, but I do."

"Hmm, don't you usually just take what you want? What's different now?"

"The difference here is your daughter loves you very much." Al explained. "She would not do anything deliberately to disrespect you."

"Now that's funny." He smirked. "She disrespected me when she began working with your street gang. She's disrespecting me now by being involved with you."

Al's eyes narrowed dangerously. "I'm sorry you feel that way. But just so you know, Morgan came to work for my organization to help dismantle it. It was her job to limit the loss of life on either side during the transition. At no point in time was she ever involved in any illegal activity. Your daughter has worked for the Attorney General, the Governor and now works for the man that will be President of this country." He took a step closer. "Now I understand why she is such an over-achiever. She could never do enough to satisfy you. Any other man would be proud of a son or daughter that's accomplished what she has." He took a step backwards. "I thank you for giving me a moment of your time." Al turned and walked off the porch.

"Hey Al, are you really going to ask Ryan to marry you?" Devin asked smiling.

Al looked over his shoulder at Mr. Williams's angry face, still standing in the doorway. "Not without your father's permission." He continued to his vehicle and pulled off.

Devin turned to his father. "You better say an extra prayer tonight that mother forgives you for what you just did." He walked in the house leaving his father at the door.

Al wasn't able to join Ryan on the campaign trail as he'd planned. It was taking him a while to deal with the thought of not making Ryan his wife. He simply couldn't do anything to widen the gap between her and her father. He wanted to make her life easier, not cause her more heartache. The same thought kept nagging at him. How could a man turn his back on his only daughter? Since his own mother had turned her back on him, he wondered if talking to Lena would help. But was he ready to open Pandora's box? Was he ready to deal with decades of hurt? Would it be worth it? For a full day, Al pondered the questions. The next afternoon when all of Ryan's brothers appeared at his front door he had his answers.

Standing on his porch was Devin, who was the oldest and the one who took the lead. "I would understand if you didn't let us in. However, this concerns Ryan and you may want to hear what we have to say."

Al looked from one brother to the other. "Are you carrying?"

"Of course," Devin replied.

"I can't have guns in my house." He raised an eyebrow. He knew Devin and Donnell, but not the two middle sons. They could be there to set him up.

Jarrell, the next to the oldest looked at Al as if he had lost his mind. "You know damn well we are not going to leave our weapons outside."

"Will you let us handle this," Donnell insisted. He turned back to Al. "Come on, man. You know Devin and me would not set you up. Besides we need to talk about Ryan."

Al opened the door and assessed each as they walked in. There was nothing threatening about them. In fact, they seemed rather at ease around him. They stood in the foyer giving him the once over. The way none of them bothered to hide what they were doing amused him. Al walked to the back of the house. "Anybody want a beer?"

"A beer would be a good start, but you have to come with more than that if you want to marry my sister," the one named Scott said as he walked past Al into the kitchen.

Al watched in wonder as the others followed. Donnell stopped where Al stood. "My mother really did house break them." He shook his head. "There is no excuse for them."

He wanted to laugh as they reached into the refrigerator to determine what they would grab first. "Hey, you have any mustard?" Jarrell asked, holding an array of cold cuts in his hand.

"Here it is," Scott answered as he tossed the plastic container across the room. Devin caught it mid-air. "Hey." Scott protested.

"The man said a beer." Devin frowned, "Put that back."

Jarrell and Scott looked at Al with pleading eyes. Al shook his head. "Help yourself. Just hand me a beer." Scott smiled and flipped a beer to him. "Okay," Al looked at Devin and Donnell. "What do you two and the stooges want?" Al asked as he sat on a stool at the counter, where the making of mega sandwiches commenced.

"Hey," Jarrell and Scott exclaimed in unison.

Devin and Donnell sat next to him on either side. "We seem to have a dilemma." Donnell spoke.

"That we do," Al nodded.

"Donnell and I know you. Neither of us have an issue with you and Ryan."

"Morgan." They all looked at him confused. "Her name is Morgan, not Ryan. She's a woman, a damn fine one at that. You all treat here like she is one of you and she's not. She is a woman through and through. Believe me—I know."

"Hey, hey, hey. That's our sister. We can do without the visual," Scott grunted as he took a bite of the sandwich that he could barely fit into his mouth.

"Look, I thought I was doing the honorable thing going to your father. He shut me down. What do you want from me?"

"We want you to marry our sister." Jarrell stated. He took half of the sandwich in one bite.

"Yeah, we do," Scott added. "I know it seems like we are unorthodox, but there is one common thread amongst us. We love our little sister."

"She deserves to be with someone that loves her for her." Jarrell offered as he swallowed the other half of the sandwich. "You know what I mean?"

"That won't happen unless your father agrees."

They all froze. "Ryan---um Morgan agrees with that?" Jarrell asked.

"Morgan has no idea I went to see her father."

All the men in the room looked at each other, then roared with laughter. "You went behind Morgan Ryan's back to talk to Dad. Man, Dad isn't the one you have to be concerned with." Scott snickered.

"Ryan is going to kick your ass when she finds out," Donnell laughed. "I'm going to make sure I'm there to see it."

"Morgan doesn't scare me." Al said. Everyone was quiet for a moment, then Al laughed and the others joined in. The group sat and talked for hours. Learning more about Ryan's childhood was not only hilarious, but also touching. While none of them could fully explain their father's attitude towards Ryan, they each had their own thoughts on the matter. All of them shared. By the time the Williams' brothers left his home, Al was more than convinced that what Ryan needed in her life was love. She needed him. That was enough to convince Al that having Ryan in his life was worth any sacrifice.

The next morning Al set out to talk with Lena. The conversation was years overdue, but a necessity if he wanted Ryan in his life. Lena sat on the veranda of her home waiting for Al. The call indicated he wanted to talk. The question she had to answer before he arrived was if she would tell him the truth, or what he expected to hear. The truth would make her a victim and she hadn't been that in over forty years. A lie would fuel her son's hatred for her.

"Lena."

She looked up from the chaise lounge to see Al standing in her home. It was his first time there. "Have a seat Al." God had given her beautiful children. Her son had the longest lashes that naturally curled. He looked so much like his father. Al's father was the first man she ever loved. People thought she was a whore. That couldn't be the furthest thing from the truth. "You wanted to talk."

"I need to know why you turned your back on us."

"Blunt, aren't we?"

"I don't have the time to ease into the conversation." Al sat back in the chair directly in front of her and crossed his legs. "I've asked Ryan's father for her hand in marriage."

The smile on Lena's face was genuine. "You asked Ryan to marry you?"

"No," he replied. "Her father refused to give his blessing. He states his reason is due to my criminal activities from the past."

"But you've paid that debt and more, Al." She stood with hands on hips. "Who does he think he is being judge and jury over my son? You want me to talk to him?"

Al almost wanted to laugh at Lena's reaction. She was ready to confront Mr. Williams over him. "No. I thought if I could understand and work through my own childhood demons, I would be better equipped to help Ryan work though hers."

Lena frowned and shook her head. "I like that girl, Al. She's good for you. You think the issue Ryan has is connected to her childhood?"

"I like her too." Al smiled. "Her father turned his back on Ryan when she was young. Very reminiscent to what you did. I'm trying to understand why. What motivating factor could be that strong?"

"So you think if you understood what happened in our lives it would help you with Ryan's father?"

Al nodded. "I do. The question is, are you willing to open Pandora's box to help me?"

Lena put her book down and chuckled. "I don't see how knowing the hell of my past will help with Ryan." She stood, "But if you want to know, we're going to need some help." She walked over to the bar, pulled out a bottle of Hennessey and two glasses. "Make yourself comfortable. This may take a minute."

Al stood, took off his suit jacket and rolled up his sleeves.

She poured two drinks, gave a glass to him, and kept one for herself. She started to walk back, but instead, placed the bottle on the table between them. "This is going to dull the pain," she said as Al raised an eyebrow at the bottle.

"I have time," he sat back.

"You really like Ryan, hmm?"

Al nodded. "I really do."

Lena smiled, then sat back on the lounge. "This will go a lot better if you just let me get through the story. You can ask questions later." Al nodded. "Well son, to answer your question there is only one emotion that has the power to make men and women act like fools. And it's as old as time. Love. It can make you do right, or it can make you do wrong. As Al Green once said."

Al smiled. "Tell me you didn't name me after him."

Lena emptied her glass, then refilled it. "No, you were named after your father. Lord, I loved that man." She snickered. "And you have the nerve to look just like him, except for the hair."

"What, no locs?"

"It was cornrows back then, but no. Epstein Albert Day would make JD look like Huey Newton."

They both laughed. "That's pretty conservative. I can't imagine you with a nerd type."

"Oh Ep was a nerd. Hell, at that time so was I."

"You—a nerd. That is a hard sell."

Lena took another drink and sobered. "I can't speak for Ryan's father. Hell, if it wasn't for this damn need to help you find happiness I wouldn't be reliving things that are best left untold." Seeing the faraway look in Lena's eyes, Al sensed now was not the time to speak.

"You've never met your real grandmother. Your grandmother John Russell was the woman that took me in when my mother threw me out. If you think your mother is beautiful now," she smiled, "when I was younger I could have won beauty pageants had little black girls been allowed.

My mother, who, I'm sure, is in Hell, was a beautiful, manipulative woman. She used her looks to marry what she considered to be the cream of the crop, a man with a Post Office job. They made damn good money back then. My father treated me like I was the most precious thing in the world. See, I wasn't just beautiful; I was smart. Not the normal straight A student smart, but I was just like you and Tracy with numbers. So he had me tested and placed in a private school. Private schools back then were expensive, but more so for a working class Black man. They would argue all the time about the money he would spend on me. He would say, 'The child has to dress nice going to that school.' My mother felt he would pay more attention to me than he did her. She would say, 'She don't need to be going to that school. It costs too much and she ain't going to be nothing but a whore.' His response was always the same. 'I'd think you would want more for your daughter.' It wasn't until I was fourteen that I understood what he meant."

"My father worked what they called the graveyard shift at the post office. One night something woke me up. I can't remember what now. But I got out of bed to go to the bathroom that was in the hallway between my bedroom and my parents' room. I heard a voice, but it didn't sound like my Daddy's, so I walked over to their bedroom and slowly pushed the door open. It was my mother with another man having sex in my Daddy's bed." Lena shook her head. "She didn't even bother to try to explain. All she said was, 'You better not say anything to your father.'" Lena swallowed. "Well, I'd learned a few tricks from my mother and whenever I wanted to get my way, I would threaten to tell Daddy about the man." She became quiet, downed her glass of cognac then poured another. "The man would give my mother gifts, diamond bracelets, earrings, clothes—you name it. After he stopped coming there was another man and another. To keep me quiet they would give me things too. Well, one of my mother's special friends as she called them, was a little more interested in me than she liked. I had just turned sixteen, when my mother knocked on my door late one night and said, her special friend, I never knew their names, had a birthday gift for me. Well, I liked pretty things as much as my mother did. So I didn't ask any questions, I went with her to my parents' bedroom. He motioned for me to sit on the bed beside him. So I did. He gave me a red velvet box. As I opened the box he told my mother to close the door." Lena swallowed down another glass, but this time she took the bottle. "He took my virginity and my mother stood outside the door while I screamed for her to help me." She turned the bottle up and took another drink. "When he was done, he told me how sweet I was and the gifts he would bring me the next time he came over. My mother came into the room afterwards and looked down at me in the bed with the meanest smile I'd ever seen. You tell your father about me and I'll tell him about you." Lena sighed at the memory, before she continued. "A month later I missed my period. My mother told my father I had let some little boy knock me up. To this day I wish I had just kept my mouth closed, but I was scared and mad that my mother let that man hurt me. So I told my father everything. About every man, every gift, and how I got pregnant. I will never forget the look on my father's face. He stormed into the bedroom and found most of the jewelry my mother had hidden. That night, he took me to John Russell's house and said he would be back. He never came back. From what I was told, when he got back to the house, one of my mother's special friends was there. My father shot both of them, then turned the gun on himself." Lena waited a moment then turned to Al with tears streaming down her face. "My daddy was a good man. He just fell in love with the wrong woman."

Al sensed she needed his acknowledgment so he simply nodded and continued to listen.

"Life with John Russell was definitely different. There was none of the fancy furnishings or expensive cars. It was just a big house filled with a whole lot of love. When I had Valarie she took care of that baby like she was her own." Lena smiled. "She took care of me the same way. It wasn't until later I found out she had always been in love with my Daddy. But he married my mother and they just remained friends. She said she would have been his lover, but he wasn't that kind of man. So having me and Valarie there was like having a part of him. She made sure I graduated from high school and encouraged me to take classes at the university. That led me to your Daddy.

"Dr. Epstein Albert Day." She laughed a little. "When he first introduced himself, I had to ask what kind of name was Epstein for a brother. He told me a smart one. Ep was a visiting professor from Harvard. Every year he would volunteer at a Black college to share his knowledge. See he had a PhD in Economics and the man was fine as all get out. Lord, that man was fine."

"To get into his class, you had to solve a formula and write an essay on the effects of the economy on Black America and be selected. I was always great with numbers, but John Russell, who insisted that I take the class, had to help with the writing of the essay. My father had told her how smart I was, especially with numbers and she was not going to let the opportunity to learn from a man of Ep's caliber pass me by. You would have thought I'd won some grand prize the way she carried on when I was accepted in that class. Anyway, I always knew I was pretty, but after the experience with the man, I stayed away from the male species. But when I walked into that class and saw that man sitting at the desk in the front of the room I knew my life was about to change."

Lena smiled, not just any smile, but one that made her look young again. Al had to smile with her. "I was barely nineteen at the time, but that man touched me without using his hands. I don't have to tell you I excelled in that class. But you know, it wasn't just a physical thing with Ep. He would tell me he fell in love with my mind. The physical beauty was secondary. I loved him because he would never let me take the easy way out when I answered questions. He would always make me think about the impact of my answers on everyday life."

"Unlike my mother, I hadn't developed the knack for flirtation. During that semester, I didn't care how much I called myself flirting with him; he paid me no mind. Now, I will tell you that was a blow to a woman that was used to men drooling at her feet. Needless to say, I excelled in his class. After that semester, he left. That summer I was heartbroken. It was my first real crush. John Russell would tell me, if it's meant to be it will happen. The next semester when I registered, certain classes had to be signed off by the Dean of the Math department. I went there and standing in the middle of the office was Ep. He had taken the position of Dean of the department. My heart dropped when I saw him. I didn't even know how to act. But unlike before, I saw something different in his eyes. He nodded and said. "It's nice to see you again, Ms. Lambert." I almost fainted, when I realized the man remembered my name. I told him why I was there. He signed the card for the registrar. He then asked if I would be free to have a cup of tea with him later. I wanted to shout hell yeah, but I played it cool. After all he was older, a professor and fine. I didn't want to seem immature, so I simply said yes. We met at the coffee shop on campus and talked for hours. Six months later we were married. We had a nice house near campus. He taught while I attended. Valarie stayed with John Russell. There was no way I could take the child away and we didn't live that far from them. A year later we had Joan. Two years after that you came along." The smile she displayed at the memory was priceless. "For five years of my life I knew the power of love." She stopped talking.

"What happened?"

She sighed. "One of his female students ran him down with her car. According to the police, he was having an affair with the girl. When he broke it off, she lost it and decided if she couldn't have him no one would." Lena shook her head, "At the time the shock of losing my husband that I loved and learning of the affair was just too damn much. Joan had his brains and you were and still are the spitting image of Ep. I couldn't stand to be around either of you. John Russell was afraid I would do something crazy so she came and took all of us back to her house. I decided then and there that love wasn't for me. Daddy loved my mother and it brought him nothing but pain and eventually his death. I loved Ep and it brought me pain and him death. I didn't need that in my life. So I buried my unfaithful husband, sold the house and moved away. I left all of you with John Russell because I knew she would take care of you. My life became about me. What I wanted, when I wanted, how I wanted it and where. Anything else, I didn't let touch me. I didn't care. I learned early if you care about something it will eventually cause you pain. I didn't want or need that kind of pain in my life."

The two sat there. The silence was like a comforting blanket in the room. "You had a hell of a life Lena."
"You think," she solemnly laughed as she glanced at him. "Don't go feeling sorry for me. I made my decisions based on what I was going through." She put the bottle on the table. "I didn't treat myself like a victim back then and I don't want to be treated like one now. What happened was in the past. The shit with my mother is in the past. I know my actions had a terrible impact on my children and I can't do a damn thing about it now. All I can do is share some wisdom with you. I wish to this day, I had taken the time to really investigate what happened with Ep. If I had, I would have learned that he never had an affair with the girl. Oh, she tried according to other professors, but it was his rejection that made her go crazy and run him over. But I was

too hurt to dig deeper to really find out what was going on. See how that affected my life and yours, not to mention Tracy. Valarie and Tracy don't know any of this and there is no need for them to know. But you," she stood, "you need to find out what happened between Ryan's father and his wife. That will tell you why he turned his back on his daughter. Mark my words."

Al put his glass on the table and stood. He walked over and stood before Lena. For the first time in his life, he took his mother into his arms and hugged her. The tears from her eyes dropped to his shirt, as he just held her tight.

Then true to form, Lena pushed him away. She pulled on his locs and smiled. "Now get out of here so I can finish my book. And whatever you do, don't let that man keep you and Ryan apart." She pointed her finger in his chest, "You hear me?"

Al smiled, "I hear you, Mother."

"Oh hell, no you don't. It's been Lena all your life. It's still Lena."

"Alright, Lena, I have one question." She looked up at him. "Are you happy now?"

Lena thought for only a second, "Yes."

He kissed her temple. "Thanks for sharing. I'll check you later."

Lena watched him walk out the door. She dropped back down to the chaise lounge opened her book and smiled at the memory of him calling her mother.

Chapter 16

Samuel flew out to meet the camp in California, while Joshua followed the assassin's trail to Austin, Texas. True to his word, the Senator had cleared the way for Joshua to see his son, Jerry.

They agreed to meet at Jerry's ranch since this was not a line of questioning he would want to be overheard at the Governor's office. Joshua had no problem with the location since Jerry really wasn't his target in this investigation.

An older Black gentleman dressed in a black suit, white-collared shirt, and wing tip shoes opened the door to the mansion. "Good afternoon sir."

"Good afternoon. Nice suit," Joshua replied. "I'm here to see Governor McClintock."

"Thank you. Special Agent Lassiter, I presume?"

"You presume correctly."

"This way, sir."

The gentleman turned, expecting Joshua to follow. "I'm an admirer of fine clothing. I see you are as well."

"I do like to look good." Joshua replied as he followed the man through the richly decorated foyer to a double doorway that led into the library of the home where he was greeted by the Governor.

"Special Agent Lassiter," Jerry extended his hand. "Welcome to my home."

Joshua shook the man's hand. "Governor."

"No please, call me Jerry." He turned to his right. "This is my wife, Eleanor."

Placing his hand on her lower back, they appeared to be the loving couple as she stepped forward, with her hand extended. "Should I call you Special Agent Lassiter or just Agent? The last thing I would want is to offend the FBI." She flashed a smile befitting the beauty queen she was.

"Joshua is fine, ma'am." He returned the warm smile.

"Then Joshua it is. That's a biblical name. Are you a man of God, Joshua?"

"My mother claims all of her children are. All twelve of us have biblical names."

"Twelve. How charming."

"Let the boy's hand go Eleanor. He has business to conduct here," Mac growled tapping his walking stick on the floor as he entered the room.

Jerry sigh a breath of frustration. "Agent Lassiter, this is my grandfather, Mac McClintock. You will find he is rather brash at times."

Every danger instinct in Joshua's body sent alert signals. This was the man he had to take down. "McClintock." Joshua spoke with a voice that clearly indicated he did not like the man.

"That's Governor McClintock to you, boy."

"Grandfather," Jerry frowned. "Agent Lassiter is an invited guest in my home, unlike yourself. If you wish to remain, you will sit down and respect my guest." Jerry turned to Joshua. "Please forgive my grandfather Agent Lassiter.

Have a seat and tell me how I can help you with your investigation."

Joshua never took his eyes from Mac. "I only have two questions for you Governor." Still holding Mac's stare, Joshua asked. "Are you involved in an assassination plot against Governor Harrison of Virginia?"

Realizing Joshua was not going to turn away from his grandfather, Jerry walked around to stand behind the chair where his grandfather was now seated. "I admire Governor Harrison. We have worked on several endeavors together. But more than that, I would not take another man's life unless mine or my wife's life was threatened."

Joshua saw the flash of anger in Mac's eyes as Jerry spoke. Still holding his stare, Joshua nodded. "I believe you Governor."

"Thank goodness," Eleanor sighed loudly.

Joshua looked up at Jerry. "Would you stop such a plot if it was within your power, even if members of your family were involved?"

"You got the balls of a bull coming to my turf accusing my family of wrong doing, boy!" Mac hit the floor with his stick. "You got some nerve looking me in the eye. Back in the day, we had ways of dealing with uppity n...."

Mac never had a chance to complete the statement. Before he could blink Joshua grabbed him with both hands by the lapel of his jacket. He held the man in the air until he was eye level with him.

Joshua heard Eleanor's sharp gasp behind him, but ignored her and Jerry's protests. "I don't like you, Mac. The next time we meet, one of us is going to die. Since I haven't given my mother any grandchildren yet, the odds are it will not be me." He dropped the old man into the chair. He looked at Jerry. "I believe I have everything I need Governor. Thank you for your Texas hospitality." Joshua turned and walked out the door.

It must have taken Mac a moment or two to get his nerves un-rattled. Joshua was almost at the front door before he heard the old man's threat. "You'll be dead before you leave Texas. Dead, you hear me boy!"

The man that greeted Joshua previously stood with the front door open. Joshua stepped out and so did the man. "Agent Lassiter, if there is a plot to kill Governor Harrison, Jerry is not involved. It's certainly the old coot. He's as mean as a rattlesnake and is just as deadly. You be careful, son."

"Thank you for the heads up sir." Joshua said as he climbed into the helicopter he had sitting on the front lawn. "Guns trump snakes," he yelled. Joshua lifted off, then landed at Austin Airport where Melissa Sue was waiting. He boarded the private jet still pissed from the encounter with the old man. They were in the air when he called Ned. "I want everything we have on Mac McClintock before I land."

"Absolute, funny you should call. Who is the master?"

"What?"

"Who is the master?"

"Do I sound like I give a damn?"

"You will, as soon as I give you my news."

"Ned," Joshua shook his head. "I'm not in the mood."

"This should lighten your mood just a touch. The picture you sent."

Joshua waited. "I'm going to break every bone in your body if you don't talk."

"Why do you have to be so violent? What about showing your brother man a little love? What the world needs now—a little love."

"Ned!" Joshua yelled. "The picture, Ned."

"Oh yeah, Dionne got me there for a minute."

Joshua dropped his head. The nerds of this world were going to be the death of him.

"I found him."

"You found who?"

"The man in the picture. You want to stay focused here."

"Who is he?"

"I don't know, but I can tell where he is at this moment."

Joshua sat up, "Where?"

"Los Angeles, California. I have satellite photos of him near the hotel where Governor Harrison is staying. I also have him at the Orange County fund raiser last night."

Joshua jumped from his seat and walk into the carpit of the plane. "Melissa Sue, how long will it take us to get to LA?"

"Two—three hours."

"Get me there in two." Joshua walked back to his seat. "Keep an eye on him. Update me every fifteen minutes."

"Anything else?"

"Yeah. Raider is in the hanger in Austin. It needs to be fully loaded. The next time I visit Texas, I'm leaving my signature."

Sunday morning church, brunch then to the office to catch up on the correspondence was Monique's plan. Simple, right? When was anything in her life simple? The first two items on her plan went off without a hitch. The preacher spoke on positivity rather than negativity, believing—not disbelieving, trust versus distrust and forgiveness—not grudges. Yes, the service was very uplifting, Monique thought as she exited the Capital South metro stop. Dressed in an Tahari power skirt and blazer, showing off her sensuous curves and the four inch heels highlighting her sexy legs, she stopped in the Bistro for brunch. As always, Monique's looks demanded attention and the fact

that she traveled alone always enticed one or two males.
Today was no different as several offered to join her. A few
she refused tactfully until this one brother came up grinning,
wearing his gator shoes and second hand suit, like he had it
going on.

Monique reverted back to her street days with a look
that said; don't even think about it. The brother went on his
merry way and Monique declared brunch a done deal.

Placing her earplugs in, the IPod blasted a little Chris
Brown, and Trey Songz mixed with a little Pharrell, showing
her fellow VA talent some love. Her hips swayed to the beat
of the music as she waved to the brothers at the guardhouse
to the Senate building.

Taking the stairs to the second floor, she began
singing along with Chris and Jordan Sparks', No Air. The
building wasn't particularly busy on Sundays. Normally,
there were a few interns playing catch up, like she was. So
seeing the Senator and a woman walking into his office suite
was quite unusual. Monique turned off the music, then
waited a moment before proceeding down the hallway.
When she reached the door she fumbled around in her
purse as if searching for the key, but she was actually
listening to see if the couple moved on into the Senator's
office. When she thought it was safe, she slowly opened the
door and slid inside.

Inside to the left of the suite was her closet-office,
she placed her purse on the floor then walked until she was
just outside of the Senator's office. The door was open, the
Senator stood behind his desk as the woman gave him a cell
phone. "The call will come through this number. Once you
receive the call, destroy the phone."

"How do I destroy it?" He asked as he locked the
cellphone in his top drawer.

"Throw it into the Potomac for all I care. Just get rid
of it." The women turned. "You know how to reach me if I
can be of further assistance."

Monique hurried back to her office, turned her music on and was standing with her back to the doorway shaking her hips. She opened the file cabinet then closed it so the noise could be heard. She was holding a letter in her hand when she felt a tap on her shoulder. Monique jumped and grabbed the bookend off the file cabinet and swung around ready to attack.

The Senator jumped back. "Hold up there little lady," he said in his southern drawl.

Monique frowned, then pulled the earplugs from her ears. "Senator," she looked around frantically. "What in the he–," she stopped and put the bookend back on the cabinet. "I'm so sorry. I didn't know anyone else was here. You scared me."

The Senator reached down and picked up the letter she dropped. He glanced at it then held it out to her. She took the document. "I see you are trying to catch up on the correspondence."

Monique gave him a small smile. "Yes sir. I got a little behind when I left early last week." She gave him a curious look. "What are you doing here? I mean I know it's your office and everything, but it is Sunday."

"I decided to catch up on a few things also."

"So you're heading to your office to work? I won't be disturbing you here will I?"

"I'm going to get a few things, then I will be out of your way."

"You're not in my way Senator, but okay. Would you mind making some noise when you leave?"

He smiled, "I'll see what I can do."

The Senator walked out. Monique slouched into her chair and prayed he bought the act. Once the Senator left Monique worked for a few hours, just to make sure he wouldn't return. The whole time she wondered why the Senator would need a disposable cell phone and who was the woman? It was the same woman she bumped into coming from the office before.

That was it, curiosity was kicking her butt. Taking a small case from her purse, she pulled one of the instruments from the case then marched into the Senators' office. It took her a minute but she got the drawer open. Taking out the cell phone, she turned it on and wrote down the number. She replaced the phone and locked the drawer. She looked around to make sure no little pieces of paper dropped anywhere to indicate the drawer had been opened. Satisfied everything was as it should be, she walked back to her office, grabbed her purse and left.

On her way to the metro station, she called in the number. "Mr. Ned, this is Spicy calling. Is it possible to have a call routed to my number from a prepaid phone?"

"For you Spicy, anything is possible." Ned replied.

She gave him the number. "I still need the call to go through. Thank you Mr. Ned."

"Will do Spicy, and by the way, call me Ned."

Monique smiled, "You're the man, Ned." She disconnected the call, never noticing the man following her onto the metro station.

The house was quiet. Mrs. Harrison had put the children to bed and Mrs. Gordon was just wrapping up the kitchen. She stepped out onto the patio where Al was sitting in a chair, staring out into the night. "You want anything before I call it a night son?"

Al held his head back and his locs fell over the back of the chair. "No thank you, Mrs. Gordon. I'm good for the night." He sat back up.

"You seem a little down. I'm a good listener."

"I know you are. This is something I have to sort out."

"All right, son. You have a good night."

"You too, Mrs. Gordon."

The listening device buzzed in his ear. He touched it to activate the audio. "What's up, Magna?"

"Just reporting in Boss. Everything's quiet on the homefront. I believe JC is sitting out on his parents' balcony. You might want to check that out."

"Will do," Al replied as he stood. Upstairs he checked all of the children's rooms before entering JC's. The first thing he noticed was the boy was not in the bed. JC ran hard during the day, so although he was the oldest, he was usually the first one to fall asleep. Al walked down the hallway to JD and Tracy's room. He found JC sitting on the balcony just as Magna had stated. In his hand was his parents' wedding picture. "What's up, little man?" JC turned and Al could see tears in the boy's eyes. He didn't say anything, he just pulled up a chair next to JC and waited.

"Something's going to happen to my Daddy, isn't it?" the boy asked looking down at the picture.

Looking at the boy's dropped head it was hard to read his eyes. "You know, when you talk to a man, you should always look him in the eyes. That's the only way you can tell if he is being honest." JC looked up at his uncle. Al smiled. "That's better." He stared at JC, whose eyes were the mirror image of his mother's but everything else, from his sharp jawline to his build was his father's. "You and I have gotten to know each other very well over the last five years, haven't we?"

"Yes sir," JC nodded his head.

"Have I ever lied to you?"

"No sir," the boy held his stare.

"I swear to you, that we will not let anything happen to your father or your mother. Now, that doesn't mean people will not try, because they will. But I think your Uncle Brian, Uncle Samuel, Uncle Joshua, Uncle Tucker and I are going to be tough to get through. And whoever is out there that wants to harm your father will have to get through us before they will get anywhere near your parents."

"They are going to try to kill my Daddy in California," JC said without flinching.

"Why do you think that?"

JC looked down at the picture. "I don't know." He hesitated. "It's the logical thing to do. If I wanted to kill a presidential candidate, I would need to get to a country where even if they found me, the government wouldn't let them take me. And it would have to be somewhere I can get to quickly. That's why I told my Dad not to go to California or Texas." He looked up at his uncle. "You know they killed John Kennedy in Texas."

It was clear to him before that JC was highly intelligent for his age, but tonight he displayed a caring nature. A normal child would simply be afraid for their parents. This child knew exactly why he was afraid and that the fear was justified. "Then it's a good thing your father is not in Texas. But his location isn't relevant. It's our job to keep him safe." Al looked out into the night. "At your age you feel kind of helpless. There are people you love and want to protect, but you're small and the bad people are usually a lot bigger." He turned back to the child. "See, I think that gives you the advantage."

"Really?"

"Definitely," Al smiled. "The adult will not expect a mere child to out think them. It's not always about your size. Sometimes you have to beat the enemy with your mind. That's what I did to protect your Mom when I was little."

The boy smiled, "How did you protect her?"

"The same way you are helping us to protect your Dad tonight." Al shrugged his shoulders. "You don't know why, but you just have a feeling something isn't right—right?"

JC nodded, "Yes."

Al pulled out his phone, "That's called instinct or as your Uncle Brian would say a hunch." He smiled and pushed a button on his phone. "Let's call in your hunch." JC stared at his uncle. Al could see the pride in the boy's eyes. "Brian, Al. Listen, we want you to follow up on a hunch we have here," He winked at JC. "This California trip is a good location for trouble. Let's double up on security." Al put his fist out so JC could give him a pound. He could see the tension in his nephew's eyes ease away. After he completed his call to Brian, Al looked down at JC. "Feel better?"

The boy nodded, "Yeah,"

"Good. How about a game of Scattergories before you go to bed?"

An hour later, Al sat at the monitor while Magna took a few hours of shuteye. Ryan was into day five on the campaign trail and he missed her sassy mouth in more ways than one. He pulled up the videoconference on one of the monitors and waited for her to answer. Hearing her voice wasn't enough to hold him over another five days, he needed to see her. When she appeared on the monitor she was dressed. "You look good girl."

Ryan smiled, as she removed her earrings. "Just came in from a rally. The Richie Richs' of the world love to write checks."

"Sounds like a successful trip thus far."

"The people out here are eating them up—especially Tracy. Everywhere she goes, checks are written before she even asks." Ryan smiled as she yawned. "You're up late, what is it, two in the morning there?"

"A little after," Al replied as he put his feet up. "Miss you."

"Awe Day, are you going to make me horny before I go to bed?"

"That was my intent."

"Just hearing your voice does that."

"Good to know. But I needed to see you."

"Really. How much do you want to see?"

"Don't tease me like that."

"Like what?" she asked as she pulled up her dress removing her revolver from her garter."

"You like hard things between your legs don't you?"

She pulled her dress over her head revealing her curvy well-toned body in just a lace bra with matching boy shorts, garter belt and stockings. "Wish it was you instead of a hard piece of metal." She stated as she walked away from the monitor to hang the dress up.

"Don't do that to me."

The hitch in his voice could be heard as she walked slowly back. "For your viewing pleasure only." She bent over releasing the stocking from the garter, then slowly undressed her legs. She threw the stocking across the bed, then slowly turned her backside to the monitor, bent to the right to undress that leg.

"So you're into teasing a brother."

"Well, as someone once told me," she leaned forward, "I'm a woman. So, I'm putting forth all efforts to embrace my womanhood." She sat on the side of the bed, placed two pillows behind her, then crossed her legs.

"Don't do it." Al shook his head.

"What?" she smirked, "Don't you want to see how I embrace myself when you're not here?"

Al closed his eyes, praying that she would end the torment, and hoping against all hope that she wouldn't.

"You're going to miss the best part if your eyes are closed."

"Morgan." Al moaned as he opened his eyes to see her spread her legs and lay back on the pillows.

Looking into the monitor, Ryan watched as his eyes became hooded. If she was there in person she could imagine his light brown eyes darkening. Her hands covered her breasts as she gave them a gentle squeeze. "Would you believe, there was only one other man before you? Making love to you made me realize he wasn't a man at all. He was just a little boy." She allowed one hand to slowly move to her stomach, circling her navel. "Do you remember your tongue right here? I do." Her tone lowered, "I remember so well, I can almost feel the texture of your tongue right now. Can you taste my skin, Al?"

Her movements had Al mesmerized. "Mmm," He moaned in response to her question. "I can taste that and more Morgan."

"That's good Al, because I want to give you more." She eased her hand under the lace trim of her boy shorts. Her body instinctively reacted when she touched herself.

He couldn't reply for the anticipation of her next actions were too strong. Helpless was not an emotion Al was used to. Yet, that was exactly what he was feeling as he watched Ryan. But like the good man he was, he knew it was time for him to take over. "Is that one finger or two?"

"That's just one."

"You're going to need another to feel like I'm partially there. Can you give me another one Morgan?"

Holding his eyes, Ryan smiled, "I can give you whatever you like."

Al smiled as he sat forward, "Is that so? I really want you to enjoy this moment, Morgan. Take your thumb and circle your bud until you just can't stand it anymore." He spoke in a low aroused voice. "Now I want you to slowly pull your fingers out." He watched as she followed his instructions. "Ease them back in." he waited, then said, "Do it again." He saw her body squirm, as she reentered herself. "That's it babe. Keep moving just like that while I talk to you." He licked his lips as he spoke. "The first time I saw you, I wanted you. Those sexy hips mesmerized me. All I could think about was how deep I could immerse myself into you. The first time we made love, when the very tip of me touched you, I lost a piece of my soul." She stopped.

"Don't stop baby, keep going." She did. "Entering you was like sliding on a glove made just for me. You were hot. Everytime I entered you, the heat of you made me want more. Can you feel the heat around your fingers?" he smiled as she nodded. "I like the way your inner muscles squeeze around me. Can you squeeze your muscle for me now Morgan." He heard her moan. "I need you to go a little faster babe—a little deeper still. That's it babe, keep going. For that juice you are about to release is as sweet as nectar, and is as necessary for the nourishment of my soul as water is necessary for the survival of my body. I can taste your sweetness on my tongue right now Morgan, but I need more babe." He watched her body heaving as she began to go deeper into herself. "More babe and more. I need all that babe, let it go. Let it flow onto my waiting tongue. Can you feel it, waiting right at your gate for me to lick every drop of your sweetness?" He not only heard her release, but seeing it made him want to fly out to California just to catch what was flowing down her thigh. He watched as she lay there, with her eyes closed.

"Damn." Was all she could say.

"Sweet dreams babe."

Al disconnected the conference and began counting the hours until he could taste her in person.

It was three in the morning when Monique's phone buzzed. At first, she ignored the sound, turned over and closed her eyes. But before she could return to a sound sleep, it buzzed again indicating there was a text message, not a call. Curious as to who would be texting at this time of night, Monique snatched up the cell and read the text: 12 Angels. "What?" Monique slammed the phone back on the nightstand, laid back down in a huff. A few seconds later she sprang back up grabbing the cell. She looked at the text again. It didn't come through on her number. The phone vibrated in her hand. It was Ned.

"Good morning, Spicy. Did you get the message?"

Pushing her hair back from her face, she replied. "Yeah, but I have no idea what it means."

"It's a code."

"Yeah, I got that. But a code for what? And who would send a code at three in the morning. I mean the Senator doesn't have the phone. It's at the office in a desk drawer." Monique questioned as she walked into her kitchen.

"Maybe the message is meant to be received tomorrow or the next day."

"Hmm, could be. Can you tell where it came from?" She asked as she prepared a cup of coffee.

"West Coast is all I can tell you at the moment. But I'll keep digging."

"That's a big area. Do you think you can narrow that down just a little?"

"I'll get back with you as soon as I have something."

"Thanks," Monique said as she sat at the counter, waiting for the coffee. "Do you ever sleep, Ned?"

"I'm here to grant your every wish Spicy. I don't sleep until you do."

"Awe, you're my personal techie."

"I handle every member of Absolute's team."

"How many members are there?"

"Five."

She yawned, "Well thanks for being on the other end. Will we ever meet?"

"Not in this life. The only reason you know Absolute is because he was instrumental in bringing you on board and you're family. If you ever meet any other members, you'll never know it. We all have our roles here. They rarely cross paths."

"But you know all of us?" She asked as the coffee finished.

"That I do, my love. Here's your info. The tower used was in Los Angeles."

"California?" Monique frowned as she sipped her coffee.

"Yeah, you know, Hollywood, land of the fairies."

She sat her cup down, "Los Angeles, the city of Angels. The code—12 Angels."

"Hum, I don't believe in coincidences. We better pass this code on."

"What coincidence? And who are we passing this on to?"

"The last time Absolute checked in he was on his way to Los Angeles. This may have something to do with what he's working on."

"He did come by the office last week to see the Senator." Monique thought for a minute, "What's the 12? It could be an address, a date, a room, time...I bet that's it Ned. It's a time. What time did the code come in?"

"Three o'clock your time."

"That puts it at around midnight LA time. But twelve could also be noon. So we know the where is probably LA, the question is the time twelve noon or twelve midnight? And what? We still don't know what all this is about or what to do with the information."

"We'll put the info in Absolute's hands. He'll know what to do. Good work, Spicy."

"Appreciate that Ned, but I want to know where this all leads." Monique ended the call and placed her cell on the counter. Sitting back drinking her coffee, the mini mystery of the text continued to plague her. She picked her cell back up to check her calendar. Nothing significant was on there.

Now wide awake from the mystery text message and the coffee, she turned on the television that hung from the cabinet in the kitchen. There was nothing interesting on until she reached the 24 hour news channel. The anchor was discussing the drop in the market and since she invested heavily, she stopped to listen. The topic changed to politics and the first story covered Jerry and his wife on the trail in Tennessee and Kentucky. His wife really was pretty, Monique thought as she watched the couple shaking hands and kissing babies. She wondered if his wife knew, all she had to do was give him a child and Jerry would stop stepping out on her. Maybe she'll send her an anonymous letter. Next up were her Uncle JD and Aunt Tracy. She had to smile because they looked damn good out there. The crowds were a little larger than Jerry's and a lot more diverse. She turned the sound up to hear the announcer's take on the Arizona and Nevada rallies. Then he announced the candidate would be in Los Angeles tomorrow speaking with community leaders at nine and at the Los Angeles Police luncheon at noon. "Talk about a contrast," the announcer said. Monique laughed, that was her Uncle JD trying to bridge the gaps. That's one thing she really did admire about him. He looked at everyone as a person. To him it didn't matter if the person was a gang member, a senator, a hooker or a teacher. Everyone was worth listening to in his book. This country really needs him to show people how to be accepting of others. Once the story ended, she was about to turn the television off when the words from the announcer played back in her mind.

Monique ran into her office to pull up the Internet on her computer. She typed in JD Harrison and Los Angeles. The story of his visit and schedule of events appeared. Grabbing her cell, she started to call Ned back. But this was family. She had to warn her Aunt Tracy. She pushed another button and waited.

"Monique?" Tracy questioned as she answered the phone. "Is everything okay?"

"No. Aunt Tracy, I really need to speak with Uncle JD."

"He's talking with some people right now. Can I help?"

"No Aunt Tracy this is very important. I really need to speak with him now." There was a moment of silence. "Aunt Tracy, how many times have I ever called to talk to Uncle JD?"

"Never that I remember. But Monique he is really busy."

"This is more important than anything he could be talking about. This is life or death Aunt Tracy and that's not an exaggeration."

"Okay," Tracy sighed. "Let me see what I can do."

Monique waited.

"Monique?"

"Uncle JD, call me from the hotel phone at this number."

"Are you alright Monique?"

"I am, but you are not. Call me now. I'll hold. Dial the number as I give them to you."

JD sat on the bed as Tracy watched. "Go." He dialed the number recognizing what it was. "Why am I calling you on a secure government line, Monique?"

"You're going to know this soon so here it is. I work for the CIA. I was recruited while at Howard. My current assignment is to unveil information on some possible bad connections the Senator may have. I believe an assassination attempt will be made on you tomorrow at noon during the Police luncheon and the Senator is involved."

"Why do you believe that?"

"A week ago the Senator was given a disposable cell phone. I took down the number and had my techie to place a trace on any calls. Tonight a coded text came through that read 12 Angels. Los Angeles is the city of Angels. Twelve noon is your scheduled event with the police department. Guns will be everywhere. The assassin will go undetected. Uncle JD, you have to cancel that event."

JD held the line without speaking. What Monique said about working for the CIA did answer a lot of questions. "What's your code name?"

"Spicy."

He laughed. "It fits. Hold on."

While she held the line, Monique walked into her bedroom closet, pulled out a pair of jeans and a top. Once the next call was made, she had to be ready to leave.

"Spicy."

Monique stood straight up. Oh hell, she thought. "Yes sir."

"Tell me what you have." After a few silent curse words, Monique told Joshua how she broke the code. "Good work, but wrong move. Your first call is always to me. Your first, your last, your everything goes through me. Am I clear?"

"Yes sir. I hear you, but this was family. Just like you, I have to protect my Country and my family."

Joshua liked the spunky new recruit. "Report in, but keep the phone call out. Clear?"

"Clear." Monique replied then disconnected the call. "Whew." She gathered her purse. Dropped her cell phone inside and pulled out her keys. Traffic should be light this time of morning. Instead of taking the Metro, she would drive to the office.

The night watchmen sat at the console in the security office and watched as Monique walked into the elevator on the top floor. Must be a booty call, he thought as he noted the time. He never saw her get off.

Chapter 17

Security was tight on a normal day' it was relentless today. Brian's security team was stretched thin. There was now a credible security threat. Like it or not, Secret Service was needed. Today, Brian not only had to ensure his staff was on point; he had to deal with and tame the superior attitudes of the Secret Service. Fifty of the agents that accompanied them on this trip were needed. There was a definite need to set boundaries on the two teams.

Brian stood in the center of the conference room of the hotel wondering when the man speaking would get tired of listening to himself. Waddell Calhoun, Deputy Director of the United States Secret Service, had taken over the meeting with a misconception. JD and James requested Brian's complete cooperation with the group of Special Agents. But his patience had just run out.

"Deputy Director Calhoun, I believe we are getting a little ahead of ourselves." Brian spoke as politely as he could. "If I'm not mistaken, your command begins once Governor Harrison moves into the White House. While we do need your men and you, the direction of this mission comes from me."

"You have a problem with being proactive on this mission, Thompson?"

Calhoun had been Brian's commanding officer when he was with the FBI. The two bumped heads then and would probably bump heads now. However, things were quite different now. This was Brian's turf. All planning, participants, and assignments went through him. Apparently, Calhoun had missed the memo. "Not at all, but it seems you are about ten years late on the proactive issue. We've been protecting the governor for a while now." He pointed to JD who was sitting quietly in a corner. "Evidently he's still alive."

"The number of death threats this candidate has received dictates our need to be here. The President understands this country would be torn apart if Harrison was killed. How many attempts were made on his life during your reign? How many bullets did you take during that time frame? How many lives were lost? I'm here as a result of a directive from The President of the United States. You want us out, talk to him."

The agents in the conference room turned to Brian, as did James with an understanding look in his eyes. James hesitated to interfere with the jockeying for position, but he knew Brian was the authority here, not Calhoun. The sooner that was established, the sooner the testosterone levels in the room would drop and they all could get to what's important—protecting JD. He looked at JD and nodded.

"Deputy Director Calhoun, if I may address the group before Mr. Thompson responds." Calhoun nodded giving JD the floor. Looking the group over, it seemed they all needed a drink or something to loosen them up. "It's pretty early in the morning and I'm sure all of us need a few hours of sleep. I can't begin to tell you the hell I will have to deal with if as much as a hair is harmed on me." The group smiled in understanding. "My wife will kill me before any assassin has a chance. We have been on this journey for ten years now and I know this is not a small undertaking. We have dealt with threats both foreign and domestic. While we appreciate and certainly welcome your participation, we all need to be very clear on the chain of command. As of today, your commander is Brian Thompson. If the good people of this nation elect me as your President your orders will then come from Deputy Director Calhoun. I understand, this is a little different than what the Service is used to and will accept the decision of anyone who wishes to step down from this assignment at this time, without prejudice. The door is open." JD waited.

"We are here to serve our country's best interests. At this moment, that's you," one agent stated. "We follow your command."

"Thank you," JD replied, then continued on. "Deputy Director Calhoun will be available as a resource, for he knows the skill level of his people. Are all the roles clear?" With the nods of heads JD turned to Brian. "Mr. Thompson, you may respond now."

Brian stood. "It doesn't seem necessary to answer your questions at this point, but I will. In ten years I haven't lost any men. I've been shot twice, once in the arm and four times in the back. The only time any of my protectees were injured was during the time I worked for the Bureau and was restricted by their limitations. In this position, I make the calls; there is no red tape. My plan is to keep that record intact."

Calhoun was clearly pissed with Brian's response. Truth or not, he didn't appreciate the jab from the past. "Clearly, my presence is no longer needed here. I'll take my leave."

Brian watched as the man walked towards the door. Against his better judgment, he offered an olive branch. "Deputy Director Calhoun, actually I do need your expertise in some areas. I would appreciate it if you'd hang around for awhile."

Calhoun nodded then took a seat.

"There is a confirmed threat against Governor Harrison. Against my better judgment, he refuses to make my life easier by cancelling the event. Therefore, to keep me from having to deal with his wife, I would appreciate it if you all will keep him alive." He saw one or two smiles break through and thought that's a start. "Okay, here's what we have. The assailant has been identified only by his alias. Frankly, I don't give a damn what his name is. I want two things from this mission. I want him stopped and I want the name of the person or person that took out the contract." He hesitated. "Let's be clear. There is a possibility that this is a foreign threat and this mission could have international implications. But more importantly, I want to make sure that every face that is in this room returns after this mission is complete. Be careful. With details on the suspect, Special Agent Lassiter, who's been on the trail of this assassin for a while now." He nodded as Joshua stood.

"I thought you wanted the man to live long enough to give us a name," one agent joked.

Others joined in and laughed. "All of us know Lassiter, kills first and then tries to ask questions."

"Any other day, I would have a comeback for you. But this day and this man are too important. Oh, by the way, your mother sends her love." The group of men and women laughed. Joshua put a picture on the monitor. "This is the last picture we have of the assassin. It was taken less than six hours ago in this hotel. We believe the attempt will be made at noon, but that is only a theory. Everyone remain vigilant at all times. The candidate and his wife will be surrounded by no less than twenty agents, one step away, at all times."

"That's a little tight," JD stated.

"Yes sir. It is. If anyone is going to take a bullet today, it will be one of us, not you." Joshua turned back to the group. "It's four o'clock. We will assemble back here at seven. Before we go, I need twenty agents to volunteer for the one-step protection detail."

Every hand in the room went up. The scene humbled JD. Brian turned to Calhoun. "Your call, director."

JD, James, Brian and Joshua remained after everyone left. "JD, I'm going to ask again. Cancel this event." Brian stated.

"This is our best chance to catch this guy and to determine who is behind the threat," Joshua objected. "JD, man I realize you really don't know me. Presidents and Directors put up with my bull for a reason. I'm damn good at my job. They put the trust of this country in my hands. I don't take that lightly. We need to follow this plan."

"Have you ever had to stand in front of Tracy and explain why something happened?" Brian argued. "It ain't easy. We are going to have hell to pay if anything goes wrong. And you are going to be the one that has to explain things to her." The other men in the room agreed.

"She's just a woman." Joshua declared. "I can't believe all of you are scared of one woman." He walked out of the room.

"Spoken just like a man that hasn't been bit," James laughed.

Al received the call at six the next morning. He called Donnell, Tucker and Magna in for the seven o'clock conference call. For extra support, the Williams brothers joined the team for the day. Donnell knew how neither Brian nor Al liked outsiders on the compound. A few more familiar the faces, was helpful. The video conference displayed Brian, Samuel and Ryan seated at the table.

"You seem to have a few extra people there Al," Brian stated.

"They showed up at the front gate with Williams. They might be helpful," Al joked.

"Might?" Jarrell laughed. "We're the three Musketeers plus one."

"Yeah," Scott added. "We're here to save the day."

"What in the hell are you dopes doing there?" Ryan asked. "Not you, Devin."

"Protecting your man," Jarrell replied.

Al sighed, "Babe, you really should have warned me about your family."

"How do they even know about you?"

"Well Al came....."

Devin hit Jarrell before he could finish the statement. "It's not important. We're here to help in any way we can."

"We appreciate that." Brian stated. "I wish I could say this is another unconfirmed threat, but I would be lying. This is a verified threat against the Governor. While we believe we have the assassin in reach, I don't want to miss anything. We have to step up security at the compound. Al, a few agents will be there within the hour. Use them as you see fit. I prefer one of our people in the house with the children. Now that you have the Williams version of Frick and Frack they can handle keeping the children occupied and protect them at the same time."

"I think we were just insulted," Scott said to Jarrell.

"Focus here people—Focus. We are working on different time zones. We are going to try to catch a few hours of sleep, then the game is on. Be vigilant people. Al, hold down the fort."

"We have it covered on this end. Bring everyone home safe."

"Will do—out."

Al disconnected the call, then pulled out his cell. Pushing one button, the call went through. "I like you in one piece. Be careful."

"Awe Day, I'm beginning to think you care."

"I do. I'll show you how much when you get home."

He disconnected the call and turned to see all the William brothers and Magna grinning at him. "Tucker, you and Devin take the command post. Donnell, take care of the agents coming in. Magna and I will show Frick and Frack around."

Ned checked for Monique's report. It hadn't come in. checking the log, his last contact with her was around three in the morning. It wasn't the twenty-four hours required by the agency before sounding an alarm, but it was well past Absolute's requirement. The problem was, Absolute had gone silent and Ned did not anticipate open communication until the situation with Harrison was finished. Normally he wouldn't invade an agent's privacy, but he needed to confirm her safety. He tapped into her security system and checked every room in her condo. There were no signs of her. The camera system to her building revealed her car was still in its parking space, but that wasn't enough. Most days she took the Metro into the office. Frustrated, Ned decided to go back to the last contact on the security cameras. Starting with the camera in her condo, he watched as she talked on the telephone, dressed, gathered her keys and walked out the door. He then switched to the security camera of the building. He watched as she entered the elevator. The elevator began its decent. It stopped on the fifth floor. A hand appeared spraying a substance, causing Monique to fall to the floor. A masked figure stepped inside with a huge army bag. He hit the button and the elevator continued down. Lifting her unconscious body, the man placed Monique in the bag, zipped it, threw the bag over his shoulder then walked off the elevator at the garage level. He placed the bag in the back of a Black SUV then drove off.

To Ned that was enough to sound the alarm. He placed the call to the Director. The Director's order was very clear. The Harrison operation took precedence. Absolute was not to be contacted until he opened communication. Ned looked at the clock. Absolute had until he followed the SUV and to get Monique's location. If communication had not been reestablished by then, he would open the gate himself.

The modern building seemed like it could touch the sky. It was difficult to determine which vehicle the candidate was in because the motorcade was extensive. The position of the vehicles was changed to ensure no one other than those in security knew which vehicle carried the candidate. The first vehicle carried six agents, who swept through the doors quickly and on alert. The Chief of Police, who had been advised of the situation only an hour before they arrived, met them at the door. Two more vehicles filled with agents arrived and filtered throughout the building. But before any of them arrived, Joshua was there. He had walked the building room by room, closet by closet. He knew the building inside out. Now, he had to think like the assassin, which was easy, for he was one of the best in the world in taking people out.

Whenever Joshua was on a job, his concentration was on that job, nothing else. The woman walking by in the six inch stilettos with legs longer than the building only piqued his curiosity as to why she was in an area of the building that had been sealed off. From his position in the tiled ceiling he followed the legs and watched as she passed a key card off to an officer. Now why would a member of the LAPD need to have an access card to the building? He touched the earpiece. "There's a long legged red head, black dress walking in your direction. Take her down."

From his location, Joshua could see every corner of the room below that was filled with men in blue. As he watched Secret Service enter the room, he knew JD wasn't far behind. The excitement in the room could be felt even from his vantage point. The Mayor stepped up to the podium and began his speech. Joshua pulled out a hand held computer, adjusted a few buttons then sat back and waited. As the body heat from the assassin came closer, the light on his monitor intensified. When the body was only a few feet away, Joshua turned the device off. He stood in the corner of the room, blending into the woodwork, virtually undetected.

The click of the door opening put Joshua on alert. His job was to take this man down without a shot being fired. But he couldn't do that until the attempt was made. Only a few seconds divided a good take down from a botched one. No longer in a position to see what was taking place in the room; Joshua had to go on instinct. When he heard the crowd erupt in applause he knew JD had entered the room. Time was up. When he heard the clip snap into place, he had to take the man down. As soon as he stepped out, the man turned with the weapon pointed at him, but by that time Joshua had dropped to the floor, kicking his legs from under him. The weapon fell to the floor, but the man moved quickly and was back on his feet.

Joshua shook his head. "I'm trying not to kill you."

The man did not reply, he simply pulled another weapon. Joshua grabbed the weapon and dismantled it with one hand. "Come on, man. Can I just handcuff you and take you out?"

The man grabbed Joshua by the lapel of his suit. "Not the suit, man." Joshua took the ball of his hands and slapped the man's ears, then gave him a head butt, and swung him down by twisting his neck. Joshua placed his foot on the man's throat and pulled his gun. "Stay still." The man attempted to kick Joshua's legs from under him. Frustrated,

Joshua pulled out a needle, pulled the cap off with his teeth, then slammed it into the man's neck. Then he sat on him. "We were doing alright until you touched the suit." Joshua contacted Brian and gave his location. He then pulled out his computer, pressed the man's fingers on the face of the device. He hit the send button, forwarding the fingerprints to Ned.

Samuel was the first to reach him. The look on his face was one of disbelief. "Did you kill him?"

"He's not dead—yet."

Samuel reached out to help his brother up as Secret Service Agents filed into the room. "How long is he going to be out?"

Joshua just looked at his brother. "Maybe an hour." He looked at the syringe. "Maybe five." It was then that his earpiece beeped. He pushed the button to activate the device. "Silent mode Ned. That means no communication from the outside. "

"Spicy was taken from her condo. I'm sending footage to you."

Chapter 18

JD and Tracy were taken directly to the airport where they boarded the plane. In the secure room used as the office, JD, Brian, Director Calhoun, Samuel and James listened as Joshua gave his report. "The assassin was hired by Miguel Santiago."

"Santiago is the right hand man to Alejandra Mateo, the head of the Mexican Cartel." Director Calhoun questioned. "What's his connection to the Governor?"

"There is no connection," James stated.

"Then why the attempt on his life? The cartel doesn't just target people without a reason," the Director questioned.

"The Cartel didn't order or request the hit. The McClintocks ordered the hit through the Cartel. Mateo turned them down. Santiago disagreed with the decision and took the contract himself."

"The McClintocks?" The Director laughed. "You're telling me that a Governor and a United States Senator are involved in this plot?"

"Ex-Governor McClintock is the master mind. The Senator probably agreed. But I'm certain Jerry is not involved and probably not aware of his family's actions." Brian stated.

The Director stood and began to pace the room. "What proof do you have that the McClintocks are involved? From what you've said, the Cartel is the guilty party in this plot."

"An agent intercepted the message sent from the assassin to a telephone in Senator McClintock's possession. The coded message gave us the location and time of the hit. That's the connection to the Senator." Joshua angrily replied. "Now that agent is missing. If the Senator is involved, you won't have to worry about proof."

JD had remained quiet as the discussion surrounded him. The facts were disturbing. If the Senator was involved, it would be a devastating blow to the country. "I prefer the details of this event remain between the people in this room." He turned to Joshua. "Do we have any leads on the agent's whereabouts?"

Joshua nodded, "I have someone surveying the area we believe she is being held."

"Is she in Texas?"

"Yes."

"Has her father been informed?"

"No sir. We thought you would handle that call."

JD glared at Joshua. "Does he know her role in all of this?" When he received no answer, JD stood. "How long have they had her?"

"Since our call last night."

"How many agents are on the case?" JD asked.

Joshua looked to Samuel and Brian, then turned back to JD. "None," he said.

"Unbelievable." JD exclaimed. "Get the damn CIA director on the phone now! We don't leave our people behind. Joshua, I want you in Texas within the hour. I don't give a damn how you get there, just do it."

"Hold on JD," James stood. "You can't demand the Director of the CIA take action on any case. You have to handle this through the proper channels."

"Calvin, what legal remedies do we have?"

"We can always contact the Governor of Texas to request his assistance."

Everyone in the room held their breath. "Actually that's not a bad idea," Joshua stated. "This would be a good way for the Governor to show he is not involved in this."

"Is there a way she can be quietly extracted?"

"Without involving the local government—sure," Joshua replied. "But you will have to make that call to her father."

JD shook his head, "We have several issues here. The stability of the government, our international relationship with Mexico, and the impact on the election all hinge on the decisions we make. To add to all of that, you want me to tell this man his daughter has been kidnapped without revealing why."

"That about covers it," Joshua replied.

"Get him and the Governor of Texas on the phone." JD exclaimed as he turned to Joshua, "You bring her back by any means necessary."

After the room emptied out, only JD, James, Calvin, Samuel, and Brian remained. "Do you think it's wise to unleash Al and Joshua on Texas?" Calvin asked.

"When Mac is involved, you need a Calvary behind you." Samuel stated. "I'm a little concerned for my brother."

"I'm concerned for whoever has Monique." JD announced.

This was definitely not her bed, Monique thought as she turned over. The breath she took solidified her thoughts, for the place smelled stale and musky. Memories of the man spraying something in her face came to surface. She sat up quickly assessing where she was. "You ain't in DC anymore Monique." It seemed like a cabin, she thought as she surveyed the room. She sat on a queen size bed, with posts. A dresser was covered with dust, indicating it hadn't been used recently. The window had frilly pink curtains that were tied back with a bow. "How cute."

Standing, she stretched to relieve her sore muscles. "Alright, how do I get out of here?" She walked over to the door and to her surprise it opened.

"Well, hello there little lady."

Monique raised an eyebrow to the heavyset man sitting at a table in an open room. "And you are?"

The man smiled, "I'm Willie Ray. The only cowboy standing between life or death for you."

"If that's the case it's good to meet you Willie Ray. You have a bathroom around here?"

"One right over yonder," he pointed behind her.

That's when she noticed the other man. Where Willie Ray looked one hundred percent cowboy, the other man was definitely a city slicker. Willie Ray had him in bulk, but he had Willie Ray in attitude. "And you are?"

"Your executioner."

"Well, it's not nice to meet you." She turned back to Willie Ray, "Is he going to let me go to the bathroom?" She watched as Willie Ray stood, and stood and stood some more. "Damn Willie Ray, how tall are you?"

Dressed in jeans, a plaid shirt and work boots, he smiled, "Six-eleven, ma'am." He walked over and just stood in front of the other man. The man stood. "I'll let the man know she's awake." He looked at her, "Walk outside that door and I will shoot you."

"Isn't he a sweetheart?" Monique walked into the bathroom that was rather luxurious for a log cabin. She took care of her needs then washed her hands as she surveyed that room. Walking back out, she found Willie Ray at the stove. "Where am I, Willie Ray?"

"A long way from home and in deep manure."

Monique smiled, "I kind of thought that." She sat at the table where he placed a tall glass of tea, with a plate of barbecue, baked beans and corn on the cob in front of her. "This smells good Willie Ray. Can I eat this without being knocked unconscious again?"

"We take pride in our barbecue." He took a seat and began eating from his plate and smiled up at her. She followed his lead. "So, how did you get yourself in this pickle?"

"I'm not sure," she replied as she tried the baked beans. "Mmm, this is good." She continued eating. "How long have I been here?"

"A day or so."

"Hmm, my man is going to be mad when he gets here."

"I figured a cute little filly like you would have a man. Well you make sure you tell him, you're still alive because of the Senator. Mac would have let that city slicker have his way with you then kill you sure as shooting."

"Why am I here?"

"I'm not sure, but we're about to find out."

She turned as the door opened and two men walked in followed by the Senator. She knew right then and there, she was going to have to fight her way out. "I take it Willie Ray has been treating you well. I see he's trying to charm you with his famous barbecue."

"It's really good," Monique said as she continued to eat. "Would you like some?"

"What I would like Monique," he said as he sat at the table, "is to know who put you in my office?"

"Anna Murphy hired me for your office and you approved it." she pointed her fork at him as she talked. "Why would you do that knowing who I was?"

"It was a good political ploy that seems to have back fired on me," he smiled that winning politician smile. "I wish I had time to play this game with you. I so enjoyed the one in the office. But it seems time is running out for either you or me. I prefer we didn't have to do an either or."

Monique put her fork down. "Senator, if I told you, you wouldn't believe me."

"Try me."

Monique smiled. "Would you believe it if I told you Jerry got me the job?" she shrugged her shoulders. "I told you, you wouldn't believe me."

"You want me to believe my son put you in my office?"

"You don't have to believe me, ask him." Monique picked up her fork and continued eating.

"If what you say is true, we have a bit of a situation."

Watching him as she took a drink, she nodded her head, "Yes, you do have a situation, Senator." She sat the glass down. "Since you had me removed from my home without my consent, some, like my father, may view it as a kidnapping. I'm sure that wasn't your intent. And I'll be happy to tell my father just that as soon as you allow me to walk out of that door."

The Senator stood, "Willie Ray, please take good care of our guest until I return."

"Senator, since we are being so reasonable, I think it would be a good idea if you returned my purse and cell phone."

The Senator looked away as he said, "I'll take that under consideration."

Once the door closed, Monique turned to Willie Ray, "Got any more barbecue?"

Al, Ryan, Joshua and Tucker reviewed the tapes from Monique's condo. Four sets of eyes were glued to the computer monitor Joshua held, examining every aspect of the tape. Joshua stopped the tape.

"What do you see Joshua?" Al anxiously asked.

Joshua pointed to the screen, "Him," he replied as he pulled out his cell phone. "Ned, get me a location on Lucifer."

"What is it?" Al asked again.

Joshua put up his hand indicating to hold on.

"He's no longer with the agency," Ned replied.

"Who is he working for?"

"Private security for Senator McClintock, however, he's also worked for Mac from time to time."

Joshua disconnected the call. "Let's go back a little ways."

"There he is again," Ryan pointed out.

"This is the last time I'm going to ask you. Who in the hell is he?" Al asked through clenched teeth. Ryan rubbed Al's shoulders, trying to ease his anger. She wondered if her father would be this concerned if something were to happen to her.

"Ex-CIA. He now works for McClintock."

"The Senator?" Ryan asked.

"Unfortunately, he works for the Senator and Mac."

"Do you think he has Monique?"

Joshua nodded, "Yes."

"All you CIA people have specialties," Ryan asked. "What's his?"

"Extracting information by any means necessary."

As cool as he could, Al inquired further, "This man could be torturing my little girl?"

"We're going to get her back," Tucker spoke for the first time. "Then we'll kill the men that had the nerve to take her."

"Monique is tough." Joshua stated, "She can handle herself with the best of them."

Al looked down, "How do you know that Joshua?" he asked in a chilling voice.

"Because, I know."

Now glaring at the man, Al asked. "Why would the Senator want Monique silenced? What does she have on him and why do you know more about this than you are saying?"

Joshua called Ned as he held Al's glare. "Give me a location on Lucifer."

"I have one better than that," Ned boasted. "It was difficult to trace Monique's face. She was in a bag. However, using our trusty traffic satellite system, I tracked our friend Lucifer from the condo to the airport. It took a little time, but I picked him up again at the airport in Austin. I was able to track him to I-35 right before Buda, Texas. One guess who has a place near there?"

"The Senator?"

"No. The Senator's mistress."

"Eleanor McClintock?"

"Bingo."

"You are the Geek-Master,"

"Thank you, thank you, thank you very much."

Joshua hung up the phone, "We have a starting point." He walked to the carpit to speak with Melissa Sue.

"Any chance Monique is working for the agency?" Tucker asked.

Al just held Tucker's glare as he felt the shiver that went through Ryan. He looked into her eyes and wondered why she couldn't do the same with him. "It doesn't matter at this point. My daughter is being held somewhere against her will. It's my job to bring her home."

Chapter 19

After giving the order to Lucifer to extract information from Monique, the Senator needed a drink. He didn't want to have the girl killed, but if she was the only one that could connect him to the cell phone, he may not have a choice. He slumped into the chair in his office thinking she would be dead now if it was his father. He never had the heart his father did, and more he wasn't sure he wanted one. The bottom line for him was seeing his son in the White House. It was something he could not accomplish, but Jerry was different. Jerry cared about people, about the country even about other countries. He deserved to be President. Taking a drink and allowing the brown liquid to smooth his ruffled nerves, was the best thing to do at that moment. For the thought of what would be happening in the guest house was not a pleasant thought.

"Father—father. Where are you?" Jerry yelled through the house as he walked into the study. He stopped and stared at his father. "Tell me it's not true." He slammed the door behind him. "Tell me you do not have Harrison's niece somewhere on this property."

"I don't have Harrison's niece on this property," the Senator replied right before taking another drink.

"Where is she?"

"What concern is it of yours?"

Jerry shook his head in disgust. "I never put you in that category with grandfather. But if you've done what Harrison is accusing, I know I was wrong. You are too smart for this. For God's sake you're a United States Senator, not some street gangster trying to protect his turf. Which by the way, do you know who Monique's father is? Do you have any idea what chain of events you have started?"

"While you decide which of those questions you want me to answer, I have one for you. Did you put that girl in my office?"

The question caught Jerry off guard. "Yes."

The Senator rose, "Why in the hell would you do that son? He slammed his glass on the desk. "You put a spy in my office."

"Monique is not a spy, Father. She's an intelligent young woman that I happen to enjoy being around."

"Are you sleeping with this girl?"

"No more than you are sleeping with my wife. But that's neither here nor there. What's important is you releasing Monique this instant. Where is she?"

"We can't release her."

"We who, and why the hell not?"

"Son," the Senator pleaded. "You have to understand. The girl knows too much. We can't let her go."

"Knows too much about what?"

"Jerry," the Senator began to explain, "We're in a bit of a pickle here. Your grandfather set a plot to get rid of Harrison."

"Get rid of Harrison how?"

The Senator ran his hand through his now graying hair. "The only way to guarantee you the White House."

Jerry turned his back, shaking his head in disbelief. "Don't say it, Father. Don't say it." He turned sharply around, "Did you have any part in this asinine plot against Governor Harrison? This is not the time to lie to me. Did you have any part in this?"

"No son," The Senator replied quite sincerely, "I happened across the information and confronted Father. You know him, son. He has that righteous indignation about him. He truly believes he is correcting a wrong by moving Harrison out of the race for you to become President."

"I don't want the Presidency that way." Jerry yelled. "I win or I don't. We don't kill people over elections. This isn't a foreign dictatorship."

"You know how your grandfather overreacts to things, Jerry. He threatened to kill me if I stood in his way."

"Father, listen to me," Jerry tried to reason. "We have to return Monique to her family. It's the only way we get out of this."

The Senator shook his head, "Son, I'm afraid it's too late. Your grandfather already gave the go ahead to silence the girl permanently."

Jerry couldn't believe what he was hearing. "You cannot be serious." He grabbed his father by the lapels, "We have to stop this from happening. Where is she, damn it?"

"You will have to ask your grandfather son. I honestly don't know where she is."

Jerry released his father and watched as he fell backwards into the chair. He began walking out backwards towards the door. "Know this," he said solemnly. "If anything happens to Monique, you and grandfather can forget about the Presidency. I'll drop out of the race. How do you think that will play in the political arena?" He walked out swinging the double doors to the office.

"Jerry—Jerry!" The Senator called to no avail. Jerry kept walking. "Hell." He picked up the phone to call

Lucifer. He had to retract the order. "Let her go." He ordered when Lucifer picked up on the second ring.

"You're sure about that. This girl can connect you to the cell phone."

"Let her go, damn it. That's an order." The Senator hung up the phone.

Lucifer was a person that took matters into his own hands when the people he worked for made stupid decisions. This was dumb. You don't leave witnesses— period. He dialed a number. "Your son pulled back. He wants the girl sent home. What do you want?"

"Bring her to me," Mac ordered.

Lucifer hung up the phone, with a sinister look on his face.

Monique tested the windows in the room. They were bolted shut. The only way out was through the front door. Willie Ray was a sweetheart, but there was no way she could take him. Time was running out. There was no way the Senator was going to let her live and she knew it. The minute he walked in the door that sealed her fate. There was no way he could let her live. As soon as he had the information he wanted, she could count the minutes she would remain alive. For whatever reason, she was nervous about the situation, but not afraid. There were many times she had been in a rough spot, but her father or Uncle Tucker always—always got her out. This time would be no different. She just had to find a way to give them time to get to her. Ned or someone had to know she was missing by now.

There was a sound at the window. Monique turned with a smile, thinking that didn't take them long. But when she looked out, it was one of the Senator's goons taking the bars off the window. *What the hell?* She thought. Then it dawned on her, they couldn't go through Willie Ray to get to her. "Willie Ray!" she screamed. "Willie Ray, help!" Willie Ray came bursting through the bedroom door. Monique pointed, "Someone's trying to come through the window."

The sound from the electric screwdriver stopped, but not before Willie Ray figured out what they were trying to do. He grabbed her by the hand, "Come with me." He walked into the other room, closing the bedroom door behind them. The evil looking devil was there with a syringe in his hand. He shoved it into Willie Ray's arm, but whatever was in it wasn't fast acting enough to keep Willie Ray from knocking the crap out of him, momentarily. Monique took the moment to haul ass out the door. The man from the window was there. Where she got the strength from, she would never know. But she kicked him dead in the balls, bringing him down to her size. Then she karate kicked him in the face while he held his balls screaming. Turning quickly she ran towards the back of the house. "Damn!" all she could see was open fields all around. No matter what direction she ran, she would be seen.

One thing she knew for certain, if she stayed in that spot, she was going to die. Instinct took over and Monique began running. The will to live took control as she ran towards the nearest wooded area. Yeah, she heard the car behind her, but damn if she was going to stop to see who was coming. The devil called out to her and she ran faster. The trees no longer looked like a blur in the distance. She could see the outline of the bark and the branches hanging heavy with leaves. Then the car curved, blocking her view and her way, but that didn't stop her. She increased her speed, took one leap, hit the roof of the car, jumped down and kept running. The devil's cursing echoed in her ears, but as long as it was behind her, she didn't care. The woods were less than a mile away. The car came to a screeching halt behind her, then she heard the footsteps running. A hand reached out and grabbed her hair and swung her to the ground.

Angry, the devil kicked her in the ribs. The pain didn't have time to register as he grabbed her by the hair and yanked her up.

"I should kill you here and now," he cursed as he pulled her back towards the car. "The reason you are still alive is because we need information." He slammed her onto the roof of the car.

She wiped at the blood dripping from her nose. "Ooh, my daddy is going to whip your ass if you broke my nose." She shook her head. "And my Uncle Tucker, he is going to kill you."

"Shut up and get in the damn car." He had the trunk open.

With hands on her hips, Monique rolled her eyes, "I don't think so."

When he reached out to grab her, she took the palm of her hand and with all the will she had left, shoved it right into his nose. He fell to a knee, reeling from the pain as she climbed into the trunk. "Now you know how it feels." The devil slammed the trunk down as Monique smiled. "That's right Billie Bob or whoever the hell you are. Taking me down is not going to be easy." She turned on her side and was shocked to roll onto her purse. Jumping almost in glee, she hit her head on the trunk top. "Ouch." She rubbed the area then reached inside her purse. She cursed, her phone was not there. But her pin, that was actually a locator, was and she immediately pulled it out, pushed the activation button and slid it into her bra. Reaching in again, she pulled out the toolbox that resembled a makeup case. She pushed that under her panties. Smiling, she settled down for the ride to allow her muscles to rest for the next battle.

The plane carrying the small rescue group had landed. The tension in the chopper with Joshua at the controls was at a low simmer. Al was always a quiet man, but his mood was almost eerie. Ryan glanced in Tucker's direction. She could read him more so than Al. The last time she saw that look was when they took his lady friend Julianna home and ran into her abductor, Jonas Gary in the neighborhood. If she had not stopped him, Jonas Gary would be dead.

The silence was so strong everyone visibly jumped when Joshua's cell sounded, with the exception of Al. He never looked up—never even flinched.

The conversation was one sided, but it was clear there was a break in the case. "What's going on Joshua?" Ryan asked.

"We have a positive location."

"Let's go get her." Ryan replied with a sigh of relief. "We're going to have her soon, Al." Al didn't reply, he simply nodded, acknowledging that he'd heard her. For a moment, she was a little hurt by his reaction, but she didn't let it show. She'd become used to being shunned by the men she loved.

The back door of the mansion had more bling than the brothers in the hood's cars. Who in their right mind would put gold on a back door? Monique frowned at the stuffed animals that lined the walls of the room she was taken to. The only thing scarier than the hoofs with eyes hanging on the wall was the old man sitting in the chair behind the desk. Monique tilted her head to the side. "You know, it might be me, but was that you in that movie, It's A Wonderful Life? Damn if you don't look like old man Potter."

The devil gave her a hard push forward. She fell forward, catching the edge of the desk to break her fall.

"You still haven't learned that pay back is a bitch, have you?"

He was about to give her a backhand when the old man spoke. "Not in this room," he demanded. He turned angry eyes to her.

"Does he roll over and bark at your command, too?" Monique joked.

"You're the whore that turned my grandson against his father. I can't imagine what he sees in a darkie."

Monique frowned, "A darkie. What is that, code for a Black person?"

"Gal, if you had any sense, you would be afraid of me. I've taken out more of your kind than I care to count. And if you don't give me the information I need, you're going to be next."

Monique looked around as she spoke. "I don't think so, pops." With her hands on her hips she surveyed the room. "People used to tell me they did things big in Texas. I can see now that was no lie. Is that real?," she asked pointing to a rifle hanging above the fireplace. She watched as he nodded to the devil. She threw her hands up frustrated, "Oh, come on now. I wasn't that bad." The devil gave her a backhanded blow that sent her to the floor.

"I don't think you understand the severity of your situation little lady," Mac sat back in his chair.

Monique wiped the blood from her mouth as she sat on the floor. "First, my nose, then my lip." She shook her head. "I might not wait for Daddy. I just might kill you myself." She balled her fist up and punched him in the balls. The devil fell to his knees howling. Monique stood nodding. "I'm a girl from the hood. We can go blow for blow if you want."

Her mistake was not watching the old man, who walked up behind her and cracked her on the head with his cane, knocking her to the floor. She wasn't unconscious, but damn if she didn't wish she were.

Outside the house, Joshua and Ryan had gained entrance to the house through the back. A black gentlemen dressed in black met them at the door. "Are you here to help that girl? Mac's going to kill her sure as shooting."

"Is anyone else in the house?" Joshua asked.

"Yes sir. The staff is here and the man that brought the girl is here."

"Get the staff out of the house." The man ran off to do Joshua's bidding.

"He didn't seem too anxious to hang around," Ryan teased. "I'll keep an eye on them."

They moved quietly down the hallway, while Al and Tucker entered the house through a set of French patio doors. Once inside, they stopped for a moment to listen.

Mac leaned against his cane as he reached down and pulled Monique up by her hair. "Listen gal, you're going to tell me what I want to know or I'll order Lucifer here to skin you alive. Who are you working for?"

Monique couldn't help it, she laughed. "Lucifer?"

Tucker walked into the room, with his gun ready, but before he could take a shot, he was watching Mac fly into the fireplace. When he turned back Al was on top of the man that was on the floor, pounding away.

Monique got up and grabbed her daddy by the waist to pull him off of the man. "Daddy, you're going to kill him!"

Al turned to Monique, lifted her by the waist and sat her aside. "Yes, baby girl, I am." He turned back to the man on the floor and continued pounding.

"Uncle Tucker, don't just stand there, stop Daddy."

Tucker raised an eyebrow. "Why?"

"Uncle Tucker!"

Tucker sighed. "Alright." He took his time strapping the gun over his shoulder then reached down and pulled Al off of the man. Then he raised his gun and shot the man in the leg.

Mac stood, wobbling as he used the mantel on the fireplace to help him up. "How dare you come into my home boy? Don't you know who I am?"

Al walked towards Monique. Mac raised his cane to strike him.

Tucker raised his gun and pointed it at Mac. "I'm trying hard not to kill you old man."

Lifting Monique up, Al looked at his daughter. "Who did this to you?"

"I'm all right Daddy," she said as she stood.

The last thing Monique wanted was her father to be put back behind bars. She knew if she told him anything he would kill somebody. She looked at Tucker, "It took you long enough to get here."

Tucker had to smile, "What made you think I was coming?"

She looked as if she was wondering why he would ask such a stupid question. "My Daddy."

Tucker frowned and turned to her. "Your Daddy?"

"My Daddy told me whenever I was in trouble you would not be far behind."

"And you believed him?" Tucker teased.

"He's my Daddy, of course I did. Right, Daddy?"

The three broke out laughing. "Who hit you?" Al sobered very quickly.

Monique reached down into her panties and pulled out her case. Inside she pulled out an eyebrow pencil and twisted the end. She took a picture of Lucifer then walked over to take a picture of Mac. A blast went off from the other side of the room.

Everyone turned to see Joshua standing in the doorway blowing the end of his gun off. "That's how it's done in the Wild Wild West boys."

"Why in the hell did you do that?" Tucker asked. "The man was already down.

Joshua walked over and kicked Lucifer over. Under his body was a small device. He picked it up then flicked it open. "Duck," he yelled as he threw the device out the window. The device exploded with a whirl of smoke surrounding it. "We're the CIA: we may go down, but we are never out."

"I know that's right." Monique said as she fumbled with placing the eyebrow pencil back in the case.

No one was paying much attention to Mac until he reached above the fireplace and pulled down the rifle and yelled, "Get out of my house you n--." Before he could turn completely around, a sharp instrument was lodged in his throat, pinning him to the mantle. His eyes were as big as the stuffed animals above him.

Everyone turned to Monique in awe. "What? I have a license to kill any enemy of this country, foreign or domestic." She put her hands on her hips. "Does everyone in this room agree that Jeremiah McClintock is an enemy of this country?" She asked with hands on hips, face bloody and eyes that dared any of them to disagree.

"Was an enemy," Ryan laughed from behind Joshua. "He's dead now."

Monique nodded, then walked over, pulled the tool from his neck and wiped it off as Mac's body fell to the floor. She replaced the device in the case. "I believe my job here is done. Take me home Daddy."

Chapter 20

The failed assassination attempt on JD Harrison was on every news channel. Scenes from Mac McClintock's ranch in Texas were broadcast across the country. Social media sites were buzzing with claims that Jerry McClintock would be pulling out of the race amidst the scandal. "It's not clear at this time what role the Governor had in the plot against Governor Harrison. However, his camp is busy disclaiming any knowledge of the assassination attempt. It's unclear what action, if any will be taken against Senator McClintock. But sources say The Department of Justice is going to request his immediate resignation. This is Victoria Morales reporting."

JD clicked off the television and walked over to the window. Placing his hands in his pockets he hung his head in thought.

Tracy walked up behind him wrapped her arms around his waist and placed her head between his shoulders. "What are you thinking?"

"That if it weren't for Monique, I might be dead."

A small smile touched Tracy's face. "And to think, you wouldn't get the cereal for the child."

They both laughed, remembering the rebellious sixteen-year old. JD reached around and pulled Tracy to his side, still laughing. "Who knew that brat would be our lifeline after the butt whipping she received."

"Well as soon as Turk brings her home we need to find a way to thank her and make sure she's safe." She sighed. "I never thought working in a Senator's office would cause her any harm."

JD didn't reply for he now knew Monique was CIA. This was only the first of many covert assignments to come.

"Do you really think Jerry was in on the plot?"

"No." JD replied without hesitation. "I think he was caught in the middle of his grandfather's scheme."

Tracy looked up. JD looked down expectantly. He could sense she had more to say. "I think you should meet with Jerry one on one. No campaign managers or advisors. Look into the man's eyes and ask him the question. If you are satisfied with the answer talk him out of leaving the race."

JD stood there holding her, staring into those eyes he loved so much, remembering another time she advised him to talk to someone. "I'm not sure Brian or Secret Service would allow Jerry in the same state with me, much less a room."

"They work for you, Jeffrey. If you request it, they will do it. Just think about it. Jerry shouldn't pay for his grandfather's sins."

His lips slowly descended to hers. The gentle sweet kiss was filled with love and pride. "Your capacity to forgive is so amazing."

"What's amazing is how after all these years your lips still spread fire through my body."

"Keep talking like that woman, and I'm going to impregnate you right in this office."

Tracy sighed, patted his chest then stepped away. "Too late for that sailor, that ship sailed two months ago. I believe our child will dock around the same time we move into the White House." She walked out the door laughing at the expression on her husband's face.

Al, Ryan and Monique arrived home late that afternoon. Joshua stayed behind to handle the aftermath of questions. Al was certain they would keep him and Tucker out of the answers provided.

His concern was now Monique. She was tough, but to be kidnapped and held against her will had to have touched her nerves.

"I'm going to run upstairs and take a shower." She called down to her father as she climbed the stairs. "I sure hope you have some real food in the house and none of that tofu stuff you've been eating."

Al watched as his daughter walked up the stairs, wondering if she was really as okay with the events of the past forty-eight hours as she seemed. Time will tell, but at the moment he had to deal with another issue. "You knew," he said as his eyes moved from the stairs to Ryan.

There was no need acting like she didn't know what he meant for she felt it coming the moment Tucker made the suggestion. "Yes."

Al couldn't explain why, but his heart plummeted. "You didn't think that was something I should know?"

His tone was so cool, so even, void completely of emotion and that it caused her heart rate to increase. "Yes."

"Yet you remained silent for—how long?"

"A few weeks," she replied standing completely still, waiting for the last shoe to drop.

"Why?"

"It wasn't my business to tell."

"She's my daughter."

"She's an adult."

The tension in the room was as deafening as the silence became. Neither was willing to budge on their stance. Al turned towards the refrigerator taking items out to cook. Ryan took that as her cue to leave. Closing the door behind her, tears formed before she could stop them. Since she rode with them from the airport, she had to call her brother to pick her up.

"You are wrong for that," Monique said from the stairs, "and you are going to have to crawl to get her to forgive you." She took a seat at the breakfast bar. "You lived by a street code. No one talks. Ryan lived by that same code. Regardless of the relationship between the two of you, telling someone else's business is not something either of you would do. You live and die by the code. Your team taught her that, now you want to hold it against her. I hope you are smart enough to know she is the one woman on this earth that can heal that heart of yours." She smiled up at her father, then tilted her head. "Go get that woman and bring her back where she belongs."

The bruises on her face were clean, but still very visible. If it weren't for the felony charge, he would have blown the man's head off that had the nerve to touch her. "Code or no, she should have told me." He leaned across the counter and kissed his daughter's forehead. "Tell me how you got involved with the CIA."

"You really should go get Ryan."

Al nodded, "I'll talk with her later. Right now, I want to know about you."

Fifteen minutes after leaving Al's, Ryan was riding silently in the passenger seat of Devin's car. He took several looks in her direction, but just like when she was a little girl, she had shut down. Well, little girls grow up, but certain things never change. Devin pulled into the drive thru of the Krispy Crème on West Broad Street. "The hot light is on," he said, but received no response.

Devin ordered a dozen assorted donuts and two coffees. He drove to his father's house and parked in the driveway. They stepped out, walked to the back yard and sat in the sand box as if it was the most normal thing for two adults to do. Devin opened the box of donuts and smiled as his little sister reached in and took the glazed, sprinkle, sweet. He waited until she reached for the third one before he spoke. "Relationships are hard. It doesn't matter if it's your father or your lover." He took a sip of his coffee and sat it back on the wooden edge of the sandbox. "Expectations are high when love is involved because the heart is such a delicate muscle. It can be damaged to an irreparable level. But you know, whenever Daddy would say, 'You can't fix this,' Mommy would say, 'You can fix anything if you work hard enough.' I believed Mommy. If I didn't, then my life would be over. I don't know what's happened with you and Al. But I know he came here to face Dad to ask for your hand in marriage." Ryan's motion of biting another donut froze as she stared at her brother. He held her glare. "I want you to think about what it took for Al Day to ask anyone for anything."

Tears fell down Ryan's cheek. Devin reached out and pulled his sister into his lap, tucked her head in the crock of his neck and rocked her back and forth. It had been a long time since his sister cried. In a way it was a happy moment, for that meant she was at least feeling something. But for the tears to be flowing because of a man, well, as a big brother that just didn't sit right—even if that man was Al Day.

Proud was an understatement as far as Al was concerned. Somewhere along the line, his little girl had grown up. She was not only a beautiful young woman, but also a true patriot. After listening to her he knew he had JD to thank for that. Monique expressed how much she admired her Uncle JD for standing up, sometimes against his own, for what he believed was the right thing. It was clear to Al that he no longer had to worry about Monique. It was also clear that Tracy was all right in JD's hands. For the first time in his life, the only person he had to worry about was himself. Tonight, he didn't want to deal with his life, for that would mean thinking about Ryan. Could he trust his heart to a woman that lived by the same code as he? The heart was a complicated device. No one was immune to its functions—no one—not even him.

It wasn't quite seven in the morning when the doorbell sounded. Al walked to the front door, looked out and saw Mr. Williams, Ryan's father, standing on his front porch. Wondering why the old man was there, Al opened the door and was surprised when a fist connected to his nose, forcing him back a few steps.

"You made my daughter cry. Are you out of your damn mind?" The old man swung again, but this time Al ducked his fist and he stumbled forward. Catching his balance, Mr. Williams turned towards Al more than ready for battle. He swung again.

Al blocked the swing. "I don't want to fight you, Mr. Williams."

"You don't. Then stand there, I'll just whip your ass." Mr. Williams went for Al's throat. Al ducked and took Mr. Williams to the floor with a tackle.

The man clasped both hands together and hit Al in the back, causing him to fall backwards. The man may be old but he still moved with speed. He was on top of Al about to punch him again when Al wrestled him over, pinning his arms to the floor. "Look, old man. I don't want to hurt you, but I will if you don't calm the hell down."

"You claimed you loved Ryan. Well you don't hurt people you love." Mr. Williams yelled.

"You hurt her all the damn time," Al yelled. "Every time you turn away from her you hurt her. Every time she tried to please you and couldn't get not one 'I'm proud of you' from you—you hurt her. So don't come at me talking about hurting your daughter when that's all you've done her entire life." Al could see the tears welling up in the man's eyes.

"She's my daughter—my baby girl. In her entire life I've never seen her cry—until you." Al released the man's hands, but remained sitting on his chest. "She looked so much like my Mary with tears coming from her eyes last night. I never could take seeing Mary cry." He wiped the tears from his face. "I can't do much to change our life, but I'll be damned if I let you get away with hurting Ryan."

"Morgan—damnit," Al jumped on the man's chest. "Her name is Morgan." He sighed as he rolled off the man's chest. He sat up against the sofa and watched the old man. "Why did you push her away?"

Mr. Williams hesitated so long Al didn't think he was going to get an answer. "She looked and acted just like Mary." The tears rolled down the man's cheeks as he sat up with his back against the wall. "She talks like her, walks like her, and is sassy just like Mary. Every time I looked at her I saw Mary. It hurt so damn bad at times I couldn't even be in the same room with her." He wiped the tears.

"After a while it became the norm. Ryan is just as stubborn as her mother was. Once she closed down, there was no getting in."

"Did you ever try?"

Williams sighed, "Not really. I was too busy working. It was the only time I didn't think about Mary. I had to work until I was bone tired before I went to bed so she wouldn't creep into my dreams." He sat there not saying anything for a few minutes. "I am proud of her— you know. Even when she worked on the street, I knew what she was doing. I've watched her grow into a strong young woman. Seeing her break down in Devin's arms hurt. She should have been able to come to me."

"You closed the door on her."

"Did you?" Mr. Williams held Al's glare. "I don't know what happened and I don't care. But the man that stood on my porch stood up for Ryan. Where is he?" Mr. Williams stood, as did Al. "I may be an ass of a father, but I'm no different than any other man. I don't want to see my daughter hurt. You came to me and asked for her hand in marriage. Not many men do that these days. I believe you love her. Don't close the door on her like I did." He turned to walk to the door. Al followed. "If you tell anyone about this conversation I'm coming back to kick your ass again."

"Like you did this time?" Al smiled.

"Yeah, just like that." Mr. Williams walked out the door.

"Back to the shades, I see," Tucker teased when he walked into Al's kitchen a few hours later. He looked around. "Where's Ryan?"

"Her name is Morgan, damnit. Morgan!" Al's temper was still a little warm.

Tucker raised an eyebrow, "Okay. Where's Morgan damnit?"

Al gave Tucker a sideways glare. "She's not here." He opened the refrigerator to give Tucker a beer.

Tucker opened the beer took a seat at the bar then asked, "Why the shades?"

Al slammed the refrigerator door, walked around the counter and took a seat, pulling the shades off, so he could see. Tucker froze with the beer bottle midway to his mouth.

Tucker finished taking his drink before speaking. "I didn't get a call. So whoever clocked you isn't dead." Chuckling, Tucker asked, "You want to talk about it?"

"Not really." Al took a drink.

"If you tell me Ryan or Morgan did that, I swear you are going to lose all cool points with me."

"I almost wish it had been Morgan, then at least I'd know she was pissed at me. Right now, I get a nod of her head then she leaves the room."

"Can you blame her?"

The look Al gave Tucker was one of betrayal. "It's clear whose side you're on."

"There is nothing in this life that would ever make me turn my back on you. That's why I'm pissed at you. You finally find a woman that knocks you off your game and your damn pride is keeping her away." Tucker took another drink. "Which brother clocked you?"

"Daddy." Nothing was said for a second, then they both laughed.

"Old man Williams finally knocked you down."

Still laughing, Al was taking a drink as he shook his head. "Not quite. Let's just say we had a serious heart to heart."

"The man clearly loves his daughter. You love his daughter, too." Tucker took the last swig of his beer. "Don't be foolish and let her walk out of your life."

"I don't know how to fix this."

"Easy," Tucker stood to leave. "Get down on your knees and beg." They both laughed.

"Easier said than done."

"I know. But I'm on my way to do some begging myself," Tucker replied as he walked towards the door. "You don't need me here anymore. In a month JD will be elected President of the United States. Tracy will have a White House full of Secret Service. Monique," he laughed, "Well, let's just say the world better look out for her. And you—my friend—are on your way to happy ever after. As for me, I'll be in Seattle until Julianna agrees to marry me."

Al reached out and shook Tucker's hand. "Keep me posted. The wedding is on me." The two had a brotherly hug and pat on the back. "Life as we've known it will change."

"Maybe for me, but you, I wouldn't be too sure. You will marry Ryan and Monique is your daughter. There is no telling what the future may hold."

"You have never lied my brother."

Chapter 21

The next week was so hectic even the children were beginning to wonder if the adults were all going crazy. Although everyone was fairly certain the threat was over, security at the compound was intensified. Secret Service agents covered every area surrounding the Brooks' Estate. At times, even Ashley complained when an agent questioned her as she walked from her home to Tracy's. On about the third day, James and JD laughed as they watched Ashley and Tracy hold a meeting with the security team. The women laid them out for causing havoc in their homes. Afterwards, Cynthia and Roz fed the agents so much food; all of them forgave the women for calling them imprudent fools and a few other choice words. Afterwards, the agents put a sign up in the bunk house that read: WHATEVER TRACY WANTS. That was their new motto, and it seemed to calm things down.

JD unfortunately had larger problems to deal with. The story of Jeremiah McClintock's death was released to the media. Senator McClintock's situation was another story. Fortunately, Jerry handled that. The media ate up the sadness the Senator displayed as he described his loss of zest for the political arena since his father's death. His concentration was now on his son and doing all he could to get him elected. However, behind the scenes, Jerry had distanced himself from his father. His wife Eleanor decided to stand with her husband.

JD met secretly with Jerry, as his wife suggested. The two men actually had quite a bit in common. He could clearly see why Brian considered Jerry a friend. They had different philosophies on how to do things, but they both wanted what was best for the country.

The next meeting JD had was going to be interesting. Monique sat with her legs crossed in front of his desk and she seemed different. The multi-colored hair, the fake nails and the tight fitting clothes were gone. Present was a very professionally dressed young woman, who, if the face didn't look so much like his wife's, he wouldn't have known it was Monique. "It's been a while."

"Why you want me here now. You ain't never cared nothing about me."

The statement grated on JD's nerves. "Your statement is grammatically incorrect. Rephrase it, and then try again."

"Huh?"

"Is that a word?"

"Is what a word?" A teasing Monique asked.

"Huh," JD replied, now smiling with her. "You just like to work my nerves, don't you?"

She smiled. "Yep. So what's up, Unc?"

JD sighed, "It's yes—not yep."

"Okay, I'm just trying to ease the tension for a difficult conversation."

JD didn't sit behind his desk, but took the seat next to her. "CIA?" he raised an eyebrow.

"Yes." She allowed a moment so it would sink in. "I'm an operative, Uncle JD. On any day, I'm what you need me to be."

"You're what the President needs you to be."

"True, but I believe in November you will be the President and it will be an honor to serve you."

The words touched JD in a way he couldn't explain. This was the same young girl that sat at his table when she was sixteen and called him everything under the sun. Now, she was willing to put her life on the line for him. "Thank you for saving my life."

"I was protecting the country, Uncle JD. But you're welcome."

JD smiled. "If I become President, you and I may have moments when we are working closely together. Will you be able to handle that?"

"Your first man will be Joshua. However, you should be comforted with the knowledge that I am being trained by the best. When he is unavailable to serve you, I will be here."

"How does your father feel about this?"

Monique tilted her head, "I'm not sure. I think all in all he's proud. But like any father, he's concerned with my safety."

"I'm sure, because I am. I guess he knows how you got into Georgetown now."

"Yes, I think he's figured that one out," she smiled.

"I want you to promise me something."

"Sure," Monique turned a little in her seat to face him fully.

"You will complete law school and take the bar in Virginia, DC, and Maryland. After you've had your fun with the CIA I may need you in a cabinet position."

"Oh, you're claiming it now," she teased.

"Let's just say, I'm optimistic." JD smiled, "Promise me."

Monique nodded, "I promise."

"Good," JD stood, "Now get out of my office so I can take care of some real business."

Monique laughed, "Okay Uncle JD." She stood to walk out, then stopped. "Uncle JD, will Ryan be at JC's birthday party this weekend?"

"I would think so. Why?"

"Well, it's been almost a week but she and daddy still aren't talking."

"Really," JD leaned against the edge of his desk. "Any ideas on how we can fix that?"

"I'm not sure, but we have to fix it. Daddy is miserable, whether he wants to admit it or not."

"So is Ryan," JD conceded, "They're back to wearing the shades and watching each other."

Monique smiled. "It's kind of cute, but they are too old for that. How did they come together the first time?"

"Al dragged her off the dance floor caveman style."

"Did not," Monique laughed.

"Yes he did," JD stood. "You know if you want it done right, get Tracy and Ashley as your allies. They'll have Al and Ryan back together before the night is over."

─◦⊱♡⊰◦─

"Aunt Tracy," Monique called from the kitchen. "I need your help."

Tracy and Ashley turned to watch Monique approach. "Sure, what do you need," Tracy asked.

"I need you to help get Ms. Ryan and my dad back together."

"They're still not talking?" Ashley asked surprised.

"No," Monique shook her head. "And it's my dad's fault."

"It usually is the man's fault," Ashley nodded as she crossed her legs. "What do you want us to do?"

"I don't know," Monique shrugged. "You two have the market on the love thing, not me."

Tracy shook her head and sighed. "It wasn't that easy getting them together the first time."

"Passion," Lena said as she and Martha walked in the room.

"Hello mother," Tracy agreed, "Passion between a man and a woman never fails when they are truly in love."

"The question is, are they in love or in lust?" Martha stated.

"I can't speak for Ryan," Lena said as she took a seat, "but Al is in love with that girl."

"If that's the case, then we have to take measures into our own hands," Tracy smiled. The women frowned wondering what she was thinking.

"Well with that, I'm leaving the details on you." Monique waved, "I'm out people."

"Later Monique," Lena replied as the others waved. "When are you rejoining JD on the trail?"

"After JC's birthday party Saturday," Tracy replied.

"Just think. In a little over a month from now JD is going to be our President," Ashley smiled. "Can you imagine that?"

Martha boasted, "Humph, Yes I can." They all smiled.

Chapter 22

Birthday boy, Jon-Christopher Daniel Harrison sat quietly in the front seat of his father's car as the big men went into the barbershop. The anticipation was getting to him as he looked up at his father, "Can we go in yet?" He asked with big light brown eyes that resembled his mother's.

"Not yet son, let's give them about five minutes, then we can go." JD replied. JC began swinging his legs, waiting patiently, as his father watched him with a smile remembering the first time his father brought him to the barbershop. But this day was special for him and JC. Last night his son came to him and told him he was ready to have his hair cut. The decision surprised JD for he knew how much his son thought of his Uncle Al. He wanted to look like and be like Al. JD had to admit, the thought of his son looking up to Al stung a little, but he had to believe his son respected and liked what he saw in his dad too. So this morning, on his eleventh birthday, JC had made a big decision and was ready to go forth. Today it was time for him to start growing up. He was no longer a little boy, but was now a young man, that's what he told his father. It was time for him to begin making his mark on the world. Letting the braids go was the first step.

"It's all clear, Governor Harrison," the head big man said. JC looked at his father and smiled. He was so excited. He was going in a little boy but would come out a young man.

JD looked at his son, "Now son, remember your promise. You will still play a little b-ball with me even after you become a young man today."

JC looked up at his father and smiled, "I promise Daddy. We will."

JD opened the car door and stepped out. He was immediately surrounded by Secret Service agents. On the other side of the vehicle, the same occurred for JC. As he reached the curb, JD took his son's hand and proudly walked into the barbershop.

The bell sounded, indicating someone had entered the shop, as greetings began pouring out. The regulars were there for their eight a.m. appointments. "JD, man what's up?" one man stood and shook his hand. "Mr. Gov.," another shouted out, with emphasis on the word Gov. "What's going on, man?"

JD shook hands, gave pounds, and a few body hugs as JC looked on. It was his first time coming to the barbershop with his dad and the one thing he took in right away was that people really did like his dad. The place was big to the young boy. There were six chairs on both sides of the room, with a mirror on the wall behind each one and a counter with different assortments of combs, electric razors and hair clippers. Some of the seats were occupied, while the majority was empty.

Two agents took up residence inside the shop, one at the back entrance and another stayed at the front as JD and JC walked to the last chair on the left. A man with a white coat that looked like one of his mother's dresses, stood behind the chair, smiling. "Well, well, well if it ain't the first family. How you doing son?"

JD extended his hand, smiling warmly at the man. "Good morning, Mr. Brown. I'm doing well, thank you."

"Now who do we have here?" the man asked looking down as he released JD's hand.

"JC Harrison," the boy proudly replied and extended his hand.

Looking a little surprised at the boy's bold reply, the man took the child's hand, "Well how do you do? It's a pleasure to meet you. What can I do for you today Mr. Harrison."

"Mr. Harrison is my dad. I'm just JC," the boy replied as his father proudly looked on. "I'm here to get my hair cut. Can you make my hair look like my dad's?" JC looked directly in Mr. Brown's eyes as he spoke.

"Son, I can make it look better." He patted the back of his chair. "Have a seat right here. Let me show you what I can do." As JC climbed up in the chair Mr. Theodore Brown looked up at JD with pride in his eyes. "Your father would be proud of you son. The young boys that come in the shop these days don't know how to pull their pants up, much less how to give a proper greeting."

"I can't take credit for that. My wife works wonders with the children," JD replied as he took a seat across from them.

The chime sounded as the entrance door opened. "B, what's up man? You're right on time." Zack, the barber next to Theo stated as Brian and his son Elliott walked in the door.

"So how many are there now, JD?" Mr. Brown asked.

"Four and another on the way," Brian yelled from his seat.

JD replied laughing, "Three girls and one boy."

"You're trying to repopulate civilization by yourself?"

"No, Mr. Brown," JD smiled as he took a seat across from his son. "I just love my wife."

"How many for you now Brian?" Zack asked.

"Number three is in the oven," Brian smiled proudly.

"Where's Calvin?" Zack asked.

"Coming across the street," Elliott replied. The men watched as Calvin and his son entered the shop.

"Good morning all," Calvin spoke as his son took his seat in the barber's chair.

"Ready for you right here, Mr. Johnson," Larry, another barber, swiped the seat with his towel. "Everybody's getting the same thing?"

The sons looked down the row at each other. JC nodded. "Yes sir. Cut it clean."

The men looked at their sons and smiled just as Douglas walked in the door.

"Doug," was echoed throughout the room.

"What it is?" Doug laughed.

"Where's your son?" Mr. Brown asked.

"Doug's been so busy raising those brothers of his, he hasn't had time to start his own family." Larry laughed. "Let's see, one is a judge over in Henrico County and the other is playing with the big boys on Sundays. Who is he with now?"

"Miami," Doug proudly replied. He looked at JD, "We're still on for tomorrow before you hit the road, right?"

"Sunday game with the boys," JD shook his head, "Wouldn't miss it."

"What are you going to do when you move into the White House in January?" Mr. Brown asked.

"They're going to have to put a big screen in the Rose Garden," JD replied. The occupants in the shop, including the Secret Service agents, laughed as the four friends gave pounds around the room.

TNT Event Planning had turned the ballroom of the Harrison's home into a literal football field. With the goal post at each end of the room and the artificial turf striped, in white lines, marking off the yards. The football cake sat at center field with two huge yellow water coolers next to it. On the forty-yard line on both sides was miniature football players dressed as the Redskins and on the opposite side the Cowboys. It didn't take long for the party to be in full swing. In addition to Tracy's children, Ashley's four were there, along with Cynthia's daughter, Jackie's son, Caitlyn's son and Ashley's cousin, Alexis' son, Jonathan. As if that weren't enough Carolyn Roth-Roberts' son, Gavin Jr. arrived.

"Hello, Gavin. My you have grown." Tracy smiled at the now five year old. "Where's your mom?"

"Talking to my granddad and Uncle JD."

"Okay, well you go catch up with JC and we'll talk later." The boy ran off.

"I didn't know Carolyn was coming," Cynthia frowned.

"Oh, come on. It's time to let the past go." Roz laughed. "You're pregnant, Tracy's pregnant, she's pregnant, I'm pregnant. All is right with the world."

Tracy, Ashley and Cynthia froze, staring at Roz. "You're pregnant?" Tracy asked.

Roz's smile was as wide as the Golden Gate Bridge and just as bright as she nodded. "Yep and we were approved for a foster child." The women screamed and hugged Roz simultaneously.

"It always happens like that," Ashley laughed. "What are you going to do?"

"Raise my babies together."

"What's going on?" Caitlyn asked with her plate resting on her eight-month pregnant stomach, while stuffing her mouth with potato salad.

Ashley laughed at the sight. "She's going to be like you in a few months."

"You're pregnant?" Caitlyn beamed.

"Yep," Roz replied.

"That's probably why this potato salad is so good."

Upstairs, the men gathered in JD's game room to enjoy a little college football before they had to join the party downstairs. JD, Brian, Calvin, Douglas, James and Samuel were watching the game as Senator Roth and now Senator Gavin Roberts walked in. "Good afternoon Gentlemen," Gavin smiled. He extended his hand to JD. "Umm, excuse me, Mr. President," he smiled at JD.

"Not yet," JD shook his hand.

"Just another month to go," Senator Roth smiled. "I knew it was going to happen."

"So did I," Carolyn stated as she walked in, smiling. "I told you ten years ago this is where you were going to end up." She kissed JD on the cheek.

"Oh God, not you again," Brian smirked.

"And good day to you too, Brian. I thought having a wife would mellow you out."

"I thought having a husband would shut you up. I guess we were both wrong."

"Look you two, a truce for the day. This is JC's birthday." JD demanded.

"Where is Tracy?" Carolyn asked.

"She's downstairs with Jackie and the rest of the ladies." Samuel replied.

"Is your wife down there?" Carolyn frowned.

"Yes. But she has to put up her boxing gloves for another seven months, so you're safe."

"Cynthia is pregnant again?" Gavin asked smiling, "So is Carolyn."

JD laughed, "So is Tracy."

They turned and looked at James. "Not as far as I know." The men laughed.

"There's going to be a baby born in the White House." Carolyn beamed, "I have to go and congratulate Tracy on such a good move. That girl is going to be a good political wife after all."

Carolyn literally ran out of the room almost knocking Monique down.

"Do you think anyone should tell her Tracy didn't do this for political reasons?" JD asked.

"No son," Senator Roth laughed. "Let her have her moment, please."

The men laughed as Monique stepped back out of the room and watched Carolyn walk away. She never forgot words, pictures or faces. Monique walked back into the room. "Uncle JD." JD walked over to the door. "Aunt Tracy said you should be downstairs in ten minutes."

"We'll be there."

"Uncle JD," she called out when he was about to walk away. "Who is the woman that just walked out of here?"

JD looked down the hall, "Carolyn, she's married to Gavin Roberts."

"Senator Gavin Roberts?" Monique questioned.

"Yes, that's right." JD replied. "Is something wrong?"

"I'm not sure." Monique shrugged, "Don't forget—ten minutes."

Tracy stepped onto the patio where Ryan and Magna stood. "We're about to cut the cake. Are you two coming?"

"I'm right behind you." Magna replied.

"What about you Ryan?"

"I'll get a slice later."

Tracy could feel the sadness surrounding her friend. "You know I love you like a sister—don't you?"

"I know," Ryan forced a smile.

"Okay," Tracy gave her a sad smile. "I'll bring you a slice of cake out later."

After the cake was cut, the men and boys decided to play a game of touch football. The teams were divided evenly with boys and men. Senator Roth and James' father Avery Brooks, who were the oldest, were placed on separate teams. Ashley's son Tony and Carolyn's son Gavin were the youngest and they too were on separate teams.

The women stood on the sidelines cheering the teams on. Pearl, JD's press secretary stood behind them with a small camera crew as they taped the activities.

"Calvin, be careful," Jackie yelled, "Don't hurt your back." The men on the turf laughed as Calvin stood up and stared at his wife.

"This isn't going to be pretty," Carolyn laughed.

"Do you have an older sister?" Monique asked from behind Carolyn.

Carolyn looked over her shoulder and frowned. "No." she frowned "I'm an only child." Tracy and Ashley looked at her sideways. "Well, I was an only child until a few years ago." She clarified.

"Hmm," Monique continued to watch the woman closely. "You're not white are you?"

Tracy, Ashley and Carolyn turned to stare at the very serious Monique. "No. Up close I can see you have some African blood in you." She tilted her head. "That's a good thing cause for a moment I thought I was going to have to take you out." Monique turned and walked away, leaving the women staring at her back.

"What in the hell was that about?" Carolyn asked with her hands on her hips.

Ashley and Tracy looked at each other. "I have no idea," Tracy replied then turned back to the game.

Afterwards, while the boys went from live football, to a Madden tournament on the big screens that were set up throughout the room, the women were ready to put their plan into motion. "Mother," Ashley asked. "Everything is set?"

"Yes it is." Martha replied.

"Caitlyn?" Ashley held up an eyebrow.

"Ready."

"Roz is everything set?"

"Good to go."

Ashley turned things over to Cynthia, who looked down at her daughter. "Samantha, do you remember what you are supposed to do?"

"Yes Mommy. I'm going to cry."

Tracy looked down at her daughter Brianna. "Okay, baby this is very important. Are you ready?"

"Yes Mommy I'm ready."

Lena looked at the group. "Using children to do your dirty work." She shook her head back and forth, sucking her teeth. "There is going to be hell to pay if this doesn't work."

"Then we have nothing to worry about because this is going to work," Tracy smiled.

Caitlyn walked out the patio door with a plate of food in her hand. Ryan turned just as she was about to trip over the door seal. "Be careful," Ryan reached out to give Caitlyn a hand.

"Oh Ryan, thank you so much. I can't see my feet or anything beneath them," She joked. "Tracy asked me to get two bottles of wine from the bunker. Can you point me in that direction?"

"Tracy sent you to the bunker?"

"Well not exactly. Tracy told Cynthia they were running out of Merlot. Cynthia told Roz that the Merlot was in the bunker. Then Roz told Ashley. I really got tired of it going in circles, so I decided to try to find the wine myself." Caitlyn smiled. "So if you don't mind, hold my plate and point me in the direction of this bunker and I'll get the wine."

"I'll get the wine, you sit." Ryan pointed to the table behind her.

"Oh, I don't mind. It will be good exercise for me."

"I'll have to deal with Brian if something happens to you down there. It's not a problem."

Caitlyn smiled so sweetly. "That is so thoughtful of you Ryan. Thank you."

Ryan smiled. "I'll be right back."

"Don't forget she wants the Merlot."

Ryan waived her hand as she walked off. "I won't."

Inside the house Brianna ran into the game room where some of the men were still watching college football, and whispered in her Uncle Al's ear. "I got to tell you a secret Uncle Al."

"Okay, what is it?" Al lifted his niece into his lap.

"Samantha fell down the steps."

Al frowned, "Where?"

Brianna almost had tears coming from her eyes. "You can't tell anybody."

Anxious, Al took the child by her hand and stood. "Show me."

"Okay," the child ran, holding on to Al's hand.

Brianna took him to the door leading to the tunnel that led to the bunker. The door leading down the steps was open and he could see Samantha with her head down. Al turned to Brianna. "You stay right here."

"Okay."

Al ran down the steps, "Samantha? Are you hurt?" he asked as he picked the child up. The girl had crocodile tears as big as a golf ball rolling down her cheeks.

"I can't find Pearlie!" She cried into his shoulder.

"Who's Pearlie?"

"My doll," she cried harder. "I want my doll."

Al held the child out from his shoulder. "Where is your doll?"

"Down there." The child pointed to the next level of steps. She looked at Al with the saddest eyes. "She fell when I fell."

Al walked back up the steps and placed the child next to Brianna. "I'll get Pearlie. You stay here with Brianna."

"Okay," the child replied.

Al walked back down the steps wondering why the children were allowed to play in the tunnel. He was going to have a talk with Tracy. He had descended to the bottom level of steps. He reached inside the doorway of the tunnel and turned on the light switch. That's when he heard the door close up the stairs.

Ryan was on the far side of the bunker in the food storage area searching for the Merlot when the lights came on. "Good timing." For a moment she thought she was going to have to walk to the tunnel to turn the light on. A moment later she thought she heard a sound but dismissed it.

She pulled the two bottles of Merlot and walked to the door. She was surprised to see Al walking through the tunnel door. The two stood there for a moment just staring at each other. She noticed the doll in his hand. "Turning to dolls these days?" Ryan asked.

"This is Pearlie. In an attempt to save her, the door from the house closed. It has an automatic lock and can't be opened from this side without a key."

Al sounded a little testy so Ryan turned away. "I have a key."

"Actually you don't," JD's voice came through the speakers. They were standing in the open living area of the bunker. Al and Ryan looked around, then at each other, curious. "All of the door locks were changed yesterday. The exits have been sealed." JD began. "I have a birthday party to get back to so I'm going to make this short and sweet. As you both know, this bunker was built for both families to survive here for months in case of an emergency situation. Well to those who love you, this is an emergency situation. There's plenty of food, water, and drinks of all kinds. I think the Merlot in Ryan's hands would be a good start. There are six bedrooms. Use one, or all six, I don't care. But you will make up and I hope it's before I'm elected President. I'm out."

"JD, open this door." Al demanded.

There was no response. "Mr. Harrison," Ryan called out. Nothing. The two looked at each other. Al laughed, then looked up and saw Ryan's face was void of expression. "Hey, I've been incarcerated before. This is a luxury hotel as far as I'm concerned. Besides it's time." He reached out and took the two bottles of wine from her hand and sat them on the table near the sofa.

"This is something totally off the beaten path for me, so if I get it wrong, don't laugh." Al got down on bended knee as he took Ryan's hand in his.

"The heart is the most essential and vital part of everything. It's the source of one's being, emotions and sensibilities. It's the center of our life. It controls you—you don't control it." He looked into Ryan's eyes. "You, Morgan Ryan Williams, are the center of my being. I love you with all that I am and all that I have. I've never begged anyone for anything in my life. Here on bended knee, I'm begging you to love me back. Please forgive me for acting so damn self righteous and marry me."

Her body was shivering from his words. The simple, yet complicated way, he expressed himself always did her in.

The tears flowed from under the dark shades as she whimpered out. "You have to ask my Daddy."

Al stood and gave her that crooked smile as he removed her shades. "I already did."

Looking into his eyes, with his locs hanging around his shoulders, she sniffled, "Did he say yes?"

"After, I beat him down."

Ryan pulled back, "You beat my Daddy?"

Al pulled her back to him. "Let's just say we had a mutual disagreement," he smiled. "I'm sorry, Morgan. I was hurt to learn you kept something from me," he said as he rubbed the sides of her arms. "I'm so afraid I'll end up like my step-dad or your father."

"I don't understand."

Al released her. He walked over to the kitchen area, took out two glasses, and filled them with wine. Walking back, with the glasses in one hand, he took her hand and led her to the sofa. As they sat, he kicked off his shoes, gave her a glass of wine and pulled her into his arms.

"I'm going to tell you two stories, one about me and the other about you."

Ryan kicked off her shoes and pulled her legs up under her. It felt good to be back in his arms. She settled in. "Okay, I'm listening."

Al told her about his childhood, his part in his stepfather's death and all he had done to provide for Tracy. He told her about his days on the street, his life in prison, he even told her about his connection to the Cartel. "I let all of that go once I went to prison. I'm sure JD has figured out it was planned for me to go to prison. It was a way for me to make a clean break. While I was away, Tucker took over dismantling the organization. He controlled the investment company we had started and he invested very well. When I was released, he sold back my share of our investment company for the same amount I had originally sold it to him for—one dollar. Neither of us has to work another day in our lives if we don't want to." He stopped and refilled their glasses.

"That's my story. Now I'm going to tell you about your father." Ryan pulled slightly away. Al pulled her back to him. "I promise, it won't be easy, but your father will never hurt you again." He waited until she settled back into his arms. Then he told her about his conversation with her father.

When he finished, she looked up at him with tears on the brim of her eyes. "My looks won't change. The voice is going to be the same. I know how much my father loved my mother. I just wanted a little of that and he couldn't give it to me."

"I know, but that is something he has to live with. You on the other hand have a chance here to close that gap and forgive him."

Ryan shook her head. "I don't know if I can do that."

"I thought the same way until a few months ago."

"What happened?"

"I sat down and talked to my mother. I listened to her story and for the first time in my life, I called her mother." Al hung his head. "Now, if I could do that, there is no reason you can't do the same. After all," he looked up into her eyes, "You're just as much a man as I am."

Ryan laughed out loud. "Really." She sat the glass on the table. "Well, Mr. Day," she straddled his lap, took his glass, and placed it on the table. "I'm afraid the man in me has been replaced."

Al relaxed back, "Is that a fact," he said as he placed his hands on her hips, bringing her closer to him. "With what?"

"A very horny woman," she said as she pushed his locs from his face. She held his face between the palms of her hands. "I love you, Al Day." The kiss she gave him was so sweet, powerful and filled with love that all Al could do was surrender his heart to her completely.

He gathered her in his arms and carried her into one of the bedrooms. They fell to the bed as he asked. "How horny are you?"

Her eyes were filled with sexual tension and happiness. "Very," she replied.

He ran his hands behind her back and pulled her weapon from the back of her pants and placed it on the table. Then he removed her black jacket, and pulled her white tee shirt over her head. "Red lace?" He smiled. "I like it." He placed kisses from her throat to the crest of her breast, as his hands roamed over her body. Her body squirmed under him as his thumbs brushed over her nipples.

"Al" she moaned.

He shook his head. "I'm taking my time. I want to make love to every inch of you," he said as he unclipped the front of her bra. He looked down at the brown globes and exhaled. His eyes had turned grey when he looked at her. "Behold the beauty of a queen." He dipped his head and captured one of her breast with his mouth, swirling his tongue relentlessly over it. Then he closed his lips around the bud and suckled until he had his fill. Not a single beat later he switched to the other and treated it with the same sensual frenzy as the last.

The need to have him inside of her was intensifying, but Al showed no signs of moving. Ryan's legs widened to feel the steel of him at her core. She wanted the jeans off now but was too weak to move Al from her breast. Truth be told, she wanted him there too. Her body just wanted him everywhere. But it seemed Al was on a mission.

When he finished with the second breast he looked up and grinned. "You are definitely a woman." He began placing kisses down her body until he reached her navel, which he paid special attention. In his mind this was the lifeline to his future children. He loved that area lavishly before unbuttoning her jeans. He literally peeled the jeans from her body and threw them to the floor. While he undressed his eyes never left her, until his pants dropped, and she looked down.

The man was raw sex appeal standing before her in all his glory. Her tongue moistened her lips as her mouth watered to taste him, but he had other plans. Kneeling at the end of the bed, Al pulled her body down to him. The only piece of clothing remaining was her red lace panties. He placed her legs over his shoulders, placed his head between her legs and inhaled. Her essence was so wet. The smell of her enticed him to no end, and he knew the taste of her was waiting. The tip of his nose touched her bud and her body jerked. He turned his head and sucked on the left thigh until she bucked again. His tongue left a trail from her left thigh to her core, to the right thigh where he sucked until she bucked again. Returning to her center he ran his tongue over the silky material covering her. "Marry me Morgan." He whispered. "Say yes."

Ryan was trying to respond to the man, but every time his tongue touched her core she was rendered speechless. All she could do was moan. He did it again, this time covering the entire area with his mouth as he continued to massage her inner thighs. "Say yes, Morgan." She nodded, but he couldn't see it. His head was still between her legs and he wasn't stopping. His soft locs were teasing the inside of her thighs as much as his tongue was teasing her core. "Please, say yes."

"Yes," she breathlessly whispered. "Yes." She could feel his smile between her legs.

He stood, ripped her panties away and thrust into her with one powerful smooth motion, filling her completely. The motion of his body never slowed as he pumped feverishly in and out of her. Their bodies slapped against each other with every love filled thrust. The explosion that ripped through their bodies was so forceful, Al fell backwards. Neither could move. Ryan was still on the bed, while Al just remained on the floor. A few minutes later, Ryan crawled off the bed and straddled him where he laid. Easing down on his still erect shaft Ryan sighed, as she moved slowly over his body. Al's hands covered her breasts and massaged them with the same rhythm.

"Should we tell them we made up?" Ryan asked as she licked her lips with each swerve of her hips.

Al's hands roamed down the curve of her body until they reached her hips. "And let all their well laid plans go to waste?" His hands helped with the movement, making the motion more deliberate. "That would be cruel." He lifted his legs to support her back as he began thrusting upwards into to her. The inside of her was silky smooth and hot as melted better. There was no way he was ready to stop. "I want to deposit all my seeds into your womb right now. Am I there?" He thrust up as he slammed her body down.

"Not yet," she whispered as her hip movements intensified. He thrust up again, this time a little more forcefully. That brought a deep moan from her. "Again," she said breathlessly. He complied again and again and again until she screamed and her body released her juices. Al squeezed her behind tight, as her inner muscles vibrated around him and he pumped into her until his body exploded.

Chapter 23

A little over a month later, on the second Tuesday of November, Jeffrey Daniel Harrison was elected President of the United States. While the campaign staff celebrated at headquarters, JD, Tracy, their family and close friends watched the results from their home. After speaking with Jerry McClintock, who conceded the race, JD made arrangements to meet his Vice-President at the Convention Center to address the Nation.

Tears flowed from Martha's eyes as she hugged her son. "Your father is watching. I know he is."

"I know Mommy, I know."

Ashley was next and she couldn't contain herself. "Now we're never going to be able to control that big head of yours." She punched him.

"Hey, I think that's a felony now," JD teased.

Brian, Douglas and Calvin stood behind him. Before he could turn to them they tackled him to the floor. Douglas sat on him as Calvin held the high school yearbook. He read what was written by JD's name. "*Of all the kids in the school, Calvin is the smartest, but JD is going to run the world."* He closed the book then bent down to where JD lay on the floor. "We knew then that you were a leader. We were with you then, we are with you now. We will be with you forever."

Douglas punched him in the arm, and then stood. He held out a hand to help JD up. They could all see the tears that welled up in his eyes. "Presidents don't cry," Brian frowned.

JD shook his head and just smiled at his friends. "Thank you for being my boys." The four men hugged, then broke away, like it was abnormal.

JD turned to James. "It's been a long run."

James smiled as he shook his hand. "It's just the beginning. I'm going to head out to the Convention Center. We'll see you center stage."

Only JD and Tracy remained in the room. He stood there with his hands in his pockets gazing at his wife. Her baby bump was now showing, but she was still the sexiest woman alive. "You make me believe I can do this job. You've given me everything I've ever asked for. You make me the man I am. I don't think you have any idea how much I love you, Tracy Alexandria Washington-Harrison."

Tracy walked over to her husband and in that sweet baby voice that he loved to hear, she replied. "Oh, say it again, Mr. President."

The grin on JD's face was priceless. He pulled his wife into his arms and kissed her so deeply, they both fell to the floor pulling clothes off. An agent walked in. "Close that damn door!"

"Yes sir. Mr. President-Elect."

Jeffrey Daniel Harrison stood at the podium, as a sea of people looked on. The Convention Center in downtown Richmond was lined with red, white and blue banners, balloons, posters, hats and any other paraphernalia available to mankind. The atmosphere in the room was more than electrifying; it was explosive. He looked to his left and saw his wife Tracy beaming with love and pride in her eyes. The intensity of the unspoken message that passed between them was more than he could handle. He stepped away from his podium, placed his arm around Tracy's expanded waistline, then proceeded to give her the most passionate kiss ever witnessed by a national television audience. The crowd cheered louder, as they basked in the joy of knowing they had just elected another African American for President of the United States, which essentially meant that the Country was progressing into becoming exactly what the Declaration of Independence states, "We hold these truths to be self-evident that all men are created equal." Americans' hearts were warmed by the knowledge that the couple standing before them truly loved each other, and The White House on Pennsylvania Avenue would once again be filled with children—an American family they could all look up to.

What was so wonderful about the moment was that when the cameras scanned over the crowd, it was to display the diverse nature of what America had become, truly one nation under God. Every ethnic group imaginable stood side by side cheering at the prospect of having a better future under the leadership of Jeffrey Daniel Harrison, President of the United States.

A hush came over the crowd as they waited to hear the words from the man who had just become the new leader of the free world. Every eye was looking toward the stage where the Harrison family and friends smiled brightly. The attendees waited patiently, anticipating the words of encouragement and hope they had become accustomed to receiving from the young man facing them.

JD returned to the podium, smiled and looked at the eager faces in the crowed. "Marrying my wife was the smartest thing I have ever done." He bowed his head and chuckled, "Her love has made me rich beyond my imagination in so many ways. The most prominent of which is being able to stand before you today and accept the faith you have placed in me, to be President of the United States of America." The crowd cheered wildly, almost in a frenzy, as JD scanned the room smiling.

One of the secret service agents whispered into the invisible communication device positioned inside his ear. "We have another President with rock star status, we need to tighten up." At the command the agents on the stage moved closer to the family, as more agents entered into the room at floor level and spread throughout the crowd. JD continued with his speech as the agents moved about unnoticed, but vigilant. Midway through the speech, JD reached down to pick up his daughter, Gabrielle who was tugging at his pants. She captured his cheeks between her small hands and kissed her daddy. As the crowd clapped, Gabrielle joined in, smiling. JD smiled at his daughter and turned back to his speech. She then laid her head on his shoulder and listened as her daddy talked.

Brian Thompson scanned the room from his position directly behind JD. His trained eyes took in each level of the room searching for anything he considered a threat to the family on stage. After scanning the top levels of seats, his eyes drifted to the rafters, where some of the television cameramen took shots of the crowd below. A stream of light caught his eye as he scanned over the cameras. It was only a split second that it took his eyes to go back to the light, another second for recognition, then one more second for his body to react before shots rang out, with center stage as their target. The loud sound of the automatic weapons continued to flow through the air like shock waves. Awe and then screams filled the room. Secret Service sprang into action, covering the children and Tracy as ordered by the President-Elect. JD covered Gabrielle as Brian immediately hit him from behind, propelling him forward.

He hit the floor with Gabrielle beneath him, and that's when he heard a heart-wrenching scream that he was certain came from Tracy. With Brian and agents' bodies surrounding him, his movement was limited and his line of sight was blocked. Reaching out he grabbed her hand, "Tracy!" he yelled out, to no avail. When the firing stopped, the room was half-empty, the crowd was still buzzing and agents were surrounding the stage with weapons drawn. JD looked down at Gabrielle, who was now crying. "It's alright Gabby, Daddy has you. It's alright." He held her tightly as he scrambled to stand. Tracy was pulling her hand from his, frantically reaching for something. Following her line of vision, he saw the blood and his heart literally stopped.

The frenzy that followed was all a blur as JD scrambled to get to the body on the floor next to Tracy. His mind snapped. Is it possible his dream and worst nightmare had all occurred on the same night? How would he live his life knowing he was responsible for the events happening at that moment? How many lives would come to an end on that night, trying to accomplish a dream?

Hundreds of Secret Service agents surrounded the people on the stage. JD was pulled to his feet as was Tracy, but she refused to move. "JC!" She cried out. An agent fell to his knees to examine the child.

"Get my children out of here!" JD yelled as he fell to the floor next to his son. "JC," he cried out.

"Mr. President-Elect, we have to move you to a safe location," An agent pleaded.

"No, get Tracy out of here."

"No, I'm not leaving my baby."

Brian rushed over to Tracy, picked her up and surrounded by agents carried her from the room. JD took JC from the agent and held him to his chest, then carried his son out of the room. In the ambulance, the EMT's were examining JC to see exactly where the wound was. There was a lot of blood on his face and his head. It was difficult to maneuver around the small, enclosed space with JD and two Secret Service agents around him, but the EMT did the best he could.

Cleaning the area around the child's face, it looked as if a bullet grazed the right side of his head. "The bullet did not penetrate the skull. The graze caused the blood."

"Then why is he unconscious?" JD asked.

"Mr. President, I don't know. He could have hit his head during the fall. But his vitals are good and strong. We'll know more when we get to the hospital."

"Get my wife on the phone. I want to speak with every one of my children in the next five minutes." JD sat there, holding his son in his arms, feeling helpless.

The ambulance pulled into the Medical College of Virginia hospital, not even five minutes later. Agents and police immediately surrounded it. The child was removed from the vehicle and taken into a secure location in the emergency room. That entire section of the hospital was closed down and off limits to anyone but essential personnel.

"Where's my wife?" JD yelled. "Get her here!"

"She's en route." One agent stated as JD followed his son into the examination room.

"The President has ordered us to take you to a secure location." Another agent stated.

"I'm not leaving my son." JD replied as calmly as the situation would allow.

"Sir, I've been ordered to move you forcefully if it's necessary."

JD slowly looked up from the seat where he held his son's hand. "Move me."

It was a dare, not permission, for the agent to take a step towards him. Unfortunately the agent didn't know the look in JD's eyes was dangerous. Before he could react to the unexpected attack, JD had tackled the man to the floor and had raised his fist to strike him when Samuel and Brian walked in. They quickly pulled JD from the agent and stood him against the wall. JD pulled away, straightened his clothes, then retook his seat next to his son.

The doctor demanded, "Everyone except Mr. Harrison—out. The nursing staff jumped to action.

"Secret Service doctor, we can't leave the President-Elect."

"Then take the stupid one out, sit in the corner, and leave the man alone while I take care of his son."

Tracy ran into the room as the agents scrambled to get out. "Jeffrey," her voice trembled.

JD reached his hand out. She took it as tears rolled down her face. "He's unconscious."

"Mrs. Harrison, the bullet grazed his head," The doctor tried to reassure her. "He is unconscious from the fall."

Tracy walked over to her son, cupped his face in her hands then kissed his cheek and spoke softly. "Jon Christopher, Mommy wants you to wake up. Baby I just need to see your eyes look into mine and I'll know you're alright." JC's eyes fluttered open, looked at his mother, then closed again.

The doctor looked at the child, at Tracy, then at JD. "Let's get him upstairs to do a cat scan."

"I'll go with you," Tracy stated as the nursing staff prepared to remove JC.

"I'm coming too," JD stood.

"No." Tracy shook her head. "You are going to find the person that is responsible for hurting my baby and then you are going to kill him."

JD looked into his wife's eyes and didn't recognize the woman that stared back. "Tracy?"

"No one harms one of my children and gets away with it. Now you find that person or don't bother to come home."

The men in the room looked on as JD watched his son being taken from the room. Tracy never looked back. "She's angry, JD. Just like you." Brian stated.

"JC is going to be alright," Samuel said, "which is more than I can say for others."

JD looked over his shoulder at Samuel. "What others?"

"Mr. President-Elect, we have a room set up for you to work from until you can see your son." The hospital administrator said.

"Where are my other children?" JD asked as he followed the men.

"All secure sir," an agent replied. "As is your mother and sister."

"Where is James?"

"James and Pearl are in the room waiting for you." Brian stated.

"Where's Calvin?"

"Calvin was hit." JD stopped and stared at Brian as he spoke. "We don't know yet."

"Is he here?"

"Yes."

"Take me to him."

"No. Jackie is with him and so is Douglas. You are needed in the situation room." Brian stated. "I will physically take you out if I have to. Don't make me."

JD stormed off, following the agents. "Who else is hurt?"

"Carolyn, Ryan, three agents and the Vice-President-elect." Brian replied. JD glared at him, "Keep walking. We'll give you a full run down as soon as you are secure." They took him to an expansive suite in the hospital that was sealed off. The hospital administrator met him at the door that was surrounded by agents. "President-Elect Harrison, your son's cat scan came back clear. There's a little swelling, but that's to be expected. Once the shock wears off, we expect he will regain consciousness. Mrs. Harrison is with him in a secure room. He will have around-the-clock care."

They walked through the double doors to a room where JD was met by James. "Mr. President-Elect, there are three dead, seven injured from the stage area. The injuries from the floor are minor scrapes and bruises. No one on the floor was shot. The names of the fatalities are on the desk." JD moved to the area James pointed to in the makeshift office, as James continued. The Vice-President-Elect and the two agents covering him were DOA.

"I want to see his wife as soon as possible and any information you have on the agents." JD sighed.

"Yes sir. Ryan was shot in the shoulder and is being cared for as we speak. If Al doesn't kill the physician, she should be released within the hour."

"She covered Tracy," JD spoke aloud.

"It's her job sir." James stated then continued. "Calvin is a little more serious; however, the attending doctor believes he will survive. As for Carolyn," James sighed, "Things are a little up in the air with her." JD looked up at James, who just shook his head. "They don't know."

"There were two gunmen, one was taken down in the response fire, and the other escaped."

JD ran his hand down his face not realizing he still had JC's blood on his hands and clothes. "What do you mean escaped?" he looked at Brian, then Samuel. "Call Joshua. I want to see him within the hour."

"Mr. President-Elect, the President is on the line for you." An agent held a cell phone out to JD.

At first JD stared at the phone, then he reached out and took it. "Mr. President." He listened as the man spoke. He occasionally nodded his head, but never replied until he said. "Thank you, Mr. President." Then the call ended. JD gave the telephone back to the agent, then sat down and sighed. He looked around. "Is there somewhere I can wash up?"

"Yes," Pearl replied as she walked in with a change of clothes for him. "Sorry it took a minute to get by Secret Service at your house. Then by the media." She sat the clothes down. "I made a statement to the media that you will speak with them as soon as you've spoken with the families involved. Take a minute, breathe, change your clothes and then we'll address the media."

"You're trying for the Press Secretary's job?"

"Natural progression," Pearl smiled, "but we can talk about it later."

JD smiled, "It's yours." JD said as he walked into the bathroom of the suite.

Pearl turned to James. "How is he?"

"Rattled, but dealing."

She turned to Brian, "How is Tracy?"

"Pissed, no beyond pissed."

"Tracy?" Pearl questioned.

"Told him not to come home until he finds and kills the person that hurt her baby," Brian stated.

A shocked Pearl questioned again. "Tracy?"

"Tracy," Samuel confirmed.

Chapter 24

Monique met Joshua at the door of the hospital. Neither said a word until they were away from any ears. "What in the hell went wrong?" he asked. "We took out the two assassins months ago."

"But we didn't take everyone out," Monique stated. "The Senator is still out there and we never determined who was feeding the information to his camp in the first place. Nor do we know who the woman was that gave him that damn cell phone. There are too many loose ends."

"The Senator is out." Joshua explained. "We've had him under surveillance since the last incident. Who was hit?"

"The Vice-President, Calvin Johnson, Ryan, Carolyn Roth-Roberts and a few agents. You still think the President-Elect was the target?"

"I don't know. But there is no chatter on another assassin."

As Joshua talked, Monique watched as an elderly couple and a woman spoke with a member of the security team. He pointed in the direction of the emergency rooms and the small group walked away. She tilted her head to the side. The woman in the group looked familiar. Joshua stopped talking; her body language was telling him that something was up. "Follow your instincts."

Monique glanced in his direction. "I'll get back with you," she said as she walked away.

"Mr. President-Elect." Joshua joined in step with JD as he exited the suite. JD stopped, "Secure area." The agents stepped back allowing a decent space between them and the President-Elect. Brian and Samuel stood nearby as they spoke. "I want the person that shot at that stage in custody before the night is out."

"By any means necessary?" Joshua asked.

It took JD a moment, but remembering his son on that stage smiling up at him one moment, then bloodied the next prompted him. "By any means necessary."

"Yes Sir," Joshua replied as JD strolled away.

"Before you kill him," Samuel cautioned his brother, "we need to know who is behind the latest threat."

"Who was on the man that escaped?" Joshua asked.

"Calhoun," Brian replied.

Joshua put a call into Ned as he walked away. "Ned, give me a location on Calhoun." He paused for a moment as a thought occurred to him. "Then run a check on him, the normal, connections, recent movements and financials."

After speaking with the Vice-President-Elect's wife and family, JD found Ryan outside the room where JC had been taken. "How's the arm?" JD asked.

Ryan glanced up at him. "Hurts like hell, but I'll survive."

"You saved Tracy's life."

"That's why you pay me the big bucks." She replied. "There were two shooters. Did they get the other guy?"

"No. Joshua is on it."

Ryan nodded, "Heard she put you out."

"Humph," JD smirked, "She's pretty angry."

"Angry or not, that's your son and wife in there. Don't you think you should be the one comforting them?"

"I wanted to be," JD sighed, "but I can't."

Ryan turned to him. "You're the President-Elect of the freaking United States of America. You can do anything you damn well please. Even piss your wife off a little. All I know is if it was me lying there, when I opened my eyes, I would want to see my mom and my dad." She shrugged her shoulders." But I'm just a security guard, what do I know?"

He kissed Ryan on the cheek. "I have no idea how Al puts up with you." He walked into the room. Tracy looked up then turned back to JC lying in the bed. Al stood.

"How's it going out there?"

"Rough," JD replied. "Seven injured three dead."

"Who?" Tracy asked without looking up.

"Vice-President and two agents."

The shocked look on Tracy's face told the anguish she felt inside. "I have to speak to Joanna."

"I spoke with her and the family and conveyed your sympathy."

Tracy nodded. "Who's hurt?"

JD walked over, picked her up from the chair, then sat back down with her in his lap. He rubbed her stomach as he replied. "A few agents, Ryan, Calvin and Carolyn."

"Carolyn?" Tracy moaned. "Is the baby okay?" JD shook his head no as he held his son's hand. "Carolyn?"

"Still in surgery, but it doesn't look good." Tracy's head fell against his. "Why?" she asked as a tear fell from her eyes.

He wrapped his wife in his arms and held her as she cried. "I don't know babe, but I'm going to find out." He rubbed her back for a moment then he wiped her tears away. "I'm going to stop in on Calvin and Carolyn when I leave here."

Tracy stood and looked at her husband who remained seated. "Go. I'll be here with JC. You find the person that did this terrible thing Jeffrey. I meant what I said. I want this person dead. I don't want them to have another opportunity to hurt my babies."

JD stood, "Tracy, you don't mean that."

"Yes, Jeffrey. I do."

For a moment JD just stared at his wife. He kissed her temple, bent over, kissed his son's forehead and left the room.

Al followed him out the door. "Someone hurt her baby. She's going to lash out at the closest person and that's you."

JD shook his head. "It's more. I think she blames me for this. Hell, I blame myself."

"JD, there's this theory referred to as the propensity for violence."

"Even the mildest mannered person will result to violence if pushed."

"So you know this." Al nodded.

"Your sister introduced it to me years ago."

"Think back to how you reacted when you found out that Munford killed your father. That should help you understand how she feels. Right now, you're hurt because it's Tracy and you're her target. In her mind, you are supposed to be their protector, so protect. You can't do it the way that I would. But you will find a way to place the responsible person's head on a platter and serve it to your wife." Al held his stare, "Do it your way—by the book."

JD nodded, "Thanks Al. Would you stay with Tracy? And by the way," he nodded towards Ryan, "Good luck with that one my brother." JD patted him on the back then walked away.

JD watched Jackie stand as he approached. She walked right into his open arms and cried on his shoulder. A moment later he took her hand and sat her back down. "Where's your family?"

"They haven't cleared Secret Service yet," she said as another tear dropped.

"I don't want you here by yourself." He turned to Pearl, "See if we can find her family and have them brought directly here." He turned back to Jackie. "What is the doctor saying?"

"He was shot in the shoulder. The bullet tore some ligaments, and they are going to try to repair what they can. They are pretty sure he's going to be alright with some physical therapy."

"I know he's going to be alright. Hell, he's going to be my Chief of Staff, he has to be alright."

Jackie smiled as tears stained her cheeks, "Have you told him that?"

"No, not yet and don't you tell."

"I won't, besides he needs to hear it from you."

"I'm sure he already knows." JD smiled.

"No, he doesn't. He thinks it will be James."

"James is my campaign manager, that's what he is good at. Calvin has been my advisor and friend all my life. Having anyone else in that seat never crossed my mind."

"You're a good man, JD." She kissed his cheek.

"Make sure you tell my wife that." He stood, "I'm going to leave an agent here." He turned to one of the agents. "Have someone find me the minute he is out of surgery."

"Any word on Carolyn?" Jackie asked.

"Not yet," JD shook his head. "I'm going to check on her now."

"Okay. Stay clear of her mother. You're not one of her favorite people."

"Thanks for the heads up," He smiled, then walked away.

"What do you think she meant by that?" Pearl asked as they walked down the hallway.

"I have no idea. Carolyn's mother is the last person I'm concerned with. Who's next?" JD asked Pearl.

"Senator Roberts. Carolyn is still in surgery. It's touch and go. They lost the baby."

JD sighed, "This job has got to get easier at some point."

Monique followed the trio into a private area secured by Secret Service agents. Two of the members of the group were rather elderly, and looked to be members of society's elite. The woman who held her interest was a little offbeat. She was elegantly dressed, but there was something not right about her. Monique was surprised when they were ushered into the suite occupied by Senator John Roth, Senator Gavin Roberts and her grandmother, Lena.

Senator Roth stood as the woman approached him. Monique missed the first exchange, for the Secret Service Agent stopped her. She flashed her credentials, then walked forward.

"Hell must have frozen over. The Worthingtons are here." John stated.

"How is she?" Elizabeth Worthington, Carolyn's maternal grandmother, asked in her normal, holier than thou fashion. No one replied. "I asked you a question and I expect an answer."

The only word missing from the question, in Lena's mind, was the word boy on the end. Her husband wasn't anybody's boy. "Who are you addressing?" Lena asked with a raised eyebrow.

"Certainly not you," Carol Worthington, Carolyn's mother replied.

"Get Gavin down here." Elizabeth commanded her husband, Edward. "We may be able to have a sensible conversation with him."

Lena's hands went to her hips as she stepped away from her husband. "Gavin's mind is on his wife, where it should be. If you want answers, I suggest you ask in a respectful manner and I believe John will answer you. If not, there's the door, show yourself out."

"Excuse me," Monique kissed her grandmother's cheek. "Hello Grand'Mere. Senator, how is your daughter doing?"

"We're waiting for the doctor to join us." John replied as Gavin walked up.

"Mr. and Mrs. Worthington," he nodded. "Carol." He spoke. "We don't have anything new at this time. They took her straight to surgery. This is not the time to cause confusion. I'll call you myself once we have news."

"I'm staying here with my daughter," Carol stated defiantly. "I want the person that caused all of this behind bars."

The doctor came out and walked over to Gavin. "Senator," he looked around at all of the people. Gavin nodded indicating he was free to speak. "We were able to stop the internal bleeding. That was our biggest concern. That's the good news. There are a few things we cannot make a determination on until she awakens."

"May I see her?" Gavin asked.

"Yes. The nurse right inside the door will direct you."

Gavin turned to John as he walked away. "I'll let you know the minute she is awake."

"Doctor," Monique called out as she flashed her credentials. "How long will it be before we can speak with Mrs. Roberts?"

"I don't want her upset."

Nodding, Monique agreed. "I totally understand. However, I believe Mrs. Roberts may have vital information concerning the events of the evening. I only have one question for her."

"She should come around in an hour or two."

"Thank you, doctor." Monique returned to the group just as Lena was explaining to the Worthingtons that their presence was no longer needed.

"We have wings in this hospital with our name on it." Edward spoke. "You don't show us the door, we, have you removed."

"Really?" Lena smirked. "Do you think you can have the mother-in-law of the President-Elect removed? Think again!"

"John," Carol looked over Lena. "What did they say about Carolyn?"

"She's been shot." John replied to his ex-wife.

"You're still the same uppity—" Edward hesitated

"Finish that thought and I'll do the same thing I did years ago." John stepped towards Edward. He looked at Carol. "You turned your back on Carolyn when she was five years old. When she became the First Lady of Virginia was the only time any of you would give her the time of day because her skin is a tad darker than yours. That dark skin didn't bother you when we were making love. It only bothered them." He pointed to her parents. "You couldn't take being shunned by your family, so you turned your back on me and her. Now you want to stand here and make demands. Carolyn wouldn't want you here and neither do I." He stated and walked to where Gavin was pacing the floor.

Lena's heart went out to her husband. She could feel the pain radiating through him. "It doesn't appear you are welcome here."

"My daughter would want me here!" Carol yelled.

"When she is able to speak, we'll ask her. Until that time it's best that you leave."

"Good evening," JD spoke after he had heard enough. He extended his hand. "Mr. Worthington." Edward shook his hand. "Mrs. Worthington," the woman nodded. JD turned to Carol. "Ms. Worthington, I'll speak with Gavin. Afterwards, I'll give you whatever updates on your daughter's condition there is."

Carol huffed, "I don't want anything from you. You're the reason that my Carolyn is hurt. That should be your wife in surgery not my daughter. "

Monique watched as the color drained from her Uncle JD's face. "I thank God it wasn't. And I pray that your daughter will survive this brutal attack. I will do everything in my power to find the person who did this and punish them to the fullest extent of the law. However, I will not stand here to be berated by a woman who wishes my wife harm. If, you would excuse me."

"You don't have to look far." The woman hissed. "All you have to do is look in a mirror to find the guilty party."

Monique watched the woman's eyes as they trailed JD. "I'll be damned," she said as the reality of the situation hit her. She stepped back to blend in with the agents that were in the area. Pulling out her cell, she called Ned. "Give me everything you have on a Carol Worthington. I want her bank account checked for large withdrawals and her movements during the last six months. And Ned, I need that now." Monique then turned and whispered something to one of the agents. Four agents immediately formed a barrier between the Worthingtons and JD.

JD stopped. "You'll get yours. You will." She smirked as she walked off with her parents trailing behind.

"What in the hell was that all about," JD asked John and Lena.

A stunned John watched as Carol entered the elevator. "I have no idea."

Calhoun watched as JD and his contingency of agents left the room. Speaking with Mrs. Harrison's agents gave him a good view of the area. Other than the agents, only Al Day and Ryan Williams remained. He knew what Day was capable of. However, Williams was another matter. While on the Harrison's compound, he rarely had contact with the woman. However, common sense told him that Thompson wouldn't have a slouch on Harrison's wife. Injury or no, she had to be a threat. "The family has been through a lot tonight." Calhoun said to the four agents standing a few feet from the door to JC's room. "Let's give them a little more privacy. You two take a stance at the end of the hallway. Don't let anything or anyone get by you without clearance from me. You two take the other end. We have men covering the stairwell. Let's be sensitive to their needs, a child has been shot."

"Yes sir," the agents replied, and then took their positions.

Ryan watched as the agents adjusted their positions, wondering why they'd moved. Looking down to the other end of the hall, the other agents had moved as well. Observing the area, she noticed that the stairwell was not been secured. She started to say something to the agents down the hallway, but the hairs stood on the back of her neck and were a clear indication to proceed cautiously. "Oh hell," she murmured as she nonchalantly stood, rolling her neck from side to side as if she was trying to relieve stress. Ryan pulled her weapon from the back of her pants and placed it inside the arm sling she was now wearing. She stepped into the room. "Al, can I speak to you for a minute?"

Al and Tracy looked up. "Sure," Al replied. He looked at Tracy, "I'll be right back."

"I need a hug," she said to Al.

Al gave her an incredulous look. "You need a hug."

"Yep, right now."

He wrapped his arms around her and held her tight. "We have a situation." She said as she placed her weapon in the front of his pants. "I don't know all that's involved, but someone is about to come through that stairwell. We need to move them."

Al looked over her shoulders to survey the situation. He cupped her face in his hands and kissed the side of her lips, "Is that Calhoun at the nurses' station?"

Ryan nodded. "Yes, he's checking his watch."

"Can you handle this?"

Ryan gave Al a look that almost made him laugh. "Alright, I'll take care of them."

Al stepped back into the room as Ryan sat back down and crossed her legs. Not knowing who was in the loop for communication, she couldn't call for help without alerting the person they needed to catch. So instead, she pushed the number nine key on her cell. That sent a signal to Brian and Samuel that there was an alert.

Samuel was in the makeshift situation room with James when the alert beeped. He looked at the cell, Ryan's name appeared. "What room is JC in?" he asked James.

James looked at his notes, "Suite 240."

Samuel nodded then walked out of the room.

Brian was with JD and Pearl when he received the alert. When he saw Ryan's name he stepped away and dialed Samuel. "What's up?"

"I'm en route to room 240."

"That's where Tracy is."

Brian took the nearest stairwell, "I'm right behind you."

As Ryan expected, a man dressed as an agent came through the stairwell door. The shoes were a dead giveaway. There wasn't an agent on staff that could afford Italian loafers. And if they could, they wouldn't wear them on the job.

The man walked over to Ryan. "Are you Ms. Williams?"

"Yes," Ryan replied. "And you are?"

"Take a look at my hand." Ryan did. "It's a dot gun. One twitch of my finger and you are out in two seconds."

Ryan looked up at the man. "What do you want?"

"I need to get into that room."

Ryan looked down the hallway. "Don't think about it Ms. Williams, just stand and open the door.

Ryan sighed as she stood. "I don't think you really want to go in there."

"Now, Ms. Williams."

Ryan shrugged her shoulders, "Okay. But I want you to remember you asked for this."

The man looked down the hallway at the agents. Once he was satisfied they had not alerted anyone, he pushed Ryan inside. She fell to the floor on her arm. "Ouch. Now, that hurt."

"Hello, sweetheart. I see you brought company." Al said from the bed where he laid with her weapon pointed at the man. He didn't ask any questions, he simply pulled the trigger.

"Oh hell, Al," Ryan jumped up as the man hit the floor. "You weren't supposed to do that. Give me the gun."

She grabbed it from him and pushed him from the bed just as the agents stormed the room. "Boy am I glad to see you guys."

Brian and Samuel ran in behind the agents. "Who is that?" Brian asked referring to the dead man on the floor.

"I have no idea," Ryan replied as Samuel bent down to the lifeless body.

An agent stepped forward. "Ma'am, we need your weapon."

"Sure," Ryan was about to turn the weapon over to the agent when Brian spoke. "I'll take that."

"Where's Calhoun?" Al asked.

The agents looked around. One stepped outside the door and looked down the hallway. "He was here a minute ago."

"I think you should locate him." Al stated, "Now."

"Where are Mrs. Harrison and her son?" an agent asked as Brian's phone buzzed again.

"I'll tell you as soon as you locate Calhoun."

Brian immediately left the room.

Standing outside near the south exit of the hospital, Joshua leaned against the building, waiting. According to Ned, it wasn't going to be long. Now, at least they knew how the candidate's itinerary was getting out. The only question that remained was why.

Calhoun ran from the building smiling when he saw the chopper waiting. The fist that came out of nowhere, breaking his nose, stunned him as he fell to the ground. He looked up to see Lassiter standing over him. "You broke my damn nose."

"Consider yourself lucky." Joshua snatched him up by his coat. "I usually kill people." He stood the director up and brushed off his clothes as he spoke. "Now, you know me. You can come quietly or, I can carry you." He smiled. "What's it going to be?"

The director stood there holding his nose. "You can't touch me Lassiter." He smirked. "You think you have me. But you and I know all I have to do is talk and I'm a free man." He pulled a handkerchief from his pocket. "Come on, let's go through your little interrogation."

Joshua knew the smug bastard was right, but that didn't mean he had to like it. He grabbed the man by the neck and slammed his head into the brick building. "The hard way you say, okay," he said as the man slid to the ground. Joshua grabbed the man's lapel and sat him up against the building. Standing over him, Joshua looked down. "I have one question. Why?"

Blood running down his face, the man shook his head from side to side. "You wouldn't understand."

"Try me," Joshua replied as he threw his handkerchief at the man.

Calhoun took the handkerchief and wiped at the blood. "I gave the agency thirty years of my life. I lost my wife and the respect of my children for the agency. I was a true patriot. What did they do? They turned their backs on me. They placed some young boy that doesn't know a damn thing about this country as Director. I have to report to him."

"Let me get this straight. You were willing to take the life of a woman and betray your Country because the agency looked you over for a promotion and a for a measly million dollars?" Joshua yanked the man up. "You're right, I don't understand. And the next time you call yourself a patriot, those will be the last words you say." He dragged the man back into the building, mumbling to himself. "I know why they passed you over. Because you're stupid. I can't even call you dumb. Calling you dumb would be an insult to dumb people."

Monique was standing at the door of the stairwell when she heard the commotion. The door swung open and Calhoun was thrown through. Monique and several other agents barely got out of the way.

Agents immediately surrounded Calhoun and Joshua, none of them sure who to apprehend. JD and John turned to watch the scene unfold. Seeing it was Joshua, JD walked over. "Joshua?"

"Mr. President. It gives me no pleasure to deliver this piece of crap to you." He stood there frustrated. "I got to tell you. I desperately want to kill this man. I refrained because I know you do not like the idea of taking a life." He said angrily. "At some point, we have to come to an understanding that sometimes the people who attack our country need to die." He threw his hands up. "That's all I'm saying."

Some of the agents didn't have the restraint that their new Commander in Chief had, as they openly laughed at Joshua's dramatics. "Would killing him make you feel any better?" JD asked, trying like hell not to laugh.

"You damn right it would!" he walked away, stopped then walked back, "Sir, Mr. President-Elect, Sir." Then he stormed off down the hallway.

Monique turned to her Uncle. "You got to love a man that is so passionate about his country."

The communication devices began going off. The same sounds had been heard before, and JD's heart dropped. "Where's my wife?" he frantically asked the agents. Samuel, Ryan and Al stepped off the elevator. JD immediately turned to Al. "Where's Tracy?"

"I'm not sure, but she's fine." Al replied.

"What in hell do you mean you're not sure? I left her and my son with you." He yelled, "Where in the hell is she and JC?"

"I'm right here Daddy," came the weak child's voice.

The sea of agents parted as Brian stepped through with JC in his arms. Tracy ran by the agents and threw herself into her husband's arms. JD hugged Tracy and kissed her cheek, then reached out and took JC from Brian's arms. He had his son on one shoulder and his wife crying into the other, hugging them fiercely. Then he inhaled and almost choked.

"Yeah," Brian folded his arms across his chest. "That was my reaction too."

"Babe," he said to his wife. "Where were you?"

Tracy turned, placing her hands on her hips as she looked at her brother. "He threw me in the dumpster."

JD looked up at Al. "I didn't throw her in the dumpster." He explained. "I threw them down the trash chute."

The night had been so horrendous; JD felt this comic relief moment was needed for everyone involved. He began laughing and couldn't stop. Holding JC as securely as he could he bent over in laughter. "I'm sorry, babe." He laughed harder at Tracy's exasperated face. After JD began laughing the others around them joined in.

Lena was worse than JD. "Tracy, it is funny." But Tracy wasn't having it.

Al didn't laugh, but he was smiling. "Look Sugie, I had to get you out of that room. Would you have wanted JC to be in there when that man came in?"

"Of course not."

"There was no other way. I had to throw you out in the trash." Lena really let go then.

JD grabbed his wife and kissed her. "I love you. I don't care what you smell like."

Tracy playfully hit him in the chest. "I love you, too."

It was a long night. JD finally had the opportunity to speak with the media and things seemed to settle down at the hospital. Afterwards, he went home to make sure each of his children were fine and to reassure them that JC and mommy were okay. He returned to the hospital, where he and Tracy fell asleep in JC's room. Around five that morning, he received word that Calvin was awake. Walking in the room, he was pleased to see that Calvin was actually sitting up talking to his wife. "Hey man. I finally got to take a bullet for you. I was beginning to feel left out."

"Man, that's not even funny." JD held out his hand, giving Calvin a pound. "You know I love you like a brother."

"I know," Calvin replied. They held each other's stare for a moment, acknowledging the mutual understanding. "What's with all the agents at the door?"

JD looked around the room. "Jackie, may I have a moment with Calvin?"

"Of course," she smiled and kissed her husband. "I'm going to check on Carolyn. Then I'll be right back."

"Alright baby." Calvin watched as she walked out the door.

JD took a chair and pulled it next to Calvin's bed. "We have a lot of decisions to make. We have a lot of positions to fill beginning with the Vice-President slot. I have to submit a name that will clear hearings."

"Those are decisions you and your Chief of Staff need to discuss."

JD nodded his head. "That's what I'm doing. Here's what I want to do."

Calvin knew JD needed him to listen but he had to stop him before he continued. "JD, you're asking me to be your Chief of Staff?"

"No. I'm the President-Elect of the United States of America asking you to serve your Country." He sat forward.

"This is what I want to do. I want to name Jerry McClintock as my Vice-President."

"He's a republican."

"I hadn't noticed," JD joked, then sighed. "Calvin, it's time for someone to take steps to unite this country. Jerry's a good man."

Calvin listened as he proudly accepted what his friend had offered him. Once that cleared his thoughts, he was stunned at what JD suggested. "Do you think the Country is ready for that?"

"We're going to get them ready." JD stood. "You have one week to get yourself well. Then we are going to hit the ground running."

Tracy was sitting in the suite area of JC's room when Pearl walked in. "Good morning Ms. Press Secretary," she smiled.

Pearl bowed, "Thank you, thank you, Mrs. Harrison-Lady in waiting."

"Is that what I am?" Tracy frowned over her tea cup.

Pearl nodded and laughed, "I'm afraid so."

"While we're in office let's see if we can change that." They laughed. "Did you get in touch with her?"

"She just cleared security. She should be here in a minute."

"Okay what else do I have to do?"

Pearl looked at her list. "You have to hire a Social Secretary, Press Secretary, and Chief of staff. Actually, once you get your Chief of Staff, he or she will handle the rest for you."

"Hey?" Monica Jackson smiled from the doorway. Monica was the CEO of Tracy's company Next Level. She was the first person she and Ashley had hired. The three of them ran that company by themselves until it grew into the multimillion-dollar company it was now.

"How is everyone?" Monica asked as she took a seat on the sofa with Tracy.

"Carolyn is still in question, but everyone else is doing okay." Tracy replied. "I know it's early in the morning, but this couldn't wait."

"Okay, what do you need?" Monica asked.

"I need you to resign as CEO of Next Level."

"What?" A shocked Monica looked at Tracy with her mouth gaped wide open.

"And I need you to do it immediately. Pearl, gave her the papers to sign."

Monica was stunned. "Tracy, what's the problem? I'm sure whatever it is we can work it out."

"The problem is I need a Chief of Staff. You're the only person I know that can keep me in line with all the stuff I will have to do. But you can't be my chief of Staff and the CEO of Next Level at the same time. So you have to resign from Next Level."

"You want me to work at the White House?"

"Yes." Tracy replied as if that was a foregone conclusion.

As soon as Monica signed the papers Pearl took the pile of files she had and put them in Monica's arms. "Have fun," she said and left the room. Monica then turned back to Tracy wondering what in the hell had she gotten into.

Before going to the area designated as his office, JD decided to drop in to see how Carolyn was doing. He was surprised to see Monique and Joshua standing outside Carolyn's door. "What now?"

"We have to question Mrs. Roberts," Monique replied.

"Why?"

"Well sir, we believe Mrs. Roberts, intentionally or not, was the person supplying your daily itinerary to McClintock."

"I don't believe that."

"Sir we know that Mrs. Worthington was the person that gave the cell phone to Senator McClintock. We just need to ask one question of Mrs. Roberts."

"No." JD responded then walked into the room.

A frustrated Monique followed as Joshua remained outside. She positioned herself near the door. The confirmation from Ned that her suspect was involved wasn't something Monique could push aside. They made that mistake one time before. She wasn't going to make it again.

JD was talking with Gavin and John, both of whom had stayed the night in the room with Carolyn. He turned when Joshua walked inside the room and stood next to him.

Before he could ask, Carol Worthington walked in the room.

"Hello again," Monique smiled.

Carol Worthington took a step back. "I don't know you," and walked towards her daughter.

"Oh, of course you do." Monique took a step in front of her, stopping her progress. "I ran into you at Senator McClintock's office." Monique turned to the men standing near Carolyn's bed. "It's true. You see I saw her myself. I didn't put it all together until now. But that's her." Monique smiled. "Oh and not only is she involved in last night's scenario," Monique shook her head. "No. She was also an intricate part of the last attempt on the President-Elect's life, too."

"You don't know what you are talking about. I don't know you. I've never seen you a day before in my life." Carol protested.

JD, Gavin and John stopped talking as they turned to the unfolding scene. Joshua stood back to watch his trainee at work. "Of course you have." Monique pulled out her handheld and turned it towards the lady. "See, my friend Ned, he's a wiz with electronics. He can pull pictures out of the air. Like this one. See, that's you the first time we met right in front of the Senator's office." She touched the screen and another picture appeared. "And here is the second time we met. Hum hmm. See." She showed the picture to JD and the other men. Then she touched the screen again. "Oh, and this is the best one." She turned the monitor back to Carol. "This is when you actually met with your accomplice." Monique turned to show a picture of Carol and Calhoun near the Capitol. "Here's what I don't get." She looked around. "You have everything. You're not a bad looking woman. You have so much money you could buy a few countries and you had another grandbaby on the way. Why would you want to kill Uncle JD?"

Carol looked around frantically as all eyes fell to her.

John step forward. "Listen, I don't know what you think you have but Carol couldn't have been involved in this." He looked at her, as if asking with his eyes for her to deny everything. When she did not respond he looked at her dumbfounded. "You're her mother. How could you do this to her?"

"John. I wasn't doing anything to her. I was doing it for her!" she tried to explain. "You allowed this. You let that whore's daughter come in and take everything away from my Carolyn. You and my parents with all their superiority shunned her as if she were something dirty. But she wasn't. She was my beautiful baby girl." She nodded her head as tears rolled down her face. "That's right, my daughter. She was the one that became the First Lady of Virginia. Not those other grandchildren of theirs that they put on a pedestal. It was my daughter, my Carolyn that put the Worthington name where it should have been. It was left up to me to protect her and give her the life she deserves. And you," she scowled at JD. "You took that whore's daughter over mine!" She pounded on her chest. "That wife of yours doesn't deserve to be in the White House. Carolyn does! She was groomed for it. None of you deserved to live after the way you rejected my Carolyn." She sobered, "I shouldn't have listened to that old man with his half-baked schemes. I should have just had all of you blown away. The next time, none of you will live."

Tracy walked into the room "What's all the commotion about?" she asked.

Before anyone could react, Carol turned. "You!" Grabbing her around the throat, Carol pulled a gun from her purse.

"Tracy," JD yelled as Gavin moved closer to Carolyn.

A cynical smile appeared on Carol's face. "You thought you had me, didn't you." She smirked. Ryan stepped into the room, applied a death grip on the nerve of Carol's neck and watched as she crumpled to the floor.

Ryan smiled as she held up three fingers. "Tracy made me watch Star Trek after the Carolyn incident."

JD grabbed Tracy as several Secret Service Agents took Carol into custody.

"Wow," Monique whispered. "The person she claims she was protecting is the one fighting for her life. Now that's crazy."

Epilogue
Six Months Later

"Whew, I'm so glad you are all here." Tracy rested against the door of the Blue Room where her friends had gathered to get Ryan dressed for the wedding. "I swear I just couldn't go any further."

"Are you in labor?" Ashley ran over to her.

Tracy nodded. "Don't even think about it." She stated as the ladies in the room looked at her. "I'm not going anywhere until Al is married. And you are going to help me."

"Tracy, how far apart are the contractions?" Cynthia asked.

"Only forty, forty-five minutes. We have plenty of time."

"Tracy, are you crazy?" Roz panicked.

"Oh she has plenty of time," Ashley waved Roz off. "Why don't you go check on things in the kitchen?"

"I'm pregnant, not stupid. You're trying to get rid of me."

"Look, we've all given birth before." Cynthia soothed Roz. "You haven't. We know that forty-five minutes is almost three hours before that child arrives. You need to have a seat, while we get this wedding started."

Ryan stood in front of the mirror in her A-line white gown and veil. "Hey we can get this show started anytime you are ready."

"Thank you Ryan," Tracy smiled as she walked the floor rubbing her back.

"So this is where everyone is hiding," Carolyn walked in. Five sets of guilty eyes and one set of very frightened eyes stared at her. "You know if I hadn't made a promise to God when I was in the hospital to treat people better, I would attempt to throw a monkey wrench into whatever you all are up to. However, I'm a better person now. So, I'll try to help. What's going on?"

All eyes turned to Tracy wondering if they should confide in her. Tracy was the first to speak. "Carolyn I need your help. Lena has taken the media hostage and I'm in no condition to stop her. Would you please try to get her under control?"

Carolyn turned to walk out of the room. "Your mother and control is a contradiction in terms. But I will do my best." She stopped and turned at the door. "Do you want me to let JD know you're in labor while I'm out there?"

Tracy narrowed her eyes at her half-sister. "When we were in the hospital you said you were sorry for the things your mother attempted to do to my family and you would spend the rest of your life making it up to us. Well, I don't need the rest of your life, just the next hour of you keeping this between us women."

"I'll think about it as I try to control your ghetto mother. However, I want to make each of you aware that you need me to pull this off."

"So what, do you want a medal for being a decent human being," Cynthia hissed.

"Haven't gotten rid of all of your baby fat, have you?" Carolyn snapped back.

"Alright you two!" Tracy snapped. "I'm not in the mood. You," she pointed to Carolyn "go get Lena and take her to the Rose Garden. And you," she pointed to Cynthia, "go over there and check on Ryan. It is 11:45. I am going to make it through this wedding before this baby comes. Now go!" Everyone moved on Tracy's command.

"I'll let the minister and the men know we are ready."

"Thank you," Tracy smiled as Roz left the room. She closed the door.

"How far apart?" Ashley asked as she smirked at Tracy.

"Ten minutes."

Ashley turned to Ryan. "Okay, if we time this right we can get you to the hospital in time to drop that baby."

Twenty minutes later on a beautiful May day in the Rose Garden at the White House, Al stood with Tucker as his best man, next to Ryan with Tracy as her maid of honor, exchanging vows. The minute the minister announced you may kiss your bride, Carolyn cried out, "Tracy!" and pointed to the ground.

A few people turned and frowned at Carolyn for interrupting the ceremony, while others turned to Tracy. "Your water broke," Carolyn cried out.

Ashley rolled her eyes to the heavens. Cynthia, who had just given birth two months ago stood in front of Carolyn. "Would you sit down and shut up." She hissed between clinched teeth.

JD jumped from his seat to gather Tracy in his arms. "Bring the car around." He shouted as he picked his wife up.

"Jeffrey we're not going to make it to the car." Tracy whispered in his ear.

"JD, she's not going to make it. We need to get her inside." Ashley stated.

"Yeah, like now JD," Cynthia added.

"Pearl," Roz called out. "We need Dr. Prentiss."

"You want me to help birth that baby?" Lena asked.

"No!" just about everyone in the area yelled.

"You knew she was in labor and didn't say anything?" JD growled at Ashley.

"She wanted to be at the wedding." Ashley defended.

Carolyn ran ahead, as agents opened the door. Mrs. Langston, JD's secretary was standing inside with Roz. "The car is waiting at the entrance."

"She's not going to make it to the car, "Carolyn stated. "Bring her in here." No one moved. "Now JD," she demanded. "Mrs. Langston would you get some sheets, please."

"The baby is coming Jeffrey," Tracy cried out.

JD took his wife into the Blue room and placed her on the sofa. "Tracy baby, please let me take you to the hospital," he pleaded as he pulled his tuxedo jacket off.

"Too late for that," Tracy laughed as she grabbed her stomach.

"How long have you been in labor?" JD yelled.

"All morning," Ryan replied. When Ashley, Cynthia and Roz turned to her with glaring eyes she shrugged her shoulders. "It's not like he can do anything about it now."

"That's not the point," Carolyn said. "The girlfriend bond is never broken, especially when it comes to husbands. You're one of us now. You don't break the bond."

Everyone in the room stopped, including the unborn child. All eyes rested on Carolyn. "What in the hell are all of you looking at?"

"Who in the hell are you and what did you do with the real Carolyn?" Cynthia asked.

"Go to hell Cynthia."

"Now that's Carolyn," Lena laughed. "You should get shot more often."

As if on cue, Tracy let out another loud moan. "Jeffrey!" she grabbed for his hand.

"I got you babe. No one thought to tell me!" He yelled while comforting his wife.

"Too late to ask that question," his mother Martha laughed. The crowd from the wedding had gathered behind them.

"Anything we can do to help?" Al asked.

"This is women's work son." James stated, "I suggest we wait outside."

"Everybody out," Ashley shouted as Pearl came to the door.

"Thank God," JD exhaled as he saw Pearl's date behind her. "Dr. Prentiss. Tell me you know what to do."

"I've done this a time or two," Theo smiled. He walked over to Tracy, pulling out a pair of latex gloves from his pocket. He took one of the sheets that was given to him and draped it over her lower body. "You've done this before Mrs. Harrison. Looks like this one is going to be natural," he smiled looking over her legs. "Mr. President, sit behind her with your legs on both sides of her body to support her back." As JD moved into position, the doctor motioned to two agents, "Push that ottoman over here and grab a few pillows to make her more comfortable." He looked up at Pearl, "Baby would you tie my hair back for me?"

The women in the room looked at each other, then at Pearl as she replied, "Of course." She took a ribbon from Mrs. Langston and tied his locs back. When she was done, she noticed the eyes on her. Hands on hips she spoke. "Is there a problem people?"

"Nooooooo," Tracy cried out as another contraction hit.

JD sat behind Tracy, "Breathe, baby breathe. We can do this."

"Oh my God, Tracy. You're going to have a baby in the White House," Carolyn cried. "What a move, girl. You may have just sealed the re-election. Pearl can we get the press in here?"

Everyone in the room glared at her as she stood there with a very serious expression on her face.

"That would be a no!" Ashley answered.

"Can we clear this room, please," JD testily asked.

Tracy patted his arm, "It's going to be alright babe," she said consoling him.

"Don't push Mrs. Harrison until I tell you to." Dr. Prentiss covered the ottoman with clean sheets, braced Tracy's legs against the edge then positioned himself behind it. He looked around. "Okay folks. I need the room clear of everyone."

"We can't stay?" Carolyn asked.

"I'm about to unclothe Mrs. Harrison. If you want to see all of that you are welcome to stay. Everyone else needs to leave. That includes the agents. Now people."

The crowd slowly filed out of the room back to the Rose Garden. "Ashley," Tracy called out, "would you tell Carolyn to stay."

Ashley smiled at her friend, "I sure will." After all Carolyn went through in the hospital, she understood why Tracy wanted her to stay. The doctors stated it was unclear if she would be able to carry another child to term. This was Tracy's way of giving her sister a little of that experience.

"Alright Mrs. Harrison, let's bring this baby into the world. This one is not waiting." The Dr. smiled. "On my command I want you to give me one big push."

Tracy nodded, "Whew—Whew—Whew." She squeezed JD's hands.

"Push babe," JD wiped her forehead with a towel, "Push."

"Only a man would rush something like this," Carolyn shook her head.

Tracy had to take a moment, shaking her head at Carolyn's comment as the doctor continued to work. "That's the head. Okay Mrs. Harrison you've done this before. It's all on you now."

JD supported her back as Tracy pushed one last time and the baby shot out into Dr. Prentiss' waiting hands. "It's a boy." The doctor announced as he began cleaning the baby with the water the agents had brought.

Carolyn ran to the door. "It's a boy!" then she came back into the room, with the EMT team that was waiting to enter.

"Carolyn," Tracy smiled as she held her baby. "Would you name our son?"

A stunned Carolyn looked from Tracy to JD, then back to Tracy. "Well," she thought for a minute as she tapped her well-manicured finger against her chin. "It has to be something Presidential, maybe William or Benjamin?"

"William," JD stated. "I don't want my son to be called Ben."

"Okay William it is," Carolyn smiled.

"William Albert Harrison," Tracy smiled down at the child wrapped in her arms. "Welcome to our family."

The hospital suite was surrounded by Secret Service agents outside, but filled with family and friends celebrating the birth of the nation's first family's son. JD sat near the bed with William wrapped in his blanket asleep, as he surveyed the room. Life just couldn't get any better. He looked over at the bed and smiled at the woman who made it all worth living. He could tell she was exhausted, yet she continued to smile at everyone as they talked about the wedding and the birth.

It was time to bring the celebration to an end. "You know life is strange." Everyone stopped talking and turned to him. "Man, look at us—the boys from the neighborhood made good. Brian, you are the man. None of us ever thought you would settle down with one woman. And look at you—married with three kids. Caitlyn, I don't know how you do it, but, God bless you for putting up with him and Cynthia." The group laughed. "Speaking of mouths."

"Hey that's my wife you're talking about," Samuel protested.

"Gee, thanks a lot honey," Cynthia smirked.

"You know I love you."

"I'm glad you do," JD joked as he rocked his son. "There were a few times I was ready to kill her. Now I know she loves Tracy as much as I do. So I guess I'll keep her. For no other reason than to decorate that big house we live in now."

"That's a good idea honey," A half asleep Tracy patted him on the arm. "Keep Roz too."

"Hell I'll keep Roz before Cynthia."

"That's right," Roz smiled up at her husband Marco. "He knows we'll always be around to feed him."

"This is true. Wherever we go, you are cooking. I'm happy to see you two about to join the world of parenthood—finally. Doug, you and Karen may want to jump in at some point."

"Not with that crazy David about to be released," Ashley stated with a huff. "Babe can't Vernon put another charge on him or something to keep him in prison?," she asked her husband.

James looked at JD. The two wondered when their wives were going to realize that they cannot produce miracles at will. He turned to those eyes he loved so much. "I'm sure we can work something out."

Ashley kissed him. "I know you will."

JD laughed. "Still can't say no to her can you?" He looked at Gavin and Carolyn. "Don't give up on having another child. I don't care what the doctors say, God controls this world."

"Carolyn you may be a pain in the ass, but you're a good pain in the ass." Cynthia smiled.

"Thank you, I think," Carolyn looked at Gavin with a frown.

"Hey, I'm grateful you two are in the same room and not fighting," Gavin teased.

"Wow, remember that," Brian laughed. "She whipped your ass Carolyn."

"She got one lucky punch," Carolyn countered.

"No," Jackie shook her head. "She did whip your ass."

"Black and blue for weeks." Calvin hugged his wife as he laughed.

"Through all the joys and pains, we are all standing in this room together as a family." Tracy said as she looked up JD with tears in her eyes. "I now have a family."

JD bent over and kissed her lightly on the lips. "All thanks to that propensity for violence." He smiled, as the two remembered the very first conversation they ever shared. JD turned to the people in the room. "It's been a hell of a journey and we owe it to all of you—The Harrison family and friends."

"I think that's our cue to leave," Brian said as they all stood. "Get some rest. Tomorrow's another day."

"Well see everyone in the morning," JD replied as the family left the suite.

When the last person walked out an agent stepped in. "Will you be staying the night Mr. President?"

"Yes," JD replied.

"Secure the area," the agent spoke into his earpiece as he closed the door.

"I can't get used to that Mr. President," Tracy mumbled as JD placed the baby in his bassinet. He kicked off his shoes and climbed in the bed beside her. After gathering her in his arms he sighed. "It takes a little getting used to. You can just call me your commander in chief when we make love."

"Who say's we are ever making love again?" Tracy looked up at him. JD simply raised an eyebrow. Tracy sucked her teeth, "Alright I know I'm always the one that can't last a week."

JD chuckled as he held her tight. "I wish my father could see me and Ash now."

"I think he would be pleased." Tracy scooted closer to her husband and snuggled in. She was ready for the peaceful sleep that awaited her.

"You move any closer and we are going to start on number six."

"Oh no," she looked up at him. "I did one through five. Number six is on you."

Hours later the press was having a field day with the news of the birth of a child in the White House. Carolyn and Gavin were center stage, doing interview after interview describing the scene. Pearl could not have put a better twist on the events if she tried. Therefore, the White House gave one simple statement. "William Albert Harrison was born at 12:16 in the Blue Room with his father and aunt assisting Dr. Theodore Prentiss. We promised you a different White House. Between President Harrison selecting Governor Jeremiah McClintock, a Republican as his Vice-President and today bringing a new life into this world inside the White House, I'd say the promise has been delivered. As he said, it's time for a truly United America."

Al clicked off the monitor as he pulled Ryan's naked body closer to him. "It was a perfect wedding." She smiled against his chest.

"Until Tracy's water broke," Al laughed "I don't think I've ever seen JD so pissed."

"Yeah," she laughed, "Especially after he realized all the women conspired with Tracy."

"You were one of them."

"Hey she's my sister now. She asked me to keep a secret and I did."

"You're good at keeping secrets aren't you?"

Ryan raised her head. "Are you upset with me again?"

Al kissed the tip of her nose. "No. You've had Tracy's back for a long time now. You two have a strong bond that neither JD nor I will ever break. And that's okay."

He squeezed her a little tighter. "Now, I can relax. My life has come full circle. Tracy is the woman she was meant to be."

"My father said you really are a remarkable man. You literally guided the life of the President of the United States. Only a man that strong was worthy of his daughter."

Al looked down at his wife, "Your father said that?"

She looked up into his light brown eyes and smiled, "Yes, he did. Know what else he said?"

"What?"

"He said, you better treat me right or he'll kick your butt again."

They both laughed. "That was the most informative fight I've ever had. I know this; he loves you deeply and regrets not being there for you."

"I know that now. But we have a little ways to go. Just like you and Monique."

"Monique is a grown woman. If something is going on with her, it's up to her to tell me. I accept that now."

"I'm happy to hear you say that," she threw her thigh over his leg and straddled him. "Where do you suppose they are?"

"Who?"

"Monique and Joshua."

"Monique—no telling. Joshua is somewhere blowing up somebody's country. But I know where they are not," he said as he rolled her onto her back.

"Where's that?" she asked with a gleam in her eyes.

Al placed kisses down her stomach until he reached the essence of her. "You know, every woman has a differ sense of sexuality. You, my queen, have a unique mixture of, cool, tough and fun." He gently spread her inner lips with his fingers and blew. "Joshua, if you're up there get the hell out of the way. I'm coming in."

Ryan laughed until he plunged deep inside of her. Then she moaned with pleasure. "Al Day, you are the man that controls my heart."

CPSIA information can be obtained at www.ICGtesting.com
Printed in the USA
LVOW040245250112

265404LV00002B/2/P